the water legacy

academy of magical creatures book two

MEGAN LINSKI & ALICIA RADES

We the authors acknowledge that the United States of America is a country formed on stolen land. We respect and honor the indigenous peoples who have lived here for centuries, and we recognize there is still much work to do to make reparations and heal the damage caused to the many indigenous nations who were first here, both in the past and today.

May we remember the atrocities once committed, create a better world in the present, and look forward together for our future.

A special thank-you to our sensitivity reader Kris Riley of the Cherokee tribe for her invaluable feedback on indigenous life and culture, as well as her commentary on living with chronic illness.

Liam

ONE

Several Months Earlier

My life was perfect, and I thought that would never change... until the day everything did.

I stood at the edge of a cliff, hundreds of feet above the raging ocean on the edge of the California coastline. The wind swept my hair back, and I could hear the harsh crashing of the waves on the rocky shore below. The ocean smelled amazing from up here, salty and pure. It was a hot, sunny day, not a cloud in the sky, perfect for the first day of summer. I could hear the rustling of the leaves as the breeze from the sea whispered through the forest.

A large castle made of white stone towered behind me, far above the woodland, stark against the towering mountains in the distance. Despite it being a mile off, it still looked huge and welcoming... it was home.

A black wolf stood at my side, a thin scar across one of his amber eyes, a hardened expression on his face. His coat was the color of dark coal, and he was so tall, his shoulder came up to my hip. His ears were perked forward, watching the water as if it were something for him to hunt.

"Ready for this, brother?" I asked, taking on a slightly cocky tone as I nudged my wolf.

He huffed. Nashoma was always so serious. I laughed and rubbed my hand over his head, scratching his ears.

"You know, it's my birthday. You could lighten up a little."

My touch caused his exterior to melt down. Nashoma barked, letting his tongue loll out of his mouth. His amber eyes glittered, and I grinned.

"Come on, then." I backed away from the cliff, and Nashoma followed. We walked until we were a good twenty feet from the cliff's edge, then stopped. My heartbeat picked up in deadly anticipation.

"No time like the present!" I said, and I bolted before he could answer. I ran at full speed toward the drop off, and Nashoma sprinted with me, side by side. Neither of us hesitated as we took a running start at the cliff...

And jumped.

My stomach bottomed out and became hollow as the feeling of weightlessness came upon me, and we started plummeting toward the ocean. I let out a *whoop* the minute my feet left solid ground, then started holding my breath.

This was the biggest fall we'd ever taken. We were at least three-hundred feet up. There was a risk we wouldn't make it. But I liked pushing things to the limit. There was something incredibly thrilling about always being on the edge of death. I *loved* it.

I glanced over. Nashoma was falling gracefully through the air, his legs held in an elegant pose. His face remained unfazed as we fell at high-speed, as if staring into the face of death just made him stare coolly back.

The ocean was approaching faster and faster. At this speed, we'd be smashed against the water if this didn't work. A thrill of exhilaration went through me as we sped downward, and soon, the surface drew too close.

But before I hit the water, I clenched my palms, and I felt a well of magic rise up within me. Instead of us smacking against the waves, the water rose up to meet us, soft tendrils spiraling out of the water, and they caught Nashoma and me, cradling us in their grasp before swinging backward and launching us even farther out to sea. We flew through the air again, this time at a lower height, and landed upon the water as it became a disk to catch our fall.

But we didn't sink. The water pushed us back to a vertical position, and it caught our feet, bubbling around us so that we were standing upon the water.

Before we could even gather our bearings, I opened my hands again and curled my fingers. The water beneath us became a funnel, swirling around Nashoma and me and sending us rocketing upward. When we reached the height I wanted, I forced the water to become a springboard for both of us, and it used pressure to launch us skyward. I could hear the water as it crashed back down to the surface below, and Nashoma and I went flying through the skies once more.

It was like time had ceased to exist, and everything was in slow-time. Nashoma was sailing over me, body poised like he was flying, while I performed a backflip. I closed my eyes and extended my arms wide, like I could fly, too, as we spun downward. A jolt of adrenaline shot through my body as I commanded the water to obey my every command and whim.

Like I said... I lived a perfect fucking life, and I loved every moment of it.

Nashoma grew close to me as we got near the water. I reached out and grabbed on to him, pulling him tightly to my body as we hit the surface. The waves became soft and broke our fall with just a thought from me, but this time, I allowed the water to submerge us deep within its depths. All around us, I saw the beautiful Familiars that the Elementai of my tribe were bonded to. All sorts of magical creatures swam throughout the ocean's depths... water monsters, with long necks and flat fins, swam peacefully besides giant multicolored fish and a blue sea dragon with fins for legs, wings, and a long, feathered tail.

Beside me, Nashoma had transformed into a water wolf. He was treading water, his feet webbed and his black coat turned to a translucent blue. His eyes had changed to an emerald green that resembled gemstones, and there was a thin green spine resembling that of a fish's that ran down his back from his neck to his tail.

He barked at me, and the sound became a bubble. I grinned at him. I had the best Familiar in the world.

A school of rainbow fish swam calmly in front of us, waving like a multicolored flag in the water. Nashoma chased after the school of fish like he did deer on land, and just as fast. When the school outran him, Nashoma opened his mouth, and a funnel of bubbles and water came jetting out at high-speed, making the fish scatter everywhere.

I chuckled, though it was hard to do while holding my breath. Beneath us, a curious sea serpent swam up to see what we were doing. Her scales were a mixture of pink and purple, and two large fins stuck out on the sides of her head like ears. Her black eyes glittered as she observed us without fear. She was young and unbonded, not much bigger than a car.

I skimmed my hand over the scales of the sea serpent, and she cooed within the ocean deep before she turned downward, most likely to go hunting at the bottom. I told the water to lift Nashoma and I upward, and we broke the surface.

When Nashoma was no longer underwater, he changed back into the black wolf I loved so much.

I leaned forward and flung my arms back behind me. The result was like a slingshot. The water sent us speeding forward at least a hundred miles an hour, waves tailing out behind us. The water supported our feet, and I swerved back and forth as we whizzed across the surface to determine direction, like I was surfing. Nashoma merely ran next to me like we were on land, the water rising to support each one of his footsteps.

I was almost out of breath with exhilaration. There was nothing better than being a Water Elementai. Not a damn thing.

We were near the beach now. I slowed us down, and we breathed heavily to catch our breath as the world spun around us. What a perfect way to start out the day.

"Hey, Liam!" I heard someone call my name, and I turned to see my younger brother, Ezra. Like me, Ezra was a Water Elementai, and he was waist-deep in a funnel of his own that held him above the ocean, though his funnel was obviously weaker than mine. He'd just graduated high school and would soon be attending Orenda Academy with me... something he hadn't stopped annoying me about since he'd got his acceptance letter.

"What's up?" I asked. I approached my brother. He was more or less my identical twin, except he was three years younger and his long black hair was a bit shorter than mine. Besides that, we shared the same brown skin, and his eyes were black, like mine.

Ezra was alone. He didn't have a Familiar yet. He wouldn't get one until he'd found one to bond with at Orenda. I'd only had Nashoma for nearly a year now, after we'd bonded late last fall. So far, it'd been the best year of my life, because of him. I told the water to glide me and Nashoma calmly over to him, and it obeyed.

"Where've you been? You've been gone all morning. Dad sent me to look for you," Ezra said as I approached.

I rolled my eyes. Dad could be over the top sometimes. "I'm twenty-one. I don't need a babysitter."

"Twenty-one *today*," Ezra reminded me. "Which is why Dad's probably freaking out. He thinks you're gonna go on a three-day bender with Jonah or something."

Which could totally happen, because that kind of thing could be expected when Jonah was involved. "Dad knows I can take care of myself," I said. "He doesn't need to be all paranoid. I'm responsible."

"Yeah, sure," Ezra said sarcastically, like he didn't believe it. He paused for a second before he added, "By the way, can you buy me some beer?"

I smirked. "That depends. Can you kick my ass to get it?"

"Oh, you're *on*." Ezra launched himself at me, and tackled me into the water. We sank under the deep and started wrestling together. Nashoma danced around us, barking in excitement as he watched the scrap.

But something weird happened. When I was messing around with Ezra, my muscles cramped, and I gasped, inhaling in a bit of water. Ezra noticed I was struggling and let go of me, and we both rose to the surface. We treaded water as I coughed, trying to regain my breath.

"Whoa. You okay?" Ezra backed off, looking concerned.

"Yeah." I recovered my breath. I wasn't very good at things that involved strength— I let my magic do the talking for me. To get back at Ezra for winning, I caused a large wave to rise silently behind him, then crash upon his head.

Ezra was pushed underwater. He broke the surface again, coughing and sputtering. "No fair!" he shouted. "Not everyone's as good as you, you know."

I snickered. Ezra thought I was showing off my magic, and maybe I was. I couldn't help it that I was talented.

We swam toward the beach, and Nashoma followed us, walking leisurely over the water. We reached the beach and walked upon the sand. The water left our bodies and clothes immediately, soaking onto the sand as we used our magic to dry us off. Nashoma shook his fur, and the water came splattering outward, leaving his fur dry and soft again.

"So what are you gonna do? Come back home?" Ezra asked.

Facing another one of my Dad's lectures about how *I was the first-born* and how *the future Water chief should be more responsible* didn't sound like something I wanted to do. "I'm meeting Jonah for lunch," I told him as we headed up the path toward town.

"I'll join you," Ezra said. "Dad will lose it if I come back without you."

There was a small bar that was still in the woods, on the edge of Kinpago. It was more or less an old hunting lodge that someone had converted into a restaurant.

My best friend, Jonah, was leaning against a tree on the outside of it. He was using his magic to play with a few leaves that had fallen on the ground in boredom, watching as they spiraled up and down on mini-tornadoes at his fingertips.

When he saw us coming, he pulled back his magic and let the leaves drop. Jonah didn't have a Familiar yet, though I felt like that time was getting close.

"About time," Jonah said as we approached. "I was worried my perfect complexion was gonna burn by the time you showed your pretty ass up."

I rolled my eyes. "Whatever you say, Jonah."

"Hey, boy!" Jonah said to Nashoma, and Nashoma barked in reply. "Look what I have for you!"

Jonah brought something out of his pants pocket. It was a tiny cupcake. He put it on the ground in front of Nashoma's paws. Nashoma barked and did a little dance when Jonah set the cupcake in front of him, spinning around in a few circles before he lunged forward and scarfed the dessert up.

"Hey, what the hell do I get?" I asked as Nashoma gobbled up the cupcake.

"A kiss, if you want it." Jonah leaned forward, his lips puckered obnoxiously. I shoved him away.

"Get out of here, asshole." I laughed.

We walked into the bar. It was a cozy place, but well-lit, with large windows and mismatched tables and chairs jostled against each other. There were all kinds of people in here— Toaqua like me, Yapluma, and Nivita, from the Earth tribe. I noticed the bar was absent of anyone Koigni... from the Fire tribe... and was grateful for that. You couldn't trust those types. All types of Familiars were in here. We had to navigate around a large stag's antlers, and apologized to a griffin as we stepped on its tail. A horse with a peacock tail moved out of the way so we could pass, and a strange creature that was half-deer, half-leopard growled as it started in on its salad, sharing it with her Earth Elementai.

This time of day, the place was packed. We had to pick a table in the middle of the room, because Jonah was so big and couldn't fit anywhere else. The three of us ordered buffalo burgers, and I started in on my first beer of my twenty-first birthday. Nashoma jumped onto a chair next to me, and I made sure to order him a steak, extra-rare.

"What do you want to do after this, Liam?" Ezra asked as he shoved a fistful of fries into his mouth. Nashoma had blood dripping down his front as he gnawed at his steak.

"I don't know," I replied. I was starving, and had already scarfed down my burger. "Go hiking, I guess."

"You *always* want to go hiking," Jonah whined. "Don't you ever get tired of looking at all the rocks and trees? It's like, the same thing."

I made a face at Jonah. I knew I grew up here, but there was something about this land that was incredible to me. This place was magical. It was like no matter how many times I'd walked around it, there was always something even more amazing to see.

"All you like looking at is man ass," I replied as a come-back. Ezra spit out his drink and laughed. Jonah didn't even bother rebuking me.

"You got that right," Jonah said as his eyes followed the back end of a Yapluma dude who left the bar. "You know me too well, Liam."

I shook my head. I liked girls, but I was quiet about it. Jonah took every opportunity he could to act horny around every male entity that was in a hundred mile radius. Thirsty didn't even come close to describing the way he behaved.

"Mom's making your special birthday dinner later. Can't miss that," Ezra reminded me.

"Not on your life." Mom's cooking was phenomenal, even if I would have to deal with a talk to Dad about tribal responsibilities once I got back home.

"And after that, we're going to get my man here *wasted*," Jonah sang, flinging an arm around my shoulders. "If you and Nashoma aren't completely hungover tomorrow, I've totally failed at my job as your bestie."

Nashoma and I eyed each other warily. If Jonah had his way, we'd be so drunk by the end of the night he'd have to carry us home. Or, more likely, hire a carriage to bring us back, because he would be just as intoxicated as we were.

We left the bar. A large female dragon waited outside of it. The dragon was gorgeous, with large horns and scales that looked like rubies. She belonged to one of the Professors at school, Professor Curt, who taught Dragonology. He must've been inside, eating. She bowed her head to us as we continued down the dirt path, but in the opposite direction of town.

My Familiar kept close to me. When Nashoma moved, he looked like a shadow gliding over the ground, silent, every step filled with intent. I couldn't wait for the day when he'd grow big enough to ride.

There were a group of Koigni in a clearing ahead, shooting fireballs at each other for practice. They barely noticed us as we walked by. We weren't important enough, I guess.

"Be careful, little brother," Jonah said as we passed them by. He leaned on Ezra to tease him. "Your magic's not strong enough to put their fire out if they attack. Stay by us. We'll keep you safe."

Ezra blushed, before his expression cleared. "Hey, Liam said that you couldn't manipulate air until *after* you got to Orenda!" Ezra protested. I smiled, and Jonah's expression became outraged.

When Jonah went to say something back, Nashoma opened his mouth. Another jet of water came out like a cannon, soaking him to the bone.

"Oh, I see how it is! No more cupcakes for you!" Jonah shouted as he tried shaking the water off his arms.

Nashoma's shoulders shook like he was laughing. He cackled, showing his large fangs.

Jonah caused a giant gust of wind to rise, drying him off quickly. It messed up his man-bun. Ezra and I were howling.

"Yeah, yeah. Fucking hilarious," Jonah muttered as he fixed his hair. He shot me a dirty look. "See how many secrets I tell you, now."

I chuckled. Jonah was being a bit ridiculous about Koigni— he was just using the rumors Ezra knew about them to try and scare my little brother. Sure, they had bad tempers, but members of the Fire tribe would never just randomly attack anyone.

...They hadn't for a long time, anyway.

I thought of something. "Jonah, I think I'm gonna ask Mia to come with us tonight," I said. "We should stop by her house and ask."

"Man, it's a guy's night!" Jonah complained. "Don't invite *her*."

Nashoma gave a growl of agreement, and Jonah nodded at him. Jonah and Nashoma had bonded over the fact they both despised Mia, but the two of them would have to get over it someday. Ezra stayed quiet.

I opened my mouth to respond, but something on the road caught my attention. A fellow Toaqua, Brittney, was struggling with a cart that had gotten stuck in a hole. Brittney's Familiar was a pink alicorn, a unicorn with fluffy wings, and she was hitched to the cart. The alicorn tried to pull it out as Brittney tugged, but the cart didn't move.

I hurried forward. "Here, let me help," I said. I lifted the cart out of the hole. As I did it, a sharp spasm ricocheted through my back. It wasn't much, but it made me gasp again, though I managed to set the cart down.

That was the second time that happened today. What the heck was going on with me? Nashoma narrowed his eyes and growled lowly, as if he'd felt something, too.

I didn't like the look he was giving me. It said he knew something I didn't.

"Thanks, Liam," Brittney said kindly. "But you didn't have to do that."

"Of course I did. You shouldn't have to do it by yourself," I told her. Behind me, Jonah groaned. Ezra watched carefully, taking notes. It went without saying that the second reason Ezra couldn't wait to get to Orenda was because there were plenty of girls around.

Brittney batted her eyelashes at me. "You're so sweet." Her expression lit up. "By the way, Mia wanted me to give you this. See you around."

Brittney handed me a note, then climbed back up on her cart, letting her alicorn pull it down the road once more.

"You're such a nice guy, Liam," Jonah said, sighing dramatically. "It makes the rest of us look bad."

"Well, yeah," I replied, not sure what else there was to say. What was the point of *not* being friendly? I couldn't imagine going around being rude and pissed off all the time.

I unfolded the note and read it quickly. My insides bottomed out. Mia couldn't hang out today— said she was busy, though she didn't clarify and she wished me a happy birthday.

"I guess it *is* going to be a guy's night. Mia can't come," I told them as I pocketed the note.

Jonah and Nashoma looked positively thrilled. I was a little disappointed, but that was okay. If Mia had things to do, I was okay with it, even if it was my birthday.

"Can I come instead?" Ezra said hopefully.

"Aw, sure," Jonah said, and he put Ezra in a headlock, ruffling his hair up. "I guess the little brother can tag along."

I wasn't really listening. I felt... different. Couldn't explain how. I noticed I felt tired. Kind of worn out. Maybe we shouldn't have gone on this walk. Nashoma watched me carefully, his head tilted a little to the side.

"Dude, I seriously can't wait to take Yapluma Magic II next

semester," Jonah rambled. "There are gonna be *so* many hot guys in that class."

"I'm just so excited to go," Ezra said. "I've been hearing about Orenda my entire life, and now I finally get to be a student! I can't wait to learn how to use my magic!"

Jonah and Ezra kept talking about classes while we proceeded forward. I walked a few steps ahead with my hands in my pockets, thinking. The path led to the mountain range, and I had a sudden urge to climb it. By this time, the skies had darkened and grey clouds had appeared. The sun was gone, and it looked like it was going to rain soon.

"Let's climb up, guys," I said. "I bet the view is incredible from up there."

"Ugh, man, stop making me work," Jonah said, but he and Ezra followed me up the mountain path anyway.

When we rounded the side of the marked path, my eyes caught something strange. There was a small blue light, glowing about twenty feet or so below us within a cave carved into the mountainside. It was so small that you'd miss it if you didn't look closely. If I had to guess, it was magic.

Nashoma saw it, too. He crouched as close to the edge as he could, seemingly drawn to the small blue light, just like I was.

"Liam, we should turn back. It's going to rain soon," Ezra said, looking up.

"I can shield you from the rain if it comes down," I told him. I peered closer. What was that crazy light shining at the end of the mountain opening? I had to reach it. My eyes scanned the mountainside. There was a thin embankment by the opening, but it would be hard to get to. We'd have to slide down to get to it.

"Let's explore that cave down there," I offered. "I think there's something inside."

"I don't know, dude. That path looks dangerous," Jonah said, staring warily at the embankment. "I doubt we can make it down."

"Where's your sense of adventure?" I asked. "You could just fly us down there if you wanted."

"Fuck you," Jonah snapped back. "You know I don't like caves."

Most Yapluma didn't. I looked expectantly at Ezra, but he shook his head.

"Fine," I said. "I'll do it myself."

I jumped down the path and landed on the tiny embankment, walking carefully along the edge. If I slipped, I had better hope Jonah would catch me. Otherwise, I'd go falling down the mountainside. There wasn't enough water within the mountain that I could use it to break my fall.

Nashoma let out a tiny whine, like he was reluctant to come after me. But he'd follow me wherever I went, so he slid down the side of the mountain and joined me as I proceeded toward the cave opening.

The edge got thinner and thinner as I walked toward the cave, but that didn't slow my steps. The blue light was drawing me in, making it hard to think. It was like I was under some sort of spell. Nashoma was pretty far behind me, now. I'd gone ahead of him without thinking. A few rocks crumbled above me and spattered dirt down, but I wiped it away from my eyes and kept going.

"Liam, you need to come back!" Ezra sounded scared. "Those rocks don't look stable!"

"I'm fine!" I shouted back, ignoring him. That was the same moment I slipped. My right foot staggered forward, meeting nothing but air. I grabbed on to a root sticking out of the side of the mountain to try and stop my fall.

The root gave way, and I heard a loud cracking sound. Everything happened so fast that there wasn't enough time for Jonah to react to catch me, and I tumbled downward, landing in front of the cave opening.

I didn't get a chance to look inside and see where the blue light was coming from. I pushed myself to my feet as I heard Jonah and Ezra telling me to get out of the way. Multiple rocks from the side of the mountainside above had come loose and were rolling toward me in a landslide.

Those rocks were going to crush me. I glanced around frantically for an escape, but there was nowhere to go. My mind froze as several large boulders tumbled toward me at high speed.

There was no chance. I was going to die.

Liam, watch out!

I felt a pair of paws on my back, and I went tumbling down the side of the mountain. I felt air wrap around my body and lift me upward before I plummeted to my death. The air lifted me backward, pulling me upward until I landed face-first in the dirt.

Two pairs of shoes were in front of my face. Jonah and Ezra. He had flown me back to where they were standing.

That sentence still echoed in my ears. Someone had called my name. The sound had been deep, and male. I hadn't heard that voice before, couldn't place it, yet it sounded terribly intimate... like I'd been hearing that voice every day since before I'd been born. I staggered to my feet, dazed. Ezra and Jonah were both staring at me, their faces pale white and horrified.

... Where was Nashoma?

When I understood where the voice had come from, it felt like the weight of the world had been suddenly dropped on my head, crushing me.

The voice telling me to watch out had been my Familiar.

I let out an audible cry and spun around. The landslide had covered up the entrance of the cave and most of the embankment, making it so I couldn't see the entrance.

I couldn't see Nashoma, either.

"Nashoma!" I screamed. He didn't answer me. My scream bounced off the sides of the mountain and echoed through the trees, vibrating throughout the entire forest.

No. *No, no, no, no, no...*

I tried jumping off the embankment and racing to my Familiar, but Jonah grabbed me. He and Ezra each took an arm, trying to hold me back.

"Liam, it's not going to help!" Jonah shouted. He sounded panicked. Ezra said something about it being too dangerous, but I barely heard him.

Jonah was a big guy, and Ezra wasn't exactly tiny, but a freight train couldn't hold me back from getting to my Familiar now. I threw them both off and slid downward, until I reached the site of the landslide.

I started throwing boulders off of him. The rocks cut into my hands.

I left large red streaks on the rocks as I sifted through them, my palms gushing blood. I didn't even fucking feel it. All I could feel was absolute terror as I tore through the rubble, hoping against hope he was okay, that he would make it through this.

I let out a cry of relief as I spotted his black fur, but it was short-lived as I heaved the last boulder off of him. Bones were poking through his fur in multiple places, and he was bleeding so much, from so many spots. He'd been crushed underneath the landslide. Nashoma was still breathing, but his amber eyes shone with a terrible agony. He was in awful pain, and it was all my fault. He couldn't even whine.

My hands skimmed over him, unsure of what to do or how to touch him, because I was pretty sure whatever I did would only torture him. "It's gonna be okay, brother. We're going to find someone to help, you're gonna make it..."

Soft footsteps landed beside me. It was Jonah and Ezra. They had followed me, even though it was dangerous for them to do so.

"Liam," Jonah said softly. His voice sounded choked. "It's... it's too late."

"No." They'd already accepted what I couldn't. Tears started dripping out of my eyes and onto Nashoma's fur. "We— we can still save him."

I heard sobs from behind me. Ezra was crying, too.

Hold me, Liam. Nashoma spoke to me. It was all he had the strength to say. His eyes pleaded with me to help.

I knew it would hurt him to pick him up, but it's what he wanted. I held my breath as I gently pushed my arms underneath Nashoma's broken body. I could feel all the shattered bones underneath my hands. I cradled Nashoma's body against me and buried my face in his shoulder. His hot blood soaked my shirt and jeans.

"Nashoma, I'm so sorry," I gasped. "Please hold on. There has to be another way."

He weakly licked the side of my face. Nashoma panted heavily for a couple of seconds, gasping for breath. I could feel his heartbeat growing faint against my own. I prayed that the ancestors would make my heart stop, so his could keep going on.

But it didn't work. Nashoma slowly went stiff, curling against me and giving a last, ragged breath. I felt his heart stop as I was clutching him in my arms.

"Don't leave," I whispered weakly. But it was too late. He was already...

Something inside of me ripped. The warmth and acceptance Nashoma had created inside of me fled, like a part of myself I could no longer keep. A hole opened up inside of me, feeling cavernous, swallowing me up until I forgot who I was and I turned into a new person. Something awful grabbed my heart and changed it, turned it black and ill. It was something I'd never be able to repair, something I couldn't fix ever again. Who I'd been five minutes ago, I could never get back.

Nashoma was gone forever. He was *gone*. And with his death, I lost myself.

I mashed my face into Nashoma's body and wept. I dug my fingers into his fur and wailed as loudly as I possibly could, though I didn't mean to. It was something that just came out of me. Every breath felt like knives were stabbing into my lungs, and I hated each one, wished myself to stop breathing just like Nashoma had, though it didn't happen. I'd never felt something so agonizing in my life, not even when my grandfather had died.

I felt Jonah's hand on my shoulder trying to comfort me, and Ezra knelt by my side, but both of them felt so far away. I felt myself grow cold... like Nashoma would soon be.

Please, ancestors, let this be a dream. Let me wake up. I'll do anything.

But this wasn't a dream. This was my new reality— a reality I had created with one stupid mistake.

There was no point anymore. My purpose, my place in this world, my reason for existing... it had left when Nashoma went away.

I'd lost my soul. I no longer had it.

He died.

sophia
TWO

Fire rose within my body, warming my skin as I stared up at the towering peaks of the Orenda Academy castle. It wasn't the heat that usually came with anger and fury. It was the comforting heat of a warm blanket on a cold winter's night. It was like a hug from a loved one. It was home.

Orenda Academy. My home.

Even after a full semester living here, after winning the Elemental Cup, after everything... it was still like living a dream. No matter where I looked, I saw magic. Out in the courtyard, a group of Toaqua were making it snow in an area the size of a basketball court. Two teams formed the snow into balls and chucked them at each other. Yapluma teammates used their air power to throw the snowballs off their trajectory. A Nivita guy threw up a wall of tightly woven grass to protect himself from flying snowballs. Across the courtyard, Koigni were combatting the chilly January air with fires burning in their palms.

Familiars of all shapes and sizes roamed in and out of the castle. In the midst of the snowball fight, a white horned canine jumped to catch the snowballs mid-air. The Toaqua Familiar shifted for a moment to become one with the snow— with water— and then shifted back again. A unicorn with a golden mane the color of a wheat field climbed the castle steps beside a Nivita girl. The unicorn's tail brushed my elbow as it entered the tall doors leading into the grand hall. A creature the size of a hummingbird with bright yellow feathers buzzed by my head before following a petite Yapluma freshman outside. Above me, a tiny Fire lizard that looked like a mini dragon swooped down from its perch upon one of the castle's gargoyles and landed on the horn of a full-sized dragon sleeping in the courtyard. The green dragon shook its head, and the Fire lizard flapped its wings and took off again.

Excitement surged through me. I was so glad to be back after a long break.

"Sophia, are you coming?" Imogen was already several paces ahead of me, standing under the big chandelier that hung from the tall, five-story ceiling. She wore a frilly pink skirt that fell to her knees, a green top that suited her curves but didn't quite suit this decade, and shiny blue boots. Her strawberry-blonde hair fell in loose waves around her shoulders. The top layer was secured with a big bow pinned to the back of her head. Sassy poked her head out of the tote bag on Imogen's shoulder and looked to Esis and me expectantly.

I readjusted my backpack on my shoulder. Esis clung to my ponytail from where he sat perched on the top of the bag. His soft white fur tickled the back of my neck.

"I'm coming," I said, stepping out of the cold air and into the grand hall. A fire burned in the massive fireplace, warming the entrance. "I'm just taking it all in again. I'm happy to be back."

Imogen smirked and bumped hips with me. "Any reason why?" She wiggled her eyebrows.

I blushed. "It's not just about *him*."

It was only like, ninety-nine percent about Liam. I hadn't seen or spoken to him in almost a month. And dammit, I missed the guy so much it hurt. I hoped he was okay. I still hadn't told him about Esis' healing abilities— for a lot of reasons. For one, I wanted to tell him in person, and I hadn't found the right time for it yet. I hoped he hadn't had any flare-ups while we were apart.

"Have you checked your schedule yet?" Imogen babbled as we ascended the stairs. "I'm finally in a class with Baine. I hope we're in the same period for our Ancient Familiars elective. We'll see who's crazy for believing in wolpertingers now..."

Imogen's voice faded into the background as my eyes fell on Liam. He stood at the top of the stairs, leaning against the banister that overlooked the grand hall. His long black hair fell around his shoulders, and he wore a tight navy blue t-shirt that showed off his biceps. My heart sped up as soon as I saw him. When his eyes caught mine, my whole body went haywire. My pulse pounded in my ears, and my breaths became shallow and heavy. Heat rose to the surface of my skin, and a warm tingle spread across me.

I had the urge to race up the staircase and throw myself into his arms, but I caught myself before I could. I forced my shaking knees to support me.

A wide smile spread across his face, sending my stomach to do acrobatic flips in my abdomen. Ancestors, had he gotten *hotter* over break?

He looked well, so happy and full of life. It was like the ancestors had infused color back into his cheeks and lips. And those eyes, those deep, dark eyes. Had they always been that gorgeous?

Esis placed his front paws on my shoulder and chittered when he saw Liam. He looked like a fat white squirrel as he jumped off my back and bounded up the stairs. Liam bent to scratch Esis behind his large ears, but Esis hopped up Liam's arm and settled himself on his shoulder. Liam laughed and itched Esis under his chin. Esis purred.

"Liam!" I greeted cheerfully when I reached the top of the stairs.

"Ladies," he nodded to Imogen and me cooly, like he was trying to hide his true emotions.

It sucked. Now that break was over, we couldn't keep using the excuse of being on the same tournament team when we hung out. My whole House was full of stuck-up Elementai. It was unusual for a Koigni like me to hang out with members of another house, *especially* a Toaqua guy.

These rules were a bunch of unicorn shit if you asked me.

"I, um, need to head to my dorm and unpack," Imogen said, gesturing to the bag she was carrying.

"Are you sure, Im?" I asked before she could get too far down the hall. "I thought we were going to get food."

"Tonight," Imogen offered. "I ate with you every day over break. I think we can skip one meal together."

Thank the ancestors. Imogen was giving me some alone time with my man... well, not *my* man. Okay, maybe my man.

"See you later," Imogen said with a wave as she and Sassy headed down the hall toward the next staircase.

I turned back to Liam, beaming. "So, what have you been up to all break?"

It was a lame thing to say, but I couldn't greet him the way I wanted to. Even in normal circumstances, the images flashing through my head weren't exactly appropriate in public.

"Let's get out of here," he suggested.

I could hardly contain my excitement as Liam led me through the halls of Orenda Academy. We passed by tall, ornate windows, elaborate tapestries, and dozens of life-sized statues of Familiars.

Liam made small talk while we walked. "So, did you have fun over break?"

"Tons!" I gushed. "I stayed with Imogen's family. Their house is the best. Her mom serves waffles every morning. It's amazing. Plus, we spent a week and a half in Guatemala. It was incredible. I knew that passport I got Junior year would come in handy someday. Amelia and I hung out while she was in town, too. She was on the *Hozho* with you over break, right?"

I was rambling to calm my nerves. It was unfair that Amelia saw him more over break than I did.

"Yeah, I saw her working a few times," Liam said with a shrug. "The whole trip was kind of boring, to be honest."

Typical Liam. He was never very good at seeing the magic in the world.

We turned down three different hallways, each narrower than the last, until we entered a hallway that ended at a staircase. The stairs led to a cluster of classrooms I'd never been in before. No one saw us, but I could hear voices at the top of the stairs. They sounded like professors.

Liam grabbed my hand and dragged me under the staircase. He pressed me against the wall with his body. *Hot damn, Liam. Now we're talking.*

"You know, you could at least take me on a date first," I teased. My heart pummeled against my rib cage.

"Shh," he hissed, placing his index finger to his mouth. He glanced upward as the sound of footsteps echoed above our heads.

I pressed my lips together, holding my breath. It was dark and dusty under the staircase. There wasn't much room for the two of us between all the classroom supplies that had been shoved down here for storage. There was a cart full of potion vials that looked like they hadn't been used for a few years, along with some boxes I couldn't see into. It was like the professors who put all this junk here forgot the place existed.

The footsteps and voices continued down the hall. Once they were out of earshot, Liam and I drew a collective breath.

I expected him to push away from me now that the coast was clear, but he didn't. He stood there staring down at me with a look in his eyes I hadn't seen before. It was full of passion, desire, and want. I stared up at him, trying to find that hint of *we can't be together* I so often saw in his expression, but I couldn't find it.

Liam Mitoh missed me.

Sure, maybe he still thought we shouldn't be together, but right now, the rules didn't seem to matter. He wanted me. And I'd be damned if I didn't want him, too.

"So, uh, about that date—?" I started to say, but Liam cut me off.

"Dates are for losers," he said before his lips connected with mine.

Kissing Liam after a month of being away from him was mind-blowing. It was like our first kiss all over again, only this time I wanted to do more— to touch more. My heart lifted in my chest, dancing to the rhythm of his kiss. My lips parted, and his tongue slid over mine as his hands roamed down my body. He tasted like a fresh snowfall. His hips pressed into my body, and I didn't even care that he was crushing me to the wall. In fact, I kind of liked it. Heat pooled in my belly as I threw my arms around him and squeezed tightly.

Esis straddled us, placing one tiny little leg on Liam's shoulder and the other on mine. It was almost enough to distract me.

Liam drew away from me far too soon. He braced himself against the wall behind me and breathed heavily. His forehead rested against mine, and his warm breath rushed across the side of my face.

Esis held on to Liam's shoulder, his blue eyes widening as he glanced between us. I blushed so hard I was half surprised fire didn't come shooting out my nostrils.

"I missed this," I whispered to Liam.

He bent down and placed a kiss to the top of my forehead, then wrapped me in his arms. My whole body relaxed, swooning into his embrace. The scent of a pine forest and a warm blanket filled my nose. I'd almost forgotten what he smelled like. It made my insides feel warm and fuzzy.

"I missed *you*," he whispered back.

Tears of joy brimmed in my eyes. I never wanted to be away from Liam that long again.

"Liam," I whispered.

"Mm?" He kept his gaze on the ends of my hair as he ran his fingers down my ponytail.

"Am I your girlfriend?" I pushed the question out before I could stop myself. I'd been wondering about it all break. We never got a chance to say what we were at the Elemental Ball. I didn't just want to be friends with benefits. I wanted to be his girlfriend, even if we had to keep it secret for now. I just wanted to be *his*, and I wanted him to be *mine*.

Liam hesitated a moment. "Are you sure you want to put labels on it, *pawee*?"

"Yes," I replied without even having to think about it.

Liam sighed and met my gaze. "You don't want to be tied down to me."

I let out a breath of disbelief. "Yes, I do."

Liam shook his head. "I'm broken, Sophia. The tribe thinks I—"

"The tribe can go to hell," I told him. "You won the Elemental Cup. Whatever shame you brought to your House before I came here is gone. You've proven yourself to the Hawkei. You didn't just survive the tournament, Liam. You *won*. That counts for something."

A ghost of a smile crept across his face. "I don't know..."

"Besides, it doesn't matter what the tribe thinks," I continued. "*I* want to be with you, Liam, broken or not. We'll find a way to make this work."

Liam glanced down, then lifted his gaze to look at me beneath dark lashes. "I'm just... nervous."

"About what?" I asked softly, reaching up to twist the ends of his hair around my own fingers. "About getting caught?"

Liam shrugged. "Well, there's that. But also, I met up with Professor Perot over break. He's going to start trying some things to make me feel better, but it's all purely experimental. I don't... I don't want you to get attached to me if it doesn't work out."

My breath stopped in my chest, and I glanced to Esis, then back to Liam. "It's too late for that. I'm already attached. And if it doesn't work out... well, that's something I'll deal with on my own. You don't have to worry about me."

"But I do," Liam argued. "I *do* worry about you."

And I worried about him. Esis could help Liam— not heal him, but help him— sort of like a treatment, a drug. But if Perot was going to be giving Liam real drugs, I didn't want Esis' powers interfering with that. What if Perot could find a cure for Liam and we screwed up his data? I couldn't do that. The least I could do was give Liam a choice. It was time to finally tell him about Esis.

Liam ran his hands through his hair. "I guess I worry because... because you're my girlfriend."

My thoughts halted in their tracks when I heard Liam say those words.

I'm. His. Girlfriend.

Could Orenda Academy get any better than this?

I beamed up at him, at a loss for words.

"But no one except Imogen and Jonah can know," he warned.

"And Amelia," I added.

He groaned. "That's too many people. My brother knows we kissed, but I'm not telling him anything else. What we're doing could be considered treason, Sophia."

"What we're doing shouldn't be illegal in the first place," I argued. "Amelia is my sister, and she's going to know something's up one way or another. I can't hide it from her unless I never see her again. And that's not happening, so..."

Liam sighed. "Okay. And Amelia. I'll do my best to hide it from Ezra."

I threw my arms around Liam's neck, intending to pull him in for another kiss, but instead, my hand hit Esis. He went flying off Liam's shoulder and crashed into one of the boxes with a hard *thump*.

"Oh my God, Esis!" My hands flew over my mouth, and I instantly pushed past Liam to scoop Esis up off the ground. He shook his head, disoriented. "I'm so sorry, buddy."

Esis blinked a few times, then looked up at me like he hadn't even realized something had happened. He just chirped and rubbed his belly.

I pulled him close to me. "I think Esis is hungry. Do you want to go get something to eat?"

Liam shoved his hands into his pockets. "I guess."

"Come on, buddy. We'll get you a hamburger."

Liam checked to make sure the coast was clear, then gestured for me to follow. He eyed Esis as we entered a wider hallway. "Do you think he's okay? It sounded like he hit the floor pretty hard. Maybe you should take him to Professor Costas."

"He'll be fine," I said.

My hands shook, so I cradled Esis tighter. He snuggled into my belly, purring. Now was my chance to tell Liam. Now that we were officially a couple, I couldn't keep this from him. I had to be open and honest with him, or our relationship was doomed for failure.

"Liam, there's something you should know about Esis," I forced out through the lump in my throat. He was going to hate me for keeping it from him this long. But we'd deal with it... because we were a couple now.

Liam stopped and turned to me just as we reached another hallway. At least a dozen people and their Familiars passed through it. "What's that?"

I lowered my voice. "The thing is, he—"

I was cut off by the sound of a *squawk* echoing down the hall. I looked behind me to see a big bird with long red tail feathers flying toward us, holding a piece of paper in its mouth. My body went rigid at the sight of the phoenix. At first I thought it was Anwara, Haley's Familiar, which meant the bitch was somewhere nearby, but I relaxed when I realized its feathers were a slightly different red and the bird was a little bigger.

The phoenix swooped down and landed at my feet. It nudged me in the leg and craned its neck out, holding out the letter to me. I exchanged a confused glance with Liam.

"Well, take it. It's for you," Liam said.

Slowly, I reached out for the piece of paper. It was made of fine stationery and folded into a trifold that was secured with a wax seal. The Orenda Academy emblem had been pressed into the wax— a shield bordered by ornate designs and divided into four sections, each with a design representing one of the four Houses.

I peeled the letter open.

Sophia Henley,

You are hereby summoned to Redbird Hall immediately.

- Annette Westfenix, Koigni Chieftess

The paper shook in my hands. The Koigni Elders were summoning me? I must've done something wrong. What if they found out about Esis? What if someone saw Liam and I together?

"You should go," Liam said.

I snapped out of my daze at the sound of his voice. I hadn't realized he'd leaned in so close to peek over my shoulder. I gaped at him.

"You don't want to keep your Elders waiting." He sounded sad. "It's probably about the prophecy. Gotta do your duty to your House and everything."

"But Liam—"

"We'll talk later," he said, forcing a smile I could tell wasn't genuine. "See you, Sophia."

Liam left me standing in the middle of the hall, frightened and completely clueless. I didn't even know where to find Redbird Hall.

The phoenix at my feet nudged me, then tilted his head. He wanted me to follow.

I glanced back at Liam one last time, but he was already long gone. My stomach knotted as I turned back to the phoenix. Esis clung to my sweatshirt. He seemed as frightened as I was.

I wasn't sure I was ready to find out what the Elders wanted from me.

26

Liam

THREE

I'd had a plan. *Sophia, look, I'm sorry, but this isn't going to work out. We're from different tribes, and it's too dangerous. It doesn't matter that I lov— LIKE you, it's just not possible.*

Oh, yeah. Also, my dad says I have to kill you.

I'd tried rehearsing it a million times over break and it only sounded more pitiful each time. It proved how badly I didn't want to do this.

Then I saw Sophia's chocolate eyes, and all that was thrown out the window. I went from *we can't be together* to PLEASE NOTICE ME. And she'd walked right over and I'd dragged her under the staircase and we'd made out again and I put my hands in her hair and I was just... done.

Then I'd made her my girlfriend. *Fuck.* And I was so damn happy about it. This wasn't how things were supposed to go.

I sighed as I turned the corner to head down to the Toaqua dorms. Well, whatever. Too late now. If I was going to be Sophia Henley's boyfriend, I was gonna ride this thing until the wheels fell off.

But I knew it couldn't last forever. One of us had to die. I hoped with all my heart it would be me first.

"Hey, son, how are you feeling?" I mocked my dad's voice under my breath. "Shitty as usual? That's great! I figured out a way to bring Nashoma back to life, and by the way, you have to kill your girlfriend."

Dad hadn't told me shit since the night of the Elemental Ball. He'd dropped the bomb that the Toaqua Elders wanted me to get close to Sophia, just so I could murder her, and in exchange they would raise Nashoma from the dead.

I doubted such a thing was even possible. Unless I saw it with my own eyes, I wasn't buying it. Dad had been stubbornly silent and just told me to be patient, that I'd be told everything in time.

It'd been over a month since the ball, and that was a long time to wait without any information. It was a cruel trick to dangle Nashoma's life in front of me like a carrot.

I walked into a back-to-school party the minute I opened the door to the Toaqua dorms. The room had been filled with snow that piled up to the ceiling in places, and students slid down it on homemade sleds. Toaqua were skating on the icy surface of the pool, and a couple of girls were arguing on who had made the best ice sculpture. Their Familiars, a blue dog with octopus legs and a horse with a mermaid tail, snapped at each other nearby. A few people built snow creatures, while others made icy designs on the window for people to stare at.

Ezra, as usual, had girls all over him. He was buried under a collection of at least ten giggling women who'd ganged up on him during a snowball fight. When he saw me, he gently pushed the girls off of him and stood up.

"Ladies, let's learn to keep our hands to ourselves," Ezra said. "There's only so much of me to go around."

He winked at one of them. No joke, she practically fell over.

I rolled my eyes. As my brother joined me, the girls backed off, which was typical. I always thought I scared girls off, but Ez just claimed I intimidated them— *in a good way*, he always hurriedly added. How the hell can you intimidate someone in a good way, anyhow?

Ezra had cut his hair short over break, which I was happy about. It made it easier for people to tell us apart.

"Like you weren't enjoying that," I said as he strolled over. He wore a wicked smile, and his hair stuck up on one side of his head.

"You can't talk. You two looked cute on the staircase earlier," he teased, and he wiggled his eyebrows suggestively.

I didn't have to ask who he meant. Keeping this from Ezra was going to be impossible. He had a tendency to be watching me even when I didn't realize he was there. Had since the day he was born, and he wasn't about to stop now.

"Keep your voice down," I snapped. "You know how people talk."

"Relax." Ezra shook his head. "You're so dramatic."

"It's not like that," I growled. "Sophia and I are just friends."

"Sure," Ezra said. "Looks like it, from the way you have to pick your jaw up off the floor whenever she's around."

"Ez, I swear to the ancestors. Don't go digging, or else."

"What are you gonna do?" Ezra snickered. "Beat me up, like when we were kids?"

"I'll damn well try."

I didn't know if I could kick Ezra's ass anymore. He wasn't exactly tiny.

"I'm ready." Ezra cracked his knuckles and took a wide stance, waiting for me to tackle him. "Come at me, bro."

"You did not just say *come at me, bro.*"

The sound of a bear groaning cut our bantering off. It was Tatum, my dad's Familiar. He lumbered into the common room, a scroll tied loosely around his neck.

Nobody really paid much attention, just moved out of the way as he passed by. I was the son of the Water Chief, so it wasn't a big deal that Tatum had been sent up here to deliver a note. Tatum stopped by me. I untied the note from his neck and read it quickly.

Liam Mitoh,

The Water Tribe Elders demand your presence at Serpent Assembly at once.

- Liwanu Mitoh, Toaqua Chief

It sounded really formal coming from Dad. Which meant that this was an official tribal summons.

"A council meeting? Do you think it's about your illness, or what Perot might've found?" Ezra asked.

Of course Ez would consider that first. I hadn't told him what Dad had said to me the night of the ball. In fact, I hadn't told anyone. "No. I'm not sure." I pocketed the note. My mind was going a million miles an hour.

"He's making progress, right?" Ezra asked. He seemed anxious. "Perot's got it under control?"

"I already told you everything. I don't want to talk about it."

Perot did a bunch more tests that didn't result in anything but taking up a lot of my break. He put me on a weird diet where I couldn't eat anything, gave me a bunch of experimental drugs and potions only to pull me off of them in a few days, and had me write down my symptoms every day in a journal Baxtor came to pick up on the weekends. When he'd made no progress, as a last resort, he suggested antidepressants.

Fucking *antidepressants*.

We hadn't even narrowed it down yet if my illness was magical or not, let alone what caused it. Right now, I was on this combination of pills and a health potion Perot invented that made me even more tired than I already was and worsened my nausea. The side effects were nearly as bad as what Perot was trying to treat.

Ezra was still eyeing me in concern. We'd shared a room on the *Hozho* over break, and he'd watched my symptoms progressively getting worse after Christmas. I'd tried to keep the sound of my gagging quiet, but it was hard to conceal much when he found me curled up on the bathroom floor more mornings than not.

He was still my little brother, and he cared. But I didn't want to worry him. I had enough people worrying about me these days.

"Everything's fine. I'm getting better," I told him, which I knew was a lie. I felt worse every day. "It's probably just about what we did in Europe."

"Then why wasn't I called, too?" His expression was puzzled.

I was running out of excuses. "Who knows? I guess it could be anything."

I was going to crack. This secret had been eating me alive for weeks. I had to tell *someone*. I could trust my brother, couldn't I?

"Maybe since you won the Cup, they want to restore you back to chief hood." I couldn't help but notice the hope in Ezra's voice. I flinched, because I felt bad. But maybe if I got Nashoma back, I could be next in line to become chief again.

That would also mean I would lose Sophia.

I avoided jumping to any conclusions. "I guess we'll find out."

I went to my dorm room and grabbed my jacket before Ez could ask anymore questions. I slipped out the back and rounded the edge of the castle, hopefully where no one would see me. I turned the snow into ice and used it to glide me toward the ocean so I didn't have to walk.

When I got to the beach, my ice bridge continued, over the sand and into the waves. All the while, I was thinking. It was too much of a coincidence that Sophia and I had been summoned by our Elders in the same day. Something was going on.

I slid over the freezing cold water before I stopped the ice bridge far off shore, somewhere in the middle of the ocean. I took a deep breath. The ice melted away from my feet, plunging me downward.

THE MAJORITY of the Toaqua tribe was underwater. Serpent Assembly was no exception, but it was away from the main tribe and not connected with underwater tunnels like the rest of the village was. I floated downward until I hit the ocean floor. A large building rose up in front of me within the depths of the sea. It was constructed of stone and glass, and had tall spires that twisted upward menacingly.

Someday I'd hoped to show Sophia how my tribe lived, though I didn't know how I could get her down here. It was a long descent to the bottom, and I didn't think a single Koigni had ever set foot in Toaqua territory.

I turned the circular lever that was on the entranceway to the hall. I swam inside a narrow hallway, then closed the door behind me and pressed a button that was on the side of the wall. The water drained out of the room, and I dried myself off as I proceeded nervously toward the second door— the one that led to the Assembly chamber. This one was silver in color, decorated with sapphires in the shape of the Toaqua House symbol. I put my hand on the elaborate door and pushed it open.

Serpent Assembly was large and open. It had a massively high ceiling with the design of a sea serpent carved into it, twirling around the room to end at the head in the middle of the roof. The floors were marble, and white pillars extended to the ceiling, decorated with silver and blue gemstones. The walls were made of glass so you could see out into the surrounding ocean. Several wooden stands were placed around the room before a giant wooden bench, where each of the five members of the Water Elder Council sat. My dad was in the middle, two Elders flanking him on each side.

I'd only been in here a few times, and it was no less intimidating than it had been when I was a kid. But I told myself to stop being a coward and walked up to one of the wooden stands like this wasn't one of the scariest things I'd done in my life, the Elemental Cup included.

I looked at the other Elders. Professor Baine was here, though he looked even more worried and disheveled than usual. His suit was rumpled and had a few stains on it, and it didn't look like he'd combed his hair. He was actually still wearing his slippers. He gave a nervous glance and pushed his glasses up his face. He didn't give me a reassuring smile, or even a nod. I peered through the glass, but couldn't see Thalassa anywhere.

Right. This couldn't be good.

Sitting next to Baine was Madame Wells. Her Familiar was a killer whale, and I watched it through the glass as he swam around the council center in a circle above us.

Wells wore her black hair in a long braid that fell over her shoulder, and a deerskin dress decorated with beads. Wells was by far the youngest Toaqua Elder, only a few years older than Madame Doya. She'd just replaced an Elder that had died over the summer, and I didn't know much about her. It was unusual that a woman had taken up residence as an Elder on the Water Council, because so far in our history, Toaqua Elders had always been male, like Koigni Elders were typically female. I wondered what she had done to deserve such a coveted position. As far as I knew, my dad had been looking at nominating someone else before she stepped in.

She watched me coolly, and I couldn't read her face. Her stoic expression bothered me, and I looked away. I made a mental note to keep an eye on her.

On the other side of my dad was Elder Poole. Poole was small, and his Familiar, a leviathan, drifted nervously directly above us in the ocean outside. Poole was my father's age and seemed shifty and uncomfortable. I didn't necessarily mind Poole, but how he'd gotten the title of Elder when he was so spineless was beyond me. Elders were supposed to be strong to protect the tribe, and Poole... was not.

At least, not personality wise. His magic was insanely good, better than most, which was probably why he'd been nominated to the council. That's the only guess I could give.

Next to him, a wrinkly Elder who was probably more ancient than the ancestors themselves scowled at me from his seat on the bench, clutching a tall walking staff. His Familiar, a gigantic kraken that was quite hideous, sneered at me through the glass— if a giant squid could sneer, anyhow. I wanted to sneer back, but that was rude, so I didn't.

I never liked Elder Malison. Don't know why, but to me, there was always something off about him. He was two weeks older than dirt and had been on the council even before my grandfather was Chief. He opposed everything my father did, so I didn't know why Dad kept him around. I'd planned on kicking him out first thing once I became Chief, but after I'd lost the chance, Ezra gladly said he'd do it for me. Neither of us liked the old bastard. He'd yelled at us all the time when we were kids.

I had to wait for Dad to speak. But it seemed like he was intent on dragging this out. He waited a few more minutes before Tatum lumbered in through the door, shaking off the water that coated his thick fur.

"Very well," Dad said. He put on his glasses and looked at some papers on his desk. "Let's get down to business. Liam Mitoh, you've been summoned today to discuss a matter of great importance."

I didn't like how Dad called me by my full name. I got that this was a formal meeting and all, but it was a stark reminder of what came first— the tribe or me.

Maybe that's why I forgot to monitor my big mouth and said, "Right. You want me to kill Sophia."

Poole gave a nervous gasp. Dad frowned, and Elder Malison said,

"Watch your tongue, boy. You forget your place. Just because you've won the Cup doesn't mean we welcome you back with open arms."

I had to *really* try hard not to flip Malison off and give him a big F.U. Madame Wells showed no emotion at all.

I swallowed. "Sorry. I'll let you explain."

I really wasn't helping my case.

Dad cleared his throat. "As I was saying, *Liam*," Dad said harshly, as a reminder to behave, "you've been chosen for a special mission, one that does concern Miss Henley."

My heart was about pounding out of my chest. Were they going to *make me* murder Sophia? Was I not being given a choice?

I wouldn't do it. They'd have to kill me first.

Dad looked to Poole. He shuffled his papers and said, "Miss Henley's performance in the Elemental Cup was... quite remarkable. She performed magic no First Year has ever accomplished before, magic that many Koigni struggle to conjure."

"And she made it look like she was going for a walk," Malison grumbled. "That sort of power cannot be contained. It must be destroyed."

It felt like the air was draining from my lungs. I was totally going to freak out.

"Let's not get ahead of ourselves," Dad said quickly, and he glanced at me. He'd probably noticed all the color had drained from my face. "Liam, before you take Miss Henley's life, we ask that you find evidence to prove that she is indeed the one the prophecy speaks of. Undeniable evidence," Dad added as Poole opened his mouth.

"Yes. I motioned for her to be killed either way, but clearly, I was outvoted," Malison said with a snide glance at Wells. Again, she didn't respond.

"Do you have any questions?" Dad asked, looking at me. It was so calm and casual. I felt like I was walking around on a different planet.

"Yeah, I have a question. Why me?" I asked. I didn't care that my tone was nasty. They were asking me to commit murder, kill someone I loved. Well, they didn't know that, but still. I wouldn't kill someone even if they were a stranger, let alone my Sophia.

"Because you're the Toaqua that's closest to her. We can't stage any accidents. It would look too suspicious," Poole spoke. "Neither can we send assassins. Koigni will be expecting it, and if we were discovered, it would set off an intertribal war, one we cannot win. No one will suspect you could hurt her after your participation in the Cup last year together, and it is obvious Miss Henley trusts you. She won't see this coming, if it's from you."

This was sick. It was so, so wrong. At the same time, I was kind of glad it was me who was chosen, because at least I knew about it and wouldn't have to fend Sophia off from any Toaqua assassins.

Baine, please help me. I looked up at the benches desperately. Baine had been our tournament mentor. He liked Sophia. Could he really throw her to the wolves so easily?

Baine must've noticed my pleading look, because he sat forward and said, "I for one think we're getting ahead of ourselves. I spent all semester mentoring Miss Henley. If she was the prophesied one, I'd certainly know by now. Her performance in the Cup was phenomenal, but surely just the mark of a strong Koigni— and probably a one-off, if you want my honest opinion."

"You wouldn't notice she was the prophesied child if she came up and told you herself," Malison snapped back.

I was grateful for Baine's support, but inwardly, I hated that I agreed with Malison. Sophia could be parading around in a t-shirt advertising she was the chosen one with a neon sign that confirmed it and Baine would be oblivious.

"Remember that this is the girl that struggled to light a candle at the start of last semester," Baine replied coolly.

"Exactly! Look how much she grew in that time! Imagine what she could do if she were given six months, a year?" Malison bellowed.

"This mission is too risky!" Baine shouted back. "Koigni will discover we've slaughtered their precious child, and it'll start a war!"

"War is already coming, you old fool!" Malison roared, pounding his walking stick on the floor. "We have to strike before they strike us!"

"Um, excuse me?" I crossed my arms, and the room's attention turned to me. "What about asking how I feel about all of this? You haven't gotten me to agree, first of all."

"You'll do your duty to your tribe," Malison snarled.

"This isn't a task. You're asking me to take a life," I emphasized.

"And for what? Because you're scared of a little girl, one that could never hurt anyone?"

Madame Wells raised an eyebrow. It was the first expression I saw her make all day.

I didn't believe what they were saying about Sophia. I didn't even care that I knew the prophecy was true. Sophia wasn't like that. She wouldn't hurt a fly. I knew that about her.

Well, okay, maybe she'd hurt Haley. But it's not like anyone else wouldn't, either.

"You'll agree, Liam, because we have something you need," Dad responded calmly.

Just then, a door opened behind me. I turned. I nearly fell over when I recognized who it was.

It was Carter and Tiara— the students who'd died after Carter crashed Tiara during Flight class last year. They were alive?

At first I thought I had them mistaken for someone else, but on closer inspection, I knew it had to be them. Carter and Tiara had been in one of my classes freshman year. I didn't know them well, but I knew what they looked like and was certain this couldn't be a trick.

Tiara was some sort of giant lizard called a lindwyrm— her scales were amethyst, and she had a long neck with a small head and a thin tail that ended in several snake heads. She had feathery wings that were all different shades of purple, a plume of smaller feathers around her head, and pointed ears. She curled her head around Carter protectively, and he held her to him, like he was scared and didn't want to let her go.

Tiara *had* been dead. She wasn't moving on the cart when the teachers had brought her in. She'd been declared dead on the scene, a wooden beam rammed through her heart.

Though there was no indication of those injuries now. She seemed like she was completely fine, like nothing had ever happened to her. Her eyes were bright and alert. The only indication she'd died at all was a long, thick scar across her chest and middle.

"This is impossible," I said hollowly. "You're dead."

"No. Well, yes, we were," Carter said, with a nervous glance upward at my dad. "The Water Council saved us."

I had to hang on to the stand to keep from falling over. Why would the Water tribe save someone from another House? Carter was from Yapluma.

"Tell him, Carter," Dad encouraged.

Carter looked nervously at him, and then at me, before hugging Tiara tighter to him.

"It was almost like a dream," Carter said monotonously. "Tiara died, and then I was dead. Everything was just... gone. I thought we were to join the ancestors, but before we could, I felt myself returning to my body. Then I woke up in the Serpent Assembly, and me and Tiara were fine."

Carter shivered. I just stared at him. Tiara nudged Carter with her head to comfort him.

"I can't go back home, you see... because it would make everyone freak out," he explained. "I've been hiding here. Toaqua has been taking good care of me."

Understandable. People coming back from the dead wasn't something that happened every day.

My mouth was really dry. I turned around to look back up at the Elders.

"Tell me how you did it," I said. "Or I won't believe it."

"That's classified information," Malison snapped. "We'll be prepared to deliver your Familiar back to you on sight of Sophia Henley's dead body."

His words made my entire form go cold. Thinking of Sophia, dead... it made me want to throw up.

What if this was all a trick? I didn't believe anyone had the power to raise the dead.

But... Carter and Tiara were standing in front of me. I'd seen Tiara's body myself. How could I deny that?

"Tell me everything, Carter," I asked, looking at him. "I want to know."

"I..." Carter balked. "I don't remember much. It was all a blur."

He started squirming. He seemed uncomfortable... almost like he was going to cry. Remembering your death and resurrection probably wasn't very comfortable.

"It's okay, Carter," Dad told him gently. "You can go."

Carter didn't waste time. He practically ran out the doorway he came through, and Tiara followed. I still had so many questions, how it happened, how it could be possible… but I doubted I'd ever find Carter and be able to ask. I bet that the Toaqua Council had hidden him someplace good, where he'd never be found.

"No more questions," Malison barked. "You can either decide if you want your Familiar back or if you'll spare an undeserving Koigni's life. That is, if you're up for the task. I'm worried you'll faint on the job."

My face burned. It'd been *so* fucking embarrassing that I'd passed out on stage for everyone to see after the Cup was over. Even though I'd won, some people still thought I was weak.

I tried to analyze quickly what I knew. Somehow, the Toaqua Elders did bring Tiara and Carter back from the dead. I didn't see how they could bring Nashoma back, seeing as how his body had been so badly broken and he'd been… gone… for some time. He'd been buried for over six months now.

But Tiara's body had been ruined, and they'd fixed that. Why would they promise something they couldn't deliver on?

I could get my Familiar back. But it was at a cost— a price I wasn't willing to pay. Sophia's life.

But it'd been my fault Nashoma died in the first place. I could fix my mistake.

How could I pick between Nashoma and Sophia? It was an impossible choice.

There had to be a loophole somewhere. "What if I prove that Sophia isn't the one? Are you going to refuse to bring back Nashoma?" I asked.

"Sophia Henley dies, or you get nothing," Malison hissed.

"Elder Malison, that is *enough*." Dad's voice was harsh and rough. The room quieted.

Dad glanced at me.

Poole subbed in, "We are prepared to restore Nashoma to life once you've either completed your mission or have provided sufficient evidence that Miss Henley isn't who we suspect she is— evidence that proves without a doubt."

Without a doubt? That was asking for the moon. They wouldn't mind if I killed her without sufficient evidence, but proving her innocence would mean finding proof that the prophecy wasn't real, or that she wasn't the one. How could you disprove something that was purposefully mysterious and left up to interpretation?

"You have until the end of the semester, Liam. If no progress has been made in that time, we will do what we must to control the situation," Dad said bluntly.

I knew exactly what that meant.

"This session is dismissed." Dad stood up, his chair scraping backward. The other Elders got up and left, each of them leaving out different doors. The only ones still remaining in the hall were me, Dad, and Baine, who'd stuck around to probably talk to me about what a great idea it was to kill my tournament buddy.

"How could you do this to me?" I asked Dad the moment he'd joined me on the main floor. "You *knew*. You had information on how to bring Nashoma back for months, and you didn't tell me."

"Liam," he started, but I took a step back.

"No. You didn't tell me a thing. You're still not. Now you're using it to try to get me to hurt Sophia. How could you?"

Dad's eyes flashed with a small sign of guilt. "You know I wouldn't do this unless it was absolutely necessary."

"You're using him as *leverage*," I said, and my voice broke. "How would you feel if I used Tatum against you to get something done?"

He winced, and Tatum grumbled behind him. Dad responded, "I know it's not right. But this must be done. For the good of the tribe. They're more important than us, Liam."

I wasn't sure who he was trying to convince, himself or me. I looked him in the eye. "Dad, if I prove that Sophia's not the prophesied one, you'll let her live, right? You won't go back on your word?"

Dad stared at me for a moment. "I promise to you that if you find evidence that shows Sophia isn't the one Koigni is looking for, I will hold the council to their word, and she will be able to keep her life. But, Liam, you have to understand... it doesn't look good for her."

Fuck no, it didn't. But I had to find a way. I took a shuddering breath. "Dad, please don't make me do this."

Dad put his hand on my shoulder. "You were once going to be chief of this tribe, son. Now's your chance to prove to me that you're the man I think you are, and do what's needed to be done for your people."

Dad dropped his hand off my shoulder and left. I was still smoldering when Tatum's fuzzy tail vanished around the corner.

Seriously? He was using me as a pawn, and all he had to say was *be a man, Liam?* I hated that type of shit.

Baine came up behind me. He was a little more sympathetic. "As I'm teaching you this semester, I've been assigned to help you with your mission."

"You mean helping me to plot to take Sophia's life?" I asked, and I whirled around. "How can you be okay with this?"

"I'm not. However, I saw her during the tournament, as we all did. It's been hard to convince the others that her magic was a fluke," Baine said kindly. He sighed. "Even I have had doubts. Sophia is a sweet girl."

"Then you see why I can't do this. She would never—"

"It doesn't matter." Baine cut me off. "The Toaqua Council can't stand by and do nothing when Koigni grows stronger every day."

Baine paused cautiously. "But Liam, you do understand." He took a heavy breath. "If you do find evidence that Sophia is the one, and it's enough to prove that the prophecy is real, you're going to have to take her life. You won't have a choice."

I stared at the floor instead of him. "How can you ask that of me?"

"Because I know you'll do the right thing. You'll put your tribe first, as all of us would," Baine said simply. "I'm hoping as much as you are that this is all hearsay and Sophia is just another ordinary girl. Yet I think we both know that isn't the case... and I want you to be prepared."

I wasn't standing around to hear anymore of this shit. "Whatever."

I jammed my hands in my pockets and turned around. I was backed into a corner. Nashoma or Sophia. I kept going back and forth between the both of them. I wanted both. But it seemed like I could only have one or the other.

"By the way, Liam..." Baine added before I got to the door, and I turned. "We sent multiple Elementai to investigate the cave after the tournament was over, and found no source of magical properties within it whatsoever," he said. "We don't know how you made it out of that cave, or what healed you. We've gone over it a million times, and only one thing is clear: you shouldn't be here right now, and yet you are."

My blood ran cold. The cave wasn't magical? But then... how could I have survived? Did Nashoma use some ancestral spirit healing powers on me when he came to help, or what? That had to be it.

I shrugged in response and said, "I don't know how I made it out of that cave. But I guess you all should feel lucky that I did."

I didn't give him a chance to respond. I was out the door and swimming upward before he got another word out.

When I reached the surface, I laid back on the water and floated there for an hour, thinking. The cold didn't bother me. I was too busy thinking about what I was going to do.

The Elders wanted proof Sophia was the one to lead Koigni to glory. That was the problem. I already *knew* Sophia was the prophesied one. I already had proof. I'd seen it myself when she'd found that totem in the cave.

I needed to work all semester on finding... or creating... enough evidence to clear her name, and I somehow had to do it while Baine was watching me. I had no idea how I was going to do this.

But... that still didn't change the fact that if the prophecy came true, our race would be in danger. There would be a war, and thousands of Elementai would die— probably at Sophia's hands. Or at least by her leadership. My tribe feared that Koigni would rise to power again and it would be the end of us all. Could I really let thousands of innocent people, and their mythical creatures, die because I loved someone? Our entire way of life, and our world, would be destroyed if the prophecy came true. Was saving Sophia's life the right thing to do, or was I just being selfish?

I had a choice to make. The woman I loved, or my tribe?

I shook that off. Maybe there was a way to reverse the prophecy somehow, make it not come true. There had to be. I could save Sophia, and I could save the tribe. Nobody had to die. And I could get Nashoma back on top of it.

Should I tell Sophia? I immediately shot down the question the minute my mind brought it up. Telling the girl I was dating I was involved in a plot to murder her wasn't going to get me any points. I wanted to keep her out of this... as much as it revolved around her. The less she knew for now, the better. It would keep her safer. I didn't want her freaking out all the time on how we were going to prove to the Toaqua Elders she wasn't a threat. That was my job.

Something else bothered me. I couldn't shake off how weird it was that I'd survived the tournament, and that I'd woken up in the cave with hardly a mark on me when I was seconds away from death only moments before. I hadn't thought about it since the tournament, because there were magical places all over earth that would have those kinds of abilities to heal, but now that I knew the cave wasn't one of them, I couldn't stop.

Sophia had said I'd already been healed when she found me. What had happened between the time she'd been gone and when she'd came back?

I didn't know. If the cave hadn't healed me in the tournament, what did?

sophia

FOUR

I would've liked to say the Koigni Elders didn't frighten me, and that after everything I'd been through with the Elemental Cup that nothing could frighten me anymore, but saying so would be a lie. My tongue felt like sandpaper as I followed the phoenix through the castle toward Redbird Hall. My first day back at Orenda Academy was supposed to be magical. It wasn't supposed to make me crap my pants. This was *so* not the reason I wanted to be changing my panties today.

The phoenix led Esis and me down a long hallway. I'd passed through it before but never had any classes down here. The hall came to a T at the end and stopped at a pair of double doors. The doors were decorated with elaborate carvings of flames and had big metal hinges on them that were twisted into artistic designs.

The phoenix stopped outside the doors and cocked its head toward them. Was I supposed to knock, or just stroll right in? I glanced down to the letter in my hand. I considered it an invitation and stepped forward. I twisted the big metal knob, and the doors swung open.

A long room stretched far back into the castle. It was at least half the length of a football field, but narrower. The ceiling reached two stories high. Candles flickered in old candelabra chandeliers high above my head, casting a dull orange glow across the room. Portraits hung from the stone walls every few feet, each depicting a female Hawkei with their

Familiar standing next to them. Some of the Hawkei had stronger European features like I did, while others looked more like the original Hawkei, before they brought other people into the tribe. One thing was clear, however. Given their expressions and the Familiars that stood beside them, each portrait was a former Koigni Elder.

At first glance, I guessed Redbird Hall was one of the castle's smaller ballrooms. Then I noticed a blackboard stretched across the wall at the far end of the room. This must've been where the third and fourth year Koigni trained.

"Come in, Sophia," Madame Doya called.

She stood at the far end of the room, where a long conference table had been set up in front of the blackboard. Four other women were seated in the chairs beside her. They all stared at me with that same pointed expression Doya always gave me. This was basically my worst nightmare. I was walking into a room of Doya clones, except none of them had her fiery-red hair.

I started down the long walk toward the conference table. It seemed to take forever. The only sounds came from the pad of my sneakers across the marble floor and a low growl bubbling up from Naomi's throat. The lioness stood in front of the conference table, glaring at me.

I looked to the Elders while I walked, trying to get a feel of what I was up against. My eyes first fell upon the woman in the middle. She sat up straight, with her head held high and shoulders back. Her expression remained stoic. She had long dark hair, high cheekbones, and full lips, and she wore an expensive-looking black pantsuit. Her features looked so similar to Haley's that it felt like I was looking at Haley thirty years into the future. The phoenix that had brought me here swooped down and landed on the back of the woman's chair. I knew instantly this was Annette Westfenix, Koigni Chieftess and Haley's mother.

I already hated her.

The three other woman didn't seem as intimidating as Madame Doya or Haley's mom, but that wasn't saying much. When you toned down the sheer fear Madame Doya sent quaking through every student who crossed her path, you were still left with a heck of a lot of terror.

Beside Annette sat a woman with a thin nose and large eyes. Her skin was impeccably smooth and her hair a shiny chestnut brown, but there was something in her features that suggested she was at least twenty years older than Doya. She wore all kinds of animal prints, from the cheetah-print sweater to the zebra-print handbag. The largest serpent I'd ever seen, measuring at least twelve feet long, draped around her neck like a giant living scarf. It was mostly black, with gold and orange patterns gracing its scales. Its eyes trained on me, and it stuck its tongue out like snakes do. I almost gasped when flames shot up from its tongue before it pulled them quickly back into its mouth.

The other two women were ancient, with matching white hair and similar facial structures. The Elder on the right had a tarantula-looking Familiar in front of her, only its body was the size of a dinner plate. The way it looked at me with all those eyes made my skin crawl. The thing could probably kill me with a single bite.

The woman sitting on the far left didn't have a Familiar at her side, which only led me to believe it was something too big to fit into the castle. It was probably a dragon. Even *I* knew fire dragons were a great sign of power for a Koigni, and no Elder would sit on the Koigni Council without the most powerful of Familiars.

I didn't know what to do with myself once I reached the conference table, so I just stood there awkwardly, squeezing Esis and glancing between the Elders.

"Sit, Sophia," Madame Doya commanded.

I did as I was told. Esis settled in my lap and peeked over the top of the table.

"It's my pleasure to introduce you to the Koigni Council," Madame Doya said, gesturing to Annette. As usual, she didn't sound pleased in the slightest. "This is Annette Westfenix, our Koigni Chieftess. To her right, Madame Benally. These two women on either end are Madame Chavis and Madame Chavis, but they prefer Lorelai and Gwendolyn, as it's easier to tell them apart that way. Thank you for joining us." Madame Doya finally took her chair beside Annette.

When no one spoke, I cleared my throat. "Have I done something wrong?"

Annette cocked an eyebrow at me. She was intense, though not nearly as intense as Doya. "Trust me, Miss Henley, if you'd done something wrong, we'd be meeting in the Elders' quarters in the Koigni village. We decided to meet here to make it more convenient for you. In response to your question, you've done nothing wrong. On the contrary, you did everything right."

I gaped at her. "Excuse me?"

"In the tournament, Sophia," Doya snapped, like I was daft.

Lovely. She was even worse than I remembered. And I'd already agreed to train with her in private this semester. Those training sessions were going to be wonderful. And by wonderful, I meant brutal.

"Your performance was quite impressive," Madame Benally said, stroking her serpent's head.

"It was?" I asked. I mean, I knew it was. My teammates had assured me First Years weren't usually capable of that level of magic. But I didn't know how much the Elders had seen from the aerial cameras— or how much they'd *felt* when I pushed against their powers.

"Yes," Annette agreed. "We couldn't be sure you were the prophesied one when you arrived here at Orenda Academy. Following certain events, namely, when you bonded with... that..." she gestured to Esis, "we were almost certain you were not the one the prophecy speaks of."

I shifted nervously.

"Your performance in the tournament made it clear," Annette said. "The ancestors, for whatever reason, chose you to elevate our House." I didn't like the proud look on her face, like she was above everyone else.

"I wasn't the only Koigni to make it through the tournament, though," I pointed out. "Surely the others showed impressive marks as well."

Annette frowned. "They made it through alive, yes, but not without consequence. Most were injured or lost their teammates. Your Fire was by far the most powerful, and the most resistant against ours."

"So, what does this mean?" I hugged Esis even tighter. Had they called me here to figure out what he was? If I was as powerful as they claimed, perhaps they suspected he was powerful, too.

"We want you to fulfill the prophecy, Sophia," Annette said simply.

A wave of emotions tumbled through me. My mind flashed back to the conversation Doya and I had at the Elemental Ball only a few short weeks ago. She assured me that if I didn't do this, the blood of thousands of Koigni would be on my hands. But I didn't want to go through with it if it meant Elementai from the other Houses would die as well. Fewer, perhaps, but the risk was still there. How could I make this type of decision?

"I don't know how to fulfill it," I said.

Doya shot me a pointed expression. "That's exactly what we're here to talk about."

"I thought you didn't know, either."

"No, we don't," Annette admitted. "But we have a way for you to find out."

The prospect of learning more about the prophecy intrigued me. If I knew more about it, maybe I could find a way to save lives before it was fulfilled.

"How?" I asked.

Annette smiled, but it didn't reach her eyes. "We intend for you to ask the ancestors yourself."

I furrowed my brow. Was this some sort of joke? "I'm not a chieftess or the daughter of one. I can't contact the ancestors on my own."

"We know a way you can," Doya cut in.

"Can't *you* contact the ancestors?" I asked Annette. "I mean, since you're chieftess."

She shook her head. "When chiefs call upon the ancestors, it only calls down the spirit guides of those partaking in the ritual. Usually, those spirit guides never actually speak to us. Talking face to face with the ancestors is very rare. We need to be able to speak to them to get the information we need. How much do you know about Hawkei history?"

I stroked Esis' fur from under the table. "I know some if it, but I'm sure there's plenty more to learn."

"On May eighteenth each year, we celebrate Ancestors' Day," Annette said. "It's the anniversary of when the ancestors descended upon the earth to gift us our powers. It is the only day of the year when a Hawkei can speak to their ancestors... and contact an ancestor who is not their own spirit guide."

"I've never heard of that. I thought only a chieftain or the firstborn of a chief could contact the ancestors."

Annette gave a sly smile. "What we're about to tell you is highly classified information. Can we trust you to keep this secret?"

They all glared at me. I felt like I might burst into flame at any moment.

"I don't think I have a choice," I forced out through a dry mouth.

Annette took a deep breath. She must've approved of my answer, because she continued. "It's true that's what most Hawkei believe, but what they don't know is that the Anichi ruins, though mostly destroyed, still hold power."

"The Anichi ruins?" I'd never heard of such a place.

"The ruins lie deep in the forest where the Soul House once resided," Annette explained. "This was the site where our ancestors descended and where the Elementai received their powers. You must go there on Ancestors' Day and contact Showana Harjo. She was the Anichi who gave the prophecy 120 years ago. You must ask her about the pieces of the prophecy we suspect the other Houses are holding secret. And you must get her to tell you what you're to do in order to fulfill the prophecy."

"Okay..." It sounded so simple, not the type of thing that all the Elders had to come to Orenda Academy to tell me about. "What's the catch?"

Madame Doya let out of a puff of air. She almost sounded amused. "There's a reason no one has been to the ruins for ages. Long ago, the Koigni Elders placed obstacles within the ruins to keep the other Houses out."

Of course. Because the Koigni were power-hungry and wanted to keep the power to contact the ancestors to themselves. Typical.

"Most Elementai know it's dangerous to approach the Anichi ruins, but they don't truly understand the obstacles that lie within," Doya continued. "Nor would they understand what it took to actually speak with the ancestors once they got there. We have fewer than five months to train and get you ready to face the ruins."

My jaw hung slack. They wanted me to face the Elemental Cup all over again! All because they couldn't put their pride aside and work nicely with the other Houses?

"Why can't you just guide me through the ruins?" I asked, in a less-than-nice tone. I was really starting to get peeved off with this whole prophecy thing. "You're the most powerful Koigni in all the tribe."

Madame Doya's jaw tightened. "Because, Sophia, *we* are not the ones the ancestors chose. They want *you*. If we go along, they may not speak to us. We can't risk that and have to wait another year to contact them again."

I couldn't believe this was happening! And Doya had already gotten me to agree to private training sessions before I knew any of this. But that didn't mean I couldn't back out...

I crossed my arms and leaned back in my chair. "Let me guess, these obstacles are pretty dangerous, huh?"

"Naturally," Annette answered.

Of course.

"However, the obstacles themselves are rather insignificant compared to the importance of the ceremony," Annette said.

"Forgive me..." How did I address her? Madame Westfenix? Chieftess? Your Highness? "...Chieftess," I went with. "But what if I decide not to do this? You're asking me to risk my life for a cause I'm not sure I even believe in."

Lorelai and Gwendolyn gasped in unison.

"How ever could you not believe in this prophecy?" Madame Benally demanded. "This is about elevating the status of your own House! This is what the ancestors want!"

I reacted without thinking. Before I knew it, I'd leaned forward and exploded. "Well, maybe the Elementai should stop trying to kill me, then!"

I immediately recoiled and pressed my back to the chair. My cheeks flushed, and the room went dead silent. I couldn't believe I'd just yelled at the Elders! Could they behead me for something like that?

Annette pressed her palms to the table and took a deep breath. She looked like she was trying to calm herself, like her head might burst into flames at any moment if she didn't keep it together. She stood, breathing heavily. Finally, her eyes sprang open. There was a fire behind them I couldn't quite explain. All I knew was that if I'd been standing, my knees would've given out beneath me. She'd definitely been holding back on the intensity. No wonder Haley was the way she was, if her mother was capable of such hostility with a simple glance.

"Sophia Henley," Annette scolded, like I were her own daughter. "I tried to play nice, but I will not tolerate such an attitude from a member of my own House. I am your Chieftess, and you will treat me and your Elders with respect if you hope to ever have a future in the Hawkei society."

Holy shit! If I thought I was scared when I walked into Redbird Hall, it was nothing compared to the fear racing through my veins now. Were all Koigni women so terrifying?

Yes. The answer was undoubtedly yes.

Esis puffed up his chest and lowered his head, pointing his nubby horns at her. I had to hold him back as his tiny little paws clawed at the table, trying to get to the chieftess.

"You will do this, Sophia," Annette demanded. "If you refuse, the Koigni will not hesitate to punish you by any means necessary."

I couldn't believe this woman! If she thought this was the way to make me comply, she was *so* wrong. "You can't be serious."

"Does she look like she's joking?" Doya snapped. Naomi bared her teeth from nearby.

I scoffed. These women were horrible! Someone needed to put them in their place. "Bring on the torture, then."

Annette straightened, looking amused. She placed a hand on her hip and turned to Madame Doya. "Who do you think should go first, Eleanor? One of her teammates, perhaps? The Toaqua boy, Liam Mitoh? Or better yet, her sister— Amelia?"

I shot to my feet. "What are you talking about? Leave my family and friends out of this!"

Annette let out a forced laugh. She cocked her head at me and gave me the fakest smile I'd ever seen. She had it down even better than Haley. "Oh, Sophia, you didn't think we'd punish you directly, did you? If you don't do this, your friends and your family will suffer first. Then comes your Familiar. *Then* you."

Esis squeaked and pressed his face into my belly, shielding his eyes from the Elders' evil stares. Madame Doya grinned proudly from beside Annette. It was the first time I thought I'd ever seen her truly smile. What kind of people were these women if this is what they found joy in?

My guts twisted at the thought of losing everyone I loved. It was so sickening to imagine that I felt like I might puke right then and there. As much as I'd love to see the Koigni Council's faces if I refused, it wasn't worth sacrificing my loved ones to their wrath.

"Fine," I bit out harshly. Fire quaked in my body, begging to escape. "Fine. I'll do this, and I'll fulfill your prophecy, but on one condition."

Annette relaxed back into her chair, but I remained standing. "That depends on the condition."

"If a war breaks out so that I can fulfill this prophecy, my family and friends get full immunity." I stepped forward and leveled my gaze on Annette. Never before had my eyes felt so hard and stone cold. I hoped she felt a mere sliver of what I'd felt when she looked at me this way. "Under no circumstances will the Koigni touch them or their Familiars."

Annette straightened her back and glanced to the other Elders. Her eyes lingered on Doya's far too long. Finally, she turned to me. "Agreed."

A huge weight lifted off my shoulders. I could hardly believe that worked.

"Which Elementai shall be placed under the protection of this agreement?" Annette asked.

Lorelai— the one without a Familiar present— grabbed a piece of paper that lay in front of her on the table and began scribbling down names.

"Liam Mitoh, Imogen Ahnild— and their entire families— Jonah Chanee, Amelia Henley, and my parents, Robert and Suzan Henley."

Madame Doya twisted her nose when I called them my parents.

Yeah, bitch, they're my parents. They raised my ass. You wanna take this outside?

"Don't forget to write down their Familiars as well," I demanded of Lorelai. She barely reacted to my tone and just continued writing.

"That's quite a long list," Annette said with a frown.

"It's a dangerous mission," I countered.

Annette narrowed her eyes, then spoke coolly. "Well, it looks like we have a deal. You will begin training with Madame Doya effective immediately to prepare for Ancestors' Day. You can work out the details together later. In the meantime..."

She stood. "I have lunch date with my daughter. Dismissed."

I couldn't get out of there fast enough. I whirled around and nearly raced down the long hall toward the door. But I barely touched the handle when Annette's voice called across the hall.

"Oh, Sophia?" she said.

I took a deep breath, forced my Fire down, and turned to look at her. I didn't reply for fear that flames would come shooting out of my mouth if I spoke.

"Don't think that just because we made a bargain that it means you've won," she warned. "We will be watching you closely. *Very* closely. There are certain things about you that don't add up..."

Even from this distance, I saw her glance down at Esis in my arms. Madame Doya smirked.

I wanted to punch the bitches. All five of them. But especially Doya and Annette.

Annette pursed her lips. "And I intend to find out why that is."

My blood ran cold. I was a freaking Koigni with fire power, and my blood *ran cold*.

Annette tossed her dark hair over her shoulder and strolled out a doorway at the other end of the room. Doya and Naomi strutted behind her like they'd never been more pleased. The other Elders followed.

I whirled toward the door, bolted out of the room, and sprinted down the hallway. Anything to get away from those monsters as fast as I could. I nearly ran into a huge Nivita guy when I rounded the corner, but he jumped out of the way and continued on down the hall.

I couldn't take it any longer. My emotions were on the verge of exploding right there in the hallway. Not wanting to hurt Esis, I set him on the ground and took several steps away from him.

Then I burst. My hair ignited like the flames on Hades' head from Disney's *Hercules*. I paced back and forth, cursing, then slammed my fists against the stone wall. My knuckles ached, but it didn't matter. I'd rather take the pain than let the Koigni Council touch a single hair on my loved ones' heads.

After kicking the wall a few more times, I finally slumped against it and sank to the ground. I curled into a ball and pulled my knees to my chest. My hair— which was back to normal— draped over my shoulder to hide my face. I was too angry to cry, so I just sat there shaking. Thank the ancestors the hall was deserted and no one was around to see my outburst.

No one except Esis. He hopped forward and jumped onto my back. His tiny little arms wrapped around my neck.

"Oh, buddy," I sighed. I tore him off my neck, which was hard, considering he didn't want to let go and he was a lot stronger than he looked. Then I cradled him in my arms and buried my face in his white fur. "I love you. I'd never let anything bad happen to you."

My mind raced with thoughts of what the Elders would do to Esis if they found out how powerful he was. They might separate us to use him for themselves. I wouldn't put it past them. They might even go after Liam and prevent Esis from healing him at all. They weren't screwing around with those threats back there.

Which meant that even though I wanted to tell Liam about Esis' healing powers, even though I was *ready*, I couldn't mention it. Because now that the Elders were watching me, it'd be too suspicious if Liam made another miraculous recovery like he did in the cave. I couldn't dangle a possible treatment in front of Liam's face and then tell him he couldn't use it. It was too cruel.

Why didn't I just spit out the truth earlier? Ancestors, I was pissed!

"Sophia!"

My head snapped upward to see Imogen rushing toward me. Thank God! A friendly face. I needed her right now.

Imogen bent to her knees beside me and placed a comforting hand on my back. Sassy stretched her head out of her bag and touched her nose to my Familiar's.

"What's wrong?" Imogen demanded. "What are you doing down here?"

Shit. How was I supposed to explain this? I couldn't tell her the truth. The Koigni Elders would hurt her if she knew. Technically, my deal didn't specify what I could and couldn't reveal to others, just that I couldn't tell them about the Anichi ruins, but I had a feeling the council would see that as a breech of our agreement either way.

So, as much as I wanted to confide in Imogen— to confide in anyone — my lips were sealed. Imogen would never know what had just happened to me.

"I— I got lost," I lied.

"Um... okay." Imogen didn't sound like she was buying it, but she didn't pry, either. "It happens to all of us. It's a huge castle. You okay?" She sat beside me, and Sassy rested her head on my knee.

I shrugged. "Just thinking, I guess."

"Want to talk about it?"

I shrugged. "I don't know. It's a bunch of little things," I lied. "A new semester. Liam. The prophecy."

Woops. I didn't mean to let that last bit slip.

"Hey, Im," I said quickly, before she could ask about the details. "You read a lot. What can you tell me about Hawkei prophecies?"

"What do you want to know?" she asked.

"Who can give them? Are there any prophets alive today? That kind of stuff."

She shook her head. "We don't call them prophets. We call them *naderei*. They're really rare. I don't think there's been more than ten or so since the Hawkei got their magic from the ancestors," she explained.

"Can anyone can become a... *naderei?*" I tested the word on my tongue. "Or just Anichi?"

She nodded. "It's not connected to Soul or Spirit magic, so an Elementai from any House could be one, not just someone who was from Anichi. They're born, not made. Chosen by the ancestors to make prophecies and the like."

"Do you think there are any *naderei* today who could help explain the prophecy?" I asked hopefully.

She shook her head. "I wouldn't get your hopes up on finding one. I think the last one the tribe had was when the prophecy was made, and even then, the only people that can understand prophecies are the people that created them. *Naderei* can see the past and the future, but they usually have trouble making sense of it," she said.

"Darn." I felt so frustrated. This was getting nowhere.

"They're usually born when the tribe's about to be in great peril. Wars, famines, things like that," Imogen stated. "So it's probably a good thing one isn't hanging around."

I wasn't so sure about that. The way the Koigni Elders made things sound, there should be a *naderei* on every block, for what the tribe was about to face.

I didn't want to tell Imogen about that, though, so I changed the subject. "So, what are you doing in this part of the castle?"

"I'm trying to find our Ancient Familiars classroom so we know where to go when classes start. So it's kind of perfect that I ran into you."

"That sounds like a good idea." I got to my feet.

Imogen sniffed the air. "Does something smell burnt to you?"

"No," I lied. I'd just been lit up in flames. Of course there were going to be lingering odors.

"Yeah," Imogen said, sniffing again. "It smells like burnt hair."

I went rigid. I quickly glanced to the ends of my hair. A half an inch of it was dark and twisted. I'd have to find a pair of scissors and trim off the singed pieces later.

I tossed my hair over my shoulder and held out my hand to help her up. "Do you want to hang out?"

"Of course, but I thought after all the time we spent together over break you'd want some time alone."

"No," I said, almost too quickly. "I want to be with you."

The fact was, I didn't want to let Imogen out of my sight. I didn't want to let *any* of my friends out of my sight. I knew I had to, because of dorm assignments and classes and all that, but the thought made me uneasy.

The only solace I got in all of this was knowing that the Koigni Elders were making a huge mistake— a mistake that worked in my favor. They were training me to become stronger. One day, I might just become stronger than they were.

One day, they would come to regret what they'd done.

Liam

FIVE

We'd gotten back to school on a Sunday, and classes started immediately the next day. Sophia hadn't sought me out after the Koigni Elders summoned her, and I didn't look for her either after I'd had that pleasant chat with the Toaqua Elders. I searched for Sophia on Monday morning in the cafeteria, but she wasn't there. I hoped to the ancestors she wasn't avoiding me. Whatever her Elders had said to her couldn't have been good.

My classes were all over the place this semester, spread all throughout the day. Baine was my advisor, and I knew he'd be pulling me in for a meeting soon about graduation next year. I was pretty sure that meeting was going to turn into a talk about how we were going to murder my girlfriend instead of my future career.

Ugh. My life was so complicated.

After Advanced Toaqua Magic III on the beach, I wandered back to the cafeteria for lunch. But before I got there, I found her. My heart skipped a beat when I finally set eyes on Sophia. She was sitting on the edge of the fountain of the thunderbird, wearing a puffy blue coat and hat, and was feeding Esis fries. It looked like she'd totally forgotten to feed herself as she held the fries up in the air, trying to get Esis to do tricks.

Esis wasn't buying it. He turned his back on her and refused to look at her until she fed him another fry. He laid on his back and she dropped them one by one into his mouth, like he was some kind of king eating grapes. The little dude totally had Sophia wrapped around his finger.

The minute I saw her, I got this weird combination of happiness and guilt. She made me feel so much better just by looking at her. But at the same time, it made me feel worse, because I knew I was lying to her.

I wanted to tell her what was going on. Something inside told me to be honest. But I couldn't. There was just no way. If I told her that I'd been assigned to kill her, she'd lose it. She wouldn't want me anymore. I couldn't lose her like I lost Nashoma. I got that it was selfish, but I just couldn't.

There had to be a way to save her. To save us. I had five months before the semester ended in May. That was enough time. I'd figure out a way to convince the Toaqua Elders she wasn't the prophesied one, then once that was over with, I'd come clean and explain everything. *After* the threat was done with. I didn't want her worrying until then.

She heard me coming and looked up. Esis grumbled as she put the fries down and stopped feeding him.

"Going to protest some pipeline?" Sophia asked as I approached.

I didn't get what she was saying, until I realized I had my *Water Is Life* t-shirt on, underneath my open winter jacket. I'd gotten it for Christmas and just thrown it on this morning. I smiled at her as I sat down and said, "You know I would."

"And I'd be right there with you." She rested her head on my shoulder. I wasn't worried anyone would see, as practically no one came this way, so I let her do it.

"I saw Jonah and Imogen in the hallway earlier. They're searching for the kirin herd before class. Apparently, they're supposed to do a project on them together for a class," I told her. "They asked me if we wanted to join them."

"It sounds like fun," Sophia said, before she hesitated. "Liam... how do we tell them about us? Should we wait for them to find out?"

"They're gonna know something's up," I told her. "Might as well just come out with it."

She nodded. "Okay. Sounds fair."

I took Sophia's hand. It was so soft and warm in mine. I liked it.

We were supposed to meet Jonah and Imogen at the tree line where the greenhouses were, which wasn't too far away. There was a valley nearby just before the mountains where the kirin liked to roam.

I spotted Jonah and Imogen waiting near the tree line as the castle loomed behind us. Imogen had on this giant, fluffy white trench coat with a huge hood that appeared to be made of fox fur but I was sure was fake. She'd never wear real fur. It went past her feet so I couldn't see her boots. The coat pretty much swallowed Imogen up. Sassy played in the light snow at her feet, looking perfectly happy as she jumped into the air, hunting for mice.

Jonah looked like he was preparing to go to the Arctic. He had a trapper's hat on, a thick flannel coat, and boots that went up to his knees. It wasn't even that cold out. Even Squeaks was sporting a purple scarf that had the word *Yapluma* written across it.

We kept holding hands as we walked up to them. They spotted us. Both of their mouths dropped open.

Imogen jumped on Jonah's back and screamed. They fell over, and Sassy wagged her tail. Squeaks did this weird bucking-dance combination thing.

Esis strutted up to Sassy like he was outrageously proud of himself and gave her a high-five with his paw. She seemed disgruntled, like she'd lost some sort of game. I'm surprised she didn't pull out bet money and hand it to him.

Yeah, the little shit won. He got us together, though it took him the better part of a year.

"I can't believe it!" Imogen screeched as she untangled herself from Jonah. She stood up, but nearly fell over again. Jonah had to catch her. "You guys are together?!"

"Yes." Sophia nudged me. "We're a couple now."

"I'm not buying it," Jonah said, and he crossed his arms. "You guys kiss, or it didn't happen."

I opened my mouth to argue, but Sophia popped up on her toes and kissed me before I could say anything. It was our first kiss in front of people, and it took the words I was gonna say out of my mouth pretty quick.

"I knew it," Jonah said smugly. "Looks like I was right all along."

"This is *so awesome*," Imogen squealed. "I can't believe you two are finally dating."

"Yes, but you guys can't tell anyone," I said immediately, with emphasis and looking at Jonah. "This isn't for gossip."

"Well, *obviously*," Jonah said obnoxiously, rolling his eyes. "We aren't *stupid*."

"That's up for debate," I responded. I trusted Jonah, but at the same time, I knew if what Sophia and I were doing wasn't illegal he'd be spreading it to half of Kinpago by now.

"We won't tell anyone. Will we, Jonah?" Imogen said with a pointed look at him.

He sighed and gave a mopey expression. "No. But it's gonna suck keeping the juiciest secret at school under wraps."

"Yeah, well, it's gonna suck for *us* more if somebody knows, so keep your mouth shut," I snapped at him.

"Yeah, yeah." Jonah waved his hand at me. "Your bark is worse than your bite."

I flipped him off with my free hand. Sophia laughed. Imogen led the way as we started through the forest.

"Speaking of sucking—" Jonah started, but Imogen shushed him. We'd reached the end of the tree line, where the valley was. We peeked out through the trees at the kirin herd.

The kirin were a mixture of a horse and a deer-type being. They had tiny cloven hooves and small dished faces with little noses. Their fur was soft, green, brown, grey and blue in color, with large manes like those of lions ruffled around their heads. Their manes were a different color than their fur, but matched whatever earthy tone it was so they could easily blend into nature in case they had to hide.

The female kirin had a singular antler in the middle of their head, while the males had racks behind their large, curved ears. Their tails were long and thin, like cattle. Some of the biggest and oldest ones had scales on their backs, which caught the light and gleamed. A few peryton were dotted among the herd and were nibbling on roots of grass.

"We have to keep our voices down," Imogen said. "They'll easily frighten. We can't have them running away."

I nodded. The kirin were incredible creatures, and really gentle. But they were shy and reclusive, so it was rare for an Elementai to bond with one.

Unfortunately, Jonah wasn't one for subtlety. He fell out of the woods, and Squeaks followed him, tripping over her own hooves and going down face-first. The noise scared the herd, and they took off running.

"Oh, dammit," Imogen groaned as Jonah and Squeaks picked themselves back up. "Now we have to follow them."

Jonah got up with a disgusted expression and tried shaking all the snow off. Squeaks took her wing and attempted to wipe off his jacket, but she didn't do much besides just smack him into the snow again. The rest of us proceed onward after the herd.

Jonah shivered. "Snow sucks. I don't like the cold."

"Me either," Imogen quipped. "Everything's dead or frozen. I can't manipulate anything."

"I don't mind it, though it's different from what we had in Utah," Sophia said.

I shrugged. I liked the snow. More water everywhere.

We finally caught up with the herd in a different part of the valley. Kirin had more power over the weather than most magical creatures did. They could control multiple elements instead of just one, and because of it, had created a small patch in the valley that was green and warm. It looked strange, like spring had been planted right in the middle of winter.

"Ah. Finally." Jonah slithered out of his thick coat and threw it on the ground once we reached the warm patch. Sophia and I kept ours on as we watched Imogen cautiously proceed toward the nearest kirin.

"Here girl," she said gently. She reached into her pocket and pulled out a few small carrots. "It's okay, I won't hurt you."

The kirin stomped her hooves and rolled her eyes as Imogen crept toward her. Her nostrils flared, and just as Imogen was about to feed her the carrot, the kirin took off.

"Nice try, Im. I'm here for ya," Jonah said. He'd kicked back and was relaxing on the grass against Squeaks. It looked like Imogen was doing all the work for their group project.

"Shut up. You're too big. You'll scare them more," Imogen mumbled. Imogen approached the kirin again, then held out her hand cautiously. The kirin nibbled gently at the end of the carrot Imogen held out, before it snatched up the treat and ran away.

Imogen tried a few more times, and eventually, she got the kirin to eat the carrots out of her hand. Sassy swished her tail jealously at Imogen's feet.

By this time, the rest of the herd had gotten curious and gathered around us, though most of them kept a fair distance. We were able to give them a few pets, but if we came any closer than arm's length, the kirin ran away.

Although the rest of us couldn't get closer than a pat on the shoulder, Esis was riding on the back of a kirin as it galloped around the field. The kirin seemed to like him. His fur blew back in the wind as it carried him in circles around the pasture. I think Esis thought he looked pretty majestic, but to me, he just looked like an overly pompous hamster.

"Esis! Get back here!" Sophia giggled.

Esis chittered and jumped off the back of the kirin, rushing toward her. He fell into a large pile of snow by accident and popped his head out of it. He looked like a giant snowball. You'd never be able to find him if not for his large eyes.

Sophia swept Esis up from the snowdrift and snuggled him to her chest. "You're so spoiled."

Esis threw his tiny arms against Sophia's chest and gave her a hug. A bit of homesickness took over me. I missed Nashoma. I was again reminded that he could be here if I really wanted him to be... but Sophia wouldn't be.

Imogen scribbled some things into a notebook she'd taken out of a giant pocket in her coat, glancing at the kirin every now and then. Jonah yawned.

While they... or, Imogen... were working, Sophia asked to see my schedule. I gave it to her and she swapped me hers, so we could compare.

"Geez, Liam. You're really busy this semester," she said quietly as she glanced at my classes.

"Am I? I didn't really notice." I looked at the rest of my schedule over Sophia's shoulder. I had Advanced Toaqua Magic III on Monday and Wednesday mornings from eight a.m. until lunch, then a quick *elective* class after. I had Hawkei Legends the same day outdoors in the woods with Professor Lopez, which I was excited about, because it went deeper into Elementai history and lore than Hawkei History did. Tuesday and Thursday mornings I'd start with Alchemy Basics. I'd signed up for it early, not because I was interested in it but because Perot taught that class and I know he wanted me in at least one of his classes this semester.

"Looks like we have Unicornology on Tuesday and Thursday afternoons together." Sophia brightened.

"Seems like your Fridays are free. Mine too," I murmured as I scanned her schedule. It was disorganized, like mine, a bunch of random classes. I thought Sophia might have a clear structure of study now that she'd been at Orenda a while, but apparently not.

She was just a freshman, I guess. She had time to pick a major.

"Fridays can be our couple day." She smiled and hopped up and down a little. "I'm so excited."

Sophia then looked closer at the piece of paper. "Are you taking *Basket Weaving II?*"

"Shut up." I snatched the schedule out of her hands and stuffed it back into my bag. "So it calms me down, big deal."

She giggled again. "That's so cute, Liam."

I was blushing, and she could totally see it. The herd paused, looking up at something we couldn't see. I was grateful for the distraction. As if they were scared by something, the kirin stampeded away. A gust of wind swept them up, and they galloped upon it, the clouds carrying them into the sky so they could hide.

"I guess that's all the research we'll get done today," Imogen said with a sigh. "This isn't going to be easy."

Well, no. You chose Jonah as your partner, I thought. Jonah and I had once done projects together back in high school. Never again.

"Wow. That was exhausting." Jonah got up off the ground and stretched. "I feel like this semester is going to be a lot of work. No time for anything fun."

"That reminds me. There's a party at Riley's house tonight," Imogen said. "All Houses. His parents are gone for the weekend and it's far enough away from the rest of the Yapluma neighborhood that no teachers are gonna find out. You guys in?"

"Hell yeah, I'm in!" Jonah said back, and his eyes widened. "How didn't I hear about this sooner?"

"Guys, we should be careful," Sophia said slowly. "We need a DD."

"We aren't going to be driving cars," Jonah said scathingly.

"Carriages aren't much better, and I know Squeaks won't be able to take us back. I remember what happened at the ball," Sophia said, and she sent a sideways glance at Squeaks. The hippogriff batted her eyes and pretended to be innocent.

"So we'll call a carriage." Imogen shrugged. "Come on, Sophia, it's going to be *so* much fun."

She bit her lip and didn't answer. Sophia was being even more cautious than she usually was, and she was practically at Girl Scout level already. It was weird. Something felt... off.

I somewhat shared her concern. I knew the Water Council had eyes on me, and Sophia was probably being watched by her Elders, too. They were waiting for one of us to slip up, make a mistake. Getting drunk would only worsen the chances we would, and we were trying to lie low.

But at the same time, Yapluma always threw the best parties. They were the fun House. I hadn't been to a party since before Nashoma died. What was wrong with having a few drinks?

"We should go. We'll be safe. I promise," I told Sophia.

"Don't you have class tonight?" she asked curiously.

"Hawkei Legends doesn't start until this Wednesday. Let's go enjoy ourselves," I said.

"Well... okay," she said reluctantly, and Imogen and Jonah cheered. We started on back to the castle, and Jonah talked the entire time about how bomb the party was going to be. Sophia and I held hands on the way back, though we had to let go once we got back onto the main campus.

We entered into the main hallway. This time of day, it was packed with students.

"Imogen and I have to head to Ancient Familiars," Sophia said, checking her watch. "See you guys tonight?"

"Yep. We'll meet up in front of the Nivita dorms," I said. That was the safest option. "See you later."

I wanted to kiss Sophia goodbye, but I couldn't here, because there were people. She gave me a gloomy smile and turned to follow Imogen. Esis waved lonesomely from her shoulder. I watched her hair bounce up and down on her shoulders.

I really liked her hair.

"Dude!" Jonah shouted, snapping me out of my reverie. "You and Sophia?"

"Keep your voice down," I hissed. I was waiting to get grilled by Jonah the minute I was alone with the guy. Luckily, it was so loud in here nobody had heard him. I started walking toward the Toaqua dorms, which were quieter and not so packed. Jonah hustled after me, not willing to let me get away.

"Details, though! I want to know everything," Jonah demanded. "I bet she's a killer in bed."

"Jonah, shut up. We haven't had sex yet. We literally just got together," I snapped.

"But the chemistry's been there for a while." Jonah waggled his eyebrows. "You won't be able to resist the call of the wild for long."

"The call of the... tell you what, when it happens, I'll send you a letter."

Jonah snorted and patted me on the back. "As long as I'm the first to know."

"I don't see how it's any of your business, anyway."

"I tell you about all *my* sexual adventures," Jonah argued.

"Doesn't mean I want to hear it."

"That reminds me, by the way, you need to be caught up," Jonah said hurriedly. I went to tell him that I didn't care to listen, but he went on before I could say no. "I tapped *so* many hot asses in the past few weeks."

"Anything remotely permanent?" I asked bluntly.

"Babe, relationships are for squares. I can't be tied down," Jonah said. "I love being single. Being in a committed relationship is for losers, no offense to you."

"Bullshit. Like you don't want to be married someday," I said, calling him out.

"Nah. I wouldn't want that. Monogamy isn't natural," Jonah said. I detected a hint of a lie in his tone.

Jonah went on and on about all the nightclubs he'd been to over break and how many dudes he'd slept with, though he couldn't give me names or actual descriptions of what supposedly happened. To me, it was an exaggerated number. I doubted he'd been with anyone at all, and the people he had come on to had probably turned him down.

I mostly blocked him out. I was counting down the minutes until I got to see Sophia again tonight, and hoping I wouldn't get called in by Baine on short notice.

I just wanted one nice date with Sophia. A fun night. Before I had to come back to reality and figure out a way to save us both.

I HUNG out with my brother in the Toaqua dorms until it was time to get ready for the party. Ezra went to the party early, because he'd said he'd promised Riley help setting up. I wasn't surprised my brother knew him. Ezra knew everybody.

I was glad this party was going to be all Houses. It would draw less attention to the fact Sophia and I were hanging out.

The girls had homework to do until it was time to meet up, so I ate dinner with Jonah. He had homework to do, too, but as usual he was putting it off until the last minute.

My heart about burst when I saw Sophia and Imogen waiting for us outside of the Nivita dorms. Both girls had changed for the party. Sophia wore a pair of skinny jeans I hadn't seen her in before, ones that hugged her legs. I didn't need to make it obvious I appreciated them. She also had on a tight red sweater that dipped down into a v-neck. I thought she looked perfect in blue, but red suited her, too. I figured it didn't matter what she wore. I'd be all over her if she was wearing a paper bag.

Imogen had on a puffy white crop top and a lavender ballerina skirt that went down to her ankles, with fur boots. Her hair had been tied up in a polka-dot scarf, and she wore purple lipstick.

"We are totally ready!" Imogen sang, and she hooked her arm in Sophia's. "Let's go."

We took a carriage to the Yapluma neighborhood, pulled by a peryton. Squeaks trotted behind us with Sassy on her back. When it stopped, Sophia's mouth dropped open as she stepped outside.

The Yapluma neighborhood was completely lit up with neon lights, loud music, and advertisements everywhere. Wherever you looked there was something colorful and outlandish going on. Performers danced throughout the streets, while live bands played on a stage that was set up every other block. Confetti streamed from the skies and coated the streets. Even though it was a Monday night, this place was packed.

But that wasn't all. All throughout the neighborhood were floating houses. Some of the buildings were on the ground, but the majority of them were up in the air. They hovered hundreds of feet above ground, and moved throughout the sky slowly as to not bump into each other. Yapluma levitated themselves up to them, or flew to them on the backs of their Familiars. People from other Houses either glumly waited for help or for the buildings to lower themselves back down again, like elevators.

"Welcome to my humble abode," Jonah proclaimed as he led the way. "You're only entering the village of the *bestest* House."

Sophia was still gaping. Esis also gazed upward from her shoulder. I understood it was a bit of a shock to see magical floating buildings flying around.

I wanted to put my arm around her, but I jerked my head instead. "Come on, *pawee*. They're not gonna fall on you."

I hoped. That had happened before, because Yapluma were careless. Too bad nobody had yet dropped a house on Madame Doya, the Wicked Witch of the East.

Sophia grinned, and she jogged to catch up to us. I tried to keep her close by as we pressed through the crowded streets. There was a bar, a nightclub, or a party store on every corner. The village itself was laid out in large, open areas where people could gather, have big get-togethers or concerts. Yapluma House ran the theme park, but it was closed for the season. Even in the dead of January, this place was still one big celebration.

"Notice something?" I asked Sophia as I caught the quizzical expression on her face.

"Well, the floating houses obviously take up a lot of magic, and besides all the fun stuff, I haven't really seen a grocery store or anything like that anywhere," she explained quickly. "This village is not really very... practical."

"Yapluma aren't one for practicality," I told her, with a sideways glance at Jonah. "Obviously."

Jonah turned off the main road and took a different path that went into the woods. We walked until we couldn't hear the bands anymore, but it was anything but quiet. The sound was replaced by the thudding of a bass, and speakers blasting electronic dance music as a giant mansion came into view.

Riley's house was huge. My family didn't live in a small place by any means, but his mansion made ours look tiny. I guessed it had to have thirty rooms or more. The House was lit up, packed with students and Familiars both. A dragon sat on top of the house, shooting off flames, while his Elementai climbed a flagpole. A couple of people were passed out in the yard, and people were drawing things on their faces with marker. I noticed that somebody had driven a carriage into the pool. Shit, this thing had already gotten crazy.

The mansion was on the ground so people from all Houses could come and go as they pleased. We managed to squeeze in the front door, where a loud crowd was gathered around a Nivita guy doing a keg stand. When he was done, he passed the nozzle on to his griffin Familiar, who happily finished the rest of the keg off. We hung up our coats, then joined the party.

People were dancing to the music. There was so much alcohol I could smell it. I looked around for a friendly face and saw Cade playing beer pong with my brother in the kitchen. Imogen went to sneak off, but Sophia grabbed her by the wrist and dragged her behind us.

Ezra was good at beer pong, but Cade was obviously better, as most of his cups were full and Ezra's were empty. My brother swayed back and forth as he tossed another ping pong ball at Cade's cups, and missed.

"How are you liking your first year of college?" Cade asked him as he flung a ping pong ball and it landed in Ezra's second-to-last cup. Ezra gagged as he chugged it down.

"Wonderful!" Ezra slurred when he was done drinking. Beer was dribbling down his chin. "I love people, man. Love all of them. Especially girls."

He staggered backward. "Girls are so amazing. They smell so good. Like, I love it when they're so small and tiny. You can just pick them up and..."

Ezra closed his eyes and hugged himself. I rolled my eyes. Sophia snickered at my side.

"I like thick women, personally," Cade added. "Curvy girls are *so* sexy."

He'd noticed we'd come up to the table and winked at Imogen. Imogen went bright red.

Cade chucked another ball, and it landed in Ezra's last cup. "I win."

Cade sat in a chair that was near him, then reached for Imogen. Imogen squeaked as Cade pulled her onto his lap. Sassy rose up on her back legs and hopped in excitement. He put his arms around her hips and held her there so she couldn't move.

Smooth move.

Imogen giggled and said, "Wow, Cade. Someone's had a few."

"Hey guys," Cade said pleasantly. "I'm glad to see you here."

"Liam!" Ezra shouted, like he hadn't seen me in ten years. He staggered toward me and launched an arm around my shoulders. "I'm so glad you could make it. So glad."

"Ezra, you're drunk." I removed his arm from my shoulder. "You've had way too much already."

"Naw," he said happily. "I'm totally fine."

I had to reach out to grab him so he wouldn't fall backwards. He swatted at his face like there were gnats flying in front of it, and I shook my head.

"You're done, Ez. Go home," I said firmly. I shoved him toward what looked like the exit. He staggered forward blindly. I worried he wouldn't be able to make it back, until a couple of Toaqua girls came and started fawning over him. Each of them put an arm around his shoulder and guided him to the front door.

Great. They'd take care of him. Sophia grabbed Jonah's and my arm and said, "We're gonna go get drinks. We'll meet up with you two in a bit."

She dragged us away. Imogen beamed at the thought of being left alone on Cade's lap. Sophia yanked us to the drink table, where my old Toaqua friend, Wyatt, was mixing drinks.

"Hey, Liam," Wyatt said. "You having anything? I'm making shots."

He held out one to me. I wasn't supposed to drink. It would only make my symptoms worse. The last time I'd drank had been at the ball, and I'd sure paid for it the next day, even though I'd never gotten drunk.

But I was sick of being too careful, of being different, and not getting to be like everyone else. I wanted to be normal. So I took the shot and downed it.

Sophia watched me, but didn't say anything. She took a wine cooler carefully and sipped it. Esis had drank two beers already by this time and wanted a third. He reached for one, but Sophia slapped his hands. "No, Esis. Pace yourself."

Esis stuck out his lower lip and pouted. Across the room, Imogen and Cade looked pretty cozy. Their foreheads were touching, and Cade had his arms around her. He was whispering something to her, and Sassy twirled around his ankles.

A bit of jealousy ran through me. I wish Sophia and I could do that in public without everyone thinking it was a crime. It almost looked like they were going to kiss, until I saw a Nivita girl stumble by and "accidentally" spill her drink on Imogen's lap. Imogen sprang up, and Cade hurried to grab napkins to clean it up.

The Nivita girl smirked and walked away. Ice cold. Imogen got up and ran out of the room. Cade followed her.

Poor girl.

"Well, well, well. If it isn't the loser team. I'm surprised they let you in," a snide voice said behind us.

I knew exactly who that was. *Of course* the bitch would be here. Haley made sure to show up at every social function whether she was wanted or not. Two girls stood behind her— Kelsey, and a girl I didn't know. Their Familiars were at their feet. Kelsey's was a jaguar while the other girl's was a basilisk, a winged boa constrictor that looped around her shoulders.

Haley was wearing this revealing dress that showed more skin than cloth, and she had a wine glass in her hand. I bet she'd made Riley have it be here special for her. She had a look on her face that said she was getting laid tonight and the rest of us weren't.

"It's Reject Team, actually," Jonah said back coldly.

"Whatever," Haley sneered. "I don't give a shit what stupid name you call yourselves. It's just pathetic."

Sophia sighed, like she was already tired of this routine. I couldn't blame her. She'd tried to rise above the drama, and Haley kept on dragging her back down to it. Her eyes instead went to the red-headed girl with the basilisk.

"Hi, Lindsey," Sophia said nicely. "Did you have a good break?"

"Yes. It was quiet. I enjoyed the break, but I missed having you around," she said pleasantly. Lindsey noticed Haley's eyes boring flames into the back of her head and said, "Anyway. I hope you're doing well, Sophia."

"Sure." Sophia gave Lindsey a kind smile. She had the good sense to get out of here before Haley started more shit. I noticed Lindsey's eyes followed Sophia until we left the room.

Or, more accurately, Sophia's ass.

"Do you know her?" I asked Sophia.

"Lindsey? She was in my Fire class last semester. I have her again, along with Haley and all the other Koigni bitches for Beginner Koigni Magic I." She sighed heavily. "I think I'm stuck with them and Doya until I graduate."

Jonah gave me a look like, *Did you see what I just saw?* but I ignored it. Sophia didn't seem bothered by the interaction with Haley, just irritated.

When we left the kitchen and went into the game room, my eyes spotted someone else I didn't like.

"Oh, wonderful," I murmured under my breath. Renar was here, along with a bunch of people from Yapluma. I had hoped he wouldn't show up. My luck wasn't that good.

"Hey, baby," Renar said, scanning his eyes over Jonah's body as we approached. His voice was like nails on a chalkboard. "I haven't seen you in a while."

"Yeah," Jonah said. The tone in his voice had totally changed. It sounded... desperate. Like a totally different person. "I really wanted to see you over break. But you never got back with me."

"I was busy, hun," Renar said carelessly. "I had things to do."

Everything was immediately forgiven. "Oh. Okay." Jonah gave a hesitant smile.

Squeaks cracked her beak and fixed one eye on Renar. It was sharp and looked violent. Jonah didn't pay any attention to her.

"Hey, baby, will you get me another beer?" Renar asked. "I'd love you forever."

"Of course. Anything for you," Jonah said back sweetly, and I almost gagged. Jonah hurried off to do Renar's bidding, while Renar gave me an arrogant smirk.

"You need to stop messing with him," I said bluntly. I made sure there was a clear threat in my tone.

"What are you gonna do about it?" Renar asked.

I didn't respond. He wasn't worth my time, and I was trying to enjoy myself tonight.

"Hey, guys," I heard Imogen say behind us. It looked like she'd lost Cade. She looked a little breathless. "What'cha up to?"

I gravitated toward one of the pool tables in the room. "Not much. Wanna play pool?"

It proved a welcome distraction for me and the girls. Renar spent the rest of the party ordering Jonah around, which got on my nerves and which I definitely knew bothered Imogen. Her eyebrow literally twitched the third time Renar made Jonah go get him another drink. It was like watching a dog jump for treats. Jonah tried to sit near Renar, but every time Jonah touched him, the guy literally sneered and tried to pull away. It was like Jonah was blind or something. He didn't notice, or at least, pretended he didn't. Squeaks sat in the corner and watched the pair of them sullenly, clacking her beak as if picturing what she'd like to do to Renar with it.

"Have you heard? Vanessa Thomas and Bren Emberly got engaged over Christmas. From Koigni," one of Renar's friends said.

She smoothed her dress and added, "They're getting married this summer."

The names sounded familiar. I knew Bren was a Fourth Year, but I hadn't heard much of Vanessa yet. She must've been in one of the grades below me.

"I can't wait to get married. I know *I'd* be the perfect husband. Wouldn't I, Renar?" Jonah asked. His voice was begging for the right answer.

Renar wrinkled his nose. "I'm sure you would."

Jonah lit up like a lightbulb. Huh. Jonah's whole *marriage and commitment is stupid* speech sure went out the window every time someone he liked came around.

Which was sad, because it was really obvious all he was to Renar was a piece of ass.

"I think it's about time I pour you into bed," Renar said lowly, and he took Jonah by the hand, pulling him to the stairs so they could find a bedroom.

Sophia stepped in, coming between them. "Hey, Jonah, you sure you want to do this?" she asked lowly, so Renar couldn't hear.

A dark look came over Jonah's face, and he said cruelly, "I can take care of myself, Sophia. I don't need you babysitting me and judging me for what I do."

Sophia's mouth dropped open, and I growled lowly at Jonah, "Watch it."

He barely glanced at me. Renar yanked again on his hand. "Come on, babe. The bed is waiting."

At the sound of his voice, it was like Jonah was mesmerized. He completely forgot about us as he let Renar lead him wherever he wanted to go.

"I'm gonna go find Cade," Imogen grumbled. She stomped off, and Sassy hurriedly followed her.

Squeaks made a sad noise of discontentment and drooped her head as she watched Jonah run after Renar. I patted her on the neck for support.

Sophia's eyes narrowed as Renar and Jonah disappeared upstairs. "I don't like Renar."

"Yeah, well, join the club," I said. "Nobody does, except Jonah."

"But why?" She played with Esis' tail contemplatively, and his ears drooped in relaxation.

"He's the type of person that can only see the best in people. Too good for his own good, as my mom always said."

"But he's totally being used," Sophia said sadly.

"I know. And I've tried to stop him before. He doesn't listen," I told her softly. "We used to get in fights about it all the time. I learned it was better to just let him go. If he wants to sleep with Renar, that's his choice. He has to learn from his own mistakes."

Sophia scowled, and said, "I guess it doesn't matter. I'm just here to have a fun time with you."

"Same here." I smiled at her. Even though we couldn't touch each other, just being around her was amazing for me.

She leaned forward. Her breasts were peeking out of the v-neck. I glanced at them quickly, and she caught me at it. Esis let out a whistle.

"Enjoying the view?" she asked coyly.

"I, uh... like the sweater," I said, not knowing what to say.

"Sure you do." Sophia smiled, and she went up to get another drink. She brought me back one, too, and we finished them off as the party continued around us. We were in our own little world, talking quietly.

By the time an hour had passed, both of us had drank more than we should've. I knew my limit... or, at least, I used to. It'd been a long time since I'd gotten wasted. Whatever I'd had at the ball I'd at least tripled. And it definitely showed. I struggled to keep myself upright as I continued to throw back more drinks.

Sophia was just as bad as I was. I was supposed to be watching her, but I'd failed horribly at that. We'd lost Squeaks somewhere between the third and fourth drink.

I don't know how, but Sophia had begged me to dance and dragged me in front of the speakers to do so. Thankfully, most of the people here were just as drunk as we were, so nobody made anything of it. A familiar face popped up among the crowd.

"Hey, have you guys seen Imogen?" Cade asked. He looked worried. "I can't find her anywhere."

I went to answer before my eyes caught something. ...Was that...

purple lipstick on Cade's mouth? I damn well know I wasn't that drunk to be seeing things.

"We haven't, we're sorry," Sophia laughed, and she staggered. I stumbled to catch her before she hit the ground. Then her expression cleared, and she said, "Do you think she's okay?"

Cade smiled at her. "Yeah, I'm sure she's fine. That's okay. I'll find her. You kids have fun."

Cade walked away. Sophia turned around and watched him go. "Hey, where is he going? Liam?"

I had already forgotten about Cade. Something else was on my mind. I giggled and poked her in the shoulder. "Hey. Soph. Sophie."

She snickered and turned around, nearly falling over herself. She stumbled into me and I caught her, but we were like two waves on the ocean about to topple over. I was so drunk.

"What?" she asked, and she snorted. "What do you want, water boy?"

I leaned down to whisper in her ear. "Let's go somewhere."

She swooned. Esis ran worryingly in circles around our feet. "You wanna get me alone?"

"Fuck yeah, I do." I grabbed her arm and started pulling her behind me, not really sure where we were going. I barely checked to make sure a room was empty before I dragged her inside and pushed her against the door.

Inside the room, there was a four-poster bed and a couch near a marble fireplace. I grabbed Sophia's wrists and pinned them above her head, against the wall. My mouth claimed hers hungrily and she eagerly responded in kind, like the need to be together had been chained up for too long and now had broken free. Our bodies moved against each other with our clothes still on, kissing like we never had before. I barely registered that Esis was perched on the mattress, glancing frantically at the door.

I remembered thinking that while kissing her, I felt like I could taste the rest of my life before everything blacked out.

THE NEXT MORNING, Sophia and I woke up on the bed. My head was pounding and I was really dehydrated. I had a really bad hangover. My body felt like absolute crap, rebelling because of the alcohol. Booze and disabilities didn't mix.

But it made it all worth it to have Sophia next to me. I had both of my arms around her and was hugging her tightly to my body. Her head was snuggled into my chest, and our legs were tangled up together. She felt so warm and soft. I loved it.

"Good morning, *pawee*," I mumbled, and squeezed her to me. This was like, the definition of heaven.

"Good morning," she yawned back. She wiped the hair out of her eyes, then sat up, the blanket falling off her shoulders.

That's when I immediately sobered up. Sophia was wearing just her bra, while I realized my shirt was off. Both of us were still wearing pants, but our shirts were on the other side of the room.

Esis was at the edge of the mattress, looking at us. His eyes darted from me to Sophia as he lifted his little hands as if to say, *I tried.*

Sophia's eyes locked on to mine, fully awake. "What... why are our clothes over there?"

My mouth went dryer than before. "Um."

"Oh my God. Liam. Did we have sex last night?"

"I don't know." My voice was hoarse. "I can't remember."

"Liam, figure it out! Did we?"

"What do you want me to do? Check my dick to see if it's been used?" I asked.

This was a nightmare. I definitely didn't want our first time to be like this, so drunk we couldn't remember it. Both of us had way too much last night. But if something had happened, we couldn't exactly reverse it...

"Well, hello, lovebirds," Imogen clipped. She sauntered into the room holding a coffee, Sassy strutting by her feet. "Beautiful day, isn't it?"

"Imogen..." Sophia's voice was strained. Im must've noticed the panicked look on both our faces, because she laughed.

"Chill out. You guys didn't do anything." Imogen sipped her coffee. "Me and Jonah slept right over there." She pointed to the couch. "You guys made out like crazy for a minute before you took your shirts off and passed out. You were both mumbling it was too hot."

"Did anyone else see?" I asked quickly.

"Squeaks and Sassy got a good show. But besides us, no."

"You and Jonah shared the couch?" Sophia questioned.

Imogen shrugged. "Sharing a sleeping space with Jonah is like sharing a bed with my sister. If I had one, anyway."

"You got that right, girl." Jonah swaggered into the room, Squeaks following. He was carrying a tray of three different coffees. Sophia got up and hurried to put her shirt on, but Jonah rolled his eyes. "Sophia, don't flatter yourself. You ain't got nothing I'm interested in."

Jonah's eyes darted up and down my chest. "Liam, on the other hand... down, boy."

"I thought you said you weren't interested in me," I grumbled as Sophia handed me my shirt, and I slipped it on. What a perv.

"I said I'd never date you. Not have a one-night stand."

"Sorry, I'm taken." I wrapped my arm around Sophia's waist to remind Jonah, once again, that I *was not gay*.

Jonah handed a coffee each to Sophia and me. It churned my stomach to drink it. My head was pounding. I was so sick. I had a hang-over from hell.

By the way Sophia looked, so did she.

"I thought you would've been sleeping with Renar," Sophia said.

Jonah blushed. "Um, he had to go back. Couldn't stay. But that's all right."

What a shitty excuse. They lived in the same dorms. They could've gone back to Orenda together and nobody would've bat an eye.

"Cade was looking for you last night, Im," Sophia said. "He asked us where you were."

I'd forgotten about that. But Imogen waved her hand and said, "Oh, it was probably nothing."

I didn't think so. But I felt like I was going to throw up, so I didn't pry.

"We have to get back to school," Sophia groaned. "We have class."

My stomach bottomed out. That was right. It was a Tuesday. And all I wanted to do was crawl into bed.

"Jonah and I are going out for breakfast before we head back. Want to come?" Imogen offered.

"We can't," I said. "We have class in a few hours."

"See you guys later, then. Don't get into anymore trouble," Jonah teased.

There were kids scattered all around the house when we made our way out, completely passed out. Looked like Sophia and I weren't the only ones who'd had too much to drink. That worked in our favor. Hopefully, nobody remembered we'd been all over each other.

The walk back to Orenda was really quiet. Yapluma usually partied until dawn and slept the day away all night, every night. I don't even think most of the stores around here opened until after noon. Even so, I didn't relax until we were on a secluded woodland path and within the safety of the trees.

"Shit. That was too close," I said, and I shivered. Sophia and I's relationship had almost been blown out of the water. We'd come so close to being discovered, and for what? A few drinks?

"It was." Sophia snuggled Esis into her coat. "We can't be doing stuff like that."

"No. We're never drinking that much ever again," I said, laying down the law.

"Agreed." Sophia wrapped her arms around herself. I tried to piece together what had happened last night, but the details were fuzzy. All I remembered was kissing her, then falling asleep on the bed. Good thing Imogen and Jonah had found us. But it could've easily been anyone.

"We totally weren't responsible last night," I mumbled, feeling bad. I really hadn't meant for any of that stuff to happen.

"It's fine. It won't happen again," she said.

"It's not just about the drinking, Sophia," I started. "We almost slept together."

She stopped and looked at me. I knew we needed to have this conversation, even though it was kind of awkward.

She put Esis on the ground. Then she sat down on a large log that was near the trail and knitted her hands together.

I sat beside her. I didn't know how to begin the conversation, so I let her lead.

"It didn't happen. So we're good," she began.

"Okay, but you do realize that we're *dating* now, right? And kissing usually leads to other things," I said.

"I get that, Liam. I might be a virgin, but I'm not stupid." Her cheeks turned pink.

"So... how do you feel about it?" I asked. I felt like I had to ask her, because my own feelings on the subject were complicated, to say the least.

"I don't know." She sighed, and Esis hugged her leg. "I wanna have sex with you, but I'm kinda waiting for something to happen."

"Like?" She had me out in left field here.

"Well... I don't really want to have sex until I get married," Sophia started.

Of course she'd be that kind of girl. It totally fit who she was. "Okay, that's fine, but you realize that's not a possibility for us," I said slowly.

"Why not?" She blinked at me.

"You know why." I sighed. We'd been over this. "We can't get married."

"Someday we could," she said hopefully. "If things in the tribe change, why not?"

I had to really resist groaning. "That's a lot to hope for. And you realize waiting for marriage isn't a short-term plan by any means."

She sighed. "Maybe I'm not explaining myself clearly." She cleared her throat. "I'm not necessarily waiting for marriage, but I want my very first time to be my last first time. I don't want to sleep with someone unless I know they're committed to me. That it's going to last forever."

"Nothing lasts forever, Sophia," I said quietly.

"I want this to," she said honestly. "I want you."

"I want you, too. But you know why I can't make a commitment. What we're doing is dangerous as it is. It's illegal," I said. "Can you imagine what would happen to us if people found out we were contemplating getting married?"

"Do you actually know anyone who has been romantically involved with a person from another House and been found out?" she shot back.

I held my breath. "Not for a long time. The last instance happened when I was a little kid. It was all over the news. But Sophia, it didn't end well. Both of them were killed."

"Are you saying you don't want to marry me?" Her eyes welled. She looked hurt.

"You act like I don't want you. That isn't the case."

Ancestors, we were already talking about marriage and our relationship was only a few days old. Not that I particularly minded. Sophia was somebody I'd run off to Vegas with on a whim and get hitched by one of those Elvis clergy. That didn't mean it was a good idea.

"You're being too cautious. This is going to work," Sophia said confidently. "You were wrong about the Cup, and you're wrong about this, too."

If my life consisted of Sophia telling me I was always wrong, fine, I'd live with that. But things weren't that simple. Esis was being surprisingly quiet between us, his ears back as he observed us cautiously.

"Look. I'm not trying to start an argument," I started.

"Yes you are, because you love to argue," she snapped back.

I held back my temper and counted to ten. "Soph, I'm really not. I'm just trying to do what's best for you. And if it's that important to you to save yourself for your future husband, I don't want to take that away from somebody you *are* going to spend the rest of your life with," I said.

"Don't say shit like that!" she said, and she smacked my shoulder. Ow. "I don't want a commitment right now, but I need one in the future, Liam. And I'm not giving up on us, no matter what happens," she said firmly.

"I can't give you what you're asking," I said simply. There wasn't anything to say back.

She glared at me. I just stared back at her. We were at an impasse. Neither of us would budge.

"Let's compromise," I said. "How about we just take things slow, and see where it leads? We don't have to get serious right now."

Her face hardened. "Fine. But sex is a hard no. That doesn't mean I won't do other stuff."

"Fine by me." I didn't want to take Sophia's virginity. I mean, I totally did, but at the same time, I would feel really guilty about it. This was obviously something that meant a lot to her. And if she didn't want to sleep with someone who wasn't going to be her husband... then I wouldn't do it.

Especially since she wouldn't be mine forever. At least now I wouldn't have to worry about a random pregnancy.

We got off the log, and Sophia slipped Esis back into her jacket. I put my arm around her on the way back to the castle, because I wanted to keep her warm and I felt like that conversation had just pushed us apart a little.

"Other stuff?" I questioned, and I shook her. "What exactly does that mean, Miss Henley?"

She turned pink. "Why don't you just wait and find out?"

"Uh-huh." And I would— patiently. I'd be here for Sophia, be here *with* Sophia, as long as I could.

But I couldn't promise forever. No matter how much I loved her, that would be something I would never be able to give.

Even though I wanted it, too.

sophia

SIX

What a great way to end a wonderful night. *I want to marry you, Liam, even though we just became official. I'll suck your dick, but that's it until you put a ring on my finger.*

Ancestors, I was lame. And the dumb part was that I knew I'd do exactly that. Because I was hopelessly in love with the guy. There was no doubt in my mind that if he'd asked me to fool around with him last night, I would've parted my legs faster than Moses parted the Red Sea.

But I still meant what I said. I didn't want to go all the way if he wasn't going to commit. And it sounded like he wasn't going to.

I didn't even know what to think. Our conversation replayed through my head all the way back to the castle. Liam had class, so he had to go. We parted ways without so much as a goodbye kiss, and I headed back to my dorm to kill some time before Unicornology that afternoon.

"What should I do, Esis?" I stroked his fur while we snuggled together in front of the fireplace in my dorm room. He looked up at me and shrugged. "He'll come around eventually, right?"

Esis shrugged again, and I sighed. "I thought you were the love expert, buddy. Now that I actually need advice, all you can do is shrug?"

He just laid his head on my chest and purred.

"Fine, you're forgiven. I just think... I don't know. I want to have fun with Liam, but I also want him to believe we can have a future together. What do you think?"

Esis stared up at me with his big blue eyes. He looked like he was about to shrug again, but resisted.

"You're right," I said, defeated. "Maybe I'm rushing this conversation too soon. We should just have fun while we can, right? Liam will have to realize sooner or later that we're meant to be together."

I checked my watch. Imogen had gotten it for me for Christmas, since undergrads weren't allowed to have cell phones. We had to keep our society a secret and all that.

"We should probably get going," I told Esis, but I didn't get up right away. Attending Unicornology meant I had to face Liam again. After our awkward conversation that morning, I wasn't sure I was ready for that. I couldn't read his expression on our way back to the castle earlier, and it made me uneasy not knowing what he was thinking. But I didn't want him thinking I was mad at him either, because I wasn't.

"Screw it," I announced, scooping Esis into my arms and standing. "Unicorns are cool, and we're not missing the first day of class for anything."

Esis chirped as he jumped onto my shoulder and we left the room. If Liam was going to sulk— and if I knew Liam, he was doing exactly that— I wasn't going to let it get me down. In fact, I'd do the exact opposite and lift him up. That's what girlfriends were for, right?

Just as I predicted, Liam was sulking when I arrived at Unicornology. The class hadn't started yet, so students were chatting away, all except Liam. He slumped low in a desk at the back of the room with his arms crossed and his hood pulled up. His eyes looked hollow, and his skin was pale. He seemed like he was caving into himself. There was a tight look drawn across his face. Every now and then, I noticed him shift uncomfortably and wince.

Last night had taken a serious toll on him.

"How's that hangover?" I asked as I slid into the chair beside him. Esis hopped off my shoulder and onto the table. He reached for Liam, but I gently blocked his hand. It killed me to do it, because I knew Liam could use his help right now, but I'd already decided we couldn't mess with Perot's data.

Liam lifted his head. His voice made it seem like it hurt to talk. "Peachy. You?"

Honestly, I felt fine. I hadn't asked Esis to help take the edge off, but something told me he'd taken it upon himself to do just that. I'd gotten *way* too carried away last night. Who knew you could get so drunk off wine coolers? They were practically soda.

"I'm definitely not getting drunk ever again," I answered vaguely.

Liam faked a pout. "But drunk Sophia is fun."

I giggled, thinking back to our make-out session the night before. It was definitely *hot*. "You just haven't hung out with me long enough. Believe me, fun Sophia can make appearances without alcohol."

Liam raised his eyebrows. "Is that so? I thought sober Sophia and serious Sophia went hand in hand."

I shrugged, glad that he wasn't dwelling on our conversation from earlier. "You just have to get me alone."

Liam bit his bottom lip as his hungry eyes roamed over me. I went beet red under his gaze.

"You can count on that," he whispered just as the professor strolled into the room.

Professor Fawn was a beautiful middle-aged woman with wild dark curls and soft eyes. Her makeup was done tastefully, though she wore every color of the rainbow, with a purple and pink top, light blue pants, and lime green heels. Judging by the twelve flower pots that lined the window and the additional three at her desk, I guessed she was Nivita. Imogen would've loved her.

"Settle down," she called.

The room quieted. The few students still standing clamored into their seats.

"I'm Professor Fawn, and this is Unicornology," she announced.

A Yapluma guy in front of us glanced down at his schedule and cursed under his breath. His Familiar, a raven-type bird, squawked. He leaned over to the girl beside him. "This isn't Hawkei Sociology?"

She shook her head, looking sorry for him.

"I'm just gonna..." He pointed to the door and slid out of his seat. All eyes turned to watch him and his raven go. He made a joke out of it and quoted the *Terminator* before he slipped out the door.

Professor Fawn smiled widely, like she was trying to hold back a laugh. "I'm guessing he *won't* be back. Anyone else in the wrong room? No? Let's get started, then. This semester, we will be covering four units: unicorn history and lore, unicorn anatomy and physiology, unicorn magic, and my favorite unit of them all, unicorn psychology."

Esis chittered from the table, like he was excited about it, too.

"There will be four reports due this semester, one for each unit," Professor Fawn continued.

A few students groaned, including Liam.

"*But,*" she emphasized, "I assure you this class won't be all essays and no fun. In fact, we won't even be starting our first unit until next week, so you can all relax a little."

The class seemed to let out a collective breath. Me? I was sitting on the edge of my seat eager to start those unicorn essays. I mean, who went to college and got to do essays on *unicorns*? This school was so badass, and these students didn't even know it.

"On Thursday, we'll be taking a tour of the stables," Professor Fawn said. "But unicorns can be a bit... distracting with so many creatures to look at. So today, I thought you might like to meet Melody."

Professor Fawn gestured to the door behind her desk, like she was presenting a prize on a game show. A large, beautiful creature strolled into the room. It looked like a horse that'd been run through a glitter machine. Melody's fur was completely white, but it shined as if it were dusted with diamonds. Her mane and tail were all different colors of the rainbow, and those too shined in the light. A long silver horn twisted out of her head and shimmered blue and purple. A group of girls in the front row swooned over the creature. I loved her already.

"We'll take turns by table, and each group can come up and pet her," Professor Fawn said.

A hand shot up at the front of the room. "Can we go first?"

Professor Fawn gave a friendly smile. "Absolutely."

The class erupted into conversation again as the first group approached the unicorn.

I turned to Liam while we waited. He sighed and pulled his hood down over his eyes. "Ancestors, it's loud in here," he complained.

Guilt rolled around in my belly. I wished I could help him, but...

There were too many *buts*. I could write a novel of *buts* at this point.

"Are you okay?" I asked.

Liam forced a smile. "It's just a hangover, *pawee*. I've been through worse. I'll survive."

"You better, because I'm not writing those unicorn essays without your help."

Liam rolled his eyes. "That's called cheating."

"Or studying," I retorted.

Liam eyed me. "You know what those study sessions will turn into, don't you?"

I smirked. "I hope so."

Liam just shook his head in amusement, but I knew him well enough to be certain he was hoping, too.

"What about you?" he asked.

I brushed a strand of hair behind my ear. "What *about* me?"

"Are you okay? You seem like you've had a lot on your mind lately."

I sighed. He could say that again.

"Is it something the Koigni Elders said to you?"

It didn't sound like he was prying, more like he was truly concerned. I wanted to tell him all about the meeting, but I knew I couldn't. I'd be putting him in danger if I revealed too much. At the same time, I wanted to spill every detail to him, to confide in him like I'd never confided in anyone before. He was my best friend. I knew I could trust him because of what had happened to us in the cave. He hadn't told anyone about the totem we'd found— the one that was tucked in my pocket at that very moment— so I knew he could keep a secret. Plus, he wasn't going to buy that my meeting with the Elders was nothing. So I settled with the only thing I felt I could tell him.

I lowered my voice and whispered, "The Elders think there might be more pieces to the prophecy."

Liam perked up in interest.

"They think the other Houses have pieces they're keeping from each other. They want me to figure out how to fulfill the prophecy." I quickly shut my mouth after that. Chances were I'd already said too much.

A horrified expression crossed Liam's face, but it quickly settled back to normal. "So, they think you're the prophesied one for sure?"

I shrugged. "I guess so. Why? You make it sound like a bad thing."

It *was* a bad thing. Why was I downplaying it? I didn't want to get involved in Hawkei politics, but it was that or watch my loved ones suffer.

"You might not be, right?" Liam asked desperately.

"Yeah, I guess so. I mean, I fit the prophecy, but it doesn't exactly mention me by name."

"Are you going to fulfill it?"

The way he looked at me broke my heart. It was like he was begging me not to— like he'd never be able to live seeing the downfall of his own House. But if I didn't do this, I'd lose him, and I'd never be able to live with that. There had to be a loophole of some sort, right?

"I'm still working on it," I told him.

He sat up straighter and reached for my hand, but he pulled away at the last second. "Do me a favor, will you?"

I nodded. "Anything."

"Keep any information about the prophecy to yourself." He spoke so ominously that it sent a shiver down my spine. "This kind of information is dangerous, even in the hands of someone you trust." He stared intently at me, not blinking. It was kind of freaky. Like he was trying to tell me something.

"Yeah," I finally said. "Yeah, I can do that."

Liam breathed a sigh of relief and smiled. What was up with him? "Good. So, about those essays..."

By the time our turn came to approach Melody, the class was almost over. Liam seemed in a better mood and even lowered his hood after I made about fifteen dirty jokes. Some were so bad Esis covered his eyes, like he couldn't watch the trainwreck in front of him.

"We're out of time for the day," Professor Fawn said, "but if the last group wants to come up, I'll stick around."

She gestured to Liam and me. Students began to file out of the room while Liam and I headed to the front.

"She's beautiful," I said lightly as I reached out to stroke Melody's nose. She tilted her head into my hand while Esis reached up from my shoulder to touch her under the chin. "Are you bonded to her?"

"Oh, no." Professor Fawn shook her head. "Sariah, my Familiar, is very shy. My first semester teaching I brought her to class, and she sat under the desk the whole time. I mean, she hardly fit, considering she's Melody's size." She laughed.

"Sariah's a unicorn, too?" I asked, running my hands through Melody's mane. Liam stood beside me, so close I could feel the heat radiating off his skin as he lightly petted her white fur.

"Yes," Professor Fawn answered. "She's a velvet earth unicorn with a gold horn. They're very rare."

"I'd love to meet her sometime," I said, because frankly, that sounded awesome.

Professor Fawn smiled kindly. "I can see if she'll come with me to class one day."

Just then, a small creature waddled into the room. It looked like a koala bear, but with the markings of a panda. He held out a paper to Professor Fawn. She bent and took it. As she began to read it, her face went pale.

"Is something wrong?" Liam asked.

It took a moment for Professor Fawn to respond. "There's been an incident with a peacock. Professor Costas has requested my help repairing her wing. Would... would you two mind leading Melody back to the stables?"

"Not at all," I answered almost immediately. "We'll take good care of you, won't we, Melody?"

"I'm so sorry," Professor Fawn said in a rush. "I'll give you both extra credit for this. Thank you so much."

She rushed out of the room, leaving Liam and me alone with the unicorn.

I continued to stroke Melody's hair. "Would it be bad if I snuck her back to my dorm room and kept her there?"

Liam smirked. "Yes."

"Aw, man," I sighed in jest. "But she's so nice and pretty."

"I'm nice and pretty," Liam said with a laugh.

"True, but you're not a unicorn, are you?" I reached my hand up to stroke Melody's horn. An array of beautiful colors danced across the surface of it when I touched it.

Liam wrinkled his nose. "Don't do that, Sophia."

I drew my hand back. "Why? Are you not supposed to touch unicorns' horns?"

"You can touch it. Just not... like that. It looked like... something else."

I snickered. "You mean, don't touch it... like this?" I curled my fingers around Melody's horn and pumped my hand up and down.

"Ancestors, Sophia. Stop it," Liam said with a laugh. He tried swatting my hand away, but I only taunted him further.

Liam opened his mouth to say something else, but before he could, Melody's entire body tensed as she let out a loud sneeze. Pink glitter shot out of the end of her horn and rained down on Liam. It coated his entire face, landing in his open mouth and everything.

I totally lost it. I doubled over laughing, unable to contain myself. Esis giggled so hard that he jumped down from my shoulder and rolled onto his back on the floor. He clutched his stomach and squeaked.

Meanwhile, Liam leaned over the wastebasket in the corner and spit glitter from his mouth. Melody didn't even seem to care, as if this happened to her daily.

"Oh my God!" I laughed. "She... she..." I couldn't get the words out between my laughs.

Liam wiped the pink glitter from his face and shook his hair out into the garbage can. He huffed and turned to Melody. "Let's get this unicorn back to the stables."

"Oh, come on," I insisted. "Aren't you even a little amused by it? It wouldn't kill you to laugh every once in a while."

Liam stared at me, completely unamused. "Ha ha," he said dryly. "I don't find it amusing that I'll be eating glitter for the next month."

"Maybe it's magical glitter," I teased as we began walking out of the room with Melody at our side. Esis jumped on her back to ride along.

Liam rolled his eyes, but his lips twitched at the corners, like he was holding back a laugh. We reached the door to outside, and he held it open for Melody and me to pass through. We stepped out into chilly air.

The woods started only a few feet in front of us, leaving this corner of the castle deserted.

I poked his side as we entered the woods. "You're no fun."

Before I knew what was happening, Liam grabbed my hand I'd poked him with and spun me around. His hips pinned me against a thick tree trunk next to the path.

Now that's what I'm talking about!

"*I'm* no fun?" he challenged. He was so close that my breasts touched his chest when I inhaled. His breath rushed across my face, and I no longer registered the cold air around us.

My knees shook beneath me. "Maybe... maybe I spoke too soon."

"Hell yeah, you did." Liam claimed my lips as his own, drinking me in. His tongue slid inside my mouth, sending my heart to do wild flips inside my chest.

I threw my arms around his neck and dragged him even closer. Heat pooled low in my belly. Liam bit my lower lip, then drew away, gazing at me with a passion in his eyes.

I giggled as happiness surged through me. Before I knew what I was doing, the words slipped out between the laughs. "I love you."

I realized what I'd said too late. Liam went rigid, and his face fell. My stomach sank. I'd ruined the moment.

"Liam, I just meant—"

His body slammed into mine, stealing the words from my mouth. He squeezed me in a tight embrace and buried his nose in my hair. It caught me by surprise.

"I know what you meant," Liam said softly. "I've waited so long for someone to say that to me. And I love you, too, *pawee*."

He drew away from me to look me in the eyes. He blinked rapidly, and tears lined his lower lids.

Concern for him swept through me. "Liam, are you crying?"

"What? No." He pressed his fingers to the corners of his eyes. "I just have unicorn jizz in my eye."

I shook my head and stifled a laugh. "We should probably get Melody back to the stables. I have another class to get to soon."

"Oh?" Liam asked as we started down the trail. Melody followed, with Esis on her back. "What class is that?"

"Koigni Magic," I groaned.

"Doya. Sounds like fun."

I rolled my eyes. "Thanks for reminding me. I'm sure she's just going to *love* having me back this semester."

"WELCOME to your second semester of Beginner Koigni Magic." Madame Doya stood at the front of her classroom in a velvety red dress, pacing back and forth and shooting daggers at the students in the front row.

Luckily, I'd gotten here early and claimed one of the seats in the back. The class was made of up most of the same students from last semester— including, of course, Haley. There were maybe a dozen new faces who'd been in the other time block in the fall. There were several new Familiars as well, since Kelsey and Lindsey had both bonded over break.

"Now that some of you have bonded and several have competed in the tournament—" Doya shot Haley a glance I couldn't read, "—I expect some of you to do better this semester than others. Several of you will be competing in next fall's Elemental Cup. You should be prepared to carry out at least Third Year level tasks."

"But we're only First Years," an unbonded girl from the front row piped up. She looked a little like Haley, with the same sleek black hair, straight nose, and full lips, but she had sweeter eyes. Doya raised an eyebrow her way, but the girl didn't even blink. Most students would be cowering under Doya's gaze.

"Yes," Doya agreed, "but the tournament does not cater to First Years. For you unlucky few who will bond before your second year, you'll have to push yourselves harder than the rest. Would you like a demonstration?"

She didn't wait for an answer. She cocked her head and started toward the training floor on the other side of the room.

Chairs squeaked across the hardwood floor as everyone rose in unison to follow her. Several students claimed a seat on the couches in front of the training area, while the rest of us stood with nowhere to sit. I kept to the back of the group behind the sofas, hoping Doya wouldn't call on me. I didn't want to wake Esis from where he slept in the hood of my sweatshirt.

"Haley," Doya demanded, snapping her finger and pointing to a spot in front of her. I breathed a sigh of relief.

Haley rushed over to her like a trained little puppy and planted her feet where Doya had pointed. Anwara ruffled her feathers from Haley's shoulder. Haley held her head up proudly and shot the whole class a smirk.

Get over yourself already.

"Haley, I'd like you to catch my fireball, like you did in the tournament," Doya said.

Haley stood at the ready, just in time for a fireball to rocket out of Doya's palm. Haley stumbled backward as she caught it between her hands. It suspended in the air between her fingers as she sustained the flames. Her eyebrows knit in concentration.

The girl beside me, the one who'd spoken up earlier, leaned over and whispered. "She looks like she's going to shit herself, doesn't she?"

I almost gagged in laugher. I had to bite my lips together to keep from making a noise. "I take it you're not a fan?" I whispered back.

The girl twisted her nose up. "No. But don't tell anyone that, because we're family and all."

My eyebrows shot up. "Excuse me?"

"Oh, sorry," she said. "We haven't been formally introduced. I'm Vanessa Thomas. I'm Haley's cousin."

I stood there dumbstruck for a moment. There was *another one?* How many Haley clones were running around Kinpago?

"Believe me, I'd look at me that way too if I were in your shoes," Vanessa whispered.

I quickly composed myself. "I'm sorry. It's not a bad thing—"

Vanessa scoffed. "You don't have to lie to me. Haley and I don't exactly get along."

That wasn't a surprise. I was pretty sure even Haley's *friends* didn't get along with her. I figured they only stuck around to elevate their status in our House. I think I could really get to like this girl.

"Good," Doya said to Haley, pulling mine and Vanessa's attention back to the demonstration. "But I think we can do better. Sophia."

I internally groaned, but I stepped forward anyway.

"You two were the only ones in this class who competed in the last tournament. Let's see what you've learned." Doya turned to me with a sardonic smile. She was freaking amused.

Haley placed a hand on her hip and glanced down at her perfect nails, tapping her foot.

Oh, it is on!

Yeah, I'd show her. I'd show her exactly what I'd learned. Esis stirred awake as I pulled him from my hood and set him on the ground. I stripped off my hoodie and tossed that beside him. Esis rubbed his eyes, then noticed me abandoning him to stand in the middle of the training floor. He immediately became alert and shot a fist into the air, cheering for me.

"Okay," I said confidently as I took my place across from Haley. "What rules are we playing by?"

Madame Doya raised a manicured brow. "Rules? In the tournament, there are no rules."

She stepped aside just in time for Haley to shoot a fireball at my head. I ducked out of the way, and it slammed into the stone wall behind me, fizzling out upon impact. I retaliated immediately, but instead of aiming at Haley, I shot my fireball at Anwara. She was a phoenix, so I knew it wouldn't hurt her.

She lost her balance on Haley's shoulder and fell backward. Her wings shot out to her sides, but there wasn't enough distance between her and the floor to catch herself. She landed on her back with a hard *thump.*

Haley took one look at Anwara sprawled out on the hardwood, then turned back to me. Fury burned behind her eyes, and her hands curled into fists.

But I was already acting, knowing that she'd be distracted by Anwara. I pictured my Fire gathering into a ball at my chest, then opened up my magical channels. Heat shot down my arms, and a stream of flames erupted from my palms. This time, I aimed it at Haley's hair.

Her hair lit up in flames, and she screamed. She spun around in circles and raked her fingers through her hair as fast as she could to try extinguishing the flames. Students laughed from the edge of the training area.

Honestly, it was a wonder Haley had survived the tournament at all. Had she not learned anything? I supposed there was a reason all of her teammates died.

I pulled my fire back since I had no intention of hurting her— not here, at least. Back in the tournament I would've, but despite what Doya said, there were rules here in the classroom. I didn't think the Koigni Chieftess would take well to me putting her daughter in the hospital.

Anwara finally righted herself. Haley had put the fire out, but her hair was at least three inches shorter and just barely fell below her shoulders.

"Not cool, loser!" she shouted, even though I was barely ten yards away from her. Her fists shook, and her jaw tightened.

I narrowed my eyes at her. "How many times does someone have to tell you that's not my name? Are you deaf, or can your tiny little brain just not process the information?"

Haley's face contorted into anger. She let out a primal scream as fire jetted out of her hands. I threw my arms up on impulse. The flames slammed into me, searing the hairs on my arms. Regular fire didn't burn me, but when it was fueled by another Koigni's magic, it was red-hot.

I ducked out of the way to avoid her flames, but she followed. Anwara joined in on the fight and shot a fireball at me. My t-shirt caught fire at the shoulder, and my body broke out in sweat. Haley grinned in satisfaction.

I tossed two fireballs her way as I darted from one end of the training area to the other, trying to outrun her stream of magic. I caught a quick glance of Doya, and she looked absolutely displeased. Esis' eyes filled with worry for me.

That's when I knew what I had to do. I stopped running and faced her flames head-on. Flames ran all the way across the room from her palms to me. My magic reached out to hers. I didn't produce fire, but I could feel our magic tangling together. Her flames broke off in two directions, shooting out to the sides three feet in front of me as if I had a force-field around me. In reality, I was redirecting her flames with my magic.

Haley glanced down at her hands in confusion, like she thought there might be something wrong with her magic. When her gaze returned to mine, she knew I had her. A moment of horror crossed her face just as I pushed against her magic with everything I had. Her flames ricocheted back at her. The wave knocked both her and Anwara off her feet.

I grinned proudly. The class responded with a mix of cheers and boos. I knew without a doubt the boos were coming from Haley's posse, namely Kelsey and a few other girls. I stole a quick glance at the class to see that Lindsey and Vanessa were among the ones who were cheering.

Doya strolled quickly into the middle of the training floor, her velvety dress billowing out behind her. "I think that's enough for today. As you can see, the tournament can be brutal. If you can't shoot a jet of fire out of your hands as Haley has done, you might as well not enter the tournament at all. Return to your seats."

I stood rooted in place for a good five seconds. All that, and she'd praised *Haley*? But I was the one who'd won! Redirecting Haley's power was *way* more advanced. What the hell?

Esis scurried over to me, dragging my hoodie behind him. I swallowed down my frustrations and bent to scoop him up in my arms. He clapped, like he thought I'd done well.

"Thanks, Esis," I whispered. "At least someone thinks so."

"I KICKED Haley's ass in Fire Class earlier," I announced to Imogen at dinner time.

She popped a ravioli in her mouth and raised her eyebrows. I was half surprised they weren't covered in glittery blue to match her eyeshadow. She was all blue and glitter today. Even her hair, which was twisted into a ballerina bun, had a bright blue scrunchie holding it up. "Seriously? Tell me all about it."

I shrugged while I unwrapped a hamburger for Esis and handed it to him. I swore it was all he ever ate. We sat in our usual booth in the corner of the cafeteria with our Familiars at our sides. The room was bustling with conversation, but no one paid attention to us.

"Do ya pit us against each other for a demonstration," I told her. "I used Haley's magic against her."

"Serves her right." Imogen snorted.

"I have to admit, I was kind of proud. Okay, really proud. Like, that's some advanced Koigni shit right there."

Esis grumbled at my language. But I'd beaten Haley-freaking-Westfenix. I could use whatever language I wanted.

"Everyone thinks she's so good," I continued, "but all she can do is conjure flames. I mean, sure, they're pretty strong flames, but that's basically it. I seriously wonder sometimes how she got through the last task."

Imogen slipped Sassy some meat under the table, then leaned in to whisper to me. "I bet her mom had something to do with that."

I inhaled a sharp breath. It hadn't occurred to me before, but it definitely made sense. The Elders had run the tasks during the tournament. Her mom could've pulled back on the fire to get her through.

"Cheats," I muttered under my breath. "Anyway, enough of that. I've been waiting to ask you something all day. What *happened* to you last night? I was worried."

Imogen snickered. "You were *drunk*."

"Drunk and worried," I pointed out. "Did Cade ever find you?"

Imogen's pale skin turned a bright pink. "Oh, he found me all right."

"Ooh." My curiosity was instantly piqued. "Do tell."

"We, uh, kind of made out."

I squealed so loud it made Esis jump. "Oh, my gosh! That's great, Imogen. So, are you two together now?" I was so happy for her.

Imogen dropped her gaze and tossed Sassy another piece of meat. "No. It was amazing, but I... I had to stop it."

My face instantly fell. "What? Why? I thought you guys liked each other."

"I know," she said in disappointment. "But I was kissing him, and all I could think about was Trace."

I winced. If Amelia popped in my head every time I kissed Liam, I didn't know if I could kiss him again.

"Not like *that*." Imogen swatted at me. "I just felt really guilty because Cade and my brother were best friends. Like, if Trace were still around, I don't know if he'd be okay with this. And I think Cade maybe felt the same way, so we stopped. I was embarrassed, so I hid from him the rest of the night."

"Aw, Im." I frowned. "You could've come found me. We would've had fun together."

"I *did* find you," she replied playfully. "You were passed out topless!"

"Shh..." I glanced around to make sure no one had heard. We both started giggling.

Eventually, Imogen composed herself. "I'm not sure Cade even remembers. I don't know how much he had to drink, but he didn't mention it when I saw him earlier. Which is good, I guess. He probably wouldn't have kissed me if he'd been sober."

"Don't say that, Imogen. He likes you."

She shrugged. "I don't know. I just wish I hadn't screwed up our first kiss."

My heart sank. I had no idea what to say to her. I wished I had a way to make her feel better.

"You'll get another chance to kiss him." I realized that probably wasn't the right thing to say as soon as it left my mouth.

"Oh, yeah," she said sarcastically. "When?"

I shrugged. "Valentine's Day? That's coming up soon."

"Sure, that'll work. *Hey, Cade. I thought we could fool around since it's Valentine's Day. Let me take you back to my dorm room and jack you off.* That'll go *greeeat.*" She rolled her eyes. "Besides, I seriously don't know if I can do this. Maybe I should just start dating someone else."

"But Cade's perfect for you!"

Imogen shrugged, but deep down, I knew she felt it, too. "Maybe I'll become a lesbian. I'm sure Jonah has some insight."

"It doesn't work that way, Im." I took a bite of buffalo steak.

She shook her head. "Whatever. I'm done worrying about Cade. It's not going to happen."

I knew Imogen was lying. Since the moment I met Cade, one thing was very clear: Cade and Imogen belonged together.

She just hadn't realized it yet.

Liam

SEVEN

The first Wednesday in February, Baxtor woke me up early with a knock at my dorm room door. The Air peacock had a note in his beak from Perot, who wanted me to come in as soon as possible. He didn't even want me to wait until after class, which freaked me out.

I was always nervous when I got these kinds of notes. The first time I'd gotten that kind of notice, I was told I had some sort of unknown disease that nobody could cure. When I'd been told that, my hearing had gone fuzzy, and I couldn't comprehend what the doctors were saying. Ever since then, an unexpected summons from someone in the health field always meant bad news. I worried that Perot had found something that would make everything ten times worse.

I knew one thing. I was less healthy than I was a semester ago, which was really bad. I didn't think I could deteriorate much more, but apparently, there was always a new rock bottom for my body to meet. Which must've meant that Perot had bad news.

I got showered and dressed quickly, then headed down to Perot's office. It felt so eerie pushing open the door to his alchemist's lab in the depths of the school.

It was too early for class, so the room was empty. Perot was at his desk. He smiled at me, so I supposed the news couldn't be too awful.

"You wanted to see me?" I asked breathlessly as I took the chair across from his desk.

"Yes. Breathe, Liam," Perot said, and he used his Air magic to shuffle through some papers. I relaxed, or tried to. He started reading something from my blood charts silently.

"Did anything I gave you help?" he asked absentmindedly, as if his mind was somewhere else.

"No," I responded honestly. His potions helped with the pain, but they made me so tired I couldn't do anything but sleep whenever I took them, and I'd secretly stopped taking the pills. They weren't helping, and I thought that when I took them I was even more pissed off than I usually was.

"I didn't think they would," he murmured while looking at the results. "And I think I might know why."

He was killing me here. "All right, what is it?" I asked.

He briefly looked up, and Baxtor cooed. "Results from tests show that many systems of your body are severely weakened. Immune, digestive, respiratory, muscular, cardiac— none of them are really working as they should. They're like dominoes in a chain, one setting off the other, and it takes a lot of energy to keep them going. It explains the fatigue and pain you experience. But before today, I haven't been able to figure out what's been causing it."

"Did you?" I leaned forward, ready for answers. I didn't want to get too excited, but it was hard not to.

"I have a theory." Perot leaned back in his chair. "Elementai DNA isn't the same as a human's. It has a special property in it, a quality within our blood that enables us to meld the elements."

"Yes. But I knew that," I said. "All magical races have something in their genetic makeup that enables them to use magic."

"Yours doesn't work as it should."

The statement floored me. I didn't understand what he was getting at. "What do you mean?"

Perot seemed thoughtful. "I haven't proven anything. But from my best guess, I think you have some sort of mutation in your genes that causes this disorder. A genetic defect that hasn't been seen before. Some kind of rare disease that's specific to Elementai, though we don't have a pool of people large enough to confirm. You really are an abnormality."

Gee, thanks, I thought bitterly. That was one thing I hadn't been called yet, though Perot didn't mean it in a bad way.

"This is the most challenging case I've ever had to work on, Liam. It's exhausting everything I know." Perot sighed in frustration, before he brightened. "However, I do find it *very* interesting. You're a puzzle I can't quite figure out."

My girlfriend would probably say the same thing. "So, why am I here?"

I didn't mean to be rude, but I was already getting exhausted from just sitting here listening to him. Talking about my illness was always the number one way to put me in a bad mood.

"I want to try something else," Perot said, and I groaned inwardly. I didn't want any more tests. He added, "Your journal's been the most help. I noticed that you seem to have the worst symptoms when you use your magic the most. Our magic comes from our blood. And I believe your genetic defect is causing your magic to pull energy from your other body systems, weakening them, instead of getting the energy from the natural world around us like it should be."

"What?" I sat back in my chair. "Are you telling me my *magic* is the reason I'm this way?"

"It would explain why you didn't have symptoms as a child. You didn't use your magic until you were older, so your body was able to keep you going," Perot said. "Did you experience any of your symptoms after bonding with Nashoma, after you came to Orenda?"

I thought about it. Come to think of it, I had spent the semester before I lost him sick a lot, but I just thought it was a really bad, never-ending cold. It'd been winter, so I figured it wasn't a big deal. "Kind of. But not like I am now."

"I figured so. You drew from Nashoma's magic, and it protected you, for the time being," Perot said. "Now that he's no longer here, you're forced to carry the brunt of it yourself."

Perot took his glasses off and threw them on the table, rubbing his eyes. "Though it still doesn't explain how you managed to survive his death. Our existences are tied directly to our souls. It's the magical force that keeps our bodies going and powers our magic. There shouldn't be a way for you to survive without drawing from him. Yet, here you are."

Perot scratched some things onto a piece of paper. "I suggest going on a cleanse. Don't do any magic for at least a few weeks, and see how it goes."

"But I can't stop using my element," I said, stunned. "My magic is who I am."

"Don't jump to conclusions, Liam. It's only a hypothesis," Perot said. "It explains some things, but not others."

"I can't do that. I have classes I have to use my magic in," I protested. I was throwing out excuses. He wasn't taking my magic away from me—no way.

"I've already spoken to Professor Baine, along with your other professors," Perot added. "They're willing to overlook anything you might have to skip for the sake of our research."

I didn't want to get an easy grade because I was sick. It didn't look like I had a choice, though. "Fine. A couple of weeks," I told him. "I don't want to go any longer than that."

"It'll breeze by, trust me," Perot said. I severely doubted him.

Perot gave me strict instructions. I wasn't allowed to so much as toss a bottle of water across the room until March. Lame. He adjusted my pain potion for smaller doses so I wouldn't sleep all the time, told me I was depressed and needed to take his suggestion and do something about it (I was not, screw him), and sent me on my merry way.

I left his office pretty pissed off. My mind was out of control as I headed back to my dorm.

What was I without my magic? I didn't even know. It was the one part of myself that I was still proud of and still holding on to, and Perot wanted me to give it up?

What if I had to make the choice between my life and my element? Could I even do that?

The answer was clear. If it came down to that, my element would win. Always. I'd take a young death over growing old without magic.

I punched my dresser, and it rocked dangerously. I had to catch it to keep it from falling over. My hand was throbbing, but I didn't care.

I lost my Familiar, my health, and now Perot wanted me to stop using my magic, too? Bullshit. No fucking way. I'd die first.

It seemed like my illness was bound and determined to take everything from me. No way in hell I'd let it. I was worth fucking more than this. And I wasn't gonna let anyone tell me what I could and couldn't do, not even Perot.

I wanted to hide in my room for a while, but I'd promised myself I'd stop doing that, so I forced myself to go to the Commons before class. I found Jonah there, eating a whole box of jelly doughnuts by himself in front of one of the fireplaces.

I plopped next to him on the couch. He offered me one, but I shook my head. I wasn't hungry.

"Fine. Be that way," Jonah said with a full mouth, and he threw one to Squeaks. She caught it in her beak and lapped it down happily. "What's up?"

I didn't want to tell Jonah about what Perot had said, though I knew I would have to eventually. Talking about that was just too much right now. So I said, "Not much. What's up with you?"

"Same as usual. Sucking dick and kicking ass."

"Great."

Though everything seemed dark right now, when Sophia came in, the world seemed to brighten up. She had an armful of books, and Esis was balanced on her shoulder. Imogen was next to her in a blue dress that had snowflakes all over it, and a fluffy pink coat that Sassy was tucked into.

When he saw me, Esis jumped off Sophia's shoulder and zig-zagged around the other people in the room to get to me.

Esis placed his arms around my stomach and gave me a hug. He must've thought I needed it. I gave him a pat on the head.

"Esis, no!" Sophia seemed a little panicked. She glanced at Imogen in a way I couldn't read, then snatched Esis up into her arms firmly. He squirmed to get out of them and beat his little fists against her hands. She ignored him.

"Why'd you yell at him? He just wanted to see me," I said curiously. Esis had given up and was now lying dramatically in Sophia's arm, blowing out gusts of wind to make his tail move in a bummed way.

"I just... I don't want him running off like that. He could get stepped on," Sophia said cautiously.

Hm. She'd never cared before, but I guess there were a lot of people in here, not to mention some pretty big animals that wouldn't notice if they turned Esis into a pancake. "Guess you're right."

Sophia carefully studied my face. "Something's wrong, Liam. I can tell."

How did she know? She'd been around me for five seconds. "I'm okay." I really wanted to reach out and grab her hand to try and prove it, but I couldn't, and it sucked. "I'll tell you everything later. It's nothing serious, I promise."

She bit her lip and seemed worried. Jonah and Imogen gave me similar looks, but didn't say anything.

Imogen broke the tension by turning to Sophia and saying, "So, you ready for Hawkei Careers?"

Sophia sighed. "No. It's my worst class."

"I was being sarcastic, Sophia." Imogen laughed. "I know you hate it, though I don't know why."

"I really do hate it." She scowled.

I wondered why, too, but didn't ask. Hawkei Careers wasn't hard when I took it. It was more of an exploration class for what you wanted to do after graduation. Why would Sophia have such a hard time in it?

"Just be like me. Decide to be a professor and *never leave*," Jonah said before he shoved another doughnut down his throat.

"Ew. No." Sophia wrinkled her nose. "I love Orenda, but I couldn't grade papers forever."

"I'm really having trouble between deciding to be a Familiar zoologist or a Hawkei fashion designer." Imogen tapped her chin thoughtfully. "Though I guess I have another semester to decide."

Everyone looked at me, and I said, "I'm here. That's all that matters."

"Your thoughts seem dark this morning," Jonah commented.

"Aren't they always?" Imogen sighed. She took Sophia's arm, and said, "Come on, we're going to be late."

"Okay." Sophia gave me an encouraging smile and a wink. "See you later, *pawee*."

That brought a smile to my face. Jonah made an obnoxious noise. "Aw. You two are too fucking cute. Spare some of us single people, won't you?"

He stood up and tossed the empty box to Squeaks. She caught it with her beak and threw the box away in the trash. We moved around a dragon and a manticore as we made our way out of the Commons. I had class in the same direction, so I walked with him. Squeaks clopped cheerfully behind us.

"I thought you were dating Renar," I said. Though I kind of doubted it. Behind me, Squeaks gave a hiss.

"Renar doesn't want to put labels on it," Jonah said lightly, ignoring his Familiar. "He doesn't think having a relationship means anything. He wants to keep it open."

That was translation for, *I want to be able to screw you and other people at the same time without consequences*, and we both knew it.

"Are you okay with that?" I asked.

He shrugged. "I'm cool with whatever he wants."

Sure he was. But I changed the topic and said, "Sophia told me she loved me."

Jonah nearly stopped in his tracks. "Whoa. For real, man?"

"Yeah." I usually didn't talk about this kinda stuff with people, but ever since it had happened, I just wanted to talk about it with someone. Like that proved it was real. Mia had never told me she loved me. I guess that should've been a sign.

"I hope you said it back."

"Of course I did," I snapped. "Why wouldn't I?"

"You guys exchanged the L-word within a month of dating? That's fast, man," Jonah said.

"Not really. We've liked each other for a while, right?"

"I guess." Jonah seemed to be thinking. "You guys really have something special. I wish I had someone who cared about me like that."

"She really is amazing." Sophia Henley loved me, and she had *said it out loud*. I couldn't stop thinking about it, the way she said it. It was crazy to me to think that somebody actually loved me, especially someone like her. I didn't deserve her.

"So, how's the sex?" Jonah asked, totally breaking me out of my happy-ass thoughts and throwing them back into the gutter.

"We haven't had sex, okay? Would you quit asking?" I hissed. "Sophia doesn't want to. She wants to stay a virgin until... you know."

"Oooh." Jonah nodded his head in clarification. "Wow. That's rough, dude."

"I don't really care about the sex. I just don't want her thinking it can last forever," I told him.

"Right. But who says it can't?" Jonah asked. He gave me a salute before he headed off into his classroom. Squeaks shook her tail at me and jogged happily after Jonah.

Him, too? They were being ridiculous. This could never work long-term.

But now he had me thinking things could be different, too. And every day that passed with Sophia, forever seemed to be a closer and closer possibility.

Maybe this could last. We'd figure out a way to make it work. What if Jonah was right and it *was* possible for Sophia and me to last?

I decided to think like that from now on. No longer would I bring up the fact that what we were doing wasn't allowed. Sophia was right. There had to be a way. A way for us to change the rules, or at least break them without facing any consequences. We *could* be together forever.

But then... even if we did manage to stay together despite tribal lines, there was always one giant, looming factor in the background. My illness. I saw the look on her face today when I said I had bad news. It was like both of us were waiting for that inevitable moment where Perot would tell me I didn't have long, and then I'd have to tell Sophia. It was awful.

The hardest part of this whole thing wasn't thinking I could die. It was thinking of leaving her when I did.

I WANTED to go find Sophia that afternoon so she wouldn't worry, but right after Advanced Toaqua Magic, Baine called me aside. We were on the beach and practicing summoning tidal waves, though Baine had told me to "supervise" some of the other students and help them with their magic instead of doing my own. It was a good excuse to cover up the fact that I couldn't use magic, though I didn't think it was going to last forever.

When all the other students were gone, Baine came close to me, his hands in his pockets. "Liam, have you made any headway in determining if Sophia is the prophesied one or not?"

Yeah, I have proof, straight from the Koigni Council itself, I thought. But obviously, I couldn't say that. So instead, I made something up. "I know Sophia was called in by the Koigni Elders," I started, and his eyebrows raised. "They uh... they want her to find something. Though they won't tell her what it is."

It was just a wild guess, but it must've hit the mark somehow, because Baine paled a little. "My office. Now."

I followed him to the castle and into his messy classroom. Baine kicked aside a few papers and items before he knelt down and opened a book. A folded piece of paper slipped out, and he handed it to me. I unfolded it quickly and read it.

The prophesied one will bring death beyond comprehension,
It it she who shall cause Toaqua's darkest hour.

Shit. That was worse than I expected. And it mentioned a female, which only confirmed Sophia's identity even more.

"That's the Toaqua piece of the prophecy. There are suspected to be four pieces, one from each House," Baine said. "We've attempted working with Yapluma and Nivita, though they're feigning ignorance. They claim to not have any pieces, but we are certain it's a lie. They're hiding their information until they have to make their move."

"You mean until they know which side is going to win," I said. Baine nodded slowly.

A war between Koigni and Toaqua. And neither of the other two Houses would interfere until they knew which side was getting annihilated, so they could join up with the winners and spare themselves from extinction. At least, that's what Baine suspected.

"*Death beyond comprehension* doesn't sound good," I started.

"It's a massacre unlike anything the Hawkei have ever seen. And if the prophecy is to be believed, Koigni will win." Baine sighed. "You understand why we have to stop this, Liam."

I did. I thought about my family, about my parents and my brothers and sisters, and what the world would be like if they were exterminated.

"The Koigni Elders. Did they say what Sophia had to look for?" Baine asked.

"Uh... I don't know. She didn't say much about it. I don't think they told her anything substantial," I started. I was going to have to do a lot of lying if I wanted to keep my girlfriend alive.

"That's good, that's good," Baine mumbled under his breath. "Then they don't know what they're looking for."

"Do you?" I asked.

Baine paused. "We should start doing these meetings in the ancestral language," Baine mumbled. "Just in case we're overheard."

I nodded in agreement. Most Elementai knew the Hawkei language, but a lot of people struggled with it, and weren't fluent. They knew enough to get by in a pinch and that was it. Hawkei was all my family talked in our house when guests weren't around. I switched over. Hawkei. *"Fine. Show me what you've got."*

He started rifling through more books, finally wrenching one out from under a pile and causing the entire thing to collapse. He really didn't care if his office was a disaster.

The book was gigantic. It took up his entire desk as he placed it on top of a mess of trinkets and devices, spreading it open. *"This is what they're looking for,"* Baine said, pointing to a page.

I looked at the drawing. It was a decorated tomahawk, with a long handle and feathers tied on to the sharp blade, and strange symbols carved into the sides. It looked positively normal.

It wasn't the totem we'd found in the cave during the Cup, that was for sure. And it made me breathe a sigh of relief.

"What is it?" I asked, completely confused.

"It's an Azaimperiai," Baine said. I recognized the ancient Hawkei— a mixture of words that meant *ancestral control.* *"It's a device that can summon the ancestors to use as an army."*

"Like in our legends?" I looked at it. It didn't seem that intimidating,

but who knew. The most powerful and magical things in our world often came in small packages.

"Yes. *They're not just stories, Liam.*" Baine shook his head. "*If Sophia gets her hands on it, it's all over.*"

"*Wouldn't the ancestors oppose killing people of their own race?*" I asked.

"*I don't believe they would have a choice.*"

I wasn't sure how the *Azaimperiai* worked, and there were no instructions on the page. I wasn't sure if Baine was totally correct about it, but I'm sure he knew more than I did, so I didn't question any further.

"*I spent nearly twenty years looking for it, and never even came close,*" Baine said in frustration. "*It's completely lost.*"

"*Are you sure it's still around?*"

"*I'm certain of it.*" He glanced at me. "*It's the last relic that Anichi left behind.*"

"*If you spent twenty years looking and didn't find it, either you're terrible at finding things or it's truly gone for good,*" I said firmly. "*No way Sophia will be able to find it just like that.*"

"*Look around you, Liam. Since Sophia's arrival, things have been happening quickly.*" Baine collapsed in his chair. "*The Azaimperiai could be calling out to her with its magic to come find it. And the longer we let this go on, the less chance we have to disrupt destiny.*"

I thought about that. "*What if she fails to find it?*" I asked. "*Doesn't that mean she's not the chosen one?*"

"*Most likely. Though we can't base our mission around 'what ifs.'*"

"*You sure are sounding like Malison, Elder Baine,*" I told him.

"*Don't call me Elder Baine. It makes me sound old. Use Professor.*" Baine wrinkled his nose.

I tried not to roll my eyes. Baine was totally old, he just didn't want to admit it.

"*The evidence is clear. Sophia is extraordinary, Liam. She's got powers stronger than any Koigni we've ever seen before, and it's not going to stop there,*" Baine said. "*She's a gifted Elementai unlike any that's ever lived. Can a threat that immense to the tribe really be allowed to live?*"

"*Looks to me like it doesn't matter what kind of proof I find or don't find, you're going to force me to take Sophia's life anyway,*" I shot back.

"We're talking about genocide, Liam," Baine said firmly. *"Even if Sophia isn't the prophesied child, wouldn't it be better to take her life to potentially save thousands, just to be safe?"*

What he said horrified me. He must've noticed, because he lifted a hand and said, *"I'm getting ahead of myself. Just... find out more about this mission the Koigni Elders have given her. I'm sure it'll help."*

I nodded. *"Sure."*

"In the meantime..." Baine steadied himself. *"You need to prepare yourself, just in case. You should feel comforted. You can give Sophia a quick death. A painless one."*

I didn't want to talk about that. *"Whatever. Are we done?"*

"For now. You can go." Baine waved me away.

Before I went, I added, *"By the way, I know Perot talked to you. We use our elements all the time in Advanced Toaqua Magic. Everyone's going to know I can't use magic. They'll think I'm weak,"* I told him.

"Lucky for you, we're having a heavy month on theory. We'll be writing more than we'll be practicing," Baine said.

Great. More fucking essays. Like I didn't have better things to do.

I tried to slam the door on the way out, but it ended up getting caught on a bunch of shit. Baine raised an eyebrow at me, so I just left.

Fuck, Baine's office should be one of the tasks in next year's Cup. Getting out of that room alive was a challenge itself. He was totally a hoarder. I was scared to see what his house looked like.

I knew the moment I was gone Baine was gonna high-tail it out of there and tell my Dad what he'd found out. I hoped I'd made the right decision in lying about Sophia finding some magical object instead of telling the truth about what she was really doing, but it seemed like I'd only made my case worse.

I thought about what Baine had told me. I sure as hell didn't want to be responsible for causing the tribe's *darkest hour.* Sounded ominous as shit.

I headed to the cafeteria to lunch, because even though I still wasn't hungry, I knew I had to eat something.

I saw Sophia leaning against a statue with Esis in her arms. Jonah was gabbing to Imogen, who was on the floor and leaning against Squeaks. Sassy, though I don't know why, was perched on Squeaks' head. They waved me over. I approached, though Baine's words had left a pretty hollow pit in my stomach.

"*Hey guys,*" I said as I approached. "*Where are we going today?*"

"Huh?" Sophia just stared at me blankly, like she couldn't comprehend my words.

"Dude. Talk American. She can't understand you," Jonah said.

I realized I was still talking in Hawkei. "Oh. Sorry." I rubbed the back of my neck, embarrassed, as I resumed speaking English. "I was talking to Baine."

"In the old language? Weird," Imogen said as she stood up. "I can read or write it, but talking it's a whole other story."

"Don't ask me to translate," Jonah said. His Hawkei was really bad.

"Will you teach me?" Sophia said, looking up at me brightly. She was so sweet.

"Sure," I said. "Though it's really hard."

I glared at Jonah. "And it's English, not American, you ass."

"We're in *America*. Red, white, and blue, baby," he said.

He was an idiot.

"Anyway, you guys wanna head inside?" Imogen said, thumbing at the cafeteria.

I hesitated. We all had the same lunch hour on Mondays and Wednesdays, and it was cool. We'd mostly spent it together, but we usually hid out in other places around the castle. We'd never eaten in the cafeteria as a group together before. Not since last semester, anyway, and that was on and off, not to mention when we were participating in the tournament and it was expected of us to talk to one another. But we'd been talking about doing it for the past few weeks, just hadn't yet worked up the courage.

"No time like the present, right?" Sophia asked, and she nudged me.

She was right. If I couldn't eat with my friends from other Houses in a school cafeteria, how was I ever going to be brave enough to defend mine and Sophia's relationship if it ever got out?

"Okay. Let's go." We headed inside and got our food together, choosing a vacant table in the middle of the room, where Houses weren't designated. As a team, we sat down together. I noticed eyes were on us the entire time, but not as many as I expected. A couple students stared, but I was starting to think people were getting used to us weird kids by now.

"Hey, Liam. What's up? Can we sit here?" My brother had come by, along with Wyatt and a group of about five other people. I noticed among his group was Cade, and the Lindsey girl we'd met at the party. The number of people following Ezra was so big, he was having trouble finding a place to sit. The only spaces left were tables around us, which shouldn't have surprised anybody.

Lindsey was the only girl among them with a Familiar. Her basilisk hovered near her shoulder and looked at me.

"Sure," I said. "Doesn't matter to me."

Ezra and Wyatt pushed a table together with ours, and his group gathered around it, sitting in chairs. People of all Houses mixed together, and inwardly, I relaxed. I was glad Ezra came over with his friends. It made it a little less weird that a bunch of people from different Houses were sitting together, and not just my team.

"So, Liam," Sophia started before I even got two bites in. "What happened this morning?"

She was quick. It must've been bothering her all day. "It wasn't much, Soph. Perot wanted to see me," I started. "He thinks he might've figured out what's going on with me."

"What's wrong with you? I could give him a list," Jonah quipped. I ignored him.

"Perot? What did he say?" Ezra nearly planted his t-shirt in a pile of spaghetti sauce, he leaned so far forward.

"It's not much, Ez," I said. Quickly, I summarized what Perot had told me this morning. Sophia's face grew concerned as I went on. Under the table, she put a hand on my knee, though it ended up closer to my thigh. It was meant to be a comforting gesture, and it was *comforting something*, all right. If she kept doing that, my dick was going to have a problem.

When I was done, Imogen muddled over what Perot had told me. "I think I've heard of this before. It sounds familiar. Give me a few weekends to go through the books at my parents'. I'm sure there's something."

"You don't have to do that, Im," I said softly, though I was kinda touched she would offer.

"Of course I do. I have to keep my buddy alive," Imogen said, and she nudged Sophia.

Sophia seemed sad. "I'm really sorry you can't use your magic, Liam."

"It's okay. It's only for a month," I told her softly. "I'll survive."

"Aw, Liam. You're so gentle and sweet around Sophia. Where's the love for the rest of us?" Cade teased.

"Fuck off." I took a fry from Sophia's plate and flung it at him. He gave me an obnoxious wink that I took to mean something.

Cade didn't know about us, right? He couldn't have, unless...

Fuck. The stables! Sophia and I had kissed by them, not thinking anyone was around when we took Melody back. Cade was always hanging around there. What if he had seen?

I forced myself to calm down. I didn't know Cade that well, but he was into Imogen and seemed like a nice guy, plus he was friends with my brother. If he knew anything, we could probably trust him.

A girl came over. She stood next to Cade and put a hand on his shoulder. She gave a smirking glance to Imogen. It was a gesture of ownership. I realized she was the girl who had spilled her drink on Imogen at the party, and the girl who had taken him away from Imogen at the ball last semester.

"Hey, babe. Why you sitting over here?" the girl asked. Her voice was high-pitched and whiny. I was instantly annoyed.

"Guys, I want you to meet my new girlfriend. This is Mallory," Cade said, gesturing to her.

Imogen's face fell at the word *girlfriend*. Mallory leaned down and gave Cade a kiss right in front of Imogen. It was brutal to watch.

"My friends are waiting for us. Can we go?" Mallory asked.

"Uh... sure." Cade got up and went to sit with Mallory in the Nivita section. Imogen's eyes followed him all the way across the room.

Jonah looked at Imogen. "I'm really sorry, Im."

"It's okay," Imogen said flatly. "It's for the best."

Sassy made a sad noise and hung her head, but Imogen acted like the whole thing hadn't bothered her. She ate her food with a rageful expression and threw death glances at Mallory between bites.

I didn't think Mallory was Cade's type. She was tall and thin, and her clothes were so boring, black slacks with a light gray top. She looked like she was going to a business meeting.

I knew Cade liked short girls who wore crazy outfits. More specifically, I knew he liked Imogen. This came out of nowhere.

I sent a questioning glance at Sophia, supposing she knew what was up. The glance she gave me said she'd tell me later.

Mallory wasn't the only one who wanted to be a bitch today. Haley walked by with her army of clones, a salad on her tray. She sneered at us like we were disgusting. Miranda was by her side, and her eyes were on Lindsey. She seemed torn between whether she wanted to join us, or stay with Haley.

Haley barked some order, and Miranda cringed. Miranda made a quick gesturing movement, and Lindsey got up. "I gotta go. See you guys."

I felt bad for Lindsey. It was obvious she wanted to hang around with us, but when Haley said jump, she knew better than to say no.

The rest of the table didn't notice Lindsey sneak out. They were all in a deep discussion about a book that Jonah had brought out of his bag to show the girls.

"Oh, it's the best. It's got dragons, and tons of hot dudes, and lots of sex," Jonah gushed before he sighed dramatically. "I wish *I* could be in a reverse harem."

Jonah had the weirdest taste in literature. He liked to read shifter romance novels where there'd be three or more guys to one girl, or short stories where people lost in the woods were rescued by multiple mountain men who didn't talk. In the past few weeks, he'd gotten Imogen into it. Our lunch conversations were going places I never wanted them to venture into. Ezra's multiple girlfriends listened with interest as Jonah described some convoluted plot from a romance book that didn't make sense.

"Jonah, you're the best," one of the girls gushed. "And it's so cool you're proud of who you are. You totally don't mind being yourself."

"I own that shit, honey." Jonah put his book back in his bag. "You gotta own whatever you are, too. Be your own star."

I rolled my eyes.

"Jonah, will you come to my dorm tonight?" another one begged.

She batted her eyelashes at him. "I would love to hear more about your books."

She was totally trying to turn him not-gay. Wasn't gonna happen, ladies.

"Nah. I gotta go to the gym later. Burn some carbs, pump some iron," Jonah said. "Plus, there's a game on tonight. I gotta prep my fantasy league."

I didn't understand how Jonah could go from total horny frat boy to overdramatic drag queen in less than point-five seconds. It was enough to give you whiplash.

As if by fate, Renar slid up to the table. You know, because he was so greasy and gross. He took an empty chair next to Jonah and, without even a hello, planted his mouth on my best friend's. I figured they'd just kiss quick and get it over with, but that's not what happened. They made out like they were long lost lovers or something. They didn't even come up for air. I saw tongue and everything. It made me want to throw up my lunch.

"Um... I have class," Ezra said with an awkward glance at me, and he slid out of his seat. His friends made similar excuses and all left, until it was just my team and Renar. Sophia pretended to play with Esis, and I tried to focus on my meal.

Squeaks was so pissed off. Her feathers were puffed up, and she ruffled them in displeasure as she watched them kiss. She looked like an overly large disgruntled owl.

Imogen sat there, quivering in rage. She was already pissed off because of Cade. I waited for the blow up.

"Can you guys go make-out somewhere else?" Imogen finally snapped. "I hate PDA."

Jonah finally pried his face away from Renar's and gave her a dramatic look. "Fine. I can see we're not wanted."

Jonah sauntered away, swinging his hips, with Renar at his heels. They picked a booth that was literally right across from us so we could see everything. I was very sure Jonah had done it on purpose. Squeaks stayed with us and refused to move, though she continued to watch Renar with narrowed eyes.

"I think I've lost my appetite. See you in class, Sophia." Imogen stood up with the rest of her half-eaten food and walked away. Sassy ran after, jumping into Imogen's bag.

Sophia stopped messing with Esis and watched Jonah and Renar go at it with a slightly horrified expression. "A little kiss is okay, but they're taking it a bit far."

"No shit," I muttered. Even if it was allowed for us to kiss in public, I wouldn't eat Sophia's face off in front of the entire cafeteria. Renar was totally making Jonah into a spectacle for all to see, and he wouldn't even commit. I totally saw Renar make a go for Jonah's pants, and I had to tear my eyes away. They were five seconds away from doing it on the table in front of everyone.

"Let's get out of here," Sophia said quietly. She stood up, and I followed. We cleaned off our table as quickly as we could while trying to ignore the scene around us. People were starting to whisper and point at Renar and Jonah, and it was embarrassing.

"Squeaks, you coming?" I asked her. She was so still, even I was scared of her.

Squeaks made a non-committal sound and ground her beak. She was five seconds away from springing on Renar. Esis patted her on the shoulder from his place on the table before jumping onto Sophia's shirt.

"Suit yourself," I told her, and we left the hippogriff behind.

When we were out in the hallway, Sophia said, "I don't get how Jonah can stand to be around Renar when Squeaks obviously doesn't want him around. If Esis didn't like you, sorry Liam, you'd be gone."

"That's okay." I laughed. "I don't expect to take the little guy's place."

Esis stuck his tongue out at me, like he'd won.

"Jonah's very good at lying to himself," I added. "He sees what he wants to see and nothing else."

"Then why can't Squeaks pretend she's happy for him?" Sophia asked.

"Familiars can't really hide emotions like Elementai can. They'll always reveal your true feelings," I told Sophia.

Sophia pondered this. "But if that's true, why does Sassy love Cade, but Squeaks hates Renar?"

"Just because they're our soul doesn't mean we're the same person.

Squeaks is supposed to be Jonah's protector, but she can't really protect him if he's choosing something bad for himself," I said.

"Hmm. I see." Sophia stroked Esis. "I suppose it's a good thing that Esis loves you."

Esis pulled away from Sophia and jumped toward me. I grabbed him in mid-air and held him to my chest. He snuggled into my hoodie like it was a nest and stuck his head out of the pocket.

"For sure. Nashoma bit Mia once. I should've taken it as a warning," I said.

At the mention of Mia, Sophia wrinkled her nose. "She sounds worse every time you talk about her."

"She's really not that bad," I said, but honestly, I couldn't remember. It was hard to recall what dating Mia had been like. I'd pretty much forgotten. I barely remembered the few times we had sex, and to be frank, it hadn't been good.

Sophia was quiet for a moment before she asked, "Liam? I don't want to make you upset, but... what happened to Nashoma?"

The question hit me hard. I thought about my Familiar, how he died and how I had the chance to bring him back.

It reminded me I would probably lose Sophia if that happened. Still, I missed him so bad it made my chest ache. "I don't really want to talk about it, Sophia. It still hurts, you know?"

She nodded. "Okay."

She glanced away. I think she believed I didn't want to open up to her. It wasn't that. I just... couldn't. It hurt too much.

I stopped in front of the staircase by the window. I glanced around—nobody was here. Quickly, I yanked her behind some curtains. She laughed.

"I gotta go, Soph. Basket Weaving." I smiled at her. She was the only person in the world I'd willingly admit that to.

"You should make me something," she said coyly as she took Esis out of my hoodie. "It would be so sweet."

She didn't need to know I was already working on it, but it was gonna take me all semester. "Maybe one day."

I gave her a quick kiss. She smelled so good today— it made me miss the ocean. Sophia deepened the kiss and put her tongue in my mouth. I made out with her for a minute before I forced our mouths apart. It was like ripping off my own arm.

I laughed. "No, we can't do that. We'll get too carried away, and I've gotta go."

She giggled. "What if I don't want you to?"

Skipping class to mess around with Sophia was really tempting, but I didn't want her to fall behind. "You've got class, too. We'll catch up later."

I gave her another kiss before I stepped out of the curtains. "I love you."

"I love you, too, Liam." She cuddled Esis, then ran off. I swear there was a skip in her step.

Like always, I watched her until she faded out of sight. Then I started up the staircase to head to Basket Weaving. The minute she was gone, Baine's heavy words almost crushed me once again.

"She's extraordinary, Liam." Yeah, I knew she was. I'd heard what had happened between her and Haley, too. The duel had been legendary, according to some Koigni First Years. She'd kicked Haley's ass all around the classroom, and Haley was no novice by any means. Word had probably made it back to my dad by now. She wasn't giving the Toaqua Elders a lot of reasons not to kill her.

One thing was pretty clear. If Sophia kept showing off her Fire, she'd only become a bigger target. I couldn't let that happen. I had to make the Toaqua Elders view her as weak somehow.

Although it killed me, I had to stop Sophia from using her magic as much as possible. If I wanted her to live, I was going to have to start sabotaging her.

sophia
EIGHT

Valentine's Day at Orenda Academy was magical. As I passed by the grand staircase that morning, I saw a group of Yapluma girls leaning over the fifth-floor balcony in the grand foyer. They blew heart-shaped bubbles that floated down around the huge chandelier. A Nivita guy handed a girl a red rose and made it bloom right before her eyes. Familiars scurried this way and that, carrying Valentine's Day cards for their Elementai's sweethearts. I even saw a rabbit Familiar hopping down the hall with a dozen pink balloons strapped to its back.

My heart lifted in my chest when I saw Liam walking toward me. It felt like my whole body was floating. I thought for a second Jonah might be playing a prank on me, but he was nowhere nearby. It was just my overactive hormones swooning for the guy who'd stolen my heart.

"Liam." I grinned widely when I met up with him. Esis chirped happily from my shoulder.

Liam wore a leather jacket. I assumed he must've been out taking his bike for a joyride this morning. Beneath that, he wore a red button-down shirt. It was one of the only days it didn't seem weird, since most people were wearing red or pink. He beamed back and held a hand behind his back.

"I have a surprise for you," he said.

"For me?" I blushed.

Liam glanced around at the passing students, then grabbed my elbow with his free hand. "Come on."

He led me down a narrow, secluded hallway. There were only three doors, two leading to separate bathrooms and one to a utility closet.

I couldn't take my eyes off his. "What's the surprise?"

"I've been thinking," he said, like we were about to have a serious conversation.

Don't ruin it, Liam. This is Valentine's Day! It's supposed to be fun.

"Thinking about what?" I asked when he paused.

He took a deep breath. "I've been thinking that maybe... somehow, someway... we can make this work long-term. And maybe make it permanent."

The air *whooshed* out of my lungs. Had I heard him right? Was Liam finally starting to believe we could be together forever?

Before I could respond, Liam pulled his hand from behind his back. He held out a bouquet of a dozen roses, but they weren't red like I expected. They were blue and orange. *Toaqua and Koigni.*

"Liam," I said breathlessly. "I love them."

I took them from his hands and pressed them to my nose, inhaling their scent. Esis leaned over my shoulder to sniff them, too.

Liam shoved his hands in his pockets and shrugged. "Yeah, well, I thought you might."

"I didn't get you anything," I admitted. "I didn't think Valentine's Day was a big thing around here."

I'd even asked Imogen about it. She'd said I shouldn't worry. She was a liar.

"And I— I've never had a Valentine before," I admitted sheepishly.

"Really?" Liam asked, surprised.

I nodded. "I guess I was never dating anyone this time of year. I want to get you something, though."

"Nah," Liam said, like it was no big deal. "You don't have to do that."

I sniffed the flowers again, and my heart swooned. I stared down at them, admiring the blue and orange tones. "I don't have to, but I want to. These flowers are perfect, Liam."

"It's no big deal. Really," he insisted. "I'm not really into flowers or chocolates and that shit. I just thought—"

"Liam Mitoh, you are *not* denying a gift from me," I demanded, stomping my foot.

Liam bit his lower lip and glanced down at my feet. Desire burned in his eyes, like it turned him on when I stood up to him.

Hell yeah I turned him on. There was plenty more where that came from.

He lifted his gaze. "What are you gonna get me, *pawee*? I'll just return it."

"Then I'll get you something you can't return," I replied with a raised eyebrow. I had no idea what that might entail... yet.

Liam smirked. "There's no time. I have class in less than half an hour."

I glanced around, wondering what I could possibly get him for Valentine's Day. Then my eyes landed on the utility closet, and something Imogen had said a few weeks ago popped into my head. I instantly knew what to do. "I don't need half an hour."

"What are we—?"

I grabbed Liam by the collar and dragged him behind me into the closet. He shot me a questioning glance, but I ignored it as I pulled Esis off my shoulder and set him on the ground outside the door. I handed him the bouquet. It was almost twice his size, but he held it up proudly.

"You keep watch, buddy," I told him. He gave me a salute, then I turned back to Liam. "Remember when I said I was open to *other stuff*?"

Liam's eyebrows shot up. My lips were on his before the door clicked shut. He tensed for a moment before his body relaxed. His hands roamed over me in the darkness, trailing up my back and then down to my butt. My hands tangled in his hair as I parted my lips. His tongue slid inside my mouth, and he dragged me closer to him. I stood on my toes and arched my back, pressing my breasts against his chest. My heart pummeled against my ribcage, and my whole body shook in exhilaration.

"Sophia," Liam moaned as he took a step forward, pressing against me.

The closet wasn't very big, barely the size of the closet in my dorm room. My back dug into the corners of the shelves behind me, and the scent of cleaner filled my nose. But I didn't care. All that mattered were Liam's lips on mine, his hands on my ass, and the heat settling between my thighs.

"I love it when you say my name," I whispered as his lips left mine and his teeth nipped at the skin on my neck.

"Sophia," he mumbled with his lips against my collarbone.

"Yes," I encouraged.

"Sophia," he said, breathing in deeply to inhale my scent.

What was it about hearing him say my name? It was so *hot*.

He drew away from me, breathing hard. I could barely see his silhouette. The only light came through a crack at the bottom of the door.

"Liam," I said breathlessly, just to hear the sound of his name on my lips.

"Fuck, *pawee*." His lips swooped down to claim mine once more. He wrapped his arms around me and lifted me off the floor.

I threw my legs around his middle, holding on to him for dear life. The taste of his lips, the scent of his hair, the feel of his skin… it all overwhelmed my senses. I could feel my love for him rising within me, overtaking every nerve in my body like its own sort of magic. Tears of happiness brimmed at my eyes. Ancestors, I loved him so much.

Liam pushed the fabric of my shirt up, exposing the skin just above my jeans. His hands trailed up my bare back until they reached my bra. He fiddled with the clasp.

I drew away from him. "Hold on. This isn't about me. This is about you."

Liam went silent for a second. "But… I— I like boobs."

I giggled. "Yeah, I bet you do. But I have something better in mind."

"Better?" Liam sounded intrigued.

I climbed down off from him. The air in here was hot.

"Hold your unicorns, water boy," I said with a smirk he couldn't see. "I can't give you everything at once." I had to make him beg for it. That's what Imogen would tell me to do, at least. For the love of the ancestors, the anticipation was killing *me*.

But I didn't drag Liam in here just to get him to second base. Like I said, this wasn't about me. I reached out my hands to find Liam's waist-band in the darkness.

He inhaled a sharp breath. "Sophia, what are you—?"

"Shh…" I was already undoing his belt. "It's okay, Liam."

"Ancestors, Sophia, they were just flowers."

I reached for the button on his jeans. "They're never just flowers, Liam. Do you want me to stop?"

I could hear the grin in his voice. "I never said that."

The sound of Liam's zipper falling filled the closet, and he let out a shaky breath. My heart pounded so hard I could hear it in my ears. Was I actually going to do this?

Liam's jeans fell from his hips and landed around his ankles. He ran his hands up my arms and past my shoulders until they tangled in my hair. Tingles spread across my skin where he touched me.

I reached out with shaky fingers and pulled back the waistband of his boxers. My fingers grazed the end of him *there*. He inhaled a sharp breath. Gently, my fingers trailed down his length, exploring him in the darkness.

Holy mother of all magical creatures! It never ended!

"Is something wrong?" Liam asked.

"No," I answered quickly. "I just… didn't know what to expect."

"I, uh, hope that's a good thing."

"Yes! Definitely yes."

Liam pulled me in closer to him. "So, what are you going to do about it?"

It sounded like a challenge. The air left my chest when I took him in my hand. *I can't believe this is happening!*

I ran my hand along his length, slow at first, until he placed a hand on each side of my face and kissed me with a burning passion. His tongue danced around inside my mouth. I couldn't help but rub him faster. I was *definitely* going to need a new pair of panties after this.

"Fuck, *pawee!*" Liam shouted as he leapt away from me.

"What?" I asked, alarmed. I must've done something wrong. It wasn't like I knew what I was doing.

"Are you trying to burn my dick off?" he hissed.

I didn't realize until that moment that my Fire had risen just below the surface of my skin. My hands were burning.

"I'm *so* sorry," I told him. "Did I ruin it?"

Liam sighed. "No. Just... try not to hurt Little Liam. I kinda need him."

My eyebrows shot up. "Little Liam?"

Liam's hands found mine in the darkness. "*Now* you're ruining it. Here, I'll show you how it's done."

Liam gently placed my hand back around him. He had me loosen my grip, and then guided me until I had the speed just right.

"Is this better?" I whispered.

"*Pawee*," he said in a light tone, squeezing my hips. "I'm living the dream here. Do you even have to ask?"

I didn't answer. Instead, I went silent. I knew if I said anything I might ruin the moment. I focused on my Fire, pushing it just low enough that it didn't hurt him, but not so far away that he didn't find pleasure in the heat. I wanted to please him. I wanted nothing more than to please him. Hell, just hearing the sounds coming from his lips pleased *me*.

Liam's hands inched up my sides until one of them found my left breast. I gasped as he cupped me in his hand. Even though there were layers of clothing between us, it *turned me the fuck on*. He squeezed harder. I took it as an invitation to increase my speed.

Without warning, his free hand fisted in my hair. He leaned his head down and moaned into the crook of my neck, his teeth biting into my shoulder to muffle the sound.

Hell yes!

He reached his peak, and his muscles constricted beneath my touch. Warmth spread across my belly, and his body shuddered against mine, curling inward. He held me tightly against him, like he couldn't stand to let me go. His fingers curled tightly against my back.

I beamed. It felt like I'd just climbed a mountain. I couldn't have been happier knowing *I* made him feel this way.

Eventually, his tremors ended. I couldn't stop smiling as Liam finally released me. He stumbled backwards, holding himself up on the shelves behind him.

"You sure—" He took a deep breath. "You've never—" Another breath. "Done that before, *pawee?*" Liam asked.

If possible, I smiled even wider. "I think I would remember that. So, was it good?"

"Was it good?" Liam scoffed. "Let's just say you can do it again."

"Sounds like fun." I reached out for him again, but he was already bending to grab the pants around his ankles.

He swatted at me playfully. "I didn't mean now."

I giggled. "Well, I guess we're just going to have to do this again another time."

Liam finished with his belt. "You can count on that."

"I will. But, um, you need to get to class." I reached for the door handle.

Before I made it out, Liam pinched my butt. I gave a little yelp and whirled around, stood on my toes, and pecked him on the lips.

"You're so naughty," I teased before I opened the door and peeked out to make sure the coast was clear. Esis was the only one in the hallway. He stood with his back to us, holding on to the flowers and whistling.

"Me?" Liam feigned. "I'm not the one who dragged you into a *broom closet.*"

I turned toward him as he exited the closet. "Yeah, well, maybe you should've."

I winked at him, but he glanced down at me with a fallen face.

"What?" I looked to follow his gaze. The hem of my shirt was covered in... *Liam.* "Oh, um... we have a bit of a situation."

Liam glanced down the hall. No one was around to see us, but he looked horrified. "Can you run back to your dorm and clean up?"

"People are still going to see!" I panicked, hoping this stuff didn't stain. "And if I try to clean up in the bathroom, my shirt will be all wet."

"Here, I've got it." He shrugged off his jacket and handed it to me.

I eyed it. "Liam, I can't."

"Sure you can." He shoved it toward me.

"What if people notice it's yours? What if they think we're together?"

"I hardly ever wear it. No one will know it's mine. It's better than..." He dropped his gaze. "That."

"True," I agreed, grabbing the jacket from his hands and slipping it over my shoulders. I caught a whiff of his scent immediately. I was *never* going to take this thing off. "There are worse ways to mark your territory than letting me borrow your jacket."

Liam smirked.

"I'm going to go wipe off before I get it all over your good jacket. Happy Valentine's Day, Liam."

I stood there waiting for a goodbye kiss, but then a group of people walked past the hallway, and Liam jumped at least a foot away from me.

"Happy Valentine's Day, Soph. I'll see you later."

He paused, then added lowly, "You can bet I'll be getting you back for that closet incident soon."

With that, he left, and Esis handed my bouquet back. I stood there to watch him go, smelling the roses again and knowing there was *so* much more to that promise than Liam would dare speak aloud.

AFTER RETURNING to my dorm to put on a new shirt, I headed to the sitting area on the third floor next to the griffin tapestry. Imogen and I met up there every Thursday morning to work on our Ancient Familiars homework. I'd be late, but I didn't think she would mind once I told her why.

When I reached the top of the stairs, I spotted Imogen instantly. She was impossible to miss with the Valentine's Day outfit she wore. It was all pink ruffles and white lace and had no shape to it whatsoever. On her head, she wore a god-awful hat that looked like a giant heart was growing out of her ears. Her face was smack-dab in the middle of it. It was huge and seemed heavy, like if she tilted her head to the side, she'd fall over. Sassy was curled up on the end table next to Imogen's chair wearing a matching pink bow around her neck.

A few passing students took notice. One guy even did a double-take when he realized Imogen was a living person and not some giant Valentine's Day decoration.

Jonah leaned over the armrest of the chair next to Imogen, chatting away at her. Squeaks was sprawled on the floor in front of him, taking up the entire study area.

"Wow, Imogen," I said as I plopped down in the plush chair across from her. "You look..."

How did I put it? The heart-shaped hat was a little over the top, even for her.

"Amazeballs?" Jonah finished for me. "The girl *slays*, doesn't she?"

I took another glance at her ruffles. Her dress looked like it belonged on a baby doll. "Yeah, I suppose she does. Don't you have class, Jonah?"

I was eager for him to leave so I could tell Imogen about what had happened between Liam and me. It wasn't exactly something I wanted to announce in front of Jonah, even though he'd probably figure it out eventually. I just didn't want to see how he'd react. At least Imogen could keep it together over this kind of stuff.

Jonah pretended to check a fake watch on his wrist. "Nah, I've got time. Besides, Imogen and I need each other today."

"What do you mean?" I asked.

Imogen curled her legs up under her on the chair and dropped her gaze. "It's a sad day for both of us. You know, because we're both single."

"But what about Renar, Jonah?" I asked.

Jonah rolled his eyes so hard I wouldn't have been surprised if he saw the back of his head. "Don't even mention him to me right now."

"You guys are fighting?" I almost hoped they were. Jonah needed to get over Renar and move on already. Renar had been stringing him along for far too long.

Jonah shrugged. "I wouldn't say *fighting*, exactly. He's just ignoring me, and, well..."

He glanced to Imogen, as if begging for her to explain.

Imogen leaned forward and lowered her voice. "I saw Renar eating a heart-shaped box of chocolates earlier today, and Jonah wasn't the one who sent them."

I felt bad for Jonah. He looked so sad that I thought he might cry. Esis noticed, too. He jumped down from my shoulder, hopped over Squeaks, and snuggled himself into Jonah's lap.

Jonah stroked him behind the ears. "Aw, thanks, little guy, but I think Imogen needs you more than I do." Jonah lifted Esis and set him on the edge of Imogen's chair.

I cocked my head to the side. "Why? What's wrong, Im?"

She breathed a heavy sigh. "I saw Cade and Mallory exchanging Valentines in the dorms this morning. Then I had to watch them suck face and everything. It was awful."

"I'm sorry," I told her. Then I added, "But, you know, *you're* the one who told him you two couldn't be together. I mean, can you blame him for trying to move on?"

Jonah gave a dramatic gasp, like he couldn't believe I'd just said that. I hardly believed it, either. It'd more or less just popped out.

Imogen scowled at me. "*You're* the one who kept insisting he liked me so much. I thought he'd at least fight for me or something. You know, like you and Liam."

Uh, oh. Irritated Imogen was coming out to play. It wasn't cool that she was taking her anger at Cade out on me.

"Are you jealous of us?" I asked, a little irritated myself.

"No, I'm not *jealous* of you." Imogen crossed her arms, clearly lying.

"Good, because you shouldn't be," I said bluntly. "Liam and I are together because I wouldn't take no for an answer. You just let Cade walk away. If you want him so bad, you should fight for him."

"You don't understand," Imogen shot back. "It's complicated between us."

"And Liam and I aren't complicated?" I hissed, trying to keep my voice low as a group of students passed through the hall.

Imogen opened her mouth to respond, but Jonah got up and jumped between us, holding both hands up in either direction.

"Whoa!" he said, like he was giving commands to a unicorn. "Time out, ladies."

Imogen narrowed her eyes at me behind Jonah's hand. Of all the girls I'd been friends with over the years, I never thought I'd fight with Imogen, and over a guy, no less. I seriously didn't know what was going through her head if she thought Cade would still go for her after she told him to back off. Unless she still thought he'd been too drunk to remember, which I was betting wasn't the case. He wouldn't have moved on so quickly otherwise.

I leaned back in my chair. "I'm just telling it how it is."

"That's the Koigni in you talking," Jonah accused.

"And that's a bad thing?" I raised an eyebrow. "In case you haven't noticed, I *am* Koigni."

"Yeah," Imogen snapped. "You are. Which means you don't understand how Nivita work. You don't know shit about me and Cade."

I reeled back as if Imogen had slapped me. She'd *never* talked to me like that before.

I scoffed and stood. "Fine. Clearly you don't want my advice."

"Come on, Sophia." Imogen rolled her eyes. "Don't be like that."

I crossed my arms. "Be like what? A Koigni?"

Imogen gaped at me. "No, like... like Haley."

My jaw dropped. Jonah gasped and threw his hand over his mouth.

What a horrible thing to say! I was so shocked that I couldn't find the words to respond.

Imogen rolled her eyes. "Whatever. If you're going to be like that, just go."

Oh, wow. Really, Im?

"Fine. I will. Come on, Esis." I turned on my heel, but stopped when I heard Esis chitter from Imogen's lap. I turned to see him snuggling up under one of the pink ruffles. He blinked a few times, as if begging me to let him stay.

"Esis," I said firmly.

He dropped his head and hopped off Imogen's chair, then waved goodbye with his little paw.

"You don't have to be so harsh," Imogen called when I turned away.

"Sophia, come on," Jonah called at the same time. "Stay. We'll work it out. I can be your couple's therapist. Oh, this'll be fun!"

I turned to call over my shoulder. "Maybe another time. See ya."

Imogen mumbled something under her breath as I started down the stairs, but I didn't hear what it was. I nearly whirled back around to demand her to repeat what she'd said about me, but I knew that was what she wanted. My pride kept me moving forward.

I'd never felt so Koigni in my life than I did in that moment. It was so unlike me that even Madame Doya would be proud.

I was still irritated with Imogen by the time Unicornology rolled around. I was all ready to open up to Liam about the whole thing and get him to back me up on how ridiculous Imogen was being, but he didn't show.

I stared at his empty seat next to me as a sinking feeling entered my gut. Was he okay? Liam didn't usually skip class unless he didn't feel well.

Shit. Could this day get any worse?

I ran back mine and Imogen's conversation in my head over and over again. She was totally jealous of me and Liam. The more I thought of it, the more I realized that Imogen might be done with me. Was I going to have to choose between my best friend and my boyfriend?

I wasn't sure I could make that kind of decision.

THAT NIGHT WAS my first private training session with Doya, and I was *so* not looking forward to it. I'd been dreading this first training session for weeks, but I couldn't exactly skip it. I had to uphold my end of our bargain, to keep my friends safe.

Even if Imogen was being totally over the top right now.

I arrived early but purposely stood outside her door until the last minute, so I didn't have to spend any extra time with her than I had to. When my watch hit five o'clock, I finally knocked.

"Come in." Her voice came from behind the door.

Cautiously, I stepped into her office. It was bigger than my dorm room, with dark mahogany bookcases lining the walls and a massive desk at the far end of the room. A painting of Naomi hung above a fireplace in the middle of the room. A nice leather couch sat atop a large red area rug next to the door, and an old grandfather clock ticked in the corner. Everything was pristine. Esis' mouth formed into a perfect O as he took in the decor.

Doya rose from her desk where she'd been grading papers, and Naomi stood beside her. "You're cutting it close."

"I'm not late, am I?" I asked innocently.

Doya glanced to the clock and frowned. "Let's get started. In these training sessions, your magic will be pushed to the limit."

"What exactly will I be up against?"

She rounded her desk and leaned against the front of it. "The barriers placed within the Anichi ruins were designed for only Koigni Elders to pass through."

I gaped at her. "You're asking me to become as strong as the Elders even though I'm just a First Year?"

Doya looked me up and down past her nose. "Yes. I am."

I straightened. "And you don't see a problem with that?"

She smirked. "You seemed to show no trouble doing so during the Cup. Besides, I will teach you the locations of the obstacles and how to avoid them, but that is a lesson for another day. The most important thing is to expand your magic enough to contact the ancestors. The power's in your blood, Sophia. It's my job to help you unlock that power."

"What does that mean? *The power's in my blood?*"

"Your parents were very strong Elementai," she said. "Speaking of them, it concerns me that you haven't asked about them much. Aren't you the least bit curious about your birth parents?"

I shrugged. For whatever reason, it bothered Doya that I still thought of my adoptive parents as my real parents. I figured she was just annoyed that I wouldn't fully embrace my Koigni heritage, but her concern seemed a little unnatural. Had she been close with my birth parents or something?

"It doesn't change who I am, does it?"

Doya pursed her lips at that.

The truth was, I didn't feel any connection to Anthony and Lucy Greyson. When Doya told me about my birth parents, it didn't feel real. She'd said they'd died shortly after I was born, but to me, it felt like they never even existed.

"No, I suppose it doesn't. Though I was close to your mother. I would expect you to offer her some respect. She did give birth to you."

Way to make me feel guilty.

"Yes, I'm sorry. You're right." I said, mostly to get off the topic. It made me uncomfortable.

Doya looked a little shocked, then said, "Well, in that case, let's move on. The first obstacle is unavoidable. It will require great physical strength, balance, and endurance, but that is going to require working out on your own time."

"I hike all the time," I said. "I'm in pretty good shape."

Doya stared down her nose at me. "Yes, well, consider more training. As for your Fire, you will have to perform a highly advanced Koigni task to complete the ceremony in order to summon the ancestors."

"What's the ceremony like?"

"Patience, Sophia. I will teach you the ceremony once you've shown your powers are ready, and we have a long way to go."

Damn. "Okay," I agreed.

"Today, we're going to focus on shaping Fire. Last semester, you learned how to shape your Fire into a sphere, but we're going to take it a step further. This is at least Third Year level magic. Eventually, you will be able to shape your Fire into anything at will."

Doya flicked her wrist and opened her palm. A fireball flew out of it but stopped in mid-air. She twisted her hand, and the flames took the shape of a lion cub. The cub bounced around a foot off the ground while Doya moved her fingers, as if she was controlling a marionette. The cub ran for Naomi and circled around her, like it was trying to play with its mother. Naomi spun around, following the Fire cub with interest.

With a simple close of Doya's palm, the Fire cub disappeared. The flames rose into the air and dissipated like they'd never even been there in the first place.

"Today, you will shape your Fire into a cube," Doya announced. "Not only that, but you will *sustain* it."

It all sounded fine and dandy until she added that last little bit.

"And if I can't?" I asked.

"Then I will be required to add more training sessions to our schedule. Frankly, I hardly have the time as it is, so I suggest you keep up with each lesson I have in store for you."

"Yes, ma'am," I answered with a salute. I *definitely* didn't want to attend any more training sessions with Doya than I had to.

She frowned. "Don't *ever* do that to me again, Sophia. This isn't a game."

I stood up straight. "Sorry." Trust Doya to not let me have any fun.

Doya's features hardened— if that were possible. She seemed as annoyed as I was about these private lessons. "Let's get started. Show me a fireball."

I placed Esis on the couch to watch. He snuggled right in, looking like he could use a bucket of popcorn for the show. I held my hands out in front of me and conjured a fireball between my palms. After a few months at this, fireballs were simple. I didn't even have to think about it to sustain the flame.

Doya stepped forward to inspect my fire. "Shaping isn't just about picturing what you want your Fire to become. It is about becoming what you picture in your mind."

"You want me to become a cube?"

Doya looked two seconds away from slapping me. "I can't teach you if you aren't willing to open your mind."

"But you just said—"

"You have to become one with your Fire," she cut me off.

I held back a smile. I loved seeing her struggle.

"Do not think of your Fire as an outside entity. Don't even think of it as an extension of yourself. It *is* you. It is *inside* of you. Don't just picture the cube. *Feel* it."

She stood behind me and placed her hands on my shoulders and squeezed them tightly. "Feel the pressure on the side of the sphere. Feel it compacting your Fire into six smooth and equal sides."

Normally, I'd object to Doya touching me, but the pressure of her hands helped me visualize what she was saying. I focused all my attention on that sphere, willing it to become a cube.

But it didn't.

"You're visualizing it as an extension of yourself," Doya scolded.

"How do you know?" I demanded.

"Because you're looking at the fireball like you're waiting for it to explode."

I didn't realize until then how tightly scrunched up my face was. I quickly relaxed.

"Remember, the Fire doesn't come from your palm," Doya said. "It comes from inside you. You will never shape your Fire if you're trying to force it externally."

"Okay, I think I get it. Just give me a minute."

Doya backed off and stood by Naomi to observe. I couldn't stand feeling her eyes on me, so I closed my eyes to try blocking her out. I pretended I wasn't in this room, that I was out in the forest. I pictured the sound of the leaves rustling in the trees and the waves crashing against the shore in the distance. In my mind, the sun was shining, and it smelled like Liam.

I took a deep breath and focused all of my energy on my heart, where I could feel my Fire power radiating from as it tingled down my arms. I pictured a box around my heart, a white cube that grew smaller and smaller with each moment, squeezing me tightly. The pressure grew until it felt like I couldn't breathe. For a moment, it truly felt like my chest had been compressed into a cube.

The sound of Doya gasping pulled me back to reality. I was surprised to see a perfectly square cube rotating around in my hand. Red and orange flames raged inside of it and across the outer surface, as if the Fire was trying to escape the box I'd put it in. At my surprise, the cube wavered, one side growing longer than the other.

"Keep it going!" Doya held up a hand to stop me.

My cube sprang back to its perfect shape. Doya and I both gazed down at it in wonder. Even Esis jumped up on the arm of the sofa to get a better look, and Naomi stepped forward. None of us could believe I'd done it.

I caught Doya glancing at the clock out of the corner of my eye. Surely she'd expected me to complete the task. But this quickly? No way.

Finally, after what felt like a whole minute, Doya relaxed. "That's enough, Sophia. I think we've made some good progress for today."

It was probably the biggest compliment she'd ever given me, but I wasn't ready to quit just yet. I felt like I could do more.

"But I'm scheduled with you for another forty-five minutes, aren't I?"

"Yes, but we don't want to—"

"Then let's see what else I can do." I closed my eyes again, wondering what else I could shape my Fire into. I didn't want to jump straight to lion cubs, but I wanted to test my limits beyond the cube. What was the next logical step?

For some reason, a three-dimensional star popped into my head. It was like the sphere, but with long points jutting out at even angles. I felt my magic expand as I drew it out into points. When I opened my eyes, the pointed star was hovering above my palm, shooting smoke out each end.

Doya's eyebrows shot up in shock. She looked thoroughly impressed.

I smirked. This was basically a call for celebration. I'd never seen Doya impressed by me before— at least, she never showed it.

"That's enough," Doya said harshly enough that I snapped my palm closed. Her expression was so stone cold that I feared I'd done something terribly wrong. "What you've just done is incredibly advanced, Sophia. I have *never* seen a First Year capable of such magic. I trust you will not go around showing this to anyone."

"Why?"

Doya sat on the couch and gestured for me to join her. I sat way on the other end, next to Esis. We weren't even close enough to touch each other, but something about sitting next to her felt intimate... like she was actually becoming my real mentor. It was weird, to say the least.

She folded her hands in her lap. "People fear those who are more powerful than they are. It is why the other Houses do not get along with Koigni well. What you did in the tournament was enough to frighten the other Houses, but they have yet to learn how powerful you truly are."

She held her head up, like she was proud of me for it. Again, *weird*.

"First Years make it through the tournament all the time," she continued. "But they *never* manipulate Fire to such an advanced degree as you've done now. You've stayed alive this long because you're sweet and don't often act upon your Koigni instincts. You don't *appear* as a threat on the surface. Which leaves me with one word of advice."

"What's that?" I asked, unsure I wanted to hear it. It sounded so ominous.

Doya leaned in to whisper in my ear. She came so close that I could smell the peppermint on her breath. *"Don't let anyone ever know you're a threat."*

She drew away, but her words echoed in my head. If no one knew you were a threat, they'd never target you. They'd never see you coming.

It was just another warning from the Koigni Elders, a warning to lie low or suffer the consequences.

At least, that's what I told myself.

But there was something in the way Doya said it that told me it was more than that. It wasn't just a warning from the Elders. It was a warning from Doya— like she was trying to protect me from something. Like she actually cared.

Which was ludicrous! But that's what my instinct was telling me. And I'd learned more than once during the tournament not to go against my instincts.

"Can I ask you something?" There'd been something bugging me for weeks now, and I didn't know who I could trust enough to ask. As much as Doya got on my nerves, something told me she needed to know about this.

"Yes," she answered in a clipped tone.

I reached for the string around my neck while I spoke. "I found this a few weeks ago during... while I was out hiking." I pulled the small white totem out from under my shirt and took the necklace off. I held it out to her. I wasn't sure why I lied about where I'd found it— since it was in the cave during the tournament— but it didn't seem relevant, anyway.

Doya took it from my hands and inspected the totem closely.

"Do you think it has anything to do with the prophecy?" I asked.

She ran a finger over the carvings, one for each House. Finally, she shook her head. "No. I don't believe it does." She handed the totem back, and I slipped it back over my head and tucked it safely beneath my shirt. "There is an object that will help fulfill the prophecy, but this is not it. The object was lost long ago. If Koigni knew where it was, we wouldn't be sending you to the Anichi ruins."

"Oh. So it's probably nothing?"

Doya shrugged. "What do you think it is?"

Something powerful. Because I'm pretty sure the ancestors led me to it. Because it was floating in mid-air when I found it. I basically lit up in blue flames when I touched it.

"I don't know," I lied. I was starting to second-guess trusting her with this information. "It just looks old."

Doya stood. "There are a lot of old relics all around Kinpago. I wouldn't worry about it. It's merely a trinket." She turned her back on me. "I think that's enough for today."

I scooped Esis up in my arms and started for the door.

"Wait, Sophia."

I turned, wondering if maybe Doya had recalled something about the totem she wanted to tell me about.

Her expression was... complicated, to say the least. "When I said don't tell anyone, I meant *anyone*. I don't care who you think you can trust."

I furrowed my brow. What was she getting at? "I know. I won't tell anyone."

"I'm serious, Sophia. Not even your boyfriend."

Her words stopped me dead. How did she know? Or was it just a general guess?

I rearranged my face quickly, hoping she hadn't read the horror that was scrawled across it. "Thanks for the warning," I said with a forced laugh. "But I don't have a boyfriend."

"Of course," she said coolly. "Just don't go trying to mix Fire with Water."

Oh, shit! She totally knew!

"I don't know what you're talking about," I feigned. My knees had gone totally weak. I needed to get out of her office *now*!

Doya's gaze flickered to the papers on her desk. *A student?* And I instantly knew. Haley had told her about me and Liam! But how did Haley know?

I wracked my brain, trying to think back over the last few weeks and whether or not Haley had seen Liam and I together. Could she have seen us leaving the closet together? Or maybe making out behind the curtains?

No. I would've noticed someone watching us, right? Unless there was a lapse in my memory, Haley couldn't have known—

That's when it clicked. There *was* a lapse in my memory. The party! Haley must've seen us and told Doya— and Doya had waited to get me alone to mention anything.

What did this mean? She wasn't going to turn Liam and me in, was she? Or would she run off and tell the council as soon as I left the room? She was probably just waiting to see the look on my face.

I was officially freaking out.

"Fire and Water don't mix, Sophia," Doya repeated. "I've seen this before, and these relationships are always doomed to go down in flames. It doesn't matter how strong a Koigni you are. These aren't the kind of flames you can ever put out."

The look she gave me was so intense. It's like she understood how I felt. But how could she? She'd never been in love.

My voice came out in a squeak. "You aren't going to report us, are you?"

Her eyes were brittle and unfeeling. "I will keep your secret, as you are too valuable to our House for us to surrender. I have informed Haley to keep this silent as well, even from her mother."

Her words shocked me. How could Haley be more loyal to Doya than her own mom?

Doya reached out to pet Naomi. "I understand what it's like to be young. There's nothing wrong with a bit of fooling around."

She acted like I owed her for keeping quiet. Which, now, I did. But her words still hurt me. What I had with Liam was so much more than just *fooling around*.

Doya's voice grew sharp and cold. "But you must understand, Sophia. Whatever you think you have with the Mitoh boy is a lie. It isn't permanent. And you need to end it. Before you *both* have to face the consequences."

With that, she tore her gaze from mine and headed to her desk. It was obvious the discussion was over.

I whirled around and rushed out of the room as fast as I could, hoping to forget the whole encounter ever happened. I threw myself behind a statue at the end of the hall, trying to catch my breath. Esis had followed me. He jumped into my arms, giving me what comfort he could.

Hell yeah, I was scared. Terrified, actually. But underneath that was a grim resolve of determination.

Doya could warn me all she wanted. She could threaten me as she pleased.

But nothing could ever keep me away from Liam Mitoh. And if she desired to tear us apart, I sure as hell wanted to see her try.

Liam

NINE

It'd only been a few days since Perot told me I couldn't use my magic, and I. Was. Dying.

I didn't feel any better, either. I knew things weren't going to change overnight, but I still expected to see some sort of progress, even if it was small. Nothing. It was vastly irritating and made me not want to talk to anyone.

Except Sophia, of course. I hadn't seen her since Valentine's Day yesterday, and I wondered what was up with her.

Valentine's Day. Fuck, Valentine's Day had been *great*. That was the hottest hand job I'd ever gotten in my life. It'd been way better than entire sex sessions with Mia. If I thought I was attracted to Sophia before, that attraction was ten times more intense now.

I was so totally in love. And it wasn't like me to say things like that, but Sophia had completely knocked me off my feet.

I was in the dining hall at lunchtime and about to go looking for her when I spotted her near the entrance. Her face was tight and worried. Esis' hair stood on end, like he'd been spooked, or wanted to fight... or both. He looked like a giant puffball as she hugged him tightly to her chest.

Her eyes caught mine, and I made my way over. She started by taking a deep breath and saying, "Liam, we have a problem."

That's never a good way to start off a conversation. "What is it?"

"Not here." She turned away, and I didn't need to be told to follow. She was walking pretty fast. Whatever she had to talk about must be important.

My stomach barreled out and become hollow. Oh, shit. Did she want to break up with me already? That had to be it. Had we been moving too fast? Fuck, I should've known to take it slow. But she came on to me, right? Maybe I should've told her no, though it's pretty hard to say no when your dream girl's got your dick in her hand...

I was a ball of nerves by the time she pulled me into an empty sitting room off one of the spires of the castle. "Doya knows about us."

I literally felt my face go white. "What?"

"It's okay, she's not going to tell," Sophia said, and she squeezed Esis tighter. "She hasn't said anything to the Koigni Elders. I'm too *precious* of a resource to give up." Her tone was bitter.

My heartbeat slowed only a little. "How the hell did she find out?"

"Haley." She chewed on her lip. "She must've walked in on us at the party, and we were so drunk we didn't notice."

"Shit." I *knew* that night was going to come back to bite us in the ass. "So, what do we do?"

"I guess you're at my mercy," someone said behind us.

It was like my whole body turned to ice. Sophia and I whipped around at the same time to see Haley standing there, her hand on her hip and looking absolutely proud of herself. Anwara wasn't with her, which was odd.

I didn't know what to do, so I just stood there. But where I froze, Sophia reacted. Her hand snapped out to grab Haley's neck, pinning her against the wall.

"Sophia!" I shouted. My instinct was to break them apart, but was that the right idea?

"If you tell anyone about us, I'll kill you," Sophia said to Haley, in the coldest voice I'd ever heard her use. Her eyes were really dark. At her feet, Esis hissed, baring his little teeth.

"Sophia, calm down," I said nervously. And she meant it, too. She really was going to kill Haley to protect us. Right now, all that was going through my head were all the places that I could help Sophia hide a body.

"Chill out, crazy. I'll keep your little secret," Haley hissed. "You forget there's stuff in it for me, too."

"Yeah? What's that?" Sophia snarled.

Haley gave an evil smirk. "*I'm* going to be Chieftess after my mom. You're supposed to help Koigni win the war, Sophia. And once that's done, I'll be the most powerful person in all of Kinpago."

What she said made sense. As much as she hated us, Haley would much rather be queen of all the Hawkei than see us go to jail. Thinking of Haley as supreme ruler over the Elementai was enough to make me wanna blow the whole town up.

Sophia still glared, but she slowly let Haley go. There were finger-marks on Haley's neck from where she'd been grabbed.

"I swear, Haley—" she started.

Haley rolled her eyes and made a dismissive gesture with her hand. "You honestly think I care about who you date? It's *disgusting* that you're with somebody from the Water tribe, but you're useful to me." She smirked. "For now, anyway."

Haley gave a nasty laugh. "Besides, it's not like it even matters that you're with Mitoh. It's not gonna last. He'd never fuck an innocent little virgin like you."

Sophia reacted. She made a fireball in her hand quicker than I could register it and swung her arm upward, intending to slam it into Haley's face.

But I couldn't let her do that. I quickly reached up and grabbed the fireball in her hand with my open palm, stopping it. There was a singeing sound and a lot of smoke. I winced and gasped loudly, because it hurt, but I'd rather burn my whole hand off than watch Sophia get in trouble for trying to kill Haley. That's not something Chieftess Annette would let go.

"Liam!" Sophia said, startled, and she took a step back. I gritted my teeth and cradled my hurt hand as Haley cackled.

"Looks like you two are getting along. I'll leave you to it." Haley sauntered off, and I tried moving my hand. It was the same one I'd burnt in the tournament, too. Sophia looked at it. It was really red, and skin was coming off in some places, but it looked like she'd extinguished it just in time before it'd really hurt me.

"I'm so sorry, Liam. I didn't mean to burn you." Sophia held her hands over her mouth. Esis sat on the floor and looked intently at my hand.

"It's fine." I sighed. "We gotta get out of here."

I hurried off to the Toaqua dorms, and Sophia followed. I told her to wait outside as I went to my room to bandage up my hand. Usually, I'd use my element to try and soothe it, but that was off-limits. It'd gone numb by the time I left my dorm.

Sophia looked really upset when I came back. "Liam, I lost my temper, it's just—"

"It really is fine, Sophia. I know all about losing your temper," I started, before I added, "but, Soph, you gotta be careful. You can't do that to Haley. She's not just any Elementai. If I hadn't been there to stop you—"

"I know, I know." She sighed and picked up Esis from the floor, cradling him. "I just thought about her telling people about us, and I lost it. I'd do anything to protect you. Including kill somebody."

Her words brought a chill to my entire body, especially the way she said them, until I realized I agreed with her. "Me, too."

We needed to get off this topic. This whole thing brought the *ride or die* phrase to a whole new meaning. "It doesn't matter, anyway. If Doya and Haley aren't going to tell because they want you to fulfill the prophecy, we're still safe. We just have to be more careful from now on."

Sophia nodded. "Agreed."

I counted the amount of people who knew in my head. Imogen, Jonah, Doya, Haley, probably Cade... not to mention Sophia still had to tell her sister, and I'm pretty sure my brother had caught on to us, too. At this rate, the entire school would know within a couple of months.

But now I was trapped no matter what way I went. If I figured out a way to prove that Sophia *wasn't* the chosen one, and the Kogini Elders believed it, too, Haley or Doya would probably report us.

And if I didn't, and kept our relationship a secret... the Toaqua Elders would expect me to kill her. Either choice I made had bad consequences.

I pushed the thought away. It was all too unbearable to think about. I still had time to come up with a plan. And I was close to forming one, though I didn't want to deal with it today. I needed time to forget.

"So, are we still on for today?" I asked hopefully. I hoped this whole thing hadn't scared her off hanging out.

"We need to go somewhere private." Sophia glanced behind her shoulder, even though we were facing the door now, like someone was going to jump out from behind the armchairs and surprise us any second.

We'd been sneaking around the castle on our Fridays together, but now with the Haley scare, I was pretty sure both of us were reluctant to be seen anywhere near each other inside Orenda. I thought quickly. "My dad has a hunting cabin in the woods. Nobody uses it this time of year," I told her. "It's really secluded. We'll be safe there."

"Are you sure nobody's going to walk in on us?" She shivered and brought Esis up to nuzzle her face in his fur.

I nodded. "I'm sure. Dad hasn't had much time to hunt, anyway, and nobody else but me and Ezra use it. He's in class today."

She nodded. "All right. Let's go."

"Did you want to invite Imogen and Jonah?" I asked. Secretly, I wanted private time, but usually how these days went was Sophia and I mostly hid wherever we could for most of the day until we went to find our friends to do something later.

"Not really. Imogen and I aren't getting along right now. We had a fight." Sophia's face hardened.

It was hard to think of Sophia and Imogen fighting. Those two were practically attached at the hip. "What about?"

"She's jealous of us, and upset Cade moved on after she told him no," Sophia said simply. "I told her if she really wanted Cade that badly she would fight for him, and it's her own fault that he's with Mallory."

"Ouch, Sophia. That's a bit harsh." I made a face.

"But it's the truth, isn't it?" She looked at me. "Our relationship isn't easy, but we make it work. Imogen could've worked it out with Cade. They're Nivita. They can be together and nobody would think it was a big deal. It's not like that with us."

Something told me Sophia was just as jealous of Imogen, for having someone she liked in the same House. "Look, this fight is stupid," I said. "You guys are too good of friends to be arguing over guys."

"She called me a proud Koigni. What's wrong with that?" Sophia continued on like she hadn't heard me. "Why can't I be proud of who I am?"

"There isn't anything wrong with it," I said gently. "I know a trait of your House is being brutally honest, and you're probably right about her and Cade. But it's not an excuse to hurt Imogen's feelings. You guys should make up."

She sighed, and played with Esis' ears. "I guess so."

I didn't think they'd be patching things up anytime soon. Nivita avoided conflict like the plague, and it wasn't like Koigni to apologize. And Sophia was becoming more and more Koigni everyday.

"What do you think I should do?" She looked to me for an answer.

I didn't know what to tell her. When Jonah and I got into fights, we usually just punched each other until one of us got over it. I knew that wasn't going to work with Sophia and Imogen.

"Let it blow over. You guys will work it out. I know it," I said.

"I hope so," she said, and let it drop. Fighting with Imogen really bothered her, though she pretended it didn't.

I was expecting to have to walk to the cabin, but when we left the castle, I noticed a familiar creature. A young dragon, thin and lithe, was spreading her wings and was about to take off. Her scales were pure white, and she had black eyes with a soft, ice-blue mane and tiny horns. Her wings were covered in blue and white feathers, and she had a tip on her tail that looked like a snowflake. My sister's Familiar wasn't much bigger than Squeaks.

I checked a small vial that was tied around her neck. She didn't have anything for me, so I supposed she must be visiting Ezra.

"Hello, Eirakari." I held my hand out to her. The young dragon sniffed it, then lashed out her forked tongue to lick it gently. She stared at me with kind eyes. "Want to give us a lift to the cabin?"

Her gentle face said she obliged. She reached out her face to smell Sophia. She let out a cold whoosh of breath, and a few snowflakes came out of her nostrils, blowing Sophia's hair back. Sophia laughed and leaned forward, kissing the dragon on the nose. Eira sighed in contentment.

Esis looked positively offended. He put his little fists up like he was ready to box.

"You want to go on a dragon ride?" I asked, smiling at her.

"Are you serious?" Her face brightened up. "I've never gotten to ride a dragon before."

"Well, this will be your first time." I hoisted myself onto Eira's back and reached out a hand to take Sophia's. She tucked a mini Fight Club Esis into her jacket, then pulled herself onto Eira behind me. I grabbed a few of the spikes that were protruding from Eira's spine. Sophia wrapped her arms tightly around my middle.

"Hold on to me, and don't look down," I told her.

Eira crouched, and then she sprang into the air. Sophia gave a cry of fright as Eira quickly took to the sky, her giant wings spreading wide to catch the wind.

Riding dragons was so much more fun than riding perytons. They escalated much quicker and were able to take bends and turns far more easily. I had to hold on tight as to not fall off as Eira looped around the castle towers and ascended, until all of Kinpago was spread out before us like a giant map.

Sophia squeezed me for dear life, but I could hear her *ooh* and *ahh* everytime Eira flew over something that was particularly pretty, and gasp whenever Eira performed an acrobatic move to show off. Eira did a loop, then a spiraling movement that made Sophia scream.

Esis scrambled out of her jacket somehow. I felt him climbing over my shoulder, and watched as he jumped down and scrambled to perch on Eira's head, looking down over the spread of the world in interest like he was king of it. When Esis sat on top of her head, Eira calmed and flew steadily as to not knock him off.

Eventually the trees grew thicker, and Eira spiraled down to land beside a two-room log cabin. Sophia slid off behind me, and I staggered when I hit the ground.

Esis was refusing to get off. He crossed his arms and pouted his lip. He wanted another go.

"Esis, down," Sophia commanded. Esis stuck his tongue out at her. She had to reach up and pry him off one of Eira's horns.

He still kicked in her arms as she squeezed him to her chest. He looked like a baby throwing a tantrum. "He doesn't listen." Sophia sighed.

"Then he's like you." I gave her a knowing smile as her mouth dropped open. I stepped toward Eira and put a hand on her shoulder. "Thanks. Pick us up again around five?"

She nodded and backed away. Eira took off again, to fly back home to Madeline.

"How do you know her?" Sophia asked as we watched her become a dot among the clouds.

"Eirakari is my sister's Familiar," I said. "Eira sometimes comes up to the school to deliver messages to me and Ezra when Tatum is busy."

"Your sister has a Familiar? I've never seen her around school. I thought she was younger than you and Ezra?" Sophia asked.

I avoided answering that. "Come on," I said. I got the key hidden in a trunk outside the cabin so I could let us inside.

"That's weird that a Toaqua would bond with a dragon," she said as I fiddled with the door.

"Eira's an ice dragon. She breathes snow and water, not fire," I told Sophia.

"Oh, yeah. I remember learning in Dragonology there are many different types of dragons, though I've never seen anything but a Fire kind in person," she commented.

I opened the door. The smell of jerky, spices, and wood hit my nose. I flicked on the lights and immediately started putting wood in the fireplace. I went to light it, but Sophia ignited the kindling before I could, then hung up her jacket.

"Thanks." I stood up and tossed my coat on an empty chair. The cabin was cramped and dark. It was decorated with a variety of taxidermy, and had old couches draped with soft blankets. There was a box TV in the corner. Thankfully, the freezer was still stocked full.

I made sure to lock the door. Sophia shivered in the briskness of the cabin. Esis had already taken one of the blankets off the couch and wrapped himself in it like a burrito.

I walked toward Sophia and rubbed her arms. "You cold?"

"Freezing." She shivered again.

"The fire will make it hot in here soon." I smiled. "In the meantime, let's see if I can warm you up."

I started to kiss her. She kissed me back, and her shaking soon stopped as I wrapped her in my arms. With her mouth still on mine, I guided her to the couch so that she was sitting on my lap. We continued making out, and Sophia pulled off her shirt. Apparently, she wasn't cold anymore.

I grabbed her breast over top of her bra with my good hand. She gasped lightly and pulled her mouth away, nibbling at my ear and trailing her teeth along my chin. Fuck, it felt so good.

But then an unwanted image broke into my head. Although this was really amazing, the thought crossed my mind of what I'd done yesterday, without her knowledge. I felt guilty, and pulled away.

She stared. "Liam, you okay?"

I forced a smile. "I'm fine, *pawee*. I'm just... really happy to be here with you."

I think she liked that, but there was something in her expression that told me she knew I wasn't really telling the truth. Instead, she just hugged me, and whispered, "You know you can tell me anything, right?"

I closed my eyes and inhaled her scent, hugging her back. "Of course."

I almost told her right then. About everything. The Toaqua Council, how I'd been assigned to kill her, the sessions with Baine. But I didn't. And I wasn't quite sure what held me back this time, except the fact that if I spilled everything, I'd lose her.

Sensing the moment was over, Sophia climbed off my lap and slipped her shirt back on, eyeing me. "Is there anything to eat in here? I had lunch, but I'm suddenly starving."

"Lots." I got up to help her look.

Sophia found a package of cookies and a bag of chips that Ezra had left behind. She turned on the TV, and we settled for watching a bunch of old movies we found lying around the cabin. She curled up next to me under a blanket, and we lay like that for hours, with my head resting on top of hers.

It was nice, just being here with her and not doing anything. It almost felt normal, like we were just a regular couple. Next to us, Esis burped and patted a protruding stomach. I knew Sophia had only eaten a few cookies. Esis had polished off the bag pretty much by himself.

Halfway through the afternoon, I started to feel bad. Like, really bad, randomly. There wasn't an explanation for it. I just felt like shit.

I tried to hide it, but Sophia immediately noticed. She sat up and let the blanket fall off her shoulders. "What's wrong?"

I rubbed my eyes. "Nothing, *pawee*. Same old shit, though it's worse today than it usually is."

"Isn't not using your magic supposed to be helping you?" Sophia asked.

"I think Perot is full of shit." I leaned back against the couch. Right now I'd give anything to make the room stop spinning.

"What can I do to help?"

"There's medicine in the top cabinet. Above the stove."

Sophia immediately got up to go rifling through it. She came back with a glass full of water and some pain meds, which I took. I was glad Eira was coming back to pick us up, because no way I'd make the walk back to the castle now. I wasn't even sure if I'd stay on during the way back.

After I drank a glass of water, Sophia stood over me in a possessive fashion. "Lie on your stomach," she ordered. "Not an option."

I was way too sick to argue. I did what she said and she straddled my back, asking where it hurt. I told her and she started massaging my shoulders. At first, my muscles reacted in agony to being touched, but as she worked, the pain became significantly less.

"Ancestors, Sophia, where'd you learn to do this?" I moaned. She was like, a total expert.

"Amelia had a phase where she wanted to be a massage therapist, before she came to Orenda. She taught me some stuff she learned, and we practiced on each other, but I honestly think she made me give her more massages than she gave me." Sophia laughed.

Esis was sitting by my head. He chittered something to Sophia and looked up at her, as if asking permission.

I heard Sophia sigh above me. "Fine, Esis."

Esis scrambled on my back and started copying Sophia, massaging my shoulder. He wasn't doing much, but he just wanted to help. With the both of them massaging me, I felt the pain go away completely. Even the burning in my hand seemed less.

This girl treated me like a fucking king, and she didn't even know what I had signed up to do to her.

"Feel better?" she asked as I sat up a half an hour later.

"A bit, actually," I said. "Thank you."

"I just want to help you, Liam," she said. "You don't have to thank me."

I really did. She didn't know. I loved her so much, but I'd already betrayed her in the most horrible way.

I EXPECTED to be sick and in bed most of the weekend, but surprisingly, after we returned from the cabin I felt fine. I'd never experienced such a quick turnaround before. It gave me hope that maybe my illness was becoming manageable, but also made me afraid, because that really did mean it was my magic that was doing this to me all along. Didn't it?

On Tuesday, I expected to see the team at our usual meeting place outside the cafeteria, but only Jonah and Imogen were there, Squeaks playing with Sassy. I hadn't seen them since we all ate lunch together last week. I looked around, but Sophia wasn't anywhere nearby. Was she really taking this fight with Imogen that seriously?

"Hey guys," I said as I approached. "Have you seen Sophia around?"

"I thought you'd know, seeing as you're her *boyfriend* and all," Imogen snapped at me.

"Whoa, hey." I raised my hands. "Don't drag me into this."

Imogen sighed. "You're right. I'm sorry, Liam. I'm just frustrated."

I could see why. Out of the corner of my eye, I could see Mallory in the dining hall with Cade. She was all over him, but it didn't look like he was enjoying it.

"Chill out, guys. I think Sophia's with Madame Doya," Jonah said.

More sessions with Doya? This wasn't good.

"What, are they having private coaching sessions or something?" I said, acting like I didn't know.

"Not really. I think she's doing makeup work. I heard she did really bad in Fire class today," Jonah whispered. "She was at the head of the class, and all of a sudden, poof. It's like she's average First Year level again."

Inwardly, I cheered. My plan had worked!

"Great. Maybe it'll take her down a peg," Imogen said viciously.

"Im," I said.

"Liam, come on. You see how she's been acting lately. Since we won the tournament, she's gotten a big head," Imogen stated.

I couldn't argue with that, but Sophia was my girlfriend. It was my job to defend her. "She's still our Sophia. She's not changing."

"You might think so, but if you'd unglue your face from hers every now and then, you'd see what I mean." Imogen stooped down to pick up Sassy. The fox yelped in protest as she interrupted her game with Squeaks. "I have to go. I have studying to do."

Imogen hurried off before I could argue back. I turned to Jonah with an outraged expression and said, "What the hell was that all about?"

"I don't know, man. Girls are too complicated. It's why I date guys," Jonah said.

Couldn't argue with that. I headed into the dining hall, and Jonah asked, "So is it just you and me today, buddy?"

"That's a good question. Are you and Renar going to make it so I can't eat?" I asked.

"No, sadly." Jonah gave a dramatic sigh. "He's been avoiding me. I think I'm too clingy."

Squeaks looked positively delighted. I made a face and said, "You aren't clingy, Jonah. Well, you are, but I'm pretty sure Renar is just being a jackass."

"I don't know. Maybe." Jonah searched the room until his eyes landed on Ezra, who was chatting it up with a bunch of people I didn't know. His mouth curled into a positively evil smile. "In the meantime, while I'm waiting for my true love to come around, why not have a little fun?"

"First, Renar isn't your *true love*," I mocked him. "Second, if you haven't noticed, the only thing Ez has eyes for are people with big breasts. Which, obviously, you don't have."

"It'll only take one time with the Jonahster to get him to come to the gay side." He waggled his eyebrows.

"Jonah, leave my little brother alone," I growled.

"I would never!" Jonah pretended to be insulted. "He's practically *my* little brother, too! I'm just... looking to help him explore a side he hasn't met yet."

I whirled around. "Jonah, I'm warning you. Don't. Touch. Ezra." I poked him in the chest for good measure.

"Fuck, I got it!" Jonah said, throwing his hands up and backing away. "Geez, you'd think you don't want him to have any fun."

"You'd corrupt him." And it was true.

I managed to steer Jonah into conversations that thankfully didn't involve him and my brother getting it on. But though I pretended like I was listening, I really wasn't. My mind was on other things. Jonah said Sophia was in Doya's class today, doing makeup work after she'd performed so badly in Koigni Magic today.

Looked like my roses worked.

The magic took a little bit of time to set in. In Perot's Alchemy class, he'd shown us a plant called *rockthistle*. It was a plant grown by one of the other magical races in the world. It enabled anyone magical to become fire retardant... except in Koigni, it had the opposite effect. In small enough doses over a long period of time, it had the ability to suppress a Koigni's power. Even being in the same room as rockthistle would damage a Fire person's magic.

We were using singular leaves off of it in class, to make a potion that healed burns for the hospital wing. We didn't use much, because it was so valuable. But after class, I'd stolen the whole thing and crushed it overtop of Sophia's flowers. Then I'd given them to her for Valentine's Day.

It wasn't poisonous, and it wouldn't hurt her, just stop her from using everything but the most basic of magic. It would hopefully be enough to convince the Toaqua Elders that she wasn't the one, but probably wouldn't influence the Koigni Elders enough to give up on the hope of her becoming the prophesied one completely.

I didn't know if it would work, not when Sophia had that damn totem strapped to her at all times. But I had to try something.

It was a temporary solution, though. The plant was magical, rare, and Perot had only had one vial of it. It grew on the other side of the world, was expensive, and took a long time to order. I wouldn't be able to find it again, which meant I had to find another way to keep her powers suppressed later on.

But what I'd sprinkled on the flowers was enough to weaken her element for a while, even after the roses died and she threw them away. The contents would come off the flowers and lay around her room, like dust, until they eventually lost their qualities and became less potent.

I really did want to give her roses. I put a lot of thought into making them orange and blue. I just wish my gift had been an actual *gift*, and not a chance to sabotage her.

I'd meant every word I'd said to her about making our relationship permanent. At least that hadn't been a lie. I felt like I had to do things behind her back, things that would hurt her, to keep her alive.

It's not forever. Soon you'll come clean about everything, once you have Nashoma back.

I still missed him so bad my chest ached. I wasn't just doing this for Sophia. I was doing this for Nashoma, too, so we could be together again.

I HEADED to Hawkei Legends under the light of a nearly full moon the following night. Professor Lopez stood outside the castle with a group of older students, rubbing his hands together. His Familiar, a hellhound that was completely made of fire, stood by his side dutifully with a proud expression. For a Koigni, Professor Lopez was actually pretty cool.

"Very well, looks like we're all here," Lopez said as he checked the faces standing around. "Let's go."

He headed into the woods. I didn't know where Lopez was taking us tonight. Hawkei Legends seemed to be held in a different place in the woods every time, which kept things interesting.

This time, Lopez led us to a small lake that parted the forests and opened into a large plain. It was close to where we'd seen the kirin.

Lopez knelt to the ground and ignited a bonfire I hadn't seen there previously. It was quiet for a moment, Lopez scanning the area for something none of us could see.

"Professor, what are we looking for?" someone asked, but Lopez shushed them. He pointed to the constellations, and people started gasping as the stars began moving.

From the skies came down creatures of all shapes and sizes. Dragons, pegasi, griffins and all other sorts of animals emerged from the night. But they weren't normal animals. They were made of stars. Their entire form was inky black and glittering, and as they touched the ground and began swooping around us, they left behind wisps of black. A large cat with horns came out of the moon, her form milky white, and began winding her way around the group, leaving misty trails in her wake. I reached out to touch one beast, a creature that had a long neck and ears as wide as its body. When my fingers skimmed over its skin, it felt insanely cold. I brought my hand away, and it glistened with the stardust that the beast had left behind. Other students around me had similar reactions, and were gabbing in excitement about how "pretty" or "awesome" they were. A wyvern made of stardust roared, and as it did so, a burst of stars came out of its mouth. People clapped in awe.

"Today's lesson will be about Starbeasts," Lopez began. "Starbeasts are creatures that are made out of space matter and stardust. They're peaceful creatures, unless provoked. In the past, they bonded with members of Anichi, and since the tribe's demise have rarely made a connection with any Elementai since."

I didn't know anyone who had a Familiar that was a Starbeast. Nobody did. They hadn't bonded with anyone in decades. Anichi critters were really rare. I didn't think there were that many left. The tribe had put a lot of them into hiding and created protective measures to ensure that the few species of Starbeasts that we did have left survived.

"Starbeasts have been known to influence planets in our solar system, as well as meteor showers, space storms, and other happenings in the cosmos," Lopez said. "It is a very lucky thing they aren't temperamental creatures; otherwise, the universe would be much different than what it is today. I doubt our galaxy would still exist."

One of the Starbeasts, the one I had pet, looked up at the sky and lifted its ears. Out of nowhere, comets began whizzing across the sky, creating an impressive display. Around me, students pointed and started making wishes.

"Now, many Starbeasts no longer bond, but does anyone know *what kind* of Elementai that Starbeasts did bond with when Anichi existed?" Lopez asked.

A girl raised her hand and said, "Spirit Warriors?"

"That's right," Lopez said. "Well done. As many of you heard growing up, Spirit Warriors bonded with Starbeasts in order to protect the tribe. They came from Anichi, and used the power of Spirit, not just healing, through totems in order to defend and rule the tribe. You all know that was a power lost when Anichi fell."

People nodded in agreement. I thought back to the totem that Sophia had around her neck and my original theory about it clicked into place. I thought it was time to tell Sophia what I knew.

After class, I headed back to the Commons, hoping Sophia would be there. She usually did my... I mean, our... homework by one of the fires there on Wednesday nights. I didn't want to wait any longer to tell her what I thought. I was relieved to see that she was there, lying on a rug with several books and notebooks in front of her. Esis sat in front of her, wringing his little hands nervously.

Imogen was also there, though she'd taken to reading a book on the couch on the other side of the room. Sassy sat in her lap, though she seemed nervous, too. At least they were in the same room together, though not anywhere close.

My attention got drawn away by a loud, screeching sound. In the middle of the Commons was Jonah, and he was standing next to Renar, who was boasting loudly that he had bonded.

Esis and Sassy's anxiety was explained in an instant. On the floor was a sheep carcass, one that had been gutted and that was bleeding all over the rug. A creature stood above it feasting, a monster that was half rooster, half wyvern. It had a rooster's head and wings, with scaly black feet and a slimy, long tail that ended in a set of poisonous barbs. It crawled on all fours, using its wings to support itself as it ripped into the flesh of the dead sheep. Familiars usually had the most vivid expression, but the black eyes of this one were cold and unfeeling.

It made my gut clench just to have the thing in here. Esis and Sassy weren't the only Familiars in the room that didn't like having a cockatrice nearby. There were quite a few other animals in here exhibiting fight-or-flight reactions that their Elementai were too stupid to notice.

You weren't supposed to feed Familiars in the Commons, but I doubt that Renar cared. The blood soaking through the carpet was going to make a shitty day for the janitors.

Renar had bonded with a cockatrice. Which wasn't surprising, because he was such a cock himself. Not to mention the thing was fucking ugly, just like his Elementai.

Still, it revealed way more about Renar than I cared to admit. Cockatrices were dangerous. Their claws were known to rip people's torsos in half with one slice, and their beaks could chomp through steel no problem. Not to mention they were ill-tempered, and vicious. I didn't know of one that wasn't a man eater and didn't have to be hunted down. They liked playing with their prey's entrails while they were still alive. People who bonded with them weren't the types you wanted to hang around.

"Alvarice is strong, probably the most powerful Familiar in all the school, I bet," Renar boasted to anyone who would hear. "I felt my Air get ten times stronger once he landed at my side."

I wondered how they had bonded. Cockatrices lived in the mountains, and were pretty reclusive. Alvarice had probably come across Renar torturing some poor, defenseless creature in the woods and decided to join in. I wonder what their bonding music sounded like. Probably the screams of dying humans or something. Too bad the monster hadn't eaten him instead.

"He's awesome, man. Really cool," Jonah said. He came too close to the cockatrice for my comfort, though thankfully, he wasn't stupid enough to try and pet it.

Squeaks stood watching Jonah fawn over Alvarice with a heated expression. If looks could kill, Alvarice would've keeled over ten minutes ago. She stood like a statue, and I could hear a low hiss in her throat.

I immediately knew the two bird Familiars were too close. Hippogriffs were proud show-offs who loved attention. And Squeaks certainly didn't like Alvarice taking away her spotlight... or Jonah.

"The tournament's going to be *so easy*. I can't wait to walk to the finish line with Alvarice doing the work for me," Renar said. He slapped the cockatrice's side, and the bird screeched at him. Several people had to cover their ears.

It was wrong, but I hoped Renar died in the tournament. I smiled at the thought.

Sophia and Imogen had both torn their eyes away from what they were doing. They were watching Squeaks, who was tossing her head in an agitated fashion and swishing her tail as the cockatrice crunched on sheep bones.

Then things happened in the blink of an eye. Alvarice shifted, and got too close to Jonah— Squeaks' territory— and she snapped.

Squeaks lunged forward. She went for Alvarice's throat, her beak wide, looking to deliver an ending blow to an artery. Alvarice had been watching her and waiting for an attack. The cockatrice lunged out of the way and threw up his talons, waiting for Squeaks to stumble into his grasp. People and Familiars both scattered out of the way as Squeaks and Alvarice went at it. Alvarice swung his poisonous barbs at Squeaks and nearly missed, though the middle of his tail caught her and knocked her down. She got back up again, lashing out with her hooves. Alvarice was clearly stronger than her, but she didn't care. All she cared about was killing Alvarice and protecting Jonah.

We had to get Squeaks away from Alvarice now, before he killed her. I think Imogen, Sophia, and I all moved at once while Jonah stood watching the fight with a dumb face. We knew better than to get in the middle of a fight between two deadly Familiars, so as a reaction, I used my element to summon whatever water was in cups scattered around the room to splash it into Squeaks and Alvarice's faces. They were surprised enough to pull apart, and Sophia managed to zap them with a bit of her fire to cause them to separate more, though I expected more from her.

Imogen manipulated a stone statue so that it walked between the two birds, blocking them from getting into it again. At this point, Jonah snapped out of it. He grabbed Squeaks around the neck and pulled her backward as Alvarice advanced.

"Squeaks, what is wrong with you?" Jonah asked as he held her back. Squeaks was still fighting to get to Alvarice.

For a minute, Renar looked like he was willing to set his Familiar on both of them before he smacked Alvarice across the head and said, "Enough! Back down!"

Alvarice cowered away, but I doubt the blow had hurt him. If anything, he merely looked more murderous, though he did as Renar commanded.

"Renar—" Jonah started in a strained voice.

"Keep that *thing* away from me!" Renar snarled. "I don't want to see it next time you come around!"

Renar stomped out of the room. Alvarice hissed loudly at Squeaks as he turned to follow his Elementai back to the Yapluma dorms.

Dammit. I had used my element. It was totally going to mess up Perot's research. It'd felt so good, though.

Jonah was checking Squeaks for injuries. Once he made sure she hadn't actually gotten hurt (which was a total miracle), he backed away from her.

"Squeaks, why did you have to do that? Now he's going to hate me," Jonah said pitifully.

Squeaks stomped her hooves a few times and shook her head, trying to get him to understand. She was still very agitated.

"That was your fault, Jonah. Squeaks warned you she was getting territorial," I said angrily. "You should've backed off. She could've gotten hurt."

"Renar had the situation under control. He would've never let Alvarice hurt Squeaks," Jonah insisted.

"Bullshit!" Imogen exploded. "I've studied cockatrices. They're incredibly violent creatures! You're lucky he didn't rip her from the inside out!"

"Just because you've read it in a book doesn't make it true," Jonah snapped back.

"Enough fighting," I said, coming between them. Ancestors, what was wrong with my team lately? "Nothing happened. Let's just move on."

Sophia said nothing, just stood there quietly. Imogen turned around and went back to the book she'd been reading, which had been tossed on the floor once she'd gotten up. I gave Sophia a look that told her we should go. She gathered her stuff without a complaint. Esis hopped on my head for a ride on the way out.

I turned around to look at Jonah. He was sitting in an armchair and looking totally... desperate. And alone. Squeaks asked for a scratch behind the ears, but he lonesomely pushed her away. She drooped her head and left him, abandoning the Commons to go who knows where without him.

There was a mass exodus of people scrambling to escape the Commons with us after the incident. Sophia waited until we were in a more secluded hallway to talk to me.

"That was..." She didn't finish.

"A mess? Yeah, I know." I ran a hand through my hair. "I don't know what Jonah was thinking."

"Thank the ancestors I don't have any classes with Renar. I couldn't focus with that creepy thing around." She shuddered.

"Me either." It made me cringe to think what would've happened if Nashoma was still around and that thing crossed his path. He'd try to kill it, as Squeaks did. The teachers were going to have a hell of a time keeping control with Alvarice in their classes.

"Why does Jonah like Renar so much?" Sophia asked. "There's something he must see in him."

I didn't answer, and it slowly dawned on Sophia. "It's because he gives him attention, isn't it?"

"Yeah. He hates being alone," I said.

"That's... sad." Sophia frowned and looked at Esis.

"He only sees the best in people. Even if he has to put on rose-colored glasses to do it," I said. "It's the only way he could love somebody as pitiful as Renar."

"I guess," Sophia said, and she let the matter drop.

"Anyway," I started. "I came to find you because I wanted to talk to you. I think I figured out what that totem is. The one you found during the tournament."

"Really?" Her eyebrows raised. "Well, what is it?"

"Not here." I led her down a hallway, one that ended in a three-tier fountain. There was nobody around. I sat down, and she took her place next to me, bringing out the totem. Esis hopped off my head and started bathing in the fountain like it was his own personal bath. For a little guy with no powers, he sure thought he owned everything.

"Are you sure it's anything? I showed it to Doya. She thought it was just a toy," Sophia began.

"It doesn't look impressive, so I can see why she thinks that way. In books and stories, they're usually portrayed as this elaborate object, though I'm starting to not think that's the case," I said as I stared down at the object. "I think what you've got there is a Spirit Totem."

"What's that?" she asked curiously.

"It's an object that Spirit Warriors used to carry, gifted to them by the ancestors and passed down through the generations. They were from Anichi," I clarified at her confused face. "The totems amplified the powers of Spirit and basically made the Warriors unstoppable. Not every Anichi could become a Spirit Warrior. Only the most powerful people in the tribe ever did, and it was the totems that made them so strong. The totems were destroyed when Anichi was taken over."

I glanced at the totem. "Or so we thought. That's probably the last surviving one."

"But if it's an Anichi artifact, why does it channel my powers? Does it only work with Spirit?" Sophia asked.

"That's what I believed, too. But I don't think anyone else but Anichi had these totems, so nobody knew what they could do if they fell into the hands of someone who wasn't from that House," I said. "The goal when Koigni found them was to get rid of them quickly, so no other Anichi could use them to become Spirit Warriors and save the tribe, not experiment to see if they worked for people of other Houses."

Sophia seemed puzzled. "Your theory sounds correct. My powers did get better once I got the totem. But they suck lately. I don't know what's wrong with me."

"It's probably just a phase. Your magic came and went last semester," I offered, lying through my teeth.

She nodded. "That's true."

I took a deep breath. "When you found that totem in the cave, you scared me, Sophia. Only a Spirit Warrior could wield that, and you did.

I doubt it would work for me, or anybody else. Having that type of power... it practically makes you a god."

Sophia fiddled with the totem. "What you say makes sense. But I don't know how I could be a Spirit Warrior if I don't have any Anichi blood. And for the love of the ancestors, I don't know why it chose me."

I shook my head. "I don't know, either."

"Why didn't you tell me this sooner?" She parted her hair back and looked up at me.

"Like I said, I was scared. And I didn't know how you'd react," I confessed. "How do you think I would take it if you told me something I was carrying around gave me ultimate power?"

"You'd probably think I was crazy. I get it." She chewed on her lip. "Do you think I cheated in the tournament, using this? Would we have died in the fire if I didn't have..."

I shook my head, and her words dropped off. "You're the one wielding the totem. It makes you stronger, but that power is still inside of you. It thought you were worthy. That's why you found it."

"Wow. That's intense." Her eyes widened.

"Yes. There's one more thing," I added hastily. "I didn't want to freak you out, but you have to be careful how you use that thing. There are stories of Spirit Warriors who died because they couldn't control their totem's power and it overwhelmed them. I would avoid using it unless you have to, Sophia. And by the ancestors, don't let anyone else know you have it. Our agreement in the cave still stands. This stays between us."

She clutched it tightly. "All right. I'll be careful."

She sighed and slumped against me. "I'm the prophesied one. I'm a Spirit Warrior. What the hell else am I that I don't know about?"

"Hopefully just those two things," I said, though I was still praying the first one wasn't true.

She moaned against my chest, and not in a way that was sexy. "When am I gonna stop finding out secrets about myself, Liam?"

"Maybe this is where it ends," I offered. It felt like a lie, though. I had a bad feeling that Sophia and I hadn't even started uncovering all the secrets about her that would eventually come to light.

sophia

TEN

I was really looking forward to sleeping in on Saturday, but Esis woke at the crack of dawn and tugged on my ear until I peeled my eyes open. "What is it, buddy?"

He chirped and pointed toward the door.

"Huh?" I rubbed my eyes and sat up. "Esis, there's nothing there. Go back to sleep."

He trilled and pointed again.

"Just another hour," I begged, tossing my head back down on the pillow.

Esis hopped over me to stand next to my face. He was so close that I could feel his fur tickling my nose. He made a two-syllable noise and smacked his paw against my cheek.

"Hey!" I cried, shooting up in bed. "What was that for?"

Esis' big blue eyes remained trained on the door.

I sighed and kicked the comforter off. It was cold in my dorm, as I wore only a pair of shorts, a tank top, and long tube socks. I hadn't kept the fire going in my room last night.

I opened the door, expecting to find nothing and to tell Esis to go back to sleep. When I looked downward, though, I was surprised to find a white envelope with my name on it lying at my feet. I bent to pick it up and eyed the smooth handwriting.

Amelia?

I glanced down the long Koigni dorm hall, expecting to see Kiwi flying away, but the hall was silent. Turning back inside my room, I shut the door behind me, then headed over to the chair in front of the fireplace. Esis bounded over to me and scurried up the chair to sit behind me. He peeked over my shoulder like he could read.

"Amelia must be back in town," I told him as I ripped the letter open. All that was inside was a folded sheet of paper. I began reading, practically hearing her voice jump off the page.

Hey, sis!

I'm on vacation from the Hozho, and I have a surprise for you!!! Meet me in the Square at noon. Can't wait to see you!

Love,
Am

I pulled the letter close to my chest. I hadn't seen Amelia in almost two months, and I missed her so much.

"Well, Esis. I was hoping to spend some time in the Koigni saunas today, but it looks like our day just got better!"

Suddenly, I felt wide awake as I headed to my dresser to pull out clothes for the day. I grabbed my lucky jeans— the ones Amelia had given me— a blue shirt, and the jacket I'd bought with the money my parents had given me. While I rushed through a shower, Esis hopped onto the vanity beside my dry bouquet of roses I was keeping for sentimental value. He grabbed my hairbrush and began brushing out his fur.

We had plenty of time before noon, but I was too excited to wait around my dorm room. With Esis perched on my shoulder, I started down the hallway toward the Koigni common room. It was still early, so the dorms were quiet. There was only one person in the common room, a girl with straight black hair who sat in one of the plushy red chairs in front of the furthest fireplace. A small blue dragon sat at her side, eating something out of her hand. I almost breezed right past them until I noticed the dragon had a twisted wing.

I stopped in my tracks. "Aisha?"

Aisha was the baby dragon who'd hung around my Dragonology class last semester. Her mother had abandoned her after she was born with a limp wing and couldn't fly. What was she doing in the Koigni common room?

The girl beside Aisha turned to look at me.

Vanessa smiled. "Hey, Sophia. You know my Familiar?"

I gaped at her, shocked by the news. "You bonded?"

Vanessa nodded eagerly and gestured for me to join her. "Just last night. I got frustrated with this dragon essay I'm writing for my Introduction to Magical Creatures class, so I went to find Professor Curt to ask his advice. He wasn't around, but Aisha was. The bonding experience was amazing." Vanessa stroked Aisha's head, looking down at her like a mother looked at her newborn.

"Congratulations," I said, sliding into the chair next to them. "This is really exciting."

Esis jumped off my shoulder to stand on the armrest. He reached out to touch Aisha's cheek. She tilted her head and nuzzled into him.

"Aww, they're so sweet," Vanessa said with a smile. "And yeah, I agree. It's super exciting."

"What was your bonding music like?" I asked.

Vanessa's eyes lit up. "I don't even know how to describe it. It was like a mix between an old flute and a guitar. I swore I heard the wind, even though we were in the castle. It smelled like rose blossoms and tasted like chocolate pudding. What about when you bonded?"

I ran my fingers through the fur on Esis' tail, recalling the memory. "I heard the birds singing my mom's lullaby, tasted my dad's homemade cherry pie, and smelled apples, like my sister's shampoo."

"Aww." Vanessa beamed. "That sounds really special."

"Yeah, but all bonding experiences are special," I pointed out.

Just then, Aisha sneezed, sending a trail of fire shooting out her nose. Vanessa and I both jumped, and Esis hopped away and hid beneath my ponytail. Even Aisha looked shocked. The room went silent for a moment before Vanessa and I both broke out into a fit of laughter.

"Wow," Vanessa giggled. "I'm glad she's not full-grown yet. Those sneezes will be dangerous."

"Dangerous?" I teased. "Aisha's one of the most gentle creatures at the school. I'd never call her dangerous."

Vanessa sighed and dropped her gaze, running her fingers over the crook in Aisha's wing. "I suppose you're right."

A silent beat passed between us. The moment instantly turned somber.

"Does it bother you?" I asked quietly.

"Does what bother me?" she asked without looking up. She suddenly seemed very interested in Aisha's wing.

"That you bonded with such a powerful creature, but that she'll never fly?" I clarified. I dropped my gaze guiltily. Esis had healed Aisha's wing last semester, but then she fell and broke it again. I knew Aisha could fly again with Esis' help, but I didn't want him to heal her, or it would arise suspicion about his powers.

Vanessa took a deep breath, then finally met my eyes. "No. It's perfect really, I guess. I mean, sometimes I feel broken, too."

"I'm sorry. I didn't mean to—"

"It's fine," Vanessa cut me off, shaking her head like it was no big deal. "It's not exactly a secret."

"Oh, um... I don't really know what you're talking about," I admitted. Esis had returned to the armrest and was playing with Aisha's scales again.

"Right. It happened so long ago, I guess no one really talks about it anymore." Vanessa tore her gaze from mine again and stroked the spines on Aisha's back. "Back in high school, my mom and I got in this huge fight in the town square. Tons of people saw, including Haley, who was shopping with us. My mom said she expected me to become an Elder someday because of our family history— with my aunt being Chieftess and all. I told her I didn't want to become an Elder if I was expected to act like any of the others on the council. I said some... not so nice things about my aunt. It, um, kind of ruined my reputation as a Koigni. My parents were so ashamed that they basically disowned me. I lived with my grandparents my whole senior year, but they weren't exactly pleased with it, either. I think they felt obligated. My parents still haven't spoken to me since then." Vanessa bit her lower lip.

"I'm so sorry," I whispered as my heart dropped in my chest.

Vanessa nodded shyly. "It is what it is. If my parents can't see that the entire Koigni tribe is overrun by pride, then that's their problem. I guess maybe I should've waited to say all that *after* I became an Elder. I might've been able to make a difference then. Now I'm just a Koigni reject no one wants to hang out with because I believe in equality among Houses."

I snickered. "First of all, *I'll* hang out with you. Second, you're not a Koigni reject. If anyone is, it's me."

Vanessa smiled. "Liar. Everyone likes you."

I snorted and rolled my eyes. "Right."

"No, seriously." Vanessa's tone lightened. "Miranda, Lindsey, Tabitha, Ben... they all talk about how much they admire you. I believe when Lindsey saw the footage of the tournament her exact words were, *I wish I look that fierce when I face the Fire task.*"

"She did not." I giggled.

Vanessa beamed, her mood lifted. "I'm dead serious."

"I'm sure." I laughed, before turning serious again. "It can't be that bad, though. Aren't you getting married?"

She nodded.

"So *someone* wants to hang out with you," I pointed out.

"Yeah, but Bren and I have been dating since my freshman year of high school. He's the only person who was there when my parents dumped me. Luckily. I don't know what I'd do without him," she said.

"That's really sweet. That you've been together so long, I mean."

"Yeah," Vanessa said with a dreamy sigh. "He's great. Now if he'd just wake up so I could tell him about Aisha. He was asleep by the time I made it back to the dorms last night."

"I'm the first person you told?" I asked, feeling bad about it. We weren't exactly close.

Vanessa shrugged. "Yeah, but it's no big deal. What time is it? I might just go knock on his door and wake him up."

I checked my watch. "It's a quarter to eight."

Vanessa stood. "I think he's slept in long enough. I'll see you around." She gave me a wave and started down the male dorm hallway.

A warmth entered my chest when I waved back. I scooped Esis up in my arms and started for doors out into the main hall.

"Well, Esis," I whispered. "I think I just made my first Koigni friend."

❧

"Sophia, my dahling."

I jumped when I heard a voice in my ear while I was loading up my plate for breakfast in the dining hall. I whirled around and smacked the creep in the shoulder. "Jonah, you jerk! Don't sneak up on people like that."

He pressed a hand to his chest and plastered a look of exaggerated offense on his face. "Well, I never! No one's ever accused *me* of being sneaky."

I laughed. It was true. His footsteps were louder than Squeak's hooves. When Esis spotted Squeaks at Jonah's side, he leapt off my shoulder and jumped onto her back. He shoved his paws into her feathers like they were reins and chirped as she started spinning in a circle. I cringed when her tail came just inches from knocking over the pile of plates at the end of the buffet.

I turned back to my food to scoop a pile of eggs onto my plate. "So, what are you up to this morning? Visiting Renar?" Ancestors, I hoped not.

"Nah. Just gotta fuel up before I hit the gym. I was wondering if you wanted to sit by us."

I followed his gaze to see Liam sitting at a table in the middle of the cafeteria. He had his elbow on the table and his head in his hand. He stared down at his full plate of food, poking at it but not taking a bite. Even from this distance I could tell he looked a little pale.

My stomach sank to see him that way. I glanced to Esis, who had one hand on Squeaks and one held high above his head, like he was riding a mechanical bull. The thought crossed my mind to have Esis heal him again, but I'd already broken my rule about that. The more I had Esis heal him, the more I screwed up Liam's chance of finding a cure. I was a terrible girlfriend.

"Is he okay?" I asked Jonah.

Jonah shrugged. "He wouldn't give me an honest answer when I asked. I thought breakfast might add some color to those pretty little cheeks of his, but he barely ate anything. Then I saw *you* and thought you could work some of your magic."

I went completely still as I reached for the tongs in the sausage tray. "Jonah, you know that—"

"Oh, not like that," he said quickly. "Though I still think you should tell him."

"But what about Perot's data?" I challenged.

Jonah shrugged. "What about it? Anyway, by *magic* I meant the fact that you're his girlfriend. He lights up every time you come in the room."

I smiled. It was a nice thought.

Jonah glanced down to the pile of sausages on my plate. "Girl, that's way too much meat. You've gotta balance your protein."

"I like sausage," I defended.

Jonah wiggled his eyebrows. "Yeah, I bet you do."

"Shut up." I nudged him with my elbow and grabbed a napkin before starting toward Liam's table.

Liam didn't even look up when I sat down. To get his attention, I tapped him with my foot under the table. He looked up, but he didn't reciprocate the game of footsy. Totally disappointing.

"Hey," I said softly. "How are you feeling?"

He blinked a couple of times, like he was trying to process the question. "Tired, actually."

I suspected it was more than that. "What are you up to today? Maybe we can hang out this morning."

Liam shrugged as Jonah slid into the seat next to him and started shoveling food in his mouth. Squeaks plopped down beside him and playfully nipped at Esis on her back.

My boyfriend had a distant look in his eyes... like he was still having trouble comprehending what I was saying. I regretted asking the question the moment it was out of my mouth. Liam ran his fingers through his hair. He looked like he was going to pass out. "Sure, *pawee*. What do you want to do?"

"Um..." The truth was, Liam didn't sound good, which made me feel like he was just saying what he thought I wanted to hear. I sighed. "You know what? I'm actually meeting up with Amelia today, so we can hang out another time. You should go back to your dorm room and get some sleep."

"Yeah, okay." He sounded so out of it— like he hadn't really heard what I said.

Liam stood from his chair. I had to hold in a breath as I watched him waver. He grabbed his plate, but Jonah stopped him.

"Hey, dude. Don't you dare waste that perfectly good food." Jonah grabbed the plate from Liam's hand and used his fork to scoop the uneaten food onto his own plate. So much for *balancing your proteins.* He blew Liam a kiss. "Sweet dreams, Sleeping Beauty."

"Yeah, yeah," Liam grumbled. "Go screw yourself."

"Gladly!" Jonah called as Liam started for the kitchens to drop off his plate.

My gaze followed him. He looked like he was going to pass out, so I nudged Esis to follow him to make sure he made it back to his room okay. But Esis didn't even notice my subtle hint before I saw Ezra rising from his chair several tables away and following behind Liam. I relaxed, knowing Liam was in good hands.

I turned back to Jonah. "It's getting worse, isn't it?"

Jonah frowned. "His health? I don't know. It's hard to say. I think he hides how he feels most of the time."

I took a bite of egg and nodded. "He's not exactly open when it comes to that kind of thing. It's always *I'm fine,* even when I know he isn't. He won't even tell me about Nashoma."

Jonah shook his head, looking sad. "It's not that he doesn't want you to know. I think it's just hard for him to think about. He blames himself."

My eyebrows knitted together. "Why?"

Jonah took a deep breath, as if contemplating whether or not to tell me. Then he shifted in his chair and leaned forward, looking sad. He lowered his voice and whispered, "Liam thinks Nashoma would still be alive if he hadn't been so reckless."

"Reckless?" I asked in shock. I could hardly picture Liam as reckless. Sure, he sometimes let his temper get to him, but he was smart and never would've put his Familiar in danger intentionally... right?

Jonah hesitated before saying, "Before you met Liam, he was kind of a daredevil. You might've even called him an adrenaline junkie."

My mind instantly replayed the day he took me out on his motor-cycle and we rode across the ocean. I could believe that.

"He was always the curious type," Jonah continued. "It was last summer, June twenty-first."

My birthday, I thought.

"We were out— me, Liam, and Ezra— and Liam saw this blue light in a cave."

"You were there?" My eyebrows shot up.

He nodded and gazed at his hands, like it was difficult to talk about. "Liam wanted to go investigate, but, well, you know me and caves don't get along."

He could say that again. He'd practically had a panic attack in the cave during the tournament.

"It wasn't safe. Ezra and I didn't want to go, so Liam went out on the ledge by himself. Of course, Nashoma followed, and... it just all happened so fast." Jonah paused and closed his eyes. A pained expression crossed his face. "The rocks started to cave in. It was a landslide. Liam was gonna get buried under them. Nashoma jumped and pushed him out of the way, but they both slipped, Liam off the side of the moun-tain and Nashoma in front of the rocks. I had to make a split-second decision. Him, or his Familiar? Obviously, I was going to choose my best friend. I got Liam to safety using my Air power, but Nashoma... he was crushed."

I gasped and threw my hand over my mouth. "Oh my gosh! That sounds horrible." Worse than horrible. I didn't have the words. I glanced to Esis, who was now grooming Squeaks' tail. A knot twisted in my chest. I couldn't imagine losing him, especially not in such a terrible way. I didn't know how Liam managed it.

Jonah frowned and glanced to Squeaks. He blinked a few times, like the thought of losing Squeaks like that made him want to cry.

"Yeah, it was horrible," Jonah said. "Honestly, I thought that was the end of my best friend, too. I'm just glad he's still around."

"Me, too," I agreed. Life at Orenda Academy would've been a lot different without Liam. I could still picture him standing in my living room when he told me I had to come here. He was the first thing that made this place seem like home. "I just hope Perot can help him."

"Agreed, but if he can't..." Jonah stared at me with a stone-cold expression. I'd never seen him look so serious before. "You can't give up on him. You hear me? He needs you, Sophia, and if you *ever* hurt my Liam Baby, you'll have to answer to *me*."

I held my hands up in surrender. "Whoa. Chill out. I don't plan on hurting him. Ever."

Jonah leaned back in his chair and stuffed a piece of bacon in his mouth. "Good. Just wanted to make sure we're clear on that. I'm glad we had this talk, Sophia."

"It's always good talking to you, too, Jonah," I said flatly.

Jonah scarfed down the rest of his food in one bite and stood. "Time to hit the gym. Gotta burn off all those extra calories. See ya later."

"Bye."

Jonah left in a hurry. It was almost like he was running away from the story itself, like the memory was too much for him.

Esis hopped off Squeaks' rear and onto the table, settling in beside me to share the food on my plate. I set down my fork and let him eat the rest of it.

The truth was, Jonah had kind of made me uncomfortable with that whole *you'll answer to me* thing. It was like he thought I *would* hurt Liam eventually. But that was never going to happen.

I looked down at Esis again, who was shoveling an entire sausage sideways into his mouth, and I realized Jonah was right. The longer I kept my secret from Liam, the more it was going to hurt him once he found out.

Eventually, Liam was going to get tangled up in my fire. The least I could do was let him be happy.

After everything he'd been through with Nashoma, he deserved that.

THE AIR WAS chilly when I made it to the town square later that day. Esis sat in the hood of my jacket, and I shoved my hands into the pockets. I took a seat on the edge of the fountain in the center of the square, waiting for Amelia's arrival, and pulled my magic to the surface of my skin to warm my cheeks. Without ceremony, something ice-cold smacked into the side of my face.

"Ah!" I yelped and shot to my feet. I just barely caught sight of a funnel of water splashing back into the icy-cold fountain. I glanced around for the Toaqua who thought it was funny to toy with me. They must've been pretty brave to try pissing off a Koigni.

Laughter erupted from behind me, and I whirled around to see Amelia standing on the other side of the fountain.

"Am!" I cried, rushing over to her and dragging her into a hug.

She laughed so hard she could barely breathe. When I drew away from her, she was literally crying.

"Ancestors, that was hilarious!" she giggled. "You looked like you were going to shoot a fireball at me."

I poked her in the side. "Watch out. I still might. That wasn't nice."

She shrugged. "Nobody ever said I was nice."

Kiwi squawked from her shoulder.

"Ha. Even your Familiar agrees with that," I said.

She crossed her arms and raised an eyebrow. "He was protesting, thank you very much."

"Sure." I rolled my eyes. "So, what's this thing you have to show me?"

She beamed. "It's a surprise. Follow me."

Amelia and I started down the street.

"What have you been up to this semester?" she asked. "Kicking ass and taking names?"

"You betcha."

"Learning anything new?" she asked.

"Oh, you know," I said. "Learning all about Hawkei careers, unicorns... and how to give hand jobs in broom closets."

"Whoa, *what?*" Amelia stopped dead in her tracks and slapped me across the shoulder.

It took me a second to realize what I'd said. What a way to tell her I had a boyfriend. Honestly, I'd been dying to tell her about Liam, but I didn't expect it to slip out like *that*.

My cheeks felt so hot I was half surprised they weren't on fire right now. "It was just the one time."

"Please tell me it wasn't some rando at a party."

"God, no! We're dating."

"Oh, good," Amelia said in relief as we started walking again. "Because if you got drunk and jacked off some Nivita guy in the woods, we'd have a problem."

"Why?" I asked, taking on a serious expression again. "Because he's not from my House?"

Amelia eyed me like she couldn't tell if I was serious or not. "*Yeah*, Sophia. You've been living here for six months. You should know how serious interhouse relationships are. Even if it *was* allowed, they'd never work out."

"You're wrong," I argued.

Amelia glared at me. "He's Nivita, isn't he?"

"Toaqua," I admitted.

Amelia pursed her lips as we entered Kinpago's Little Chinatown. "Seriously, Sophia? Do you know how dangerous that is?"

"Of course. No one will stop telling me that. But it doesn't matter, Am. We're in love."

"That's what they all say, until something more important comes along," she muttered.

"Which isn't going to happen to us, because the only thing more important than the person you love is your Familiar, and he doesn't have one," I argued.

Amelia's eyes widened. "Mitoh?! You're dating Liam Mitoh?" She made it sound like a bad thing.

A lump rose in my throat. I thought Amelia would be happy for me. She was the one raving all about hot guys in other Houses when she'd told me about Orenda.

Was she *jealous* that I actually had the courage to date one of them?

"I love him," I told her, like that would change her mind.

"I'm sure you do, but that excuse isn't going to please the Elders."

I dropped my gaze to my feet, thinking about what Vanessa had said this morning... how she could've made a difference if she'd become an Elder. "Yeah, well, the Elders have to die eventually. Maybe whoever takes their place will be more tolerant."

Amelia frowned. "I doubt it. It's been like this for generations. You need to break it off with this guy."

I gaped at her. How could she say that?

"This is just wrong on so many levels, Sophia. You can't sneak around and hope everything's going to be okay. The Elders will find out one way or another and prosecute you for it," Amelia ranted. Her preaching was annoying.

"But it shouldn't be a crime in the first place," I argued.

"Does that really matter?" Amelia asked. "It doesn't change that they disapprove. You can't be too careful."

"Can we not fight?" I begged. "You're only in town for a few days."

Amelia cocked an eyebrow. "Are you going to take my advice?"

"I'll think about it," I lied. I'd been really looking forward to telling her all about Liam, and she didn't even want to hear about him. I quickly changed the subject before she could press any further. "How's life on the *Hozho*?"

That put a smile on her face. "Really good, actually. Employees don't have to pay for anything on the ship, so we get access to the pool, ice rink, amusement park, and all that on our off hours. And we get to do tourist stuff when the ship comes into port. We stopped at the Grand Canyon two weeks ago. There's a tribe out there versed in hypnotic magic that one of the Nivita diplomats had a meeting with."

"Did you get hypnotized?" I asked as we reached the forest on the edge of town.

"Girl, I didn't take a job as a concierge for the money. Let's just leave it at that."

I laughed. "So, where are we headed?"

"I told you, it's a surprise." She held a blue scarf out in front of me.

"What am I supposed to do with that?" I asked.

"Put it over your eyes. What good is a surprise if you can see it coming?"

I groaned. "Really, Am? I won't be able to see where I'm going."

"I'll guide you."

I sighed and gave in. We walked for what felt like another twenty minutes while she told me all about her travels on the *Hozho*. I talked about my winter break and classes, all while blindfolded.

Eventually, she stopped and pushed down on my shoulders. "Sit."

"That out of shape?" I teased. My fingers met a damp log, and I sat. "I can keep going."

"Shut up, missy." She poked me in the side. "We're here."

I removed the blindfold and glanced around, but I saw nothing but trees all around us. "What do you mean *we're here*? What's the surprise?"

Amelia stuck her fingers in her mouth and whistled so loud I had to cover my ears. A few moments later, I heard the sound of footsteps scuffling through the dry leaves on the ground. I turned to see two creatures running toward us, a dog and a cat.

Or more accurately, a coyote and a bobcat.

I shot to my feet, unable to believe what I was seeing. "Oliver?! Bruno?!"

I scratched both their heads as they reached us. Seeing them here nearly knocked the breath out of me. It could only mean one thing. I lifted my gaze to see two figures approaching in the distance. Tears sprang to my eyes, blurring my vision, and my hands shot over my mouth. I grabbed Amelia by the shoulder to keep from falling to my knees.

"Mom? Dad?" The words barely came out as tears started to fall down my cheeks.

My mother stretched her arms wide, and I couldn't take it anymore. I jumped over the fallen log and sprinted over to her. A *whoosh* of air flew out of her lungs when I slammed into her and squeezed her tightly. I pressed a kiss to her cheek, then flung my arms around Dad's neck. A second later, the three of us were wrapped in a group hug. Esis hopped out of my hood and onto my mom's shoulder, where he threw his tiny little arms around her neck. I wanted to tell them how much I missed them, but I couldn't find the words.

Eventually, Amelia approached and stood beside us. We pulled apart.

I wiped the tears from my cheeks. "Am, I can't believe you pulled this off."

She grinned. "Surprise!"

"Mom. Dad." I half-cried, half-laughed. "I missed you two so much."

"We missed you, too, honey," Mom said.

Dad placed a comforting hand on my shoulder. "You have no idea. We're so sorry we never got to say goodbye."

"I'm sorry I ran away." My throat hurt as I held back the tears. It was so surreal, seeing them after everything that had happened. I was still trying to swallow that they were part of this world, that my parents were Toaqua and grew up here.

"How are you here?" I asked. "I thought you weren't allowed in Kinpago."

"That's why we had to meet you out here," Mom said.

"How long are you here for?" I wanted them to stay forever. I'd hide them in this forest if I could, just to visit them whenever I wanted.

"Just the afternoon," Dad said. "We can't stay long. It's risky enough being here as it is."

"Then why are you here?" I asked. "Don't get me wrong. I'm super glad to see you, but..."

"Because we need to talk to you." Mom wrapped an arm around me and guided me back toward the log as she spoke. "We saw the footage of the tournament."

"You did?" I almost cringed. Was that a good thing or a bad thing?

Dad nodded and sat beside me on the log. Mom took the other side, and Amelia leaned against a nearby tree. Esis hopped down from my mom's shoulders and approached Bruno and Oliver on the ground. They both sniffed him, like they weren't sure what to think of him.

"You were amazing," Dad said, rubbing my back.

My chest lifted in pride.

Mom took my hand and squeezed it tightly. "We're *so* proud of you."

That brought on a new wave of tears I couldn't hold back. Mom pulled me into another hug, and I rested my head on her shoulder.

"You fought so well in the tournament," Dad said. "We realized you weren't the little girl we thought you were anymore."

I laughed, mostly to keep myself from crying. This whole thing felt like a dream. Never in a million years would I have guessed that Amelia's surprise was to see my parents again. It was just so overwhelming... and amazing.

"And so," Dad continued, "we thought you should finally know what really happened eighteen years ago. We thought you deserved to hear it from us."

A wave of adrenaline shot through my chest, but it quickly settled.

"You're going to tell me the truth about my adoption?" I could hardly believe it. For the last six months, it felt like I'd never know, like it'd always remain a mystery.

Mom nodded. "Yes, but before you hear what we have to say, you should know that we have always loved you as our own."

"Um... okay." I believed her. I knew my parents loved me. But the way she said it sounded like there were parts of the story I wouldn't want to hear. "I can handle anything."

I hope.

Dad started slowly. "Your birth mother, Lucy Greyson, died giving birth to you."

"And my father?" I asked.

Mom dipped her head and took a deep breath. "The night after you were born, Toaqua came for you. They knew of the prophecy and wanted to kill you, so you couldn't fulfill it."

My guts twisted. It sounded like something Koigni would do, not Toaqua.

"This sparked a conflict between Koigni and Toaqua," Mom continued. "Your father was killed, and your biological grandparents— on your mother's side— became your legal guardians."

Mom paused for a moment, and I nodded for her to continue.

"They approached us and asked us to take you and protect you," Mom explained.

"What? Why?" I asked. Koigni, working with Toaqua? It didn't sound right.

"We were friends with them," Dad said. "I'd already been stationed in Utah as part of my job to the tribe and was set to leave a week after you were born, so it was easy to get you away without arousing suspicion. And we already had Amelia, so they knew we'd take good care of you."

"So, your job with the state...?" I started as pieces began falling into place.

"It was a diplomatic position," Dad finished for me. "There are Hawkei stationed all around the States working for the government. My job was pretty low-key, so no one ever really checked in on us. We agreed to take you because we believed it was wrong to kill a child, no matter what the prophecy said or what House they were. As your guardians, your grandparents signed the paperwork that allowed us to legally adopt you."

"But no one knew, right?" I asked. "People think you stole me."

Mom nodded. "It's better that way. What your grandparents did by giving you up to a Toaqua family... it would be considered treason among the Koigni. They told people they didn't know what happened to you the night of the conflict, whether you were taken or killed. We don't want the Koigni knowing they had any involvement in what actually happened."

The muscles in my shoulders tensed. "But you could come back! If people knew the truth, you wouldn't be exiled anymore."

"Sophia," Dad said softly, shifting uncomfortably on the log. He was always the type to avoid conflict. I could tell my tone was making him nervous. "We told them we found you in the chaos and didn't know you were the prophesied child when we took you. It's best if people keep believing that."

I lowered my voice. "I just don't get why it's better. I want to see you more often."

"It's for the greater good," Dad promised. "We were pardoned because you came back to Orenda, as per the Elders' offer. But your grandparents wouldn't be so lucky if people found out what they did. We have a life outside of Kinpago. You don't have to worry about us."

"But what about your Familiars?" I pressed. I'd say almost anything to get them to stay.

"They were part of the deal when you came back. Remember?" Mom said. "We're lucky they look ordinary. Otherwise, the Elders would never let us take them outside of Kinpago. It's one of the reasons your father got his job in the first place."

"You lost it, though, didn't you?" I asked softly, staring up into my dad's soft eyes. "After they found out about me."

"Don't worry about it," Dad replied.

I let out a breath in disbelief. "How can I not worry about you? I miss you."

Mom ran her hand down my ponytail. "We know, honey. But your dad is right. You don't have to worry about us. Save your energy for protecting yourself."

"What do you mean?" I asked. It sounded ominous.

Mom sighed. "After we had some time to cool down and talk about it, we realized that Orenda is what's best for you right now." She gestured to Esis, who was cleaning his ears after Bruno and Oliver decided they weren't interested in him. "You've bonded, and you're learning how to use your powers. Amelia was right about that. But it's still dangerous here for you."

I lifted my gaze to Amelia, who straightened when she heard her name.

She cleared her throat. "About that... I'm sorry I didn't tell anyone before I turned Sophia in. I just knew she'd never make it as an Elementai without a Familiar, and I acted impulsively."

I twisted my hands in my lap. "You don't have to apologize. You were only trying to do the right thing."

Amelia nodded, but I saw a hint of guilt pass over her features.

"Besides," I said, "I love it here at Orenda. I mean, I miss home, and I miss you guys, but Orenda Academy is amazing, too."

My family all nodded in agreement, as if they were thinking back to their years at school.

After a moment of silence, Mom's expression turned serious. "Just don't get too comfortable, Sophia. I meant it when I said this place is dangerous for you. You must choose your friends wisely."

I gave a nervous laugh, not sure what she was getting at. "Don't worry, Mom. My friends are cool."

"I would hope so," she replied seriously. "Because one of these days, you're going to have to choose sides. And I hope we raised you well enough that you choose the right one."

Liam

ELEVEN

"I don't know what you want me to tell you. Sophia's magic is failing her. To me, that's a pretty obvious sign that she's not the person you're looking for."

I was in Serpent Assembly, once again attempting to convince the Toaqua Elders that Sophia was a fluke and that they needed to look elsewhere for the prophesied one. It was the second meeting, and I only had two more before the Elders made a final decision at the end of the semester.

I hoped I was making progress, but neither Poole, Malison, or Dad looked fully convinced. I still couldn't read the expressions on Madame Wells' face, but no matter what I found out, she ceased to be impressed.

Dad looked to Baine. "Elliot, can you confirm that Miss Henley's magic is weakening?"

Professor Baine made a face. "It is true. Signs are showing that Sophia's Fire isn't as powerful as it once was. I've been watching her closely, and she's been performing... quite badly in her Koigni classes."

"If that's accurate, then she never should've been able to survive the final task during the tournament," Malison shot back. "She's hiding something."

"Elder Malison, please." Dad rubbed his eyes. "Miss Henley has no idea we're keeping a close eye on her, but she knows her own Elders expect her to perform well. She has no reason to hide her magic."

"Unless your boy told her she's being watched," Malison snapped back.

"I haven't told her anything," I shot back. "It would violate our agreement, and obviously, she would never trust me again if she knew I was here talking to you."

"He does have a point," Poole piped up. Malison shot him a glare, and he went silent again.

"Have you discovered anything else while you've been following her?" Dad asked.

I winced when he said that. It made it sound so... wrong. But it was way more than following. *Yeah, Dad. Actually, she's a bomb kisser, she's got a great ass, and she gives some really killer hand jobs. Her boobs are nice, too. But, uh, that's probably not important. And you'd totally kill me if you knew.*

"I... I know Sophia's been taking private lessons with Madame Doya," I said. It was scary to admit.

"What for?" Malison snapped.

"As far as I know, they're to help her become more powerful," I said coldly. "But they're not going to help if she's not able to wield her magic in the first place."

"Hm. A likely story," Malison grumbled.

"What if Sophia didn't hold back the flames during the tournament? What if the Elders just made it look like she did, to show off that she might be the prophesied one?" I suggested. I'd been planning this for a few days now— redirect them.

"That would make sense," Dad muttered. "Sophia wouldn't have to know, either. They could make her believe she did it."

I didn't tell them no way that was a reality. I could literally feel the power coming off of Sophia during the tournament. It'd definitely been her. But the less they knew...

"Preposterous!" Malison said. "Why would they do such a thing? Their tribe has been waiting on the arrival of the prophesied one for years."

"Perhaps they got tired of waiting," Madame Wells suggested. The council turned to look at her as she spoke for the first time. I'd nearly forgotten she was there.

"Are you talking about a poster child?" Dad asked.

Wells nodded. "Precisely. It may not matter what child they choose to fulfill the prophecy, merely that they were born at the time the prophecy said they would be. The Koigni would use anyone as an excuse to attack the other tribes and start a war."

"Then we need to kill her anyway, and take away their symbol of revolution," Malison said.

Shit, shit, shit. Had my plan backfired?

"That'll hardly work, Elder Malison," Madame Wells said plainly. "We get rid of one, Koigni will just find another and another to take Sophia's place, and it'll be a never-ending trail of bodies. It would be much easier to discredit her."

I breathed a sigh of relief. Shit, Dad saw.

"These are all theories. We're getting closer to finding out if Miss Henley is the prophesied one, but we still have no confirmation of anything substantial," Dad said. "Elliot, have you uncovered anything else that may bring us closer to a conclusion?"

"Liam has told me that Sophia mentioned to him the Koigni Elders have asked her to find a certain object," Baine said. "I suspect that they've asked her to locate the *Azaimperiai*."

Fuck you, Baine, for bringing that up.

"Don't be ridiculous," Dad started. "It's been gone for decades."

"But if they got their hands on it, Liwanu, what could it cost?" Baine insisted. "This isn't something we should discredit."

Dad looked at me. "Son, what do you think?"

He was trusting me to tell him the truth. Which was weird, because so far, he acted like he didn't.

"As far as I know, Sophia hasn't gotten any closer to finding anything important. And if she did, she'd tell me before she told her Elders. She... doesn't like them very much," I said. "She's frustrated. Her magic doesn't seem to be working for her like it should, and I think her Elders are disappointed in her so far. I know Doya is."

"If Sophia feels resentment toward her tribe, we may be able to work that toward our advantage," Madame Wells said. "We could convince her to come to our side. Fight for Toaqua instead of Koigni."

"Prophecies can't be changed, Madame Wells," Baine said lowly. "They will always go the way they are spoken unless they are prevented from happening. No matter how Sophia feels about her Elders, if she's the one, she won't be able to change her fate."

In my head, I sarcastically thanked Baine for making things sound even worse than what they already were.

Dad nodded introspectively. "There's enough doubt for this to go either way. Now we need definitive proof. I want you to start sneaking into these meetings with Doya and watching them, Liam. Everything Doya tells her, I need you to report back to Baine. If her Elders lose interest, we have our proof that she is not the one."

I bowed my head. "Yes, sir."

"Session dismissed." The Elders disbanded from the bench. Dad moved quickly toward the door.

"Hey, Dad?" I asked, stopping him. "Am I getting any closer to getting Nashoma back?"

Dad hesitated, then he said, "You're doing well, son. It won't be much longer. I promise."

Tatum grumbled at me, and bumped me with his head. I gave it a scratch before he lumbered after Dad.

I got excited. Dad *promised me*. He never promised anything unless it was true. He always kept his word. I was getting Nashoma back! It was only going to take some time.

Time, and some major obstacles to overcome. How the hell was I going to sneak into these meetings between Sophia and Doya? If Doya found me, she'd burn me to a crisp, then probably feed me to her lioness while she laughed.

I was really glad I'd managed to avoid telling them that Sophia was a Spirit Warrior on top of everything. It was too much to hope for that Baine would keep his mouth shut on the *Azaimperiai*.

But I was *so close* to saving Sophia's life. All I had to do was figure out how to convince the Koigni Elders to stop believing in her, and turn their attention elsewhere. Not easy by any means, but doable. I just had to come up with a good enough plan.

When I reached the surface in the ocean, the skies were dark and the waves were churning. I had to use my element to get back home, thank the ancestors, because I was dying without it. Strangely enough, I felt *better* when my element was used. I'd been feeling pretty crappy lately, but the minute I stood on the edge of the ocean and used my magic, I felt better.

I didn't think Perot's theory was wrong that my magic weakened my body, but it wasn't entirely right. It hurt me, but I needed it, too.

The rain was pouring down. I used my magic to steady the large waves around me so I could get back to shore. It was a pretty big storm. I couldn't remember the last time it'd rained this hard at Orenda. Some Toaqua out there must've been showing off.

When I got back to the Toaqua dorms, it was full of people *oohing* and *aahing* at something. I looked over the crowd to see what it was. Ezra was in the Toaqua common room, and he was soaking wet. It looked like he'd been out in the rain.

Except this time, he wasn't alone. There was a large yellow bird sitting on his shoulder, its tail hanging all the way down to the floor. The bird had long plumage on the top of its head and blue feathers intermingled with the gold ones. The bird's torso was almost as big as Ezra's, and his talons were big enough to carry off a large animal without a problem. I bet his wingspan was at least twelve feet. When he shook his feathers, sprinkles of rain and small bolts of lightning flashed off of them.

Ezra saw me and waved me over. "Liam! Look, I've bonded! This is Dyami. Isn't he fricken sweet?"

Dyami chattered his beak at me in a pleasant greeting. "Wow. A thunderbird," I said, impressed. "I guess it was you guys who caused the rain outside."

"Yeah," Ezra said proudly. "Awe man, you should've been there. There were like, electric guitars everywhere, and Dyami just came out of the sky with all this lightning around him. It was totally badass."

All the girls Ezra liked were swooning over Dyami and stroking his feathers. Apparently, Ezra wasn't the only one who was impressing the ladies.

Thunderbirds brought rain and could cause storms whenever they wanted to. They were known as some of the most powerful Familiars alive. Ezra's popularity was about to shoot way up. He was gonna get laid every night of the week.

"Did you tell Dad?" I asked.

"Not yet. But man, he's gonna be so excited." Ezra reached into his pocket and pulled out a strip of raw meat. He threw it to Dyami, who snatched it out of the air and scarfed it down. "I don't know how I'm going to keep him fed. He eats a lot."

"He's like you, then. A total fatass." I grinned.

"Shut up," Ezra said, and Dyami squawked. He grabbed a piece of Ezra's hair and yanked on it.

"Ouch!" Ezra said. "Fine, here, have some more. But it's all you get until dinner."

Ezra gave him another snack. Dyami scarfed it down like it was nothing at all and started pecking at Ezra's head for more. Ezra tried swatting him away. It was really funny to watch.

Thunderbirds got huge. In a year or two Dyami would be the size of a small dragon, and big enough for Ezra to ride. It was a fitting Familiar for someone who'd someday be chief.

"Maybe he just sticks with you because you feed him," I suggested.

"Wouldn't surprise me," Ezra grumbled. Dyami nuzzled his head against Ezra's neck and he grinned. "But he is really cute, though."

I wouldn't really call Dyami cute. If he came for me, I'd start running.

I'd thought about all the people that had bonded in the last month. Renar, Vanessa, and now Ez. It'd go like that at Orenda. You'd have months at a time where nobody would bond at all, and then a crazy three-week stretch where everybody bonded at once.

I watched Ezra mess around with Dyami, and it hit me. My brother would be in the tournament this fall. He'd have to survive and prove that he deserved to live, just like I did.

I immediately felt scared. But I reminded myself he'd be better off than I was. Having a thunderbird by your side was a hell of a lot better than nothing at all. And by that time, Dyami wouldn't exactly be a pushover. A thunderbird would be an asset to any tournament team.

Ezra would probably be selected for one of the better ones. He'd have a good chance of making it out alive.

"Hey, Liam?" Ezra sounded hesitant.

I looked at him. I was spacing out again.

He looked a little nervous. "Is the tournament... hard?"

I didn't want to lie to him. But he had months to prepare, and I didn't want him to freak out too much in the meantime. "It's not easy," I said. "But you've got a strong Familiar. You'll get through it."

He nodded. "It's just... I'm not really worried about myself, more who I'm teamed up with. I think if someone's in trouble, I'll have to save them. You know?"

I grabbed his arm. "Listen, Ez. If something happens out there, you play it safe. Don't try to be a hero."

Ezra looked at me blankly. "Okay."

Some girl got his attention, and he changed the subject so he could talk with her. I left with a knot in my stomach.

I thought the worst thing about the tournament was actually being in it, but that was wrong. Now I knew that it was watching people you loved participate.

I didn't want my brother to put himself in danger for someone else. If one of his teammates was dying, I didn't want him to sacrifice himself to rescue another person. I wanted him to run away.

But Ezra wasn't that kind of kid. He was like me. Which was the exact thing that would get him killed out there.

I'D BEEN FEELING like a shitty boyfriend lately, because I was always in bed. I hadn't been spending as much time with Sophia as I usually did because I was sick all the time— sicker than usual.

I knew I was getting worse. It wasn't encouraging. But I was at the point I was kinda sick and tired of being sick and tired. I wanted to take Sophia out for the day and pretend I was normal... act like I wasn't living on a complicated timeline that involved proving her innocence and finding a cure for myself.

I planned on taking her out for a hike today. It'd been a while since

I'd gone for a walk, since I'd pretty much been in my room. Today I felt... okay... which meant I had to take advantage of it while it lasted.

Sophia was sitting on a bench by the Toaqua dorms when I came out, waiting for me. Esis was brushing her hair, which she'd left down. She'd worn hiking boots and a thick coat.

She was so pretty. I loved looking at her.

Esis peeped when he saw me coming. He ran to me and sat on my shoulders, brushing my hair instead.

"Dude, hands off," I said, prying Esis away and handing him back to Sophia. I was touchy about my hair, and he acted like it was his personal property. Had since the day I'd met him, actually.

Sophia laughed. "Good morning to you, too."

"Good morning." I nudged her with my shoulder. "You ready?"

"For sure." She beamed. "I can't wait to spend time with you."

"I missed you, too." There was no one around, so I took a quick chance to plant a kiss in her hair. Esis made an argumentative sound, like I was messing up his work.

"I have a question," Sophia asked. "Jonah said you used to be an adrenaline junkie. What did you use to do?"

"Talking about me again, huh, *pawee*?" I pinched her side, and she squeaked.

"Hey, I didn't bring it up. Jonah made you sound pretty cool, but you're lame now," she teased.

"I'm not lame. And I did pretty much every extreme sport there is," I said. "I used to do a lot before I got sick. Dirt bikes, four-wheeling, hang gliding, skydiving, surfing, you name it. Cliff-diving was kinda my favorite. I think that's why I don't like regular sports too much. There isn't enough risk."

"You know how to surf?"

"Of course I know how to surf," I said. "I'm Toaqua, I'm from the West Coast, and I literally live in the water."

"You're such a California boy," she said, rolling her eyes and giggling.

"I'll teach you how during the summer," I said. "You'll love it."

"Along with all the other things," she added. "It's really scary, but I want to try skydiving and bungee jumping, too."

"We'll start you off with cliff diving." I could control the water that way and save her if she made a bad fall.

It made me nervous to think about her doing extreme sports, but at the same time, it was awesome that I'd finally found someone daring enough to do this stuff with. Everyone else was too chicken-shit— except for Jonah, who was okay with skydiving, but that was a total cop-out. He could control the Air if he needed to in order to float safely down to the ground. If there wasn't a chance you could die, what was the point?

Sophia was Koigni, which meant that she was crazy and she'd try anything once. She was way different from cautious Toaqua girls. None of my other girlfriends wanted to do extreme stuff with me.

"Esis can come, too!" Sophia said, holding him up. "I'll make a little pouch in my jumpsuit he can fly in."

Esis held out his arms and pretended to skydive. Sophia laughed and swung him through the air like a little doll, making *whooshing* noises like he was falling through the air.

I shook my head and laughed. "Ancestors, *pawee*, you're such a dork." And this was the woman the Toaqua Elders were terrified of.

We rounded the corner to the main entryway, but stopped in place when I'd realized I'd made a mistake. Aw, shit.

Clusters of little booths were set up here and there in the main hall, and it was packed with people and Familiars both. Orenda put on a miniature wedding expo every year for all the people who were engaged and getting married in the spring. I'd made every plan to avoid it, but I'd forgotten it was today, and I'd brought Sophia right to it. Shit.

I was a guy, and this kinda shit made me wanna run like hell, but the hiking trail started outside the main doors, and this was the quickest way through. So I sucked it up and went down the stairs, walking right through the middle of the expo.

To my surprise, Sophia didn't stop to look. She kept pretty close to me at a steady pace, like she was more interested in getting outside than staying in.

"You're not distracted by all this?" I waved my hand around.

"I was never a girl who was into dreaming about her big wedding," Sophia said. "I always wanted something simple."

Hm. Interesting.

Of course, Jonah was there. He was the furthest away from getting engaged out of all of us, but he was talking to vendors like he was going to be walking down the aisle next week. He wore a pink scarf and was swinging it around to show it off. Squeaks wore a similar scarf, though she had the good sense to leave it alone, as she kept on getting whacked accidentally in the face by Jonah.

We bumped into Vanessa and a tall Koigni dude by one of the honeymoon booths. Aisha was by her side and was blowing out little smoke hearts.

"Sophia, hi!" Vanessa waved. She looked exceptionally happy. "I want you to meet Bren, my fiancé."

She grabbed his arm and smiled at us. At Bren's side was his Familiar, a chimera. It had a lion's body and a real snake for a tail, with bat wings and three heads; one a lion, one a goat's, and one a dragon's. It hissed at us, but it was somewhat of a pleasant hiss, so I don't think it was unfriendly.

"Nice to meet you. Vanessa's told me a lot about you," Bren said as he shook both of our hands. "You guys did great in the tournament. I was really impressed."

"Wow. Um... thanks," I said, surprised.

He noticed my tone and leaned in. "Don't worry. Not all Koigni guys are self-obsessed jerks," Bren said. "It's just the ones that are suck up all the attention."

Sophia laughed. "You've got that right."

"I've seen you two hanging out a lot. Maybe we could all go out together sometime!" Vanessa said. "It'll be like a double date!"

The way Vanessa was smiling at us... it's like she knew we were together. But that couldn't be, right? Still... she'd used the word *date*. I hoped no one else heard that.

"We'd love to. Liam and I were just going hiking," Sophia said, and she waved a goodbye. "Catch you two later."

Vanessa and Bren gave us equally friendly smiles. It was a bit weird, coming from a couple of Koigni. They were like the perfect couple. I could see them with a white picket fence and a couple of kids in a few years.

"Did you tell her about us?" I asked Sophia as we walked away.

She shook her head. "No. But Vanessa and I have been hanging out," she told me. "I think she can tell we like each other."

"I hope that doesn't become an issue." I glanced back over my shoulder, but Vanessa and Bren had already forgotten about us. They were looking through a honeymoon catalog.

"She's nice, and really fun. She wouldn't tell even if she knew," Sophia said. "She hates the Koigni Elders just as much as I do."

"That's good." I glanced over to the other side of the room. In one of the booths, Imogen was selling veils, bouquets, and decorated shoes that I was pretty sure she'd made herself. Girls were obsessing over them. It looked like she was selling a lot, but she kept on glancing over here every few seconds. "But don't forget about your friends from other Houses."

Esis gave a low trill. Sophia said, "I would never."

I noticed that Sophia wasn't wearing her bracelet that Imogen had given her at the Elemental Ball. Sophia had hardly taken it off before their fight.

It'd been a few weeks. It was high time to end this. "Don't you think you should make up with Imogen?" I asked Sophia as I caught her staring at Im's table.

"What? No." She pushed her lip out and shook her head. "Why would I do that?"

"You miss her."

She opened her mouth to answer, then closed it. When she couldn't argue that she didn't, she said, "She's the one who started it. She should apologize."

"A Nivita will never apologize first. Not because they don't want to, but because they're afraid of conflict. They'll avoid a fight at all costs," I told Sophia. "You're gonna have to be the one to reach out to her if you wanna end this thing."

She scratched her head. "But she was kind of a bitch about you."

"I don't really give a shit. It doesn't hurt my feelings," I said. "You're both in the wrong. Just say you're sorry and get over it."

She took another glance at Imogen before she turned away. "Okay."

I let out a sigh of relief, until it got sucked back in when I faced my worst nightmare. I thought awkward encounters were over for the day, but apparently not, because it looked like my past had come back to haunt me.

"Shit," I said. I would've grabbed Sophia's hand to whirl her around and drag her the other way, but I couldn't, because that would look too obvious and it would attract attention. I said Sophia's name, but she didn't hear me and kept walking. Which lead me right where I didn't want to go.

"Liam! Hey!" a girl called my name. Sophia turned around, and she caught sight of the one person I hoped to the ancestors she'd never meet.

Gritting my teeth, I turned to face her and attempted to be polite. "Hello, Mia."

Mia gave me a plastic smile, one I didn't return. Not much about her had changed. Her black hair was still straight and long, and she looked like she still tanned, though I didn't know why, since her skin was the same brown color as mine. Her nails were manicured and she had about ten pounds of makeup on. I noticed she still carried a love of designer labels and high heels. I was pretty sure Micah must've bought her bigger boobs, because *no way* were they that size when we'd been dating. I was standing at least three feet away from her, but I could smell her perfume from here.

Sophia recognized the name. I swear to the ancestors, literal flames lit up in her eyes. Oh, hell.

"How've you been? I haven't seen you in a while," Mia cooed. Her voice was irritating to me now. Ancestors, I just wanted her to shut up.

"I've been fine," I said dully. We hadn't had a class together since we'd broken up, thank the ancestors. I hadn't even seen her around the Toaqua dorms very much, since we had different schedules. This was the first time she'd said hi to me since she'd dipped on our relationship. Why was she talking to me now?

When I realized she hadn't even acknowledged Sophia at my side, I knew.

"Mia, this is my... friend, Sophia," I said, and I pulled Sophia over to me. Sophia didn't like that. She shot me a glare, but what was I supposed to do? I couldn't call her my girlfriend in public.

"I've heard. You two were tournament partners. You did really well together," she said.

It didn't seem like a compliment at all. Mia added, "I'm sorry you fainted on stage. That must've been awful. Ezra told me you've been getting sicker. Your life is so hard. I don't know how you manage. I just feel so bad for you."

I hated her fucking pity. And I bet Ezra hadn't told her a damn thing. My brother couldn't stand her.

I didn't know what to say, but Sophia filled in for me. "Well, you shouldn't feel bad for him, seeing as he's a tournament champion. Didn't your team come in second-to-last place your year?"

Holy shit. How had Sophia known that? Mia's eyes flashed, but she made no other indication that Sophia's comment bothered her. "You're the Henley girl, right? From Koigni. I'm sorry your *parents* took you away from your tribe. That must've been dreadful. I imagine you're still not used to being the outcast, poor thing."

Sophia went to respond, but before she could, there was a snapping at her feet. Taryn, Mia's Familiar, was jumping up and trying to get Esis. Taryn was a canine-hybrid that looked like a cross between a coyote and a wolf. She had white and black spotted fur like a snow leopard, and a jeweled sapphire set in the middle of her forehead. Esis hissed at Taryn and bared his teeth from Sophia's shoulder.

"Taryn, down," Mia said. "That's not polite."

Taryn backed off, but her Familiar growled at me, which wasn't unusual. Taryn and Nashoma had gotten into it on more than one occasion. We'd had to separate them from killing each other once.

"Micah and I are getting married next year," Mia announced. Apparently, she'd gotten bored with the backhanded compliments. She held up her hand to show us a gaudy diamond ring, then shoved it in my face. "It'll be a huge wedding, right after graduation. The entire Toaqua tribe is coming. It's going to be the most elaborate wedding in all of Kinpago."

She was really working hard to make me see that she'd moved on, which I didn't get. She'd dumped me, not the other way around.

"Congratulations, Mia. I'm happy for you," I said. And I was. She was out of my hair and in Micah's now.

"Thank you," she said, batting her fake eyelashes. I swear one of them was gonna come off. "I'm just glad we remained such good friends. You know, after everything that happened."

I could literally feel the heat coming off of Sophia next to me. Esis' hair was standing on end.

Mia looked me in the eyes. "I know things didn't end well. But I hope you don't still miss me."

You know, I always was a sucker for girls with big brown eyes, but Mia's seemed so dark and unfeeling compared to Sophia's.

I knew then. Mia could come crawling back to me and I'd never take her back. She'd left me at a time when I'd needed her the most. Sophia would never do that.

Miss you? Bitch, I didn't give a shit about you. Not anymore.

I opened my mouth to tell her just that, but before I could, a brawny dude with hooded eyes muscled his way in beside us. "Babe, let's go. This shit's boring."

I used to think Micah was one of my best friends, but now that I really thought about it, I never really liked him— more or less just put up with him. We'd only hung out because he ran in the same circle as Wyatt and the other Toaqua guys my age. In reality, he was a dick.

"Hun, do you remember Liam? We're just talking about how close we are," Mia said.

"Yeah, whatever," Micah said. "Come on."

"But—"

"Mia, I said *let's go*," Micah said sharply. He turned to leave. Mia cringed, and she followed without saying goodbye. Taryn trotted behind Mia with her tail tucked between her legs.

Thank the ancestors. I was pretty sure Sophia was gonna blow up in about two seconds.

Though when I turned back around, she still seemed like she would. Fuck.

"Really, Liam?" she asked me. "Her? You liked *her*?"

I was at a loss for what to say. "I... used to."

Jonah smelled drama. He'd left Squeaks behind and made his way over to us from Imogen's table. "O.M.G. I saw and heard everything. What a bitch!"

Sophia shook her head in disgust. I hurried to follow her while Jonah, damn him, decided to tag along.

"She looks like a Hawkei," Sophia said as we made it outside. "Someone you'd like."

"You look like a Hawkei. We're all different," I said. "And I like you, not her. That should be apparent."

Sophia shook her head. "How could you be with someone who's so selfish? It's totally not who you are."

"Honey, that's why he *was* with her," Jonah said. "Liam gave her everything, and Mia totally sucked him dry. Emotionally and financially, but never sexually."

"You don't have any right to be talking about relationships, Jonah," I said. Fuck, this was embarrassing.

"But he's right, isn't he?" Sophia persisted. She stopped at the hiking trail and turned to me. "She doesn't exactly look like a simple girl."

"Mia... likes nice things," I admitted.

"She's a total gold digger," Jonah said nastily. "Why can't you just say it?"

"Fine. Mia wants somebody to take care of her. She doesn't want to work," I told Sophia, ignoring Jonah.

"So she wants to be a trophy wife and be kept," Sophia said.

I'd never really thought of it like that. "I guess." I shrugged. "Not like there's anything wrong with that. Everyone has different goals."

"Excuse me while I go puke," Sophia said, and she made a gagging noise. Jonah nodded in approval. "Is the guy she's engaged to the one she cheated on you with?"

I nodded. "Yeah. That's Micah."

"He didn't seem very... nice." Sophia seemed puzzled. "And he's kinda ugly. What's he got that she's interested in?"

"His daddy owns half of Kinpago and he's got a billion-dollar inheritance coming his way," Jonah piped up.

"Oh, that makes sense." She nodded. It's like they were having this conversation without me even being around.

"Jonah, if you don't mind, I'd really like to take my girlfriend on a date. *Alone*," I emphasized. "Can you spread drama somewhere else?"

"Ugh, fine," he said dramatically. "It's clear I'm not wanted. But Sophia, you should know this." He pointed at her. "Mia's a man eater. And your man got devoured alive, chewed up, and spit back up by the likes of her."

Jonah swaggered off, flipping his scarf behind him. Sophia started up the hiking trail without waiting for me. She was still mad. "Ugh. Liam, how could you sleep with someone like her?"

I didn't have an answer for her, so I stayed quiet as we continued up the hiking trail. Sophia continued venting. Esis jumped off her shoulder and into the trees around us, leaping from branch to branch.

"I wish you hadn't," she said. "I wish you could've saved yourself for *me*. I know you didn't know I was coming, but..."

She sounded really hurt. I felt guilty.

"If it helps, I never really enjoyed it," I said. "It's not like being with you. She always made me feel so... desperate."

"Do you still miss her?" she asked. "Would you still be with her if you had the chance?"

I grabbed Sophia so I could turn her around and she'd look at me.

"You want to know the truth? She broke my fucking heart," I said. "And that's more than I've ever told anyone. More than I've even said out loud."

I shook her. "Yes, I cared about her. But I *love you*," I emphasized. "There's a huge difference."

"I didn't like the way she talked to you," Sophia said softly. "It was cruel."

"She thinks she's being kind." I shook my head and let her go. "She doesn't realize it's belittling."

"Oh, she knows, Liam. Don't pretend like she doesn't." Sophia's face turned pink, and it wasn't because of the cold. "When she was saying that stuff to you, I wanted to light her hair on fire."

"I could tell." I kicked a wayward rock off the trail. "I don't like it when people say they feel bad for me. I don't like being told I have such a hard life." I looked up. "It makes me feel like a victim."

"Then what do you like to hear?" she asked.

I thought about it, then I said, "That I'm strong. That I can handle it, and that all the bad things are gonna pass. That this won't last forever. Maybe that I'm brave."

"You *are* brave." She grabbed my hand and squeezed it. "You're still the bravest person I know."

That felt good to hear. "Can we forget about Mia and just have a good time? Thinking about her kind of ruins my day."

"Agreed." Sophia started up the hiking trail and let it drop, thank the ancestors.

We made our way up the hiking trail at a pace that felt really slow. I had to stop to rest a lot. I didn't like it, but Sophia actually didn't care that we took our time. Every time I had to take a break, she'd just keep on talking about our classes, or what she was doing with Vanessa, or that she worried our professor was going to catch on that she was doing both of our essays.

I worried that it would get annoying to her, having to stop all the time, but she didn't seem to care.

It made me feel relieved.

When we almost got to the top of the mountain we were hiking, Sophia said, "I've been wanting to tell you something, but I had to wait until we couldn't be heard. I saw my parents the other day. Amelia brought them."

"You did? Sophia, that's dangerous," I said.

"I know. But listen." She told me all about how her real grandparents gave her away to the Henleys. I didn't know what to think of it. Toaqua and Koigni being friends? Something was up there.

There was a lot more snow up here, seeing as how we were close to the top. Sophia turned around to go back, but I said, "Wait."

I used my magic to summon creatures out of the cold. A bear made of ice and snow came up out of the large drifts collected around us. Esis danced around it and tried to fight, but he only ended up knocking himself backward. He popped out of a snow pile absolutely covered, looking grumpy.

"Climb on. It'll take us to the top," I said.

"I thought you weren't supposed to use your element?" Sophia asked.

"Fuck it," I said. "It doesn't matter. I don't think it makes me any better. If anything, it just makes me worse."

Sophia got on top of the bear and motioned for Esis to jump on. I climbed on behind her, and the snow bear started ambling its way upwards. We were nearly vertical as we climbed, but I made sure to anchor the bear's feet into the rock and freeze it as it took each step so that we wouldn't go sliding off.

When we got to the top of the mountain, we slid off the bear. The snow bear laid down, to wait for when we headed back down. Esis smacked his tail in its face and huffed.

Sophia went to the edge of the cliff and gasped. From here, the mountains went on in three directions for miles. The ocean looked huge and curled around the edge of the earth. The view really was spectacular.

"Did you know about this place?" Sophia asked me. I sat on a flat rock near the edge that acted as a bench.

"I used to come up here a lot on my own," I admitted. "Though I haven't, since Nashoma..."

I trailed off. Sophia sat beside me. She took my hands in hers. Esis started making little snowballs at our feet. "Jonah told me how he died. I'm so sorry."

"It was my fault," I said. "I'm the reason he's gone."

"It's not your fault. It's just something that happened," she said.

"I know that's what you believe, Sophia, but you're going to have a hard time convincing me that's not true," I said.

She leaned against me. It was cold up here, and she helped me to keep warm. She was quiet for a moment before she added, "I think he would've wanted this."

"Yeah," I said. "*Inavita naan.*"

"What's that?"

"It's an ancient Hawkei saying. It basically means, *life goes on.*"

"Will you teach me Hawkei?" she sat up. "I would like to learn how to speak it."

Esis was throwing snowballs at the snow bear. They hit it in the face, but the snow bear ignored it.

"Well, you already know what *pawee* means," I told her, and smiled. "*Ei amashini ve.*"

"What does that mean?"

"I love you."

Her expression brightened. "How do I say it back?"

"There are a lot of ways. Like, if I was to say *ve ni ei toaqua*, it would mean *you are my water*. It literally means you are my life."

"Is there a Koigni version?" she asked eagerly.

"Eh... I think so. Let me remember it." I thought for a moment, then said, "*Ve havi ei koigni biksku animorte. You keep me warm against death*. Literally, the meaning is *you sustain my life*."

"Oh." Sophia gave me a smile. "Liam, *ve havi ei koigni biksku animorte*."

I took her face in my hands. "Sophia, *ve ni ei anichi un ei inavita. Ve ni te shanlis all manti un te solae all noctee. Ve ni ei pawee un te aymare au ei inavita. Ve ni ei tatum un ei todi ei teryah hootum. Ve ni nizra*."

Sophia took a quivering breath. "I don't know what you just said, but it was really hot."

"You are my breath... my spirit... and my existence. You are the sunrise every morning and the stars every evening. You are my soulmate and the love of my life. You are my ocean and you keep my world safe. You are beautiful."

Jackpot. There were little tears forming in her eyes. Her lip quivered. "Do you really mean all that?"

"I didn't pull it out of my ass for nothing."

"You just made all that up?"

"Yeah. It's how I really feel."

Sophia threw her arms around me and hugged me. Her mouth was on mine before I even had time to react. She kissed me, and I could literally feel how much my words had affected her. She was so hot that it felt like her body was going to burn through our clothes. She reached for the lump in my pants and grabbed on to it, squeezing hard. I groaned.

A snowball collided in both of our faces, and we sprung apart. Esis was launching them at us now, instead of the snow bear. He made a noise of discontentment.

"Okay, fine, I get it," I said, wiping snow off my face. "Keep our clothes on until we get back inside."

Sophia laughed. Esis chattered at us like he agreed.

"Speaking of which, it's getting colder," I said, and I shivered. "The snow doesn't really bother me much, but we should probably head back."

"You just want some," Sophia said coyly as she climbed back on top of the snow bear.

"And what's wrong with that?" I asked. I was rocking a half-hard on. Rad. Esis was such a little cockblock.

By the time we'd nearly made it back to the school, Sophia had more questions about the ancient Hawkei and their language. I thought it would be a good idea to ask if she could sit in on one of my Hawkei Legends class sometime. She'd heard something about ancestral names, though she wasn't sure what they meant.

"Every Hawkei has two names, the name your parents give you and the name your ancestors call you," I say. "You get your ancestral name through a special ceremony once you turn sixteen for guys, or um, for girls—"

"I'm guessing it's when we get our period?" she says.

"Yeah." I nodded.

"Do you have a special name the ancestors gave you?"

"Yes. But I'm not supposed to tell. Not yet, anyway."

"Are there rules?" Sophia asked.

"Not really. Every tribe and family has their own ideas about it. A lot of people come out right away and tell everyone," I say. "Mitoh men usually don't announce it until after they get married. It's tradition."

I paused for a moment, then added, "Which means no one will ever know."

"You're an asshole." She laughed, and punched my arm.

Sophia sighed dreamily. "I wish I could've gotten an ancestral name. It's like one more thing I missed out on growing up."

"You didn't miss your chance. You can someday," I say. "But you would have to talk to a Fire Elder to set that up, since your birth parents are gone and your adoptive parents don't have any standing with the tribe anymore."

"Yeah. Not gonna happen." She made a skeptical noise. "I'm not about to ask any of those bitches. Doya might be treating me nicer lately, but I'm pretty sure she'd sneer at me if I asked."

"You'll get your chance someday," I told her. "Don't let your tribe hold you back."

We spent the rest of the day hanging out in the Commons. Although we couldn't touch each other there, which sucked, it was nice being in each other's company... though I couldn't lie that the memory of her hand on my dick earlier was in my thoughts all fucking day.

We stayed there until after midnight. A movie we'd been watching had just finished, and there was no one else around. We were free to touch each other again, and were lying side by side on the big couch in front of the TV, under a blanket Sophia had grabbed from her room.

Esis was rolling on the floor. He'd eaten all of our popcorn and was currently patting a full belly.

When she'd gone back to her dorm to grab the blanket, she'd also changed from her hiking clothes into a skirt. A fucking skirt. I don't think I ever saw her wear one until that day. She was obviously hoping for something.

"So, about earlier..." I started, as a shitty way to begin a sexy conversation. I needed to work on my game.

"Oh, yeah," Sophia said, proving that dirty thoughts hadn't left her mind, either. She went to unbutton my jeans, but I stopped her. She gave me a confused look.

"I think it's my turn." My hand trailed from her knee and up her thigh slowly. Her eyes widened as I grabbed the waistband of her panties and started slowly dragging then downward.

"Esis, keep watch," Sophia told him. He jumped off the couch and scattered to the middle of the room.

This was risky. There were multiple entrances to the Commons on all sides. Esis couldn't watch them all. There was no guarantee he'd be able to warn us in time. We could get caught.

But that only made it hotter. My heart was practically skipping beats already with the thrill of the risk. Plus, I'd been dying all day to touch her. I was horny as hell, here.

Sophia lifted her hips as I pulled her panties off of her. I balled them up and tucked them into one of the cushions so they wouldn't get lost, pulled the blanket over her, then returned my hand to her thigh.

Her body was trembling as I came close, though I wasn't sure if it was because she was turned on or scared. She seemed nervous.

I moved slow when I reached her, even though every nerve in my body was going haywire. I put two fingers on her and started rubbing gently in a circular motion, ignoring the demands my body was screaming out at me. Fuck. She felt amazing.

"This okay?" I asked. I was really nervous. The last time a guy had touched her here, it'd been terrible for her. I remembered what she'd told me about her prom. I wanted to make sure this would be something she liked, not a repeat of that horrible night.

"Hmm," Sophia hummed. Her eyes were closed, and a soft expression of relaxation had come over her face. I mean, she *looked* like she enjoyed it, but that wasn't enough for me.

"I need to hear you say yes, Sophia."

"Yes," she breathed. She rolled sideways so that she was facing me, her head buried in my shirt and eyes closed. "Keep going."

I worked slowly, massaging her lightly until soft sounds started to come out from her mouth. I wanted to make this as pleasurable for her as possible. I made sure to watch her every expression in-between trying to concentrate, to make sure I didn't cross a line.

Sophia arched her back, and the blanket slid off of her. Her skirt was bunched up around her middle. My eyes immediately went downward. She really was beautiful down there. And everywhere, period. How the fuck did I get so lucky?

Sophia was looking at me, looking at my hand on her. I felt my face getting hot. I must've appeared guilty, because Sophia giggled. "It's fine, Liam. You can look."

"I... I don't want you to think I'm a perv."

"You're my *boyfriend*. You worry too much." She sighed, giving a smile. "Stop. I'm loving this."

I let out a breath. I didn't realize how tense I was. I forgot that even though this was about her, I could enjoy it, too.

And, even better. She'd given me permission to watch. I rubbed her and tried to record the image of her in my mind as she wriggled beneath me.

"Should I keep going?" I breathed. I wouldn't go any farther until she told me it was okay.

"Please, Liam," she begged.

Oh, she wanted me. Badly. And I was never very good at withholding anything Sophia wanted.

I made sure she was ready, then I teased her at first before I went in. I slowly slid a finger into her and almost passed out from the pleasure of it myself.

Sophia whimpered softly and wiggled. Shit, she was so tight. I wonder what she would feel like on my...

Don't think about that, I scolded myself. This was just fooling around. It was way different from us actually having sex, something neither of us were ready for and I wasn't sure would ever happen.

Fuck, she hadn't even touched my dick and the feeling of her on my hand made me want to come right then and there.

But this wasn't about me. This was about giving her a good experience, and making sure she was comfortable.

When she started squirming on the couch, I knew she was ready for more. I worked up to speed and her moans started getting loud. Suddenly, she gasped and started calling my name. I quickly put my hand over her mouth to muffle the sound so we wouldn't get caught. I couldn't keep the grin off my face as I watched her dissolve into bliss by my touch.

It felt like it went on for minutes. When she was finally done, her legs were quivering. She went to sit up, but I put a hand on her shoulder and held her back down.

"I don't think so," I leaned down and whispered in her ear. "You're not done yet."

I slipped another finger in, and she let out a tiny noise of surprise and contentment before I was at the same pace I'd been at moments before. I made sure she came at least twice more. On the third time, she begged me to stop and then turned inward, crawling against me and curling up against my chest.

It was like she needed to be in my arms, needed me to hold her.

And I needed her, too. Always.

I held her tightly to me as she shivered. Her voice shook when she spoke. "Ancestors, Liam. That was so good."

"I'm glad you liked it." I hadn't noticed, but I'd been holding my breath since we'd started. I'd been so worried she would freak out on me and hate it. It hit me that was the reason I'd waited so long to touch her.

I buried my face in her hair and pretended like the rest of the world didn't exist. I pretended like this could last forever and I could always have her. I pretended for a moment I didn't have to choose between her and Nashoma. Because at this point, it was an impossible decision.

"Your turn," she said, and I was snapped out of my thoughts. I felt a thrill go through me as she started undoing my belt. She reached for the button on my pants, but there was a loud *bang* and the sound of footsteps. Esis squeaked. Sophia quickly pulled on her panties while I ducked down so nobody saw me.

We looked over the edge of the couch, but there was no one there. Esis shrugged at us.

"We'd better get out of here," I said. "It's really late. We're already taking a risk."

"But I want to stay," she complained, like there wasn't an inherent risk we'd be found out.

"Sophia, no," I said, in a tone that told her I meant business.

She rolled her eyes. "Fine."

We got off the couch. Esis scrambled after us and jumped onto my back, scurrying upward to curl around my neck. Sophia and I held hands on the way back to the Koigni dorms.

"I feel kind of bad." She giggled. "What we did was dirty. Other people use that couch."

"I highly doubt we're the first people to fuck around on those couches, trust me," I told her. The stories Jonah told me made me wonder why the cushions hadn't gotten up and walked away by now.

When we stopped in front of the Koigni dorms, my heart dropped like a rock. We should be sleeping together after the moment we just shared. Not apart.

"Liam?" Sophia stared at me with those big chocolate eyes, and Esis clambered down from my neck back to her shoulder.

"Yeah, *pawee*?" I tilted my head at her.

"I just want to say thank you." She smiled at me. "I could tell you put a lot of thought into making this the best it could be for me."

"I just didn't want you to feel unsafe," I stammered. "You know, because of—"

"You could never hurt me, Liam," she told me softly. She raised up on her toes and gave me a kiss. "I trust you with my life."

When she said that, it fucking hurt. Because she trusted me and loved me so much, and she had no idea what had been going on in my head over the past few months. I wanted to tell her to stay away from me, that I was no good for her and I would only hurt her. But I didn't.

She peeked out from behind the doors and gave me a smile. "Goodnight."

Her words echoed in my head as I faced the closed door. *I trust you with my life.*

I really wished she didn't.

I woke the following morning still daydreaming about Liam's hands all over me. The man was a god, I tell you. He knew exactly what to do with his fingers, which might've bothered me— the fact that he was more experienced than I was— if it hadn't felt so amazing. I was still thinking about it when I ran into Vanessa in the hall on my way to breakfast.

"Hey," she said with a smile, petting Aisha's head beside her. "Where are you and Esis headed?"

"Breakfast," I answered. Esis rubbed his belly from where he sat cradled in my arms.

"Awesome. Us, too. Mind if we join you?"

"Not at all."

Vanessa and I fell into step side-by-side on our way out of the Koigni dorms and into the main hallway.

"How'd classes go this week?" she asked.

I shrugged. "I'm supposed to submit the topic for my big Hawkei Careers project on Monday, and I still don't know what I'm going to write about."

Vanessa tilted her head. "Still undecided on your major, then?"

"Yeah," I said disappointedly.

Her shoulders slumped. "Me, too. I took Hawkei Careers last semester and BS'ed my whole project."

I laughed. "What'd you do it on?"

"I claimed I wanted to be a unicorn medic," she admitted. "But only because I was taking Unicornology, so the essay was simple. Now I'm thinking about maybe majoring in potions, specifically medical potions."

"That sounds kind of cool," I said as we turned down another hall. "I was thinking of doing mine on Fire creature care. I think I'd like working with Fire animals, but..."

We entered the cafeteria. It was quiet this morning since it was still early.

"But what?" Vanessa asked.

I put Esis on my shoulder, then grabbed a plate and followed behind Vanessa in the buffet line. "Well, you've seen me in class lately. My Fire's been acting all wonky. I had this amazing training session with Doya, then *boom*. It's like I took two steps forward and ten steps back. Maybe I'd just do better with a more generic career path."

Vanessa glared at me like there was no way she was letting me give up. "Has something else been going on in your life lately? Something you're stressed over?"

I chuckled as I scooped a pile of breakfast potatoes onto my plate. "Are you my therapist now?"

"No," she replied with a smirk. "I just think it could be affecting your magic."

I followed her over to the drinks to fill my glass with apple juice. "How so?"

"The same thing happened to me last semester. I was really stressed during midterms, and all of a sudden it was like I could hardly conjure a flame. I mean, it was my first semester and I wasn't bonded yet, so it was hard enough as it was. And then it stressed me out even *more* because people expect so much from me, being related to the chieftess and all."

Vanessa and I finished filling our trays and headed over to the Koigni section.

"You really think it could be stress?" I asked as I sat across from her. Esis hopped off my shoulder to sit in the chair next to me— even though he couldn't even see over the top of the table there. Aisha curled up like a dog at Vanessa's feet.

"Absolutely," Vanessa said, taking a sip of orange juice. "So, are you stressing over anything lately?"

I thought about it for a minute. There were plenty of things that could go on that list, but the more I thought of it, the more I realized something.

"I guess it all started when Imogen and I got into that fight," I admitted while poking at my food. Esis tugged on my arm, and I handed him a piece of bacon. He scarfed it down in under a second.

"You should make up with her," Vanessa encouraged.

I sighed. "Yeah. Everyone keeps telling me that. But she's been avoiding me as much as I have her. She doesn't even sit by me anymore during Ancient Familiars."

Vanessa set her fork down and crossed her hands over the table. The look she gave me made me pause. "Look, Sophia. I don't think you understand how lucky you are to have Imogen. I'd kill for a friend like that."

I furrowed my brow. "But we're friends."

She shook her head. "Not like you and Imogen are. You two went through hell in the tournament together. You have a special bond because of that."

"I don't know about that," I said. "Everyone goes through the tournament, and they aren't all best friends with their teammates."

"That's because they resist forging that bond," Vanessa argued. "It's because they're afraid what other people will think. Well, you know what I think?"

I lifted my gaze from my food to look up at her. "What do you think?"

"I think it's awesome. I think what you and Imogen have is really special, and I would hate to see you give it up."

A soft smile touched my lips.

"This isn't just about your magic, Sophia," Vanessa said.

"I *am* going to make up with her," I promised, just as I'd told Liam.

"When?" Vanessa challenged. "If you let this go on too long, you and Imogen might never make up. Don't give up your best friend over something so stupid."

Guilt settled like a bowling ball in my stomach. She was right. Liam was right. Everyone was right. I just hated to admit it.

"Right after breakfast," I decided, even though I didn't *really* want to.

But I wanted Imogen back, so I was going to have to get the conversation over with sooner than later.

I DIDN'T KNOW where to find Imogen this early on a Saturday morning. Usually we met up for breakfast, but today I didn't see her in the dining hall, so I headed for her dorm room instead. Technically, I wasn't allowed in the Nivita dorms, but I didn't care because she was my best friend.

At least, I hoped she still was.

There were a few people in the Nivita common room, but they were all curled up in reading nooks set into the walls with their noses in a book, buried within the various types of plants growing throughout the room, so they didn't even notice me pass through. I stood outside Imogen's door for a full minute, trying to work up the courage to knock.

Eventually, Esis got frustrated with me and reached his paw out and knocked for me. It barely made a sound. I sighed and knocked on my own.

Imogen answered almost immediately, but the bright smile on her face immediately fell when she saw it was me.

"Oh," she said flatly. "What do you want?"

"I, uh, wanted to talk."

Imogen turned from the door, leaving it open so I could step inside. She crossed over to her dresser to put earrings in her ears. This morning, she was dressed in a white t-shirt that had been painted with the number *1* on it in all sorts of colorful puff paint designs. She wore short athletic shorts made of floral fabric, with long tube socks every color of the rainbow. Her hair was up in two curly pigtails and secured with the puffiest scrunchies I'd ever seen.

Sassy sat on the bed wearing a vest painted in the same design as Imogen's shirt. Esis immediately hopped off my shoulder and jumped on the bed next to Sassy.

My eyes scanned the room. It was more colorful than the last time I'd been in here. Pink polka-dotted curtains now covered the window, and blue string lights had been twisted inside purple tule that was draped high along the walls. The bright yellow bedspread her parents had given her over break covered the bed, and she'd hung two posters of runway models in God-awful outfits on either side of the window. Craft supplies scattered the floor in the corner, and I spotted the puff paints she'd used to decorate her shirt.

"I'm listening," she said as she began filling the tote bag I'd given her with various items. I couldn't read her tone.

"I came to apologize."

Imogen slowed as she gently placed a water bottle in her bag. She strolled over to the door like she hadn't heard me and swung it shut. She turned back toward me with her arms crossed. For a short girl like her, she could look pretty frightening when she wanted to. She gazed at me expectantly.

How did I put this into words? For one, I hated confrontation almost as much as my dad did— unless it was Haley. I lived for threatening that bitch. Two, I really didn't want to do this. But if I wanted Imogen back, it was my only choice.

"I'm sorry for what I said about you and Cade," I started with, picking at my nails.

Imogen raised her eyebrows. "Is that all?"

I contemplated it for a moment. "No. I'm sorry I've been a crappy friend lately."

I hadn't realized it was true until I said it out loud.

"The fight we had never should've happened in the first place," I continued. "You're my best friend, and I don't want to fight anymore."

Imogen's shoulders relaxed. "Me either."

"Can we put all this behind us?" I asked. "It's stupid anyway. Our friendship is stronger than arguing about a few boys."

Imogen smirked, like she couldn't argue with that. "I'm sorry, too,

Sophia. I shouldn't have said that thing about your Koigni pride. But... I kinda thought that's why you've been avoiding me."

"*Me?* Avoiding *you?*"

I paused for a second.

"Okay," I caved. "I guess that's kind of true. I'm just sick of it. I want to sit by you in Ancient Familiars again and have lunch with you and hang out with you to do our homework and all of that."

Imogen smiled. "Me, too."

"So, we're good?" I asked. "We can put all this petty stuff behind us?"

Imogen looked up at me with sad eyes, then nodded. "Yeah, we're good."

Then she threw her arms around me and drew me into a hug. I knew then that she'd forgiven me.

"Besides," she said as she pulled away, "you were kind of right."

"I was? About what?"

Imogen plopped down on the bed. "About letting Cade walk away. I thought about what you said, and I think you were right. I should've fought for him."

I sat beside her. "You still can. It's not like him and Mallory are getting married or anything."

"Oh, ancestors!" Imogen cried, throwing her hands over her face. "Don't put that image in my mind."

I laughed, and she dropped her hands to reveal a smile on her face.

"What have you been up to lately?" she asked. "I feel like I've missed so much."

I blushed so deeply I could feel my face heating. "Yeah, you have. I met Mia."

Imogen's jaw dropped dramatically. "The bitch Liam used to date?"

I nodded as disgust fell over my face. "She's horrible. I don't know how Liam could've ever dated her."

Imogen cupped her boobs and wiggled her eyebrows at me.

I swatted her. "Yeah, yeah. I saw them. Her boobs are huge. I swear to the ancestors that has to be it, because her personality sucks."

Imogen laughed. "Well, it doesn't matter much anyway, does it? I mean, Liam's with you now."

I shrugged. "Yeah, but she'll always be a part of his life. You don't really forget about the person who took your virginity."

Imogen lowered her voice and leaned into me. "Speaking of which...?"

I blushed an even deeper shade of red. "God, no! Imogen."

"But something *did* happen!" she accused, pointing to my face like it gave it all away. Which it totally did. Her eyes widened, and her mouth formed into a perfect O.

I bit my lower lip. "Let's just say Liam knows what the hell he's doing."

Imogen snickered and threw her body onto the bed face-down. She laughed into the comforter, then lifted her head to say, "Oh, my ancestors, Sophia. You didn't! How'd you two even get into each other's dorms unnoticed?"

My face pulled into such a huge smile that my cheeks hurt. "Um... we didn't. The first time was in a supply closet."

Imogen's eyes got even bigger, which I didn't think was possible. "Oh, lord! *The first time?*"

I nodded. Meanwhile, Esis and Sassy where playing a game of *catch the other one's tail.*

"The second time was in the Commons," I admitted.

Imogen's nose curled up. "Ew, Sophia. People sit on those couches."

"That's what I said!"

Imogen laughed so hard that she had to clutch her stomach. "Girl, I'd beg you to tell me all the details, but I'm actually headed down to the courtyard to play soccer with Jonah. You wanna come?"

"I didn't know you played soccer."

"Oh, this is Elementai Soccer. Believe me, it's nothing like you've ever seen before."

"Elementai Soccer? Do you play with your elements or something?" I asked.

Imogen sat up straight. "Yep. And your Familiars. It's like regular soccer, but with a few tweaks to the rules. An Elementai can't touch the ball except with their element. Familiars can do whatever they want with the ball, and you can tackle anyone on the field, Familiar or Elementai."

"Sounds fun... except..." I glanced to Esis, who was trying to wrestle Sassy to the mattress and failing miserably. "I'd probably light the ball on fire, and Esis would get trampled."

Imogen shrugged. "You can still come watch."

"What if I get bored?"

"Draw or something," Imogen suggested. "I know you love art."

I smiled at the idea. "I don't have anything to draw with."

Imogen stood and dug in the top drawer of her dresser. "I got these for Christmas and never used them. Here you go." She handed me a sketch pad and a box of colored pencils.

"Thank you. I guess I'll come along and root for your team."

Imogen finished packing her bag and swung it over her shoulder. I followed behind her into the hall. Sassy jumped of the bed to follow, forgetting completely that Esis was on her back. He held tight to her tail for support. I scooped him up before he could fall off, and he pressed his paws to the side of his face like he was dizzy.

"Do you and Jonah have a team name?" I asked.

"The Glitter— I mean, um... our soccer team is the Unicorn Force."

"Unicorn Force," I repeated. "Sounds cool."

Imogen smiled proudly. "Just wait til you see us play."

WHEN WE MADE it down to the courtyard, we found Jonah, Ezra, and Liam standing in a wide and open grassy area. There were a few other people on the far end of the clearing, but it was pretty quiet this morning. The weather was nicer than it'd been lately. It almost felt like spring. Ezra was stroking a big yellow bird on his shoulder, while Jonah rolled a soccer ball from one hand to the other. Squeaks' eyes bounced back and forth in her skull as she watched the ball. Liam was just chilling with his hands in his pockets, talking to the two of them. His eyes lifted and caught mine, and my heart flipped in my chest. The things he'd done to me last night flashed through my memory, sending heat to pool between my thighs.

Damn, I wanted him again.

When the boys saw us coming, they waved. Relief crossed their faces when they saw Imogen and I were together. It was obvious we'd made up.

"Hey, Im!" Jonah called when we stopped beside them.

Esis jumped out of my arms and hopped up on Squeaks' rear, smacking her butt until she started spinning around in a circle.

"Hey, Soph," Liam said, knocking his shoulder into mine and smirking proudly. He was still thinking about last night, too. I could tell.

"I recruited a few people," Jonah said, gesturing to Ezra and Liam. "Cade should be here shortly."

Imogen's eyes lit up, until Jonah added, "And his girlfriend."

He realized what he'd said a second too late as a disappointed look crossed Imogen's face. "Hey, Im," he said to distract her. "Do you want to do the honors?" He gestured to either end of the unmarked playing field.

That got Imogen to smile. She handed Jonah her bag and said, "Gladly."

I didn't know what they were talking about until Imogen aimed her hands at the ground. A good thirty yards away from us toward the front of the castle, grass began to grow high out of the ground. It wove together, creating a dome-like structure. As she started on an identical structure on the other end of the courtyard, I realized she was creating the goal posts. While she worked on them, I spotted Vanessa coming down the front steps and making her way over to us with Aisha at her side.

"Hey, Sophia. Do you guys need another teammate? I'm always up for a good game of soccer," Vanessa said.

I glanced to Jonah. "Um, I'm not sure. I'm not going to play. Just here to draw." I held up the sketchpad and pencils Imogen had given me.

"Hey, the more the merrier," Jonah said. "But only if you join my team. Dragons are rad."

Vanessa's eyes brightened. It was like it'd been years since someone asked her to be on their team. I felt bad for her.

"Not fair," Ezra complained. "So I'm stuck with a couple Familiarless teammates and a hamster." He stuck his finger in Esis's direction.

"Excuse you, jackass!" I snapped.

Liam's hand snapped over his mouth, stifling a laugh.

"He happens to be a..." I almost said *kurble*, but I caught myself before I could announce to the whole world our little secret. "A very good Familiar, thank you very much."

"I don't care whose team I'm on," Vanessa said with a shrug.

Ezra pushed past Jonah and draped an arm over Vanessa's shoulder. "You can be on my team, beautiful. Then after we win, we can celebrate with—"

"Hold up there, cupid." Vanessa ducked out from under his arm. "I'm engaged."

Ezra looked horrified. "Whoa. I'm *so* sorry."

Vanessa only laughed. "I'm flattered, but no."

Liam and I exchanged a glance and tried not to lose it. Watching his brother get shot down was definitely a new one.

"In fact, there's my fiancé now." Vanessa waved to Bren, who'd just stepped out of the castle and looked like he was searching for someone. His chimera was following. He relaxed when he caught sight of her. She gestured for him to join us.

"Okay," Jonah said, calling everyone's attention. "We're just waiting on a few more people. Let's split up into teams. I've already claimed Imogen and Vanessa. Liam, you game?"

Liam shook his head. "Nah, I think I'll sit out with Sophia."

Jonah rolled his eyes. "Come on, man. You two can fool around— I mean, hang out— anytime."

Liam shot him a death glare for slipping up in front of everyone. It wouldn't have mattered with just Jonah, Imogen, and Ezra around, but Vanessa and Bren didn't know about us— and we didn't intend for them to. Luckily, they didn't seem to catch his meaning.

Nearby, Ezra was eyeing up Bren's chimera. The thing looked terrifying at first glance, but the expression on each of its three heads suggested it was a gentle creature unless provoked. It suited Bren well. He was tall and muscular, the kind of guy who could snap you like a twig, but had a sweet, caring smile.

"Soccer," Bren said when he finally reached us. "Sounds like fun."

"Hey, dude," Ezra greeted, extending his hand. "Looks like I'm your team captain."

Jonah groaned.

"Hey, you got the dragon," Ezra said. "Seems only fair. Besides, you already have three Familiars on your team."

Jonah sighed. "Fair enough. Do you want Cade or Mallory when they get here? They're both unbonded."

"Cade," Ezra said without hesitation.

Jonah grumbled. "Why'd I let you take first pick?"

I glanced back up toward the castle to see a guy with broad shoulders and dark hair coming out the door. Mallory wasn't by Cade's side, but someone else was.

The creature was the size of a cheetah and was red, yellow, and green in color, with spiral patterns and polka-dots in its fur. It looked like a cross between a canine and a feline, with big, pointed ears, large paws, and a fluffy tail. Its eyes reminded me of sapphires ringed in an emerald green. It had large, feathery wings on its back, and its shoulders rolled as it walked.

Imogen went completely still as her eyes locked on Cade and the creature walking at his side. She looked entranced by both of them.

Ezra's jaw dropped. "Whoa, my man! Did you bond?"

Cade beamed as he reached us. "I did. Just yesterday."

"What *is* it?" Vanessa asked in wonder.

"It's an *alebrije*," Imogen answered, unable to take her eyes off the creature.

"Yep," Cade said proudly, petting its head. "Her name's Arabelle."

Sassy padded over to Arabelle and stretched up her nose to sniff her. Arabelle sniffed back, then licked Sassy on the end of her nose. They seemed to like each other.

"*Alebrije?*" Jonah repeated, butchering the name. "I've never heard of them before."

"They're rare around these parts," Imogen said. "They originate from Mexico and can come in all different shapes. Professor Rodriguez is bonded to one that has a dragon's body, lion's head, and owl wings. And it's just as colorful as Arabelle. Of course, you'd know that if you paid attention to anything besides dick, Jonah." Imogen stepped forward and let Arabelle sniff her hand, like she hadn't just given Jonah the biggest burn of the morning.

Jonah placed a hand on his hip and snapped his fingers. "Hey. No one says that's a bad thing."

"I say that's a bad thing," Liam joked.

"Ha ha," Jonah said dryly. "We gonna do this thing or not?"

"Yeah, let's do this!" Vanessa clapped.

"Hey, Cade," Jonah said. "Where's the girlfriend?"

"Oh, um..." Cade dropped his gaze to Arabelle. "She's actually not my girlfriend anymore."

Imogen froze the same time my eyebrows shot up. *Now's your chance, Im!*

"Oh, she's not?" Imogen asked innocently, scratching Arabelle behind the ears, which the *alebrije* seemed to like. "What happened?"

Cade bent to one knee and joined Imogen in scratching Arabelle behind the ears. Their fingers touched, and I saw them both shoot apart like they'd been electrocuted. Liam and I exchanged a glance. He'd totally noticed, too.

"Arabelle bit Mallory," he admitted.

"Oh, no." Imogen drew in a breath of surprise, but it sounded fake. I could tell she was thrilled by the news.

"Which wouldn't have been a big deal," Cade said, "if Mallory hadn't slapped Arabelle right afterward."

This time, Imogen's intake of breath was genuine. I also gasped, my eyes widening in horror. I couldn't imagine harming someone else's Familiar.

Cade shrugged. "I guess it just wasn't meant to be. Arabelle seems to like you, though." He winked at Imogen, and she went bright red.

"Yeah, well, she probably knows I'd never slap her," Imogen said.

Cade shot her a charming smile. "And that's one of the things that makes you so great."

"Okay, love birds." Jonah stepped between them. "We're losing daylight here. Cade, you're with Ezra. Imogen, you're with me. Squeaks and the chimera..." Jonah looked to Bren for his name.

"Kingston," Bren replied.

"Right." Jonah nodded. "Squeaks and Kingston will kick off. Everyone good with the rules?"

Everyone spread out to take their places on the field, while Liam and

I headed to sit on the front steps near a lion statue to watch. Esis looked around the field in confusion when I called his name, like he was trying to figure out which position to play.

"Esis," I called more sternly. "I don't want you getting hurt. We'll just watch."

He slumped over to me in disappointment.

"Why aren't you playing?" Liam asked. He sat beside me on the stone steps so closely that our legs touched. My skin heated there. I worried I might burn a hole through my jeans.

I shrugged. "I'm not really one for contact sports. I'd rather draw. And I really don't want Esis getting squashed out there."

"Pft." Liam waved his hand like it was nothing. "He'll be fine."

Esis scurried around in front of us, gathering clumps of grass, though I had no idea what for. Out in the field, Jonah gave a command, and Squeaks immediately kicked the ball. It rolled between Kingston's legs before Squeaks tripped over her own feet and face-planted into the ground. Sassy was on it a moment later, using her nose to roll it toward the goal. It looked like Jonah was using his Air power to push it along.

About halfway to the goal, Ezra's thunderbird dropped from the sky and grabbed Sassy between his talons. I gasped.

"Relax," Liam said. "Sassy and Dyami won't hurt each other."

Cade used his Earth power to create a slope in the dirt, which the ball rolled up, then promptly started in the other direction. Kingston rushed for the ball and kicked it. It went flying across the field toward the goal, but Squeaks jumped in front of the goal just in time, spreading her wings out to stop the ball. It made a loud smacking noise as it bounced off her wings. Aisha kicked the ball, then Arabelle intercepted it, sending it back in Squeaks' direction. Dyami swooped down and grabbed the ball in his talons and carried it over the field.

"Can they do that?" I asked Liam.

He smirked. "Anything's fair game as long as an Elementai doesn't touch the ball."

I was starting to like the Hawkei's version of soccer.

Dyami let go of the ball just in time for it to soar into the goal. Squeaks tried to stop it, but she missed. Ezra, Bren, and Cade cheered.

On the ground below Liam and me, Esis had finished twisting his dry pieces of grass together. He held them up like pompoms and jumped up and down like a cheerleader. I snickered. He was just so darn cute.

As the game continued, Esis cheered for everyone, no matter which team they were on. I opened up my sketchbook to draw the scene before me.

"You didn't tell me you could draw," Liam said after a while.

"Oh," I looked up from the sketchpad and set down the green colored pencil in my left hand. "I don't really. Imogen gave these to me. But I figured if cameras weren't allowed at Orenda, I could at least document the moment somehow."

"Yeah, it's a dumb rule," Liam said, scrunching up his nose.

"I don't know. I guess I get it. The Hawkei would have a problem if people were posting pictures of their Familiars all over the internet."

Liam smirked. "It wouldn't be the first time. Luckily they're usually written off as hoaxes, but some college kids ruined it for the rest of us a few years back by posting pictures of dragons on social media."

"That's why only grads get phones and cameras?" I asked.

"Yeah," Liam said. "Apparently, we're not trustworthy enough to handle it until we have a piece of paper in our hands." He rolled his eyes.

"If I had a camera, I wouldn't share any of the pictures with anyone. I'd just want it for myself, you know? My dad used to have this really fancy camera he let me use when I would go hiking back home. I kind of got into photography for a while, but I had to give it up when I came to Orenda."

Liam dropped his gaze, looking sad. "I'm sorry."

"Don't be. It's no big deal."

Liam leaned forward and rested his elbows on his knees. "But you gave up so much to come here. I didn't realize you'd given up all your hobbies, too."

"Well, not *all* of them," I pointed out. "I still get to go hiking all the time. And I've picked up new ones. You know, like doing your homework."

Liam snorted. "Not that I want you to *stop* doing that, Sophia, but that's not exactly a hobby. You need to do something besides schoolwork. Get out and relax a little."

I nudged him with my elbow. "There's always hanging out with you."

He smiled. "Again, not a hobby, though I'd like to do more of that."

We weren't just talking about *hanging out*, either.

"I don't know," I said with a shrug. "I hang out with Imogen, too. You know, before we fought. Which is over now, by the way."

"Eating dinner and doing homework are not hobbies," Liam said sternly.

"I could say the same thing about sleeping." I shot him a teasing glance.

He smirked playfully. "Fair enough, but I have hobbies."

"Right. Basket weaving," I said like I'd just remembered.

He wrinkled his nose at me. "Don't go announcing that to the whole world, all right, *pawee?*"

"It's not like it's embarrassing, Liam. I'm sure Jonah's hobbies are *way* more embarrassing than that."

"Jonah's hobbies are..." Liam stared out into the field, where Jonah was getting issued a foul for touching the ball. "I don't even want to picture some of that shit."

I threw my head back and laughed. "No, let's not. That's probably for the best."

The game was back in session moments later. Somehow, Jonah had negotiated his way out of a penalty. The ball flew around the field on its own accord— literally, like Jonah was using his Air magic to make it float.

Cade threw up a wall of dirt to block the ball from his team's goal, and it bounced in the opposite direction. Bren threw a fireball at it, which gave it an extra boost so that Arabelle could kick it toward the goal. Aisha intercepted it and smacked the ball hard with her good wing, sending it back toward the other end of the field. Ezra ran in front of the ball to block it from their goal— which was totally against the rules— but he never reached it before Imogen sprang out of nowhere and tackled him. The ball rolled into the net, earning Jonah's team another point.

Imogen quickly hopped up from the ground and dusted herself off, but Ezra stayed put, his face buried in the crook of his elbow. My stomach sank. Liam and I both shot to our feet, realizing at the same time that something was wrong. Liam rushed out onto the field, and I dropped my coloring supplies and scooped up Esis to follow behind him.

Imogen's hands shot over her face as she apologized profusely.

Liam knelt down beside his brother and placed a hand on his shoulder. The rest of the field had gone silent.

"You okay, Ez?" Liam asked gently.

Ezra lifted his head and sucked a deep breath. "Twisted my knee on the way down."

Esis squirmed in my arms, but I held on to him firmly.

"You're going to have to sub in for me, bro." Ezra clapped Liam on the shoulder.

"Uh, your team would be better off without me. I'm kinda crippled," Liam said sarcastically.

"You look fine to me," Bren said, not realizing what Liam went through on a daily basis.

Liam cringed. I could tell the statement bothered him. If I didn't hang out with him all the time, I wouldn't know he was sick, either. He looked perfectly healthy on the outside.

"Come on," Vanessa encouraged. "It'll be fun."

"Yeah, bro," Ezra said as he got to his feet. "Loosen up for once. It'll be fine." He began hobbling away to the steps.

"Hey, Ez." Liam rushed to his brother to help support him.

Ezra held up his hand to stop him. "Nah, I've got this. You go play."

Liam looked over to me. "Fine. Only if Sophia plays on my team."

"Oh, Liam. I— I don't know."

"Come on, Soph." His eyes pleaded with me. "We're up against a hippogriff and a dragon. We need your help."

"Okay," I agreed, but I only did it because I could tell how much he didn't want to run around the field without me. "Just... everyone be careful with Esis. Don't trample him."

"Who would trample such an adorable creature?" Jonah said, wiggling his fingers at Esis like he was going to tickle him. Esis let out a half-scream, half-laugh, already preparing for it.

"Okay, let's go!" Bren called.

Esis jumped out of my arms, and I suddenly found myself running around the field totally unsure of what to do. I'd played soccer in gym class before, but this was like soccer on steroids. Vanessa's and Bren's fireballs whizzed by my head, and the ground rocked beneath my feet. Familiars moved so fast that I could hardly keep my eye on the ball. Like I said, I wasn't into contact sports. I was more of the hiking-biking-camping kind of girl.

But the more I got into it, the more fun I had. I threw a fireball at the ball a few times to send it in a different direction, and I tackled Imogen to the ground to keep her from using her Earth power on Liam. He pulled water up from the ground and shot a blast of it at the ball to send it into the goal— which he wasn't really supposed to do under Perot's orders. But that didn't seem to matter to him anymore these days. When he was playing, he had a huge smile across his face, like he was having the time of his life.

I was surprised to see that Esis was handling the game well. At one point, the ball was headed straight for him. I was afraid it would run him right over and flatten him like a cartoon character, but he scooped the ball up and held it above his head while he ran across the field. Sassy chased after him. It was the funniest thing I'd seen in my life, I swear.

By the time we finished and Jonah's team had won, I was sweating, and Liam's hair was stuck to his forehead. He draped an arm around me and leaned into me, almost squashing me.

He seemed really happy. But at the same time, he also looked... not good. I couldn't describe it, but I just had a feeling something was off with him. He stumbled, and I had to catch him.

"Liam!" I said in alarm. "Are you okay?"

He inhaled deep gulps of breath. "I'll be fine, *pawee*. The game was fun."

Except I could tell he felt like shit. It was probably the most he'd exerted himself all year.

"You're lying," I accused. "Liam, you need to eat something. You look really pale."

"Nah, I'll be fi—" Liam didn't finish his sentence before his eyes rolled back in his head and his knees buckled beneath him. I tried to catch him again, but he crumbled to the ground. It all happened so fast that I could barely process what was going on. One second he was standing there talking to me, and the next he was sprawled out in the grass.

"Help!" I cried. Panic rushed over me like an ocean wave. I completely choked up and had no idea what to do. I felt useless.

Everyone else looked up from where they were chatting at the other end of the field and quickly rushed toward us. Ezra rose from where he sat and limped our way.

After what felt like a lifetime later but must've only been a few seconds, Liam's eyes fluttered open. There was a moment where his eyes were completely blank, like he wasn't fully with me. Then he blinked a few times and looked at me.

"Fine," he finished. "I'll be fine."

"Liam, we should get you—" I started, but Ezra cut me off.

"Back to your dorm," he said, glancing at me.

Everyone else arrived just then and came to a stop beside Liam. Liam groaned, looking embarrassed.

Jonah held out a hand for everyone else to keep their distance, then bent down and helped Liam to his feet. "Ezra's right. You need to rest."

Liam blinked a few times, like he wasn't seeing straight. "Yeah... that's probably best."

I could catch the disappointment in his tone. I felt so bad for him.

Liam turned his head back to me. "Don't worry, *pawee*. These two will take care of me."

"But Liam... I want to help."

"I know," he whispered. "But I gotta give Ez and Jonah hell. You go have fun. Celebrate."

"But we didn't even win," I countered.

"It's okay. I enjoyed myself anyway." He shook his head, then his cloudy eyes cleared as he realized something. "Oh, Sophia. I forgot to give you this." Liam reached into his pocket and handed me a small piece of folded paper.

I reached for Liam's arm to help support him, but Ezra cut in before I could and looped his arm under Liam's. Jonah basically supported both of them.

I glanced at the paper he'd given me. By the time I looked up, Liam was already on the move again. Esis scurried up to me and gazed up at the piece of paper, then looked to Liam. Imogen placed a comforting hand on my shoulder, but she didn't say anything.

"What's up with him?" Bren asked as he gestured at Liam, genuinely concerned. Nobody said anything, because nobody really knew what to say.

"Um... come on, hun. Let's play another game," Vanessa suggested. She could tell I didn't really want to talk about it.

Bren and Vanessa started up another round of soccer, this time two-player. I was left standing alone with Imogen.

"Why don't you think he wants my help?" I asked Esis softly.

Esis looked at me with sad eyes. Even if he could talk, I didn't need the answer. I already knew why Liam pushed me away. He didn't want to trouble me with his illness. He thought he was a burden. Which kind of hurt me, because no matter what he went through, I wanted to be there for him.

"What's that?" Imogen asked.

Sighing, I turned back to the note in my hand. I unfurled the ripped piece of paper and began to read his scribbled handwriting.

You. Me. Next Friday night. Wear a dress.

A smile touched my lips. Liam wasn't pushing me away. He was asking me on a date.

THIRTEEN

I wish I could say what happened that week, but I was in and out of it so often that I honestly couldn't remember much.

I passed out a few more times. I slept a lot. I missed a lot of class.

By the end of the week, I was feeling better and more like myself again, but it was kinda scary to think about all the stuff I'd spaced out on. I'd literally been walking around like a zombie all week. My clearest memory went back to the day of the soccer game before it blanked out.

Playing soccer with everyone had been so much fun. I really missed doing stuff like that. I wanted to be active again. But the whole reason I'd sat out in the first place was because I worried something bad could happen. It should've been fine for me to play, but I pushed myself too hard, and I embarrassed myself, again.

I didn't want to be Superman. I just wanted to do the same stuff everyone else could.

But something else worried me. Last semester, I would've been able to play a game of soccer just fine. After all, the tournament was ten times worse than that, and I'd gotten along mostly okay until the end.

I knew what it meant. I was getting worse.

The first week of March I got another letter delivered by Baxtor from Perot. I headed down to his office hoping he'd have something other than disappointment to offer me this time.

Perot seemed somber. "Sit down, Liam."

I did as he said, and he immediately launched into business without messing around, which I liked. "As far as the data shows, you're in the clear to begin using magic. It seems that your element has a different effect on you than what I thought."

"So I can use my element again?" I said. Not that I'd been following the rules much— I'd been cheating the past week or so.

Perot nodded. "Yes. But be aware it's more or less poisoning your-self. Your magic is hurting you, but it's clear that *not* using it harms you more severely in the short term. It's a case of you having to use the very thing that's killing you slowly, to keep yourself alive."

"That's typical." I crossed my arms. "So if I can't stop using the thing that's killing me, how do we get closer to figuring out how to offset the symptoms?"

I didn't want to say *find a cure*. I wasn't that optimistic.

"We need to find a way to replace the magic that's being drained," Perot says. "Though I'm not sure that's possible. You can't exactly trans-fuse magic. It's not something that's transferable." Perot rubbed his face. "Not since the days of Anichi, anyway."

"What do you mean?" I asked.

"That's how they used to heal. Anichi transferred their powers into the bodies of their patients, and the patient's own systems would be bolstered by the magic, using the Spirit element to heal itself." He shook his head. "That's impossible for anyone that isn't from the Soul House."

"Aren't there other magical races that can heal?" I asked.

"Yes, but their powers are different from ours. They wouldn't be able to help you, Liam. Our magic comes from Spirit, and Spirit is what your body needs to repair itself."

Perot looked different than he ever had. He seemed... sad. "Liam, I want to tell you something. This is difficult for me to say, as you've become rather like a son to me since we've started these sessions. I know you're young, but I'd advise you to start thinking of..."

Perot dropped off. It felt like every organ in my body— heart, lungs, everything— stopped working then.

"Just say it," I said. "I can take it."

Perot's voice was heavy. "The data is clear. Your organs are failing, Liam. Every system. And I don't know how to fix it."

That was like a punch to the gut. My head went kind of foggy. It was hard to hear what Perot was saying as he continued.

"There's been a lot of damage already, and it's only getting worse. If we can't find a way to stop the deterioration... there's no way to repair what's already been done... I'm sorry..."

He kept saying he was sorry. I wanted him to stop. It was like he was talking through a fishbowl, or far away. It was hard to comprehend. I heard his words in disconnected sentences. "What?"

"I'm saying you might want to get your affairs in order," Perot said gently. "Just in case it doesn't work out. I'm not sure how much time you have. Months. A year, maybe."

I'd said a similar thing to Sophia at the start of the year. *Just in case it doesn't work out.*

Sophia.

I stood up. My legs were wobbling. "Thank you for trying to help me, Professor." I headed for the door. It was like I was drunk.

"I'm not giving up yet, Liam!" Perot called after me, but it barely registered. My mind was too busy frantically whirling with what I was gonna do.

As I left the room, it felt like my head was buzzing with a hive of bees. My head kept jumping from place to place. I didn't know what to do.

Maybe I wouldn't need to bring Nashoma back after all. What was the point? He'd just die again right after I did, which, according to Perot, wasn't going to be much longer.

Fuck, how was I gonna tell my family?

How was I gonna tell *Sophia?*

Fuck yeah, I was scared. I didn't want to die. But what nobody told you about dying was that leaving the people you loved behind was the worst part of it. I wasn't ready to be without them. And I knew they weren't ready to be without me.

I didn't really know where I was gonna go, but my legs carried me to the Toaqua dorms. I saw my brother sitting on the couch with Dyami perched on his knees, laughing at a joke somebody told him. It was early, so there weren't that many people in here.

Seeing Ez fucking killed me. What was I gonna say to him?

Ezra was smiling. He was having a good day. He'd always been such a cheery kid. Kinda dumb, yeah, but the guy had a heart bigger than California. The news would crush him.

I decided then. I'd keep it quiet from my family, for now. When stuff started getting really bad, I'd tell them the bad news. But I didn't want them to worry right now. There was no need for it.

"Liam, hey," Ezra said, and he got off the couch. Dyami went fluttering into the air and landed on a nearby perch. His friends went off to swim in the pool, leaving us isolated on the other side of the room. "I got a problem."

It physically fucking hurt to look at him. "What is it?" I asked in a leadened tone.

He took it as my usual pissed-off-ness and didn't notice. "Well, I like Marina, and she's really sweet, but I like Kaida, too, and she's so funny. And they're both pretty hot. Thing is, they're jealous. I promised them I'd take them both out for a date on Saturday, but I forgot, so now I've gotta let one of them down. Which one do *you* like better?"

I wished I could be like Ezra, where my biggest problem was which girl to take out on a Saturday. I rolled my eyes. "I swear to the ancestors, I don't know where you get this obsession with girls from."

"You tell me. Sophia sounded like she liked it when you guys were getting it on in the Commons." Ezra grinned.

My face turned fucking red. "What the fuck? How do you know about that?"

"I walked in on you guys."

"That was *you?*" I said, recalling the loud noise from that night.

"Hey, I'm the least of your worries," Ezra said, throwing his hands up. "You should be glad it was me and not somebody else."

I guess that was true, but it was still embarrassing that it had been my little brother. My tone turned suspicious. "Hey... what were you doing out so late that night, anyhow?"

"It was a Friday night. Everybody stays up late," he said.

"Sure," I said. I bet he'd been coming from or going to the same thing me and Sophia had been doing. Hypocrite.

"Relax. I'm not going to tell anyone." Ezra leaned in. "So, was it good?"

"Shut up." I shoved his face away. Ezra laughed.

He then turned serious. "Oh, uh, by the way... Mom wants you to bring Sophia over. Tonight, for dinner. We're celebrating me bonding, but she made it clear she wants Sophia there."

"What? No," I said immediately. "Why?"

"You tell me." Ezra shrugged. "She says it's because she wants to get to know your tournament partner better, but if that were really true, she'd invite Jonah and Imogen, too. I personally think she suspects something."

"You didn't tell her anything, did you?"

"Me? No." He shook his head, then paused. "Unless Maddie said something to her."

"That has to be it," I said under my breath. Madeline and her stupid visions. I hoped to the ancestors Maddie's magic hadn't shown my innocent little sister anything too explicit.

But I hardly thought Mom needed her prophetic daughter to tell her anything. Mom was the type of person who knew everything, didn't matter what tribe you were from. She was friends with everybody, including the professors at Orenda, and therefore always heard news first and had the best gossip.

Mom also ruled the house. Bringing Sophia over was definitely not a request.

"Fine," I grumbled. "I'll bring her. Is Dad gonna be there?"

"Yeah. You'd better hope to the ancestors he doesn't find out about you two," Ezra said. "Let's just pray *he* doesn't walk in on you."

"You wanna see him blow his fucking top? Because I don't," I said. "I'm not stupid enough to screw around at home."

"Can't say I would blame you. Sophia is *sexy*." Ezra nodded in approval. "She's going to be the hottest sister-in-law ever."

"Do you ever stop talking?"

The room wavered again. I reached out and put a hand on the wall to steady myself.

"You okay?" Ezra's brows knitted together.

"I'm gonna go lie down," I mumbled, and I moved around Ez to go to my room. I laid on my back on my bed and formed a water ball out of what had been left sitting in a glass, then weaved it above me, making it churn and form into different shapes, tossing it from one hand to the other. I used to do this for hours when I'd gotten my powers. It helped me think.

Perot said I was dying. Not something I didn't know, but also, I didn't know I was dying so quickly. He said I had a year, at most. I was twenty-one years old. How could I have less than a year to live?

Did it change things when it came to the Toaqua Elders and their plot to murder Sophia?

No. It didn't change a damn thing. It didn't matter if I was dead or not. If they thought Sophia was the prophesied one, they'd find someone else to take her out after I was gone. And the next person might not be so reluctant to do what they asked.

I wouldn't be around to protect her. Which meant I needed to do what I could, now, and find a way to convince the Toaqua Elders I was committed to this thing— committed to killing her if I couldn't prove her innocence.

I had to buy her some time with what little time I had left. Fuck, how was I supposed to do that?

One thing was for sure. If I didn't have long, I didn't want to lie around in this bed all day and wait to die. I forced myself to get up and take a shower, because I hadn't earlier, and got ready to go find Sophia. I found myself playing with the droplets in the shower. Hadn't done that in a while.

We'd talked about meeting in the Nivita gardens yesterday, which was the one thing I did remember, thank the ancestors. By the time I got out there, it was nearly noon. I hoped I hadn't kept Sophia waiting for too long. It was a gorgeous day, hot for March. Spring was finally coming back to Northern California.

The Nivita gardens were beautiful and filled with every type of flower, including hedges shaped in the sculptures of various magical creatures. One large hedge in particular in the shape of a tree was in the center of the garden, surrounded by a huge maze. It was ironic that there was a plant sculpted in the shape of another plant out here, but hey, it wasn't my garden.

There were a lot of Nivita in the garden with their creatures, tending the plants and playing with their Familiars. The garden was loaded with butterflies of all sizes, some small, and some almost as big as a small child. They terrified some people, but I didn't have a problem with insects, so I just moved around them.

I remembered that Sophia and I had our second kiss out here during the Elemental Ball and smiled. That'd been a nice memory.

I spotted Jonah and Imogen before I did Sophia. They'd built some sort of wooden runway and were ordering Squeaks and Sassy to walk back and forth on it, changing various outfits every time they got to the end.

But they weren't the only ones. Jonah was also changing outfits, and was prancing up and down the stage like it was his personal walkway. People in the garden pointed and stared, but fuck them. At this point, it'd started to become a compliment for the Reject Team.

My eyes searched the garden for Sophia. I found her in front of the stage, a textbook and a bunch of papers gathered around her as she sat cross-legged in the grass. She'd worn a dress like I'd asked, a pretty blue one that looked really nice on her. It got me excited that she'd worn one just for me. I couldn't wait to get to *that* later.

Esis kept on pointing to various pictures in the book she was reading, but she shook her head each time. He looked frustrated.

She hadn't noticed me yet. I pictured her face when I told her the news that I was dying, and how it'd fall apart.

I couldn't keep this to myself. It was too hard. Fuck, it felt like I was gonna explode just carrying it around. Or wither away inside. I just wanted the whole world to know without me having to explain it to them.

When I caught her eye, I knew I couldn't lie to her. This was too big a burden for me to shoulder by myself. I wasn't even that strong. I wanted to tell her. And I knew I needed to.

But not today. I'd put it off today. I wanted to forget and be happy.

I sat next to her on the grass. "Hey," I said. I nudged her, and she looked up. Her confused expression instantly cleared.

"Hi," she said. "I'm glad to see you. I worried you weren't coming."

"I'm feeling fine today," I said, already knowing what she was getting at. I pointed at her papers. "What's with that? It's our day. No homework, remember?"

"I know." She stroked Esis' ears back, and he grumbled. "But this project's due next week, and I haven't even started."

That wasn't like her to be behind. I went to ask her what was up, before I heard exaggerated arguing above us.

"Jonah, just put it on," Imogen said, waving a really ugly scarf his way.

He shook his head. "Nah, hun. Purple's my color. Red's my color. Mauve is most definitely *not* my color."

"What are you guys doing?" I asked.

"I have to do a project for my Hawkei Fashion Design and Merchandising class, so I chose a runway show," Imogen said, turning to me.

"And I'm the star, *obviously*," Jonah put in. "We're practicing."

"But it's my grade, so you should do as I say," Imogen put in.

Jonah took his hair out of his man bun and shook it. "Then you should pay me more, darling."

"I'm not paying you anything!"

"You guys will work it out." Sophia dug around in a picnic basket by her side. "We packed a lunch. You hungry, Liam?"

I shook my head. I didn't want to eat. I threw up everything that I took down lately if it wasn't water or toast.

Jonah and Imogen came off the stage, and Sophia distributed sandwiches. Esis took three for himself and sucked them down in seconds before he gave a few to Squeaks and Sassy. Imogen argued with Jonah about the fashion show, and he argued back with a full mouth. I kept watch on the other people in the garden and played with the strands of Sophia's hair when nobody was looking.

Sophia kept working throughout lunch until she slammed her book shut and said, "Ugh! I hate this! Somebody kill me."

My stomach lurched, though it'd only been a joke. Jonah swallowed his fifth sandwich and said, "I could try to oblige, but it probably wouldn't work out."

"I don't think there's a murder weapon lying around you could use," Sophia joked back.

"Not like that. There are lots of ways an Elementai can kill people," Imogen said.

"Ooh." Sophia wiggled her eyebrows. "Tell me. I totally love those crime shows on TV. This is like, way better."

My friends were fucking morbid. Nothing like having a fashion show and then discussing murder in excessive detail.

"Well, Koigni have it easiest, obviously, because they can just burn you to death, and Nivita can crush you and strangle you with roots, but Toaqua and Yapluma can *get away* with it," Jonah said.

"How so?" Sophia asked.

"Well, a Yapluma can take all the air from your lungs and suffocate you. But it's really hard to do. Not a lot of Yapluma are able to, you know, because of the natural magic that flows through an Elementai's veins that protects them," Jonah said. "Toaqua are the same way. They can make all the water in your blood rush to your heart. It's quick and painless, but most Water Elementai can't harness enough energy to fight against the body's natural impulses, and, if the victim is magical, the magic that's naturally in the blood."

"It sounds hard. I understand why most Toaqua can't do it," Sophia said.

"Liam can," Jonah said, and I cringed. "He used to do it all the time when we were hunting with his dad. Kill animals quickly after we shot them, so they wouldn't suffer."

"Liam, you're really talented," Sophia said, almost in awe. I wished she wouldn't take it that way. The ability to kill someone easily was nothing to celebrate.

"Yeah, he is," Jonah said, with a side glance at me. "Good thing he's sick, otherwise, the rest of us would be in fucking trouble."

"I was made that way so the rest of you would have a fighting chance to keep up," I said. I couldn't resist giving a smirk.

Thankfully, Imogen and Jonah went back to what they had been doing after that, so we stopped talking about how to kill people. Sophia returned to her project, but now that the topic had been brought up, I couldn't get it out of my head.

If I had to do it... if the Toaqua Elders forced me to kill Sophia... that would be the way. I'd rush all the blood to her heart. She wouldn't even feel it. She'd be here one moment, and gone the next. I'd do it to her and Esis at the same time, so that neither one of them would know what was happening to the other, and they could go together.

I think if I had to stop Sophia's heart it would stop mine, too. Maybe... hopefully... my illness would kill me off before it got to that point.

Like I had that kind of luck.

Sophia kept on letting out impatient huffs, and Esis did the same whenever she did. This was getting annoying. I saw that the textbook was for Hawkei Careers. "Are you still having trouble with that class?"

"Yes." She slumped her shoulders. "I can't pick anything I want to do for the rest of my life. I'm going to fail."

"You're not." I took the book from her and closed it, tossing it aside. "How about you try talking about it instead?"

"I feel like I should just know." She put her head in her hand and looked at me. "How did you figure out what you wanted to do?"

"It was chosen for me," I started. "But it didn't really matter. Deep down, I always wanted to be chief. I don't really know what's left for me now, because that's impossible."

"So, what are you going to do now, since you can't be?" she asked.

It hurt to hear the question, because my automatic response was, *"No worries, I'll probably die before I graduate,"* but I forced out, "I'll go wherever Dad puts me. It doesn't matter where. I always wanted to serve the tribe."

"You deserve to be chief. You're a good leader. We wouldn't have made it through the tournament without you," Sophia said.

"Bullshit, you would've," I said.

"No we wouldn't have!" Jonah called back, overhearing us. Then he went back to shaking his ass. It looked like the runway session had turned into practice for a strip show. Squeaks and Sassy were copying him. Imogen looked like she was having a crisis.

There was something Sophia wasn't telling me. "I don't buy that you have no idea on what you want to do," I said. "Everybody has at least one small dream. Even if, apparently, it's to be a professional stripper like Jonah."

Sophia laughed aloud before her face became worried. "It's stupid."

"I won't think that it is."

She sighed and laid backward on the grass, throwing her arms over her head. "Okay. I haven't told anyone this, but all I really wanted to be since I was a kid was... well... a mom."

"Really?" I was surprised. "You don't seem like the barefoot and pregnant type."

She gave a half-hearted laugh. "That's because I hide it. I totally am."

She let out a huff, and Esis started braiding the hair that had fanned around her head. She kept talking, rambling now. "I can't imagine having a career because when I look into the future, all I see is me having kids. I always wanted this big family. I didn't really want to go to work, but not because I wanted to be lazy. I just wanted to stay home and raise children. But in this country, I didn't think it was possible. Families need two incomes to survive now. Unless I married a guy with a bajillion dollars, it's impossible." She sighed in frustration.

"I see." Sophia had given me a lot to think about.

"Is that dumb?" Her eyes searched me. Her expression was worried, like I was gonna judge her or something.

"No." I looked at her. "I don't think that it is."

Secretly, I thought that it was kind of hot. I'd always wanted a big family, too. When I was dating Mia, she was fine with staying home, but it was because she didn't want to work, not because she wanted to have a bunch of kids. She'd told me she'd have one child to fulfill the requirement to pass on the chief hood, and she was done. I'd been disappointed.

Mom had stayed home to raise us, and it was a good thing, too. Dad was so busy with the chief hood that he needed her help all the time. I didn't think our family, or the tribe, really, would've gotten along without her if she was busy working a job instead of helping my Dad. I'd wanted someone like her to be my wife. My mom meant a lot to me.

"You should do your project on being a stay-at-home parent. Really," I added as Sophia gave me a skeptical look. "Do it on how crucial children are to the tribe."

"I'll totally fail. You don't get paid for having kids," she said.

"No, but it's still important," I told her. "And you're not making any headway as it is. The project is due soon. You'll fail anyway if you don't turn anything in. What do you have to lose?"

She bit her lip and started up at the sky. "I guess you're right. Thanks, Liam, for helping."

"Anytime." Sophia could ask for my help whenever she wanted to. Even though I was Water and she was Fire, the closer we got to each other, the more perfect of a fit we seemed to be. Our values and what we wanted long-term out of life matched up. If we were from the same tribe, things would be so different.

But she wanted kids. Even if Perot managed to figure out a miracle cure and I survived, that was something we could never have. But that's the one thing she wanted out of life, to have a family. If she was with me, that couldn't happen.

Could I really take away her dream? That wasn't right.

So we just don't have kids. Simple, she'd said in the gardens last year, like it was.

No, Sophia. Not so simple. Was she really willing to give that all up for me? Man, she crazy-loved me.

Imogen was at her limit. "Stop, stop, stop," she said, bringing the fashion show to a screeching halt. "I need to redo some of these outfits. You ripped them, Jonah."

"Oops," Jonah said, looking at the hole in his pants he'd torn. "Sorry, baby cakes."

Imogen packed up her things and complained that the repairs would take her all afternoon. Jonah was going on about how there were tryouts for the school's college soccer team later. Sophia and I didn't have anything else to do before dinner, so we said we'd come watch. We made our way down the staircase so we could get to the soccer fields out back. We were interrupted when we ran into a group of people in the hallway that I never wanted to see again.

When Jonah saw them, he screeched to a halt. A vaguely disguised expression of horror flashed across his face before he quickly rearranged it into a pretend mask of happiness.

"Motherfucker," I muttered under my breath, and Sophia heard.

"Who's that?" Sophia whispered to me as a group of people approached.

"Jonah's family," I said back quickly, then kept my mouth shut as they stopped in front of us.

Jonah's parents were both short, barely five feet, very thin, and small. They wore clothes that boasted how expensive they were, and had equally tight and pinched faces that looked like they sucked on lemons for a living. His mother, Joyce, had a small monkey perched on her shoulder, while at his father Jacen's side walked a Tasmanian devil.

His sister Jenny was the same as they were. She had her hair cut short and couldn't have weighed more than a hundred and twenty pounds. Her girlfriend, Charity, was by her side and holding her hand dutifully. They looked like the perfect couple. Jenny had a wolverine at her feet, while Charity carried a tiny rabbit in her free arm.

Jacen and Joyce Chanee were the most self-important bigheads that I'd ever had the displeasure to meet. Why did these assholes have to show up here? Orenda was the one place Jonah could get away from them and their shitty influence.

Squeaks eyed them hatefully. She stood close with her body wrapped around Jonah and her wings posed at the ready, as if to fight them like she had Renar's Familiar, Alvarice.

Even though Jonah towered over all of them, he seemed to shrink five feet in their presence. "Hi Mom, hi Dad," he said weakly. "What's going on?"

"Where were you yesterday?" Jacen barked, without even a greeting. Jonah visibly cringed.

"I told you guys I had homework to do. I've been really busy with school," Jonah replied weakly.

"That's no excuse. I don't understand how you could do this to us. Since you've come to school you never visit." Joyce sniffed.

Jenny gave a grin that could make honey taste sour. "He probably thinks that he's better than us now, seeing since he won the Cup."

"I do not," Jonah mumbled meekly, but it was so small that you could hardly hear him.

"That's no excuse. You think you're so great now that you can abandon the family?" Jacen asked.

Though all of us were standing right there, his parents continued to yell at Jonah. They didn't even act like we were alive. My knuckles cracked. Sophia snaked her hand out to hold mine. Squeaks blocked it, so nobody could notice.

"We need you at home. There are things that need to get done," Jacen snapped. "You're coming with us."

Jonah was apprehensive. "But there's soccer tryouts today, and I kind of wanted to—"

"Didn't you hear me? You're needed," Joyce demanded. "Stop being so selfish and think of your family for once."

Jonah hunched his shoulders. It looked weird, such a big person trying to hide. "Oh, um... I guess it's okay," Jonah said. "I didn't really want to make the team, anyway."

I frowned. Jonah really wanted to play sports this year. He'd been going on about it all semester every time he had a chance to.

Jacen moved forward, as if to grab Jonah and pull him behind. "Don't make a scene. Let's go."

Squeaks let out a low sound, almost like a warning. Her tail was lashing. Jacen noticed and took a step back.

"I gotta go, guys," Jonah said, and he waved to us. "See you later."

At least he acknowledged us. Jonah followed his family with a hung head. It took everything I had to stand there and not have a total freak-out. Squeaks' hoof steps were loud and direct as she clopped behind Jonah, her beak at the ready.

Squeaks wouldn't let anything happen to him. It was still bullshit, though.

None of us really knew what to say. Imogen stood there with an armful of clothes, looking dazed, like she'd been punched in the face.

"I've gotta get this stuff done," Imogen said quietly, and she held up the pile of outfits she carried. "See you guys later."

Imogen headed off, Sassy at her heels.

Sophia dropped my hand and said, "*They're* Jonah's parents?"

"Yeah. Aren't they such great people?" I said sarcastically.

"But... but Jonah's so nice," Sophia said, not understanding.

"I know. He deserves better than them." I shook my head. "Don't bring it up to him later, okay? It'll just upset him."

"Okay," Sophia said quietly. She'd been holding Esis, who was still staring at the door Jonah had walked out of. "Well, I guess there goes our plans for the day."

"Not entirely," I said. "I've been meaning to tell you, my mom invited you over for dinner tonight."

"Dinner?" She raised an eyebrow. "Like, at your house? A Koigni in the middle of Toaqua tribe grounds?"

"I know, it's weird, but just go with it," I said. I pulled on the edge of her skirt and said, "Follow me. I have a surprise for you."

"A surprise?" she said. Esis' ears perked up in interest. I could totally read her tone.

"Stop being so horny," I said, and she laughed. "It's a different kind of surprise."

I took her near the Toaqua dorms, where there were a bunch of large pillars we could hide behind. I went back to my room and came back with a wrapped gift.

"I wanted to give you something," I said, handing it to her as I sat beside her on a stone bench. She took it, and Esis sniffed the wrapping paper.

"Are you going to stop buying me presents?" she asked, giving a coy look up.

"Never. Open it."

Esis did the work for her. The greedy bastard grabbed the paper and ripped before Sophia could even try to open it. It was a good thing, too. She was one of those annoying people that carefully took off the wrapping paper by the tape, piece by piece, just so she could reuse the paper.

"A camera!" Sophia lit up as Esis tossed the wrappings to the floor.

"Go ahead, take it out of the box," I encouraged.

I liked giving her presents. Her eyes sparkled as she opened the camera and examined it, putting on the matching extended lens.

"Holy guacamole, Liam," Sophia gushed. "This camera is crazy expensive. You had to have spent like, a grand on it."

"You're welcome. And please don't ever say *holy guacamole* again," I said.

"It's too much. I can't accept this," she said, handing it back.

"Take it." I pushed it toward her again. "It hardly put a dent in my savings."

I had a lot of money in there, and the tournament winnings only made it more cushy. Plus, the camera wasn't enchanted, or sabotaged, like the flowers had been. It'd just been a plain old camera. It was an actual gift, from me to her.

"Just be sure to keep it hidden," I said. "If the Elders find it, they'll go nuts."

"I'll be careful." Sophia put it into the matching case that I got for her. "I can't believe this. It's not even my birthday." The smile wouldn't leave her face. Esis took the camera out of the case and started playing with it, acting like he was some big shot photographer.

"It doesn't need to be your birthday or a holiday to get you something," I said, then as an afterthought, added, "Hey, what day *is* your birthday?"

The prophecy said something about it, but I forgot, because I tried to push that damn thing out of my mind as often as I could.

"June twenty-first," she said.

"What? No way. So is mine," I said, surprised.

"Really? That's so much fun. We have matching birthdays." Her smile got wider, before it fell. "Didn't... Nashoma die on your birthday?"

I sighed. "Yeah. Kinda ruined my birthday for the rest of my life." I gave a slight smile. "Now we can just celebrate yours instead. I like that better."

"No. We should celebrate it together this year," she offered, before adding, "If that would make it better?"

I nodded. "It totally would."

Summer was coming. It would be so much easier for us to be able to sneak around. We'd be able to hang out as much as we wanted.

"You wanna try it out?" I said, gesturing to the camera. "I charged it before I gave it to you, and I know the perfect spot."

"Sure." She took the camera away from Esis and put it back in the case. "Let's go."

We snuck out of the school. I took Sophia to a really thin trail that wound through the trees and had a lot of foliage we had to cross over. It was really reclusive, which meant no one would find us.

"It's so cool you know all these hidden trails," she said.

"I've spent my whole life exploring this place. I know where everything is," I told her.

The trail ended at a beach. There were a variety of large trees growing oranges by the shore, and they were full of rainbow-colored parrots that squawked in the trees. When they flew, they emitted light beams from their wings, which reflected off the water. Large sea turtles clustered around the seashore, their shells made of diamonds.

"Wow. This is incredible," Sophia said. She immediately started snapping pictures of the birds and all the unique wildlife. I sat and watched her play with the camera while I rested. The walk had taken a lot out of me. Esis got on one of the turtles and tried riding it like he was in a rodeo. It didn't move very fast.

"Better than the waterfall?" I asked when she sat down next to me in the sand. There had to be like a hundred pictures on there by now. I hoped she hadn't snuck any of me.

She shook her head. "Nothing's as special as the waterfall. That's our place."

Esis had given up on the turtles and was in the trees, eating as many oranges as he could. When the birds tried to take the oranges from him, he threw them at the parrots.

She turned so her knees were on me. "So, Mister Mitoh, why did you want me to wear a dress today? You know I don't wear them."

My heart skipped. I'd had this idea kind of spur-of-the-moment after a couple of fantasies got the best of me. I didn't know if we were ready to go this far, and I almost made up an excuse.

But then I remembered I was dying. It was time to live it up.

"Lean back and I'll show you," I said.

Sophia obliged, lying down in the sand. I moved over her and threw the top of her skirt up, so that she was still sitting on the bottom of it. My head dipped down. I pulled her panties slowly off with my teeth, then tucked them into my pocket for safe keeping.

"Liam, what are you— oh, *fuck.*"

My mouth was on her before she had the ability to finish that sentence. I kissed her like I would her mouth, and she writhed beneath me as my lips and tongue moved. I grabbed her ass and palmed it in my hands so I could go deeper, and Sophia started seriously moaning. She was loud, louder than she'd been in the Commons, but she could scream out here all she wanted because we were far away from school. Nobody would hear us out here but the parrots and the turtles, who were probably pretty creeped out by now from us coming here and sexing up their beach.

She tasted fucking amazing. I couldn't really describe it, except that it was sweet and I wanted more. I moved slowly at first, so she could get used to it without being overstimulated, then worked up a good pace. She came once, but I wasn't satisfied with it, so I kept it up until she did it again, stronger this time.

I didn't know what I was doing. Mia had never let me do this to her, so it was my first time too, but dammit, I was going to do it right.

Sophia reached down. She grabbed my shoulders before she tangled her fingers in my hair. Apparently, I was doing a good job, so I kept it up. I experimented by pushing my tongue inside her, and she gasped. Her legs went up to lock themselves behind my head and push me inward. Her body was shaking by this point. I reached up under her dress and bra and palmed her right breast as I continued, softly sucking the parts I knew were the most sensitive.

She started calling my name again, and her voice sounded near tears. I didn't stop, just made my movements more rapid. Without hardly thinking, I put a finger inside her almost instinctively and moved it back and forth as I worked my mouth over her. The result was the strongest orgasm I'd ever seen her have.

"Come here," Sophia gasped, pulling on the front of my shirt, and I obliged.

I lay next to her and she practically shoved her hand down my jeans. By that point, I was harder than a rock and about ready to burst. It only took a few pumps from her hand to give me a major orgasm. I rolled on top of her and kissed her mouth hard as I came. She eagerly responded back by rolling beneath me, wanting more.

The thought crossed my mind that we were alone out here and could do anything we wanted. I'd only need twenty minutes before we'd be able to go at it again. In that desperate moment, I imagined what it'd be like to be inside of her.

By the look in her eyes I knew she was thinking of that, too. I doubted her ability to restrain herself when she obviously wanted more, even if it went against her morals.

But we needed to stop. I wasn't forgetting Sophia's desire to be engaged before any of that happened— or at least deeply committed. I was committed to her, but not in that way yet. Not in the way she wanted me to be. For that, we needed a plan... or for things to change.

I tumbled off of her, my back in the sand. We laid there for a few minutes, catching our breath.

"Well?" I gasped. I was dying to know what she thought.

"I think I'm gonna start wearing dresses more often." She giggled. Sophia swept a hand through her hair and said, "I guess that's one benefit of dating a guy who isn't a virgin. They're experienced enough to satisfy you every time."

"I actually hadn't done that before. I kinda guessed what to do," I admitted.

"No way was that your first time." She looked shocked.

"I swear to the ancestors."

"Well, you're a pro at it," she said. "But that's actually kind of sweet."

"I mean..." I shrugged, and I took her panties out of my jeans so I could hand them back to her. "I know I can't give you my virginity, but I at least wanted to give you my first *something*, seeing as how you're giving me all your firsts."

"I didn't give you my first kiss," Sophia said as she pulled her panties back on. "But that wasn't special, anyway."

"My first kiss was like in kindergarten. I can hardly remember it."

"You're such a player." Sophia snickered, and called for Esis. He came down from the trees practically waddling. One more orange and he would've rolled down to us.

Sophia checked her watch. "It's getting late. We should go."

"Right." I stood up and held out a hand to help her up.

We stood at the edge of the water. Sophia held Esis and said, "How are we supposed to get down there, anyhow? I'm Koigni. I'll drown."

"Working on it," I said. I dug in my pocket and pulled out a handful of brown capsules. "I always carry some of these. These are pills filled with powdered coralreeds. They'll slow down your heart rate so you can hold your breath for longer," I said. "Toaqua take it to improve their lung capacity. Since you're Koigni, I think you should take a double dose. It should last up to thirty minutes."

I stood by the water and held my hand out over it. "By the way, you should probably not tell anyone about those. They're supposed to be a Toaqua tribe secret."

Sophia downed the pills and gave the rest to Esis. I took one of my own before I motioned at the water, using my element to call out to the creatures below. Sophia came close, and out from the water came two creatures.

They looked like horses, but they had both fur and scales, and where their back legs were supposed to be were long fishtails. In place of ears were fin-like extremities. They were basically equine mermaids. One was a pale blue, while the other was a deep green, both of their colors matching the sea. They came onto shore and nickered at us, ears perking pleasantly.

"They're beautiful," Sophia said, reaching out to stroke one.

"They're hippocampi," I told her. "They work for my dad. They'll take us to my house. The blue one is Cascade and the green one is Topi. Climb on."

I got onto Topi, and Sophia climbed abroad Cascade. Esis hopped onto Cascade in front of her, and Sophia grabbed ahold of Cascade's long, silky mane, which looked like seaweed.

"Hold on," I told her.

Cascade immediately dove downward, and my mount followed. The hippocampi swam forward in powerful strides, and I had to flatten myself against my ride so I wouldn't be blown off. The creatures swam forward in the water, around schools of fish and sharks until lights started dotting the ocean ahead of us.

After about ten or so minutes of swimming, Esis pointed. All around us, buildings were rising out of the coral and seaweed. The Toaqua village was full of tall glass towers, with interconnecting tubes that allowed people to walk from one building to the other without swimming. Toaqua rode their Water Familiars all around. It was crowded this time of day. We almost ran into a guy riding a large manta ray, and a woman with a giant sea serpent. The towers were decorated with designs of shells, waves, and water creatures. Some buildings were constructed out of sunken ships, or made in designs that looked like jellyfish. Under the ocean, the entire city looked like a vibrant underwater kingdom.

I watched Sophia carefully as we swam through town. If she showed any signs of struggling to breathe, I'd grab her and rocket her up to the surface. But she looked fine. Her eyes were wide with delight at all the beautiful sights the Toaqua city had to offer.

She loved it. It made a warm feeling grow in my chest. For as Koigni as she was, Sophia had a lot of Toaqua traits.

The hippocampi started tilting upward, and we hung on. When we got back onshore, I dried Sophia off before I removed the water from myself.

We were on the beach again, but this was a secluded beach, far out to sea. We stood in front of a mansion made of yellow walls, glass, and stone, on a private island that was hundreds of feet across in all directions. Tall golden towers spiraled up to the sky, and there were two pools on either side. Trees lined the brick pathway to the front door.

"Is this where the Toaqua tribe holds meetings?" Sophia asked, looking around.

"What? No, it's where I live," I said, caught off-guard.

"That's your *house*?" Sophia squeaked.

"Yeah? What of it?" I asked.

"You live in a freaking *palace*."

"No I don't. It's just a house," I said, irritated.

Sophia made a skeptical noise. "Yeah, okay. A house fit for a prince. You didn't tell me you were practically Water tribe royalty," she mumbled.

"Don't say that." I wrinkled my nose. "It's not a big deal."

Esis had his mouth wide open. He craned his neck back to look upward at my house.

I opened the front door. Sophia was still mumbling about how her house back in Utah would fit inside mine three times over. Inside, the house was painted in light blue, yellow, and white tones. The floors were dark hardwood, and the house was decorated with things like oars, life preservers, throw pillows, and large plants. There were other things, too, like tribal drums. Mom loved interior decorating. A lot of rooms opened up to the beach, and there was a lot of light from all the windows.

"You have a fucking *chandelier*," Sophia hissed.

"So do a lot of people," I snapped back. I raised my voice and said, "Mom! I'm home!"

Out from the kitchen stepped Haloke Mitoh. Mom wore a long blue sundress and was covered with flour. She was blasting Hawkei music in the kitchen as loud as she could, and it looked like she'd been dancing to it. She had a long black braid that went all the way down her back, and didn't have any shoes on.

Mom was eight months pregnant and about ready to tip over. That didn't stop her from hurtling toward me at lightning speed.

"Liam, sweetheart!" She kissed my cheek and patted my hair, getting flour in it. "How are you doing, honey?"

"Fine, Mom," I said. I turned and said, "This is Sophia, by the way."

"Sophia!" Mom screamed her name like they'd known each other forever and they hadn't seen one another in years. She threw her arms around my girlfriend and hugged her as tightly as her pregnancy would allow. "I'm so glad to finally meet you! Liam talks *so* much about you."

I turned a little pink. Sophia seemed a little surprised by Mom's forwardness, but that didn't stop her from saying, "Oh, does he?"

"Yes. He very much enjoys talking about you." Mom's eyes sparkled when she saw Esis. "And who is this little one?"

She tickled Esis under his chin, and he sagged his ears in delight. She pulled out a cookie from her dress and handed it to him. He immediately scarfed it down.

"That's Esis," Sophia said. "And he's going to be your best friend now."

Mom clapped her hands. "Sophia, would you mind helping me in the kitchen? I need to get these biscuits made for dinner. I would very much enjoy it if you helped."

Without waiting for her to respond, Mom took Sophia's hand and frolicked to the kitchen. Sophia's face was bewildered, but the look I shot back at her told her to just to go with it.

I heard fighting somewhere down the hall. Katie and Christian were both eight, and they were arguing again.

"It's mine!"

"No, it's mine!"

"Agh!"

It sounded like they were gonna draw blood. I headed down the hall to pull them apart and saw that Christian had something in his hands. They were playing with Dad's ceremonial arrows again, which they were *not supposed to touch.* These two had an affinity for everything that was violent.

"Hey, stop that. You're going to poke your eye out," I said crossly. I wrenched the arrow out of his hands. "Don't you know not to take things that don't belong to you?"

Christian grinned. "Ooh, Liam's back. And he brought his *girlfriend.*"

"Shut up," I said. "Just mind that you don't have one."

"Oh, I got all the ladies lining up for me, don't worry," Christian said, brushing off his shirt.

He was like a little Ezra in the making. What a nightmare.

Katie hit him on the back of the head. "You do not! All the girls at school hate you."

"Well, all the boys at school hate *you,*" Christian said back. "So there."

She shrugged. "Good. Life's better without men, anyway."

Christian's mouth dropped open. It was fun watching his smart-ass get put in his place.

Then Katie turned her sass on me. "Hey, Liam, where *is* your girlfriend?"

"I didn't say she was my girlfriend, Katie. You know she's from Koigni," I said slowly.

Katie grinned deviously. "You didn't deny it."

"She's probably hiding from your ugly mug, Katie. You scared her away," Christian taunted.

Katie punched him in the face and took off. Christian tore off after her and they started chasing each other around the house. I let them do it. As long as they weren't killing each other, I was good.

I returned the arrow back to where it was supposed to go and made sure the door was locked. When I came back, it looked like Mom had completely forgotten about making dinner. She'd pulled out a scrapbook and was going through it with Sophia, pointing at pictures.

"This one is so cute. Liam was such a sensitive baby. He always wanted to be held," Mom gushed. "He was the sweetest little thing. I remember he came home crying from school once, because another girl in his class started crying and he couldn't make her happy. It was just too much for him. He was quiet, you know? But always kind."

"Mom, quit showing Sophia my baby pictures," I grumbled. Sophia giggled.

"Oh, hm?" Mom looked up. "I suppose I should be finishing up dinner. Go ahead and give Sophia a tour of the house, dear. And get your sister. It's almost ready."

"Gladly," I mumbled under my breath. I turned out of the kitchen and Sophia followed me. Esis stayed behind. Mom was tickling him on the counter.

"You talk about me, huh?" Sophia whispered to me as we started for the staircase.

"Only to Mom," I said. "Can you drop it?"

Her smile was huge. "Okay."

The house tour didn't take long. Sophia acted all impressed with it, but this is where I'd grown up, so I was kind of over it. I avoided going into my bedroom, because it was still kind of messy in there, and I knew if we went in there the temptation would be way too great to mess around again, even with my mom and siblings here.

Sophia had stopped before a long headdress that was displayed in a glass case on the wall. It had hundreds of feathers on it and was decorated with all sorts of blue, white, and black beads.

"Wow," Sophia said, impressed. "Whose is this?"

"It's my dad's. Headdresses are for important people in the tribe. You have to earn them. Every feather designates something you did to glorify your House name, or help members of your House," I said. "When you have enough, you can make one of your own to wear at tribal ceremonies."

"It's beautiful." Sophia took a step back from it. "Do you have one?"

I shook my head. "I'm too young. I was collecting feathers for mine, but mine were taken away when..." My voice trailed off.

"When you lost Nashoma," Sophia finished for me.

I nodded. She didn't press. We turned into a different room, one that had a lot of glass vials with multiple bubbling concoctions and open windows. A seventeen-year-old girl with wavy black hair and long sleeves sat on top of an ice dragon, mixing various potions at her desk. Eirakari rumbled a hello when she saw us.

"Madeline, it's dinnertime," I told her.

She spun around. Her face brightened up when she saw me. "Liam!" She jumped toward me to give her a hug, and I held her. Out of everyone at home, I missed Maddie the most.

Maddie pressed closer to me. "Don't worry, Liam. It's not what you think," Maddie said into my shirt, quietly so Sophia couldn't hear. "It's going to be okay."

A bit of hope rose in me. I bent down so I could whisper to her. "How do you know?

She shook her head. "Perot's right, but he's wrong, too. You'll see."

My mind whirled. This is why I didn't believe in prophecies and that kind of shit. They were unpredictable and all over the place, and Maddie was wrong sometimes. How could Perot be right and wrong about me dying at the same time? It didn't make sense.

She let go of me and turned toward Sophia. "You must be Sophia. Hi. I'm Madeline."

Maddie gave Sophia a hug, too. Sophia returned the gesture politely and said, "It's nice to meet you."

Maddie gave Sophia's hand a squeeze. "You're going to pass your Hawkei Careers project, by the way. Your teacher's going to give you an A, so don't worry about it."

Sophia's mouth gaped open. "How did you—?"

"Just trust me." Maddie winked. "And by the way, I don't care if you know my secret. I already know you can be trusted."

Maddie headed off. Eira followed, and I felt a rush of cold air as she passed by. Sophia was rubbing her arms to warm up.

"Your family is very... huggy," she said.

"Yeah, we are." I laughed. "Feel like you're part of the family yet?"

"Yeah." Sophia rubbed her arms. "Liam, what's up with Madeline? She's kinda…"

"Weird? Yeah. She bonded and got her magic really early, when she was still a toddler," I said.

"Wow." Sophia stopped in her tracks, eyes widening. "Is that even possible?"

"For someone like her? Yes. Maddie… sees things?" I said, not sure how to put it. "She's called a *naderei*."

"She can see the future?"

"Kind of. And the past. She's the same type of person who made the prophecy a long time ago."

"Does she know what will happen in your future if you ask?" Sophia asked curiously.

"It's not like she can request what she wants to see. It just happens," I say. "She can't control it. Half her visions don't make sense to her, most of the time."

"How did she bond?" Sophia asked as we made our way back down to the kitchen.

"Mom works with water and ice dragons, or at least, she used to before she had me and Ezra," I told Sophia. "She kept working part-time until she had Maddie. Eirakari was a sick dragon baby she brought home one day that bonded with Maddie. Mom kept her here under the ruse that she was too sick to be on her own, then said she got too attached to separate from the family."

"I'm supposing Madeline's powers have to remain a secret," Sophia stated.

I nodded. "Can you imagine what the tribes would do if they knew? They would try to use her for her gift," I told Sophia. "When she's old enough and goes to Orenda, we'll stage a bonding so that no one suspects anything, and she'll be able to compete in the tournament."

Sophia had a thoughtful look on her face. "It seems like your family has a lot of secrets, Liam."

I couldn't really respond to that. An obnoxious voice with a lot of yelling told me that Ezra was here. His volume went up by a hundred whenever he walked in this house.

"This place is always loud," I mumbled under my breath. In the dining room, it was absolute chaos. The twins were throwing things at each other, and Ezra was talking loudly to Madeline about something I didn't care about. Dyami, who looked like he hadn't gotten used to the noise yet, was sitting on a statue of a dolphin in the corner with his feathers ruffled.

"Where's Dad?" I asked, noticing his seat was empty.

"Your father isn't here yet. He's running a little late," Mom said as she placed food on the table.

Thank the ancestors for that. Hopefully, he wouldn't show up at all.

Mom's cooking was amazing, and out of everything, it usually didn't make me feel sick. I decided to take a few spoonfuls. Her food was worth the risk that I'd toss it up later.

"Where is your Familiar, ma'am? Is she hiding?" Sophia asked Mom.

"My Familiar is a kelpie, dear. She lives in the sea, and in our pool in the basement," Mom said, piling more food onto Sophia's plate. "Here, honey, have some more. Don't want you going hungry."

Sophia already looked stuffed, but Esis started shoving what she'd been given into his mouth. I didn't know how Esis kept on packing it away when he had eaten his fill of oranges earlier. What exactly was he preparing for, hibernation?

Mom glanced at me. "Liam, honey, you're looking a bit tired. Why don't you go lie down after supper?"

Mom always noticed when I was feeling ill. I couldn't hide it from her, and it sucked. "I'm fine, Mom. Really."

"Hm." She pursed her lips together. "Well, if you don't feel okay, I don't want you going back up to school tonight. Sophia, you're welcome to stay as well. You can sleep in Liam's room with him. I don't mind."

Sophia nearly spit up the water she'd been drinking. Ezra wiggled his eyebrows at me, while Madeline and the twins giggled. Well, Mom had made it clear she didn't give a shit if we were together.

But Dad had to come home sooner or later, and he was going to flip his lid if he saw me cuddled up to the same girl I was supposed to kill for him. Not gonna happen. I'd have Sophia drag me back to school first.

"We'll be fine, Mom," I said. My face was burning. I hoped it didn't show.

Then the door slammed open. Everyone in the room turned to see my dad standing in the doorway, Tatum behind him.

The atmosphere totally changed when Dad showed up. It got silent. And awkward. Really awkward.

Dad's eyes locked on Sophia for what felt like a full minute before he looked to me. I could literally read the questions that were going on in his head. He wanted to know what she was doing here, and why. I guessed Mom hadn't told him Sophia was coming.

"Liwanu, come sit down. We have a guest," Mom said.

Dad behaved when Mom was around. He sat down across from us

"Hello," Sophia started politely. "I'm Sophia. You must be the Chief of Toaqua. I'm pleased to meet you."

Dad just looked at her. I wanted him to say something, but he didn't. Esis thumped his tail against the table and ate another biscuit, chattering at Dad.

Good thing Mom and Ezra were extroverts. They kept chatting so it wasn't quiet in here. Even the twins noticed the tension and were eating silently.

The only one who wouldn't leave Dad alone was Esis. He'd crawled to the other side of the table and kept poking Dad in the arm like a science experiment. Dad didn't know what to make of it and tried to ignore him, but Esis kept prodding harder. Sophia was totally embarrassed and kept trying to call him back over, but he wouldn't listen.

Mom was always the talkative one and Dad was usually silent, but this was over the top. He didn't say a single thing throughout dinner, just kept eyeing me and Sophia like he was trying to figure out what was going on.

"Hey, Liam, are we going snowboarding this year?" Ezra said. "Season's almost up."

"What? Oh, no, I don't think so," I started. "I think we waited too long."

"Liam was always my wild child," Mom said fondly to Sophia. "He was uncontrollable."

"Yes. I think the past year has settled him down." Dad spoke for the first time, looking at me.

A coldness settled in me. He made it sound like that was a good thing. This past year had been the worst of my fucking life. I'd lost my Familiar, I'd been made to participate in the stupid tournament, and I'd gotten sick. I hated this year. The only thing that had made it good was Sophia. I wanted to tip over the table.

If Dad thought that the past year had made me controllable, he was dead wrong.

The minute he was done eating, Dad got up and said, "Liam, we need to talk in private."

I didn't say anything, just stood up and followed. Tatum stayed behind. We headed to his office, and he shut the door behind us.

"Liam, what's happening here? Is this some sort of plot?" Dad asked immediately the moment we were alone.

"Good to see you too, Dad." I leaned against his desk. "And before you ask, Mom invited Sophia here, and I know better than to tell her no."

Dad groaned and rubbed his face. "I should've known your mother had something to do with this."

"Does Mom know about what you asked me to do?"

"What? No." Dad looked shocked I would ask.

"I'm not surprised." Mom definitely wouldn't approve of her oldest son becoming a killer. She'd be disgusted with Dad for even asking me.

"Do you know what you're doing, bringing her here?" Dad hissed. "She's in more danger here than anywhere else. If Malison were to know she were in our waters—"

I sighed and looked skyward. "I know what I'm doing, all right?"

"Have you discovered anything else?" Dad pressed.

"No. Will you please stop asking?" I said. "I'm working on it."

"You're running out of time!"

"You don't need to remind me!" I said. It was more of a yell than anything. I ran a hand through my hair quickly. I was getting so stressed out. It was making the room waver. I had to put a hand on the desk to steady myself, and Dad noticed.

"I think you need to sit down," he stated.

"I think you need to stop pressuring me!" I shouted back. "Do you even care about how I feel?"

It was a two-part question that I wasn't sure he completely got. In a low voice, Dad said, "If you aren't able to do the job, I can find someone that can."

"It's not about that," I snapped. "I can do it. I just don't want to take an innocent life."

There was a knock on the door. "Liam?"

Sophia poked her head in. I was about to freak out, but she must've not heard what I said, because she just stated, "Your mom wanted me to tell you that if we're going back to school, we should be leaving soon. It's getting really dark."

"Thanks, Soph. I'll be there in a minute," I told her softly.

She quietly shut the door. When I turned back around, Dad's expression had totally changed. It was like he was in shock.

He'd seen the way I'd looked at her, how gently I'd spoken to her—how I'd used a pet name. Most people would miss it, but most people weren't my dad. He knew me pretty well. And I'd made it totally obvious by accident.

Dad rubbed his face, like this was his own personal hell. "No. No, no, no, Liam. I was afraid this was going to happen."

"You don't know anything, and you can't prove it, either," I said viciously.

Dad was shocked about how defensive I got. "Liam—"

"You wanna lock me away, fine, but let her go. My life's already ruined. She hasn't done anything," I said.

"I'm not going to turn in my own son!" Dad bellowed. "But by the ancestors, Liam, you're playing with fire! You have a duty to your tribe!"

"I have a duty to myself, what makes *me* happy!" I shouted back. "I've been miserable since Nashoma died, I deserve something that makes my life worth living!"

"And if she's the one the prophecy speaks of? If she starts another war, another genocide, and she destroys your tribe? What then? Are you willing to give up your House, your family, for your own selfish feelings?" Dad asked harshly.

"I haven't figured that out yet," I said lowly. "And you're assuming Sophia is the one the prophecy speaks about."

Dad laughed, but it had no humor in it. "Liam, open your eyes," he said. "I know there's evidence on both sides, but do you really think that this is going to work out?"

I shook my head. "It doesn't matter. I told you I was going to prove Sophia's innocence, and I will. You asked me to get close to her. Well, Dad, I'm as close as I'm ever going to get."

Dad gave a growl of frustration. "I just wished you and Mia had worked things out."

"That was never going to work," I said. "Mia and I were completely incompatible, and everyone but me saw it from the get-go. You know it. Mom even said so." Mia was the only person Mom could never quite warm up to.

"Your mother and I were arranged," Dad started.

"You got lucky. Mom's amazing. Mia, not so much."

Dad looked heavenward, like he was pleading with the ancestors themselves. "Why can't you just pick someone from Toaqua?"

"Because I don't want any of them. I want Sophia. Sorry." It was the first time I'd really said that out loud, and it felt empowering.

"Why do you always have to be so rebellious? You have been since the moment you were born. You should be with someone from your own tribe!"

"Well then, you should've chosen better for me." I crossed my arms. "You couldn't have picked a worse fit if you tried. I almost feel like you did it on purpose."

"That's not fair, Liam. I owed Mia's father a great favor," Dad said firmly.

"So you give him a favor back. You don't pawn off your eldest son," I shot back.

"I have great love for my children, but a chief puts his tribe first!" Dad shouted back.

I wanted to tell him right then. I wanted to tell him I was dying, that it wasn't fair and that I hated he was using me to try and make the Elders happy.

But it wasn't going to do any good. Dad was never gonna see the light of day. I couldn't make him see it. And now that he knew about us, the only thing I could do was work even harder to prove that Sophia deserved to live.

I was done with this conversation. I backed away. "Don't worry, Dad. I'll get your damn evidence. Then I want you to stay the hell away from us."

The office door banged on the way out. I immediately started looking for Sophia. I was glad Mom mentioned that we should be on our way. I wasn't really feeling that bad, but I'd use my illness as an excuse any day to get the fuck out of here.

Sophia was standing in front of a picture in the hall, Esis on her shoulder and her head tilted to the side.

"I helped your mom do dishes," she said as I came beside her. "Your family's really fun."

I didn't answer. I stared at the picture Sophia was looking at. It was a picture of me and Nashoma. He was in my lap and licking my face while I laughed. It'd been taken last year around this time, but it felt like ages ago.

I wasn't even the same person in that photo anymore. That boy's eyes were different. The light hadn't gone out of them yet.

"Is this Nashoma?" she asked.

"Yeah," I said.

"He's pretty big," she said. She tilted her head the other way. "I didn't know he was black. He's so beautiful."

"He was." I turned away from the photo. It hurt to look at it. "Can we go?"

"Yeah." We said quick goodbyes to Mom and my siblings. Ezra was gonna stay the night, as he'd already started cleaning the beer out of the fridge.

When we left the house and walked toward the water, Sophia spoke up.

"I heard you guys shouting," she said. "Was it about me?"

"No," I lied. "Me and my dad just have a... complicated relationship."

"Oh." She chewed on her lip. "I have a feeling your dad doesn't like me very much."

"Forget about my dad. Mom loves you," I said, trying to redirect the conversation.

"She seemed to." Sophia tapped her chin. "She kept calling me *shantee*. It was strange."

Oh, fuck no. "She did not."

"What does it mean?" Sophia asked.

My face turned red. "Never mind. Don't ask."

Dammit, Mom. She was probably already picking out flowers for our wedding, knowing her. What had Maddie told her? No, even worse, what had Maddie *seen*?

"Okay..." Sophia said, drawing out the word. "Thanks for bringing me to meet your family. I feel like I could really fit in here."

"You're welcome, *pawee*." And she totally could. It didn't matter that she was Koigni. She did fit in here. She belonged. And I wanted her to keep belonging.

Dad knew now that I would do anything, fabricate anything, to prove Sophia was innocent. Which meant from this point forward I needed to come up with undeniable proof that she wasn't the prophesied one, and rub it in the council's smug faces.

I was done playing around. It was time to get desperate.

sophia
FOURTEEN

"Tell me, Sophia, what's been on your mind lately?"

Doya almost sounded like she cared. She led me down a narrow trail through the forest, far away from the school for one of our many private training sessions. The sun had fallen low in the sky, and the air was chilly. I used my Fire to warm Esis, who was curled up in my arms.

"I don't know," I lied. The fact was, there was a lot on my mind lately. It'd been over a week since I'd visited Liam's house, and I couldn't stop thinking about it, along with my parents' visit, the approaching Ancestors' Day, my failing powers, my upcoming finals... the list went on. But I wasn't about to tell *her* any of that.

Doya remained emotionless. "The fact is, Sophia, your powers have failed to impress me lately."

Naomi glanced back at me with a frown. I didn't even know cats could frown.

"You don't have to remind me," I grumbled, pushing aside an evergreen branch as the trail narrowed.

"I originally thought that perhaps you exerted yourself too much in our first training session and that makeup sessions would help, but clearly, I was wrong."

Doya led me out of the trees and into a secluded clearing. It was only about an acre in size, with long dry grass covering the ground and various logs and stumps strewn here and there. Doya breezed over to one of the dry logs and sat on it gracefully, which surprised me, because she seemed like the kind of person who would do anything to avoid getting dirt on her dress. Naomi stood alert, her eyes glaring out into the trees like she was standing guard. Doya gestured to the empty spot beside her, inviting me to sit.

I approached cautiously, but sat beside her anyway. It was a little uncomfortable to say the least, considering I was pretty sure this was the closest I'd ever come to her in my life.

Doya crossed her legs and turned to me. "We're running out of time, Sophia. You have so much more to learn— to master— before Ancestors' Day. If the Elders think this is some sort of ploy—"

"It's not a ploy," I snapped before softening my tone. "I wouldn't do this on purpose. I know what's at stake."

"I know you wouldn't," Doya said softly. I'd never heard her speak so gently to me before. It was a little unnerving, like she was toying with me or something. "I'm saying that the Elders might *see* it that way. If you don't want them to fulfill their threats, we must find a way to break through whatever's been holding you back so you can complete your task."

It suddenly clicked. She wasn't acting like this because she cared about my well-being. She only cared about me fulfilling the prophecy. I never thought I'd live to see the day she resorted to kindness to manipulate me.

Yet she was still staring at me like she expected a response. I had to give her *something*.

"My friend and I were fighting for a while," I admitted, "but we've made up now."

Doya raised a curious eyebrow. "You think you can perform advanced Koigni magic again?"

I thought about it for a moment, then nodded. "I don't see why not."

The truth was, my powers had gradually started improving after Imogen and I made up, but I still had a long way to go before I was back to where I'd been during that first training session.

"Nothing else has been on your mind then?" she asked.

Nothing I'm going to tell you.

"No," I lied.

Doya pressed her lips together. "Good. Then we can see what kind of progress you've made these past few weeks."

She stood and spun toward me, her dress billowing around her. "On your feet, Sophia."

I did as I was told and set Esis on the log to watch. He turned his ears down like he was disappointed to be set down.

"To contact the ancestors, you will have to learn how to conjure lightning," Doya said.

"Lightning?" I gaped at her. "Are you joking?"

"I never joke, Sophia," she replied flatly. She could say that again. "The ceremony is different for each House depending on their element. For a Koigni, it requires lightning, but it is very advanced and complex. Only the best Koigni are capable."

"So, only the Elders?" I asked.

"No. There are maybe a hundred Koigni who can do it, but compared to the thousands of us living in Kinpago, the percentage is quite small."

"And you want me, a First Year, to do this?" I couldn't believe she was suggesting such a thing.

"You *are* the prophesied one." Doya cocked an eyebrow, as if begging me to challenge the assertion. "I think you're capable of anything you put your mind to."

Oh, wow. A compliment from Doya. That never happened.

"You just need to get over yourself first and actually *put your mind to it.*"

There it was. Finally, she was starting to sound like herself again.

I shifted my weight between my feet. "So I just have to... believe in myself?"

Doya smirked. "It's a bit more complicated than that. What you need is *focus.* Now that you and your friend aren't fighting anymore, you can do that, can't you?"

Woops. I shot myself in the foot with that one. By the look she gave me, I could tell she knew I wasn't being completely honest with her. It was like she was just waiting for me to finally crack and admit what was bothering me. But that was just it. There was no *one* thing.

"Shall we get started?" Doya didn't wait for an answer. She walked to the center of the clearing with Naomi at her heels.

I instructed Esis to stay put on the log and followed behind her. I didn't want him getting hurt during training.

"Conjuring lightning is different than conjuring fire," Doya said. "We create lightning not through flames, but through heat. It works by superheating a column of air so much that it becomes ionized plasma, promoting electrical conductivity and resulting in a static discharge. The light is mostly a result of the heat."

"Um... okay." So far I was following along.

"Just be careful you don't overheat the air, or you could ignite the atmosphere."

My eyes widened. "That doesn't make me feel better."

"Don't worry," Doya said with a wave of her hand. "No one has ever done it before. It fails more often than it works, anyway. You have to have enough of an electrical imbalance in the atmosphere. If you try too hard, you'll deplete the imbalance and it will no longer work. There are ways to replenish the electrical imbalance using thermal updrafts, or thermals, but that takes time. It's far more advanced, and we won't get into that today. I'll not bore you with the scientific details. I choose to focus on the magical aspect."

Now I was totally lost. Good thing I wasn't being tested on any of this.

"Remember what I told you about *becoming* the shape you envision?"

I nodded.

"Well, forget about it," she said in a clipped tone. "For now, anyway."

Doya closed her eyes and lifted her hands up to the sky. "We don't *become* lightning. We focus our heat, but you have to do it without producing flame. They are not one in the same, and you must separate them in your mind."

"Okay." I closed my eyes as she had done and tried to imagine my heat and my flames as separate entities.

"Can you see the heat inside of you?" she asked. It sounded like some sort of riddle.

"Um... no."

I peeked my eyes open briefly to see her staring down her nose at me. She huffed and closed her eyes again, turning her chin to the sky.

"The reason this task is so difficult is because you cannot focus your magic externally until you first master focus of your internal self."

Doya was one to talk. That lady had the emotional maturity of a plant. She couldn't control her anger if her life depended on it. I didn't get how she'd become so powerful, and an Elder, no less.

"And once you master that..."

A blinding light flashed across the clearing, and then a deafening *crack* echoed around us. I cursed and ducked my head, covering my ears.

Doya smirked proudly. "Once you master that, you can do almost anything."

Esis sprinted across the clearing and jumped into my arms, his eyes the size of saucers. I squeezed him tightly and whispered in his ear, "It'll be all right, buddy."

"Now you try," Doya demanded.

My mouth hung open. "Lightning?"

She raised her eyebrows, waiting for me.

My palms grew clammy. Did she seriously expect me to pull a lightning bolt out of my ass or something? This was super advanced stuff I wasn't ready for.

"I'm going to do it again, and when I do, you have to focus," Doya said. "Got it?"

"Yeah," I agreed, but I wasn't exactly certain what I was supposed to focus on.

Doya aimed her hands at the sky again, and almost instantly a second lightning bolt cut across it. I didn't flinch this time as thunder rumbled above our heads.

"Feel that?" Doya asked.

I focused on the air around me and noticed a slight shift in pressure. Electricity sizzled through the air. If I were Yapluma, my Air senses would be going haywire right now. Is that what she wanted me to feel?

"I think I get it."

"Think?" Doya challenged. "Or know?"

I thought about it for a moment, then dropped my shoulders. "Neither. I don't feel anything."

Doya frowned, then lifted her chin and said, "Burn me, Sophia."

"Excuse me?" I gaped at her.

"You need to learn how to focus your heat. Without using your flames, I want you to burn me. Right here." She held up her palm and pointed to the center of it.

"I— I can't," I stammered.

Doya pursed her lips. "You mean, you don't desire to hurt me?"

Oh, I did. Big time.

"All you have to do is focus," she pressed. "Heat the air between us, and burn me."

I breathed a large sigh and set Esis at my feet, then faced Doya with my palms out. Picturing my magic inside of me, I drew heat to the surface and focused it in my palms. My hands warmed, and I tried to push that warmth out into the air around me. Doya stood still, looking unimpressed. So I pushed harder, concentrating until my whole body grew hot and sweat broke out across my brow.

Suddenly, flame erupted from my palms, shooting directly toward Doya. She jumped out of the way, and Naomi growled at me. Esis clapped at my feet, like he thought I'd actually accomplished something.

Sorry to break it to you, buddy.

My stomach sank, and Doya glared at me.

"You're not focusing, Sophia," she snapped.

"I don't know what I'm doing yet," I shot back. "You're asking me to move mountains before I've picked up a stone!"

Doya sighed. "This isn't Nivita magic."

Oh, wow. Sarcasm. I never thought I'd hear such a thing from Doya's mouth.

"Can we just maybe back up a step?" I asked in a calmer tone. "Maybe start with separating heat from flame?"

Doya took a deep breath before finally saying, "Fine, but I want to see you actually make some progress tonight. We're not leaving here until you do."

"Yes, ma'am."

Doya guided me through visualization techniques to help me better understand my magic, and then she discussed ways to help me focus it.

"Picture your magic like a string," she said. "It's not merely a ball of yarn you haphazardly throw into the air. It's a single strand you can guide wherever you please. Do you understand?"

I nodded.

"Good, now use that against me." She held her palm up again. "Burn me."

I closed my eyes and tried to picture my magic like a string as she'd instructed. I envisioned it rising through my body and snaking out of my arm, through my palm, and across the air between us.

Focus, focus, focus, I repeated to myself.

A split second later, a blast of orange light crossed the back of my eyelids, and a wave of heat swept over my skin. Doya shrieked, and I opened my eyes to see a fireball had shot out of my hands and landed in the grass beyond her. Flames licked into the sky, eating away at the dry grass.

Doya quickly threw out her hands and calmed the flames with her magic. Then she whirled toward me, fuming. "You aren't focusing, Sophia! Do you have any idea how important this task is?"

I took a step back, almost stumbling over Esis' tail. He curled his lips back over his teeth and growled at her. I bent to scoop him up in my hands and held on to him protectively. "I understand."

"No," Doya snarled, taking a step closer to me. Naomi followed, glaring at me. "The fate of the Koigni rests in your hands. If you can't contact the ancestors to learn how to fulfill the prophecy, our whole House could perish!"

"I know!" I shouted back, though I didn't really care about that. I'd save Vanessa and Bren, but the rest of the Koigni could go to hell. All I really cared about were making sure my friends survived this whole thing.

"Then you need to *focus*," Doya snarled. Her hands fisted at her sides.

"You keep saying that. It's not like I'm not trying." I took another step back to distance myself from her. She looked two seconds away from bursting into flames.

"Try harder. You need to stop letting other people distract you."

"No one's distracting me," I argued.

"I could list a dozen people who are keeping you from realizing your full potential, Sophia." Doya took a step closer and started counting off on her fingers. "Your Nivita and Yapluma friends. The Mitoh boy. Your sister. Your *parents*."

I gasped. How did she know about that?

Doya stood so close to me now that she loomed over me, her nostrils flaring. I held my breath and shrank away, hiding Esis in the crook of my elbow.

Doya glared down at me so hard I thought her face might crack like stone. "I have eyes and ears everywhere, Sophia. I'm not keeping your secrets as a charity gesture. So figure out how to find your focus, or so help the ancestors, I will not hesitate to use them against you."

I swallowed down the lump in my throat, willing myself to say something. But I didn't have anything. Doya had me backed into a corner, and the only way out was to perform the most advanced Koigni magic the Hawkei had ever witnessed. It was hopeless.

Doya scoffed and finally backed down, but it did little to comfort me. She looked at me with such disdain that I swore I could *feel* it coming off her in waves.

Then I heard something. A snap in the bushes. Something had stepped on a branch. My eyes glanced to the left, and I noticed a shadow move, though I couldn't make out what it was.

Doya hadn't heard. She was still fuming. It must've been some animal.

I stood up straighter, but my voice came out small. "I— I can try again."

Doya held up a hand to stop me. "Don't bother. I can't handle continuing to watch your failure."

Doya whirled around and stomped away from me, leaving Esis and me alone in the clearing to contemplate everything she'd said.

Failure.

The word echoed in my mind. Is that what I was? A failure? Had I failed to protect my friends and family?

I slumped over to the dry log and fell down on it, feeling totally disconnected with my body as her words bore their way through me. Esis spread his arms out and tried to hug my belly, but he couldn't even reach around my front side.

With Doya gone, I pulled the totem out from beneath my shirt and stared down at it. If what Liam said about this totem was true— that it was supposed to enhance my powers— then I should've been capable of what Doya was asking, shouldn't I? I was the prophesied one. I was supposed to be amazing.

And yet... I wasn't.

Maybe the problem wasn't with the totem or the prophecy. Maybe, like Doya said, the problem was me.

Tree branches reached out onto the narrow path, scraping along my skin as I hurried back to the castle once I found the strength to rise to my feet. I was so angry at Doya that I could set this entire forest on fire. Seriously. Who did she think she was, threatening everyone I loved, everything I held dear? And to have the gall to tell me *I* was the problem when she couldn't teach worth a crap.

"I don't get why she hates me so much," I muttered to Esis.

I broke out of the narrow trail and started on a wider one up toward the castle. Esis sat perched on my shoulder and began chittering in my ear and tugging on my hair.

"Ow! Esis." I swatted at his tiny hands. "Stop. That hurts."

I continued up the trail until I broke out of the trees and reached a rocky ledge that overlooked the beach. Esis screeched in my ear, bringing my footsteps to a halt.

"What. Is. It?" I snapped.

Esis blinked a few times and then pointed out toward the beach. In the dimming light from the sunset, I saw several figures moving around the rocky shore. Upbeat music played from an old boombox someone had brought out, and I could see Jonah and Squeaks shaking their butts to the music. Then Jonah stopped and pointed over to Ezra and Dyami, who stole the show and showed off with some break-dance moves.

A dance-off. My friends were having a dance-off. I was *so* not in the mood right now.

But then I spotted Liam sitting on the rocks watching, and I couldn't resist making my way down to them.

By the time I reached the beach, Imogen and Sassy were showing off their moves. Imogen wore a beaded skirt that made noise when she shook her hips, and she shimmied her shoulders, using her boobs to her advantage. Cade was totally staring down her shirt, and she didn't even notice.

"Hey, Liam," I said softly as I approached.

His face lit up when he saw me. "Hey. Where have you been?"

I sighed and sat beside him on the rock. Esis jumped down from my shoulder and settled on my lap. "Don't ask."

"Doya?" he guessed.

"What gave it away?" I grumbled.

"Oh, I don't know," he teased. "You just have a... glow about you."

I wiped at my forehead. "It's called sweat."

Liam chuckled. The sound of his laughter helped ease my mind a little.

"So, what are they up to?" I asked, gesturing to the other four dancing in the sand with their Familiars.

"Ez thinks he's going to win the tournament in December, and he claimed he'd have the best moves the Elemental Ball has ever seen. So of course, Jonah had to challenge him."

"Sounds like fun," I said.

"Yeah, and the fun continues. Squeaks and Sassy are planning a sleepover," Liam said.

"Oh, okay," I said with a forced laugh. "And Cade won't be jealous of Jonah?"

Liam rolled his eyes. "It's not like that, Soph. And besides, Jonah's not going with them. I guess he has to go to his parents' house later."

I should've been dancing and laughing with my friends, but after Doya chewed me out, I just couldn't bring myself to do it.

"How do they stay positive all the time?" I asked Liam, feeling totally defeated. "I mean, don't they see what's happening all around them?"

Liam shrugged. "They do. I think it's just their way of holding on when times get rough."

I nodded. I wished I could let go the way Jonah and Imogen did.

Liam shifted on the rock to face me. "Hey, Soph. You okay?"

I purposely didn't answer. "You wanna get out of here?"

"Yes," he answered far too quickly.

I cracked a smile. "Not like that, Liam."

Not that it hadn't been good the last time we'd fooled around. In fact, it was *amazing*. I just wasn't in the mood right now. I wasn't in the mood for much of anything. I felt too defeated.

"Come on." Liam glanced around the beach and decided it was safe to take my hand. He laced his fingers through mine and started leading me toward the trees.

"Esis," I called, pulling his attention away from the dancing. He started and hopped over to me, following at my feet.

"Do you want to talk about it?" Liam asked once we were in the privacy of the trees.

I shrugged. "It's just... Doya. You know how she is. She blames me for not being good enough, and—"

Liam held up a hand. "On second thought, I'm not sure it's best to tell me."

My shoulders dropped. Was I annoying him by complaining about her?

Liam stopped in the middle of the trail and turned to me with a fallen face. "The thing is, Sophia, I have something I need to tell you."

I bit my lower lip. Whatever it was didn't sound good. My eyes darted to Esis, who scurried up a tree and then sat on a low branch to watch us.

"Um, okay. What is it?"

Liam raked his fingers through his hair, pushing the long strands away from his face. He glanced around, then gestured to a large rock not far from the trail. "You should probably sit down for this."

Oh, man. He was going to tell me something horrible, like that erectile dysfunction ran in his family or something. We'd never have sex.

I followed him off the trail and sat on the rock beside him.

"The thing is, Sophia—"

The rock shifted beneath us, and I jumped to my feet to keep from tumbling over. Liam shot up beside me and held an arm over my chest, like he was protecting me. We both relaxed when we saw the creature stand. It looked like a rock, with a hard gray shell and moss growing on the top, but its joints moved easily. It had four legs and a wide nose like a cow. Pine needles hung out of its mouth like it'd been grazing. It shot us a disgruntled look and then trotted off into the forest.

My heart rate slowed, and I turned back to Liam. "That was interesting."

He nodded, but he didn't look at all interested. He probably grew up with those things all over the place.

"Sophia..." Liam reached out and took my hands in his. I didn't need to use my magic to warm my skin, because Liam's touch did that for me. It was like he had a power all himself. Liam dropped his gaze to my hands and began rubbing the backs of them.

I suddenly became very concerned. "What is it, Liam? You can tell me anything."

When he lifted his gaze, his eyes were brimmed in tears. "I know. I just don't want to hurt you."

"Hurt me?" My tone was laced in pain already. Was Liam breaking up with me? Tears rose to my eyes, and it felt like a heavy weight had settled on my chest. Just the thought of losing him made it impossible to breathe.

"I just... I love you so much, *pawee*." His voice cracked.

Oh, shit! He *was* breaking up with me. I didn't think I could handle it.

"I love you, too," I whispered.

Liam's lips swooped down to meet mine, and his hand came up to support the base of my neck. I threw my arms around him and dragged him in closer until my breasts were pressed against his chest. If Liam was breaking up with me, this could be the last kiss I ever got from him. I wanted it to last forever.

All too soon, Liam drew away from me. He rested his forehead on mine and breathed deeply. "I love you, but—"

"Liam, don't," I pleaded.

"But... I'm dying."

The words were like a punch to the gut. My mind went blank. I was totally confused. He wasn't breaking up with me, but I was losing him nonetheless. But what did he mean by that?

"We're all dying, Liam," I said. "I mean, someday we'll all die."

"I know." Liam's expression was hard, his eyebrows knit together. It was like he was trying to hide his true emotions behind the only mask he knew how to wear. "But I'm dying faster than most."

The knot in my chest tightened. "I know you're sick, but you don't know—"

"Perot told me," Liam interjected. "He said my organs are shutting down. I could have months, maybe a year..."

"Oh, my God!" I threw my arms around him again and squeezed tightly. He gasped, so I loosened my hold on him. Tears began to flow down my cheeks and soaked into his t-shirt. I could hardly find the strength to breathe, it broke my heart so badly. It felt like the weight of a mountain was pressing down on my chest. He wasn't breaking up with me, but this was worse... so much worse. "I'm so sorry."

Liam ran his hands over my back. "You're the only person I've told so far."

"This is so unfair." I cried into his chest. The words couldn't begin to describe how I felt. It was far worse than unfair. It was cruel.

Esis jumped down from the trees and landed on my shoulder. I glanced up for a moment to see him stretching his arms around Liam's neck. He'd miss him, too. I just knew it.

Liam sniffled, then buried his face in my hair.

"I don't want to live without you, Liam," I whispered. Life would be pointless without him. He was like the air I breathed and the water I drank. He belonged in my life, and I just couldn't imagine a world where he no longer existed.

"I know, but I've already had more time here than I should've. When Nashoma died, I should've... I should've—"

"Don't say it, Liam," I warned.

Liam was still around for a reason. He had to be. Otherwise the ancestors wouldn't have let him live this long. Maybe it was my narcissism talking, but I couldn't shake the feeling that they'd kept him around for *me*. And if they were just going to take him from me right away, what was the point in that?

No. I wouldn't let that happen.

I reached up and stroked Esis' tail. Esis stared down at me with watery eyes. I lifted my lips at the corners, and he nodded back in understanding. Then he pressed a small palm to Liam's forehead.

Liam didn't notice anything out of the ordinary, but I knew that somewhere inside of him, Esis' powers were helping him heal.

To hell with Perot. To hell with the Elders. To hell with anyone who suspected anything from a "miraculous recovery." Liam was here for a purpose.

And I'd be damned if he died before he got to fulfill it.

I'd be damned if he died at all.

So I wasn't going to let him.

Liam

FIFTEEN

I woke up the next morning feeling... good. Really good. Better than I had been for a long time.

And it was totally weird. I got ready, expecting to start feeling shitty again any moment. But I didn't. I was tired, but other than that, I was fine.

I even felt hungry. I was hungry all the time, actually, but this morning my stomach wasn't rolling. I went down to the dining hall and ate breakfast, and actually kept it down this time.

I could actually eat stuff again. So weird.

It was a Sunday, so the dining hall was quiet. I was about ready to head out to find Sophia, because I was trying to spend as much time with her as I could these days, when I ran into Baine in the hallway.

"Liam. Just the man I wanted to see," he said, and he put his arm around my shoulder. "Come. We have things to discuss."

Great. This was the last thing I needed. I glumly headed with him, mentally ticking down the minutes in my head. I only had so much time left, and I didn't want to spend a second more than I had to with Baine.

Thank the ancestors, he didn't take me to his office this time. We went to a secluded classroom instead, and Baine locked the door behind us.

"Koigni has spies lurking around the castle. We can't be too careful." Baine began the meeting in Hawkei, and I quickly switched over.

"Spies?" I asked.

"Koigni has grown suspicious that Toaqua has taken it upon themselves to eliminate Sophia.

We're being watched," Baine stated. *"We know that they haven't yet figured out you've been assigned to the task, but they're getting close. You need to be cautious, Liam. If they get any idea you're the one that's supposed to end her life, they'll stage an accident to take you out first."*

This was getting intense. *"So, what am I supposed to do?"*

"Nothing, at the moment. Any action would arouse suspicion," Baine began. *"You're safe, for now. From what it appears on the outside, you two are just good friends."*

So Dad hadn't told Baine about me and Sophia. Honestly, that'd been one of my biggest fears.

"Our own spies have uncovered that the Koigni Elders have asked Sophia to complete some sort of task, as you've mentioned before, but we've ceased to discover what it is. However, we know that it is approaching soon, most likely before the semester is up. Has she mentioned anything to you about what it could be?"

I shook my head. *"She hasn't said."*

"Dammit." Baine rarely swore, so he must've been aggravated. *"Another dead end."*

I knew Sophia had been assigned to something big. I'd figured as much, after Chieftess Annette had summoned her the first day of the new semester. But she hadn't mentioned a thing about it. It kind of hurt that she was keeping it secret from me, though I believed she had to have her reasons for it. I wished she could open up and tell me.

I wasn't one to be pointing fingers. I'd been keeping secrets from her, too.

Baine crossed his arms. *"Have you learned anything from these sessions with Madame Doya?"*

I shook my head. *"There's been only one that I've seen so far, and no. The only thing I've witnessed is that Sophia can't do what Doya's asking her to."*

I'd stopped watching Doya's session with Sophia yesterday before it was over. I felt guilty spying on her, and it became obvious that she wasn't going to be able to conjure lightning very quickly. So I'd abandoned my post and walked back to the beach early. The way Doya had yelled at her made me pissed, and to make it worse, Sophia had nearly seen me. I'd stepped on a branch by accident and gotten her attention. I'd come very close to being caught.

But even though Sophia hadn't managed to conjure lightning, she'd shown potential. Which meant the rockthistle had worn off. Taking her powers again wouldn't work, as I had no way to do that. Which meant I needed to come up with another plan— one that would turn her own House against her.

And it needed to start with the Elders.

Baine scratched his beard. *"Hm. If Sophia continues to show little potential, the Koigni Elders will get angry. They don't want to lose their opportunity."*

"How is that our problem?" I asked. *"My job is to figure out if Sophia is the prophesied one or not, and the evidence I've seen all semester is that she's not."*

Baine sighed. *"We have one last option. I've reviewed the footage from the tournament several times over the past semester. One in particular has caught my attention. You were dying when you went into that cave, Liam, and you walked out as if nothing had ever happened. Sophia went after you, and you both were gone for a considerable amount of time."*

Baine leaned forward. *"Is there something you're not telling me?"*

Shit. Shit, shit, shit. Think of something, quick!

"I don't remember anything," I lied. *"All I can recall is passing out in the cave, and waking up, and Sophia was there. Then I was fine, and we just left the cave. That's it."*

"That's too simple," Baine said in frustration. *"There must be an explanation for all of this."*

He tapped his face with his finger, then brought it away in a sudden stroke of clarification. *"The powers of Anichi would be the only thing that could heal you, in that state. Sophia is Koigni, which means that she had to come in contact with some sort of Anichi power to restore your health."*

The fucking Spirit Totem. That's what healed me. It had to be. It was close enough to work its magic on me, since it'd been in the cave. Sophia just didn't know. But how was I supposed to keep that from Baine?

"*So... you're saying Sophia is carrying something from Anichi?*" I feigned.

"*She must be. You need to find out whatever she has, Liam, and bring it to us,*" Baine said. "*Then we'll be able to close this case for good.*"

"*And Sophia's name will be cleared, and I'll get Nashoma back, right?*" I asked.

Baine hesitated before he said, "*It seems that way. If we can verify her powers are a result of her obtaining a powerful magical item, and not from her own strength, she would cease to become a threat.*"

This was my ticket out of this mess. "*All right. I'll see what I can do.*"

"*Don't take too long, Liam,*" Baine warned me as I headed for the door. "*Sophia's time is almost up.*"

Didn't I know it. But at least I had hope now. The Spirit Totem was the key. I didn't know how I was going to pry that thing off of her. It was always on her. She never took it off.

But I had a solid plan now. I'd get the Spirit Totem off of her and show it to Baine, tell him Sophia's powers came from there. Then I'd learn about whatever task the Koigni Elders had put her up to, and I would come clean. I'd tell Sophia the truth, and convince her to fail her mission so that Koigni lost interest in her as the prophesied one and Toaqua left her alone. The Koigni Elders would be so furious with Sophia for dishonoring her House, they'd want nothing more to do with her. And Toaqua would turn their attention someplace else.

Nashoma would be back by my side. Sophia would be mad, at first, but eventually she'd forgive me when she learned I did everything I could to save her life. It was iron proof.

I went to wait outside the Koigni dorms, but when I was there I found Esis, not Sophia. He had a note tied around his neck and waved to me, running over.

"Hey, little buddy." I picked him up and untied the note from around his neck. It was from Sophia. She wanted me to meet her on the cliffs near the beach.

"That's weird," I said. I put Esis on my shoulder and said, "I'm not one to refuse a lady. Let's go."

Sophia was sitting on a rock on the cliffside, taking pictures of the ocean with the camera I'd gotten her. I noticed that she was wearing the totem around her neck, tucked beneath her shirt. She took it off sometimes when we fooled around. Maybe—

Fuck, I felt like a dirtbag even thinking about it. How could I get her naked just so we could mess around, then snatch it from her before she noticed? It was totally wrong.

"You're looking a lot better," Sophia commented as I came near. She snapped a picture of me with Esis, and I frowned. She knew I didn't like taking pictures.

"I'm feeling a lot better, actually," I said, and handed Esis off to her.

Sophia beamed and petted Esis fondly. "I'm so happy to hear that. You have no idea. Maybe you're getting better."

I didn't say anything. Since I'd told her I had an expiration date, we'd resolved not to talk about it. I didn't want to give her false hope in case this was a fluke. Which I really hoped it wasn't.

Then it clicked. I hadn't been spending a lot of time with Sophia lately, because I'd been feeling awful. But in the past week I'd really been pushing myself to see her more, just because I knew I had months left with her, not years. If the Spirit Totem was what had healed me in the cave, being in its presence should be enough to keep me alive now, right?

Things were getting even more complicated. I couldn't hand over the totem to Baine if that's what was preventing my death.

It didn't matter. I could decide later. Either way, I needed that totem.

"I hoped that you'd be well enough for some cliff diving," she told me. She put her camera in her bag and have me a mischievous grin.

I was surprised. "Are you sure you're up for it?" I asked. "It's not for the faint of heart."

"I'm really scared, no lie. But I also want to live it up, you know?" she said. She put her hands on her hips and said, "No time like the present. As long as you do it with me."

I shrugged. "All right."

Sophia slipped off her socks and shoes, and I followed her lead. Then she took off the totem that was around her neck and hung it on a tree branch nearby. "Don't want this getting lost."

I had an open window, but it could wait until later. I guided her to the cliff's edge. "Don't be too scared," I told her. "If anything happens, I'll use the water to catch you."

Sophia swallowed and nodded. "Right."

This cliff wasn't very big, only twenty or so feet tall. I'd jumped here before multiple times, so I knew it was deep enough, and safe. But Sophia was pale white.

"Always jump feet first, and remember to hold your breath," I said. "Try to relax. You can do this. I know you can."

Sophia was taking deep breaths. I grabbed her hand and said, "We'll do it together. Okay?"

She nodded again. It was like she couldn't speak.

"On the count of three. If you're going to hesitate, please let me go before I jump. Ready? One... two... three!"

We ran at the edge of the cliff full-speed. I thought she might back out at the last minute, but she didn't. She just held on to my hand tighter as we jumped off the edge of the cliff and went sailing downward. A rush of adrenaline went through me as the sensation of being weightless came over me.

This was what being in love with Sophia felt like. Jumping and falling.

We let go before we hit the water, and sank in deep. I surfaced before she did and panicked a little when I couldn't see her, but she came up laughing. It was March, so the water was still super cold, but Sophia didn't seem to mind.

"That was awesome!" she said. "Again!"

We jumped off the cliff together a few more times. By the end of the afternoon, Sophia was jumping all on her own. I was sitting on a rock and watching her. She seemed to be enjoying it even more than I was.

When she'd begun the climb back up, I eyed the totem. It was still on the same branch she'd left it before.

It would take her a few minutes to get up here. This was my chance.

I went to grab the totem, but I heard the scratching of little nails on the rock, and hissing. It was Esis. He stood in front of the totem with his hair on end, warning me not to come closer. He totally knew I was trying to take the totem.

"I need it, all right? You don't understand." I tried reaching for it again, but Esis lunged forward and bit me.

I gasped. Ouch. He'd never done that before. He didn't draw blood, so it wasn't a real bite, just a warning. I shook out my hand and said, "Fine. Have it your way."

He gave me a surly look. I guess I should've been thankful that he and Sophia couldn't communicate telepathically yet, because he'd totally rat me out.

Sophia had reached the top. She shook out her wet hair and said, "What a rush. I'm totally up for anything now."

"Not anything. Start slow." I laughed. I was totally going to turn her into a daredevil by the end of the year.

If I had that long.

Sophia slipped on her shoes again and looped the totem back around her neck. "We should head back. I'm starving."

"Agreed," I started. We'd skipped lunch. I used my magic to dry us off, and I took her hand so we could walk together, at least part of the way.

Esis stayed securely on her shoulder. His big eyes told me to back off as I eyed the totem around her neck.

Taking the totem had just gotten ten times harder. There was no way Esis would let me get anywhere near it.

We headed back to school and saw someone leaning up against the wall outside the greenhouses. It was Jonah. But he didn't look like himself— not like Jonah. You wouldn't understand unless you saw it. He looked like... a different person. A sadder one.

It wasn't until he lifted his head and saw us coming that I knew why. Jonah had a huge black eye, and a bruise that ran across the right side of his face. It was swollen and red. It looked like someone had taken their Air magic and just whipped it at him.

"Ancestors, Jonah." Sophia's tone was shocked as we approached. "What happened to you?"

Jonah's face was straight. "Squeaks kicked me in the face last night when we were sleeping. No biggie."

"Oh." Sophia said, but her eyes were troubled.

Jonah didn't bother looking my way. He knew he couldn't fool me. There were no hoof marks.

"We're just about to get dinner," I offered. "You wanna come?"

"I'm not really that hungry," Jonah said.

Okay, now I knew there was something wrong. Jonah ate like a hippogriff and never stopped.

Sophia interceded. "Well, we're supposed to be meeting up with Imogen later in front of the Nivita dorms. She wanted to tell us something. See you at six?"

"Sure," Jonah said offhandedly, and he went into the castle without another word.

Sophia and I glanced at each other. We didn't say much as we headed inside to grab dinner. We sat alone in a booth in the corner of the room, but nobody paid us much attention. People had gotten used to always seeing us together.

Sophia narrowed her eyes as she picked at her salad. Esis wasn't eating, which was bizarre— he was watching me instead.

"Didn't... Squeaks spend the night with Sassy at Imogen's last night? And didn't Jonah go home to see his parents?" Sophia asked.

I fiddled with an empty plate, which I'd consumed in minutes. My appetite really was back. "Yep."

She frowned. "Why doesn't Jonah fight back?"

"You ever try hitting your mom or dad, even if they're hitting you first?" I asked her. "It's not as easy as you think."

Sophia sighed. "I guess it would be hard, even if they were coming at you. I couldn't imagine my parents hurting me."

"Me neither." I always had great parents. Dad could be a bit of a hardass, but he never raised a hand to me. Mom neither. I think she'd cut her own hands off first.

Jonah wasn't so lucky.

"Who do you think hit him?"

"His dad, his mom, maybe both? Probably both," I confirmed.

"How awful." Sophia looked like she wanted to cry.

I sighed. Stuff started flooding out of me. "I remember Jonah's parents never used to let him out of the house. He'd have to sneak out to see me. He was like their little slave," I said. "He tried so hard to make them proud when we were growing up, but no matter what he did, it was never good enough."

"What horrible parents." Sophia shuddered. "I can't even imagine."

"I don't consider those types of people parents," I said. "He really had trouble his first semester at Orenda. He couldn't handle not being told what to do all the time. He wanted to drop out and go live back home."

"Why?" Sophia was stunned. "Why would you want to go back to that?"

"He didn't know any better. When you grow up in a prison your entire life, freedom scares the hell out of you," I told her. "I told him to stick it out a year, and if he still wanted to go home, he could."

I smiled at the old memories. "After that first semester he just... blossomed. He became confident. He was so happy. I was the first person he came out to. He was freaking out. He thought I would hate him because he was gay."

"He should know you better than that." Sophia tilted her head and stroked Esis.

"That's what I told him." I smiled a little wider. "You should've seen him. He used to be so shy about dating guys. Now he practically paints rainbows everywhere he goes."

Sophia laughed. "Now everybody knows."

"Yeah." I grinned. "He made the announcement to all of Kinpago after he bonded with Squeaks last summer. I think she was the one who convinced him to be who he really was. He rented out this stage in the middle of town, dressed in drag, and lip-synced to Lady Gaga. It was... really something."

"Oh my gosh." Sophia put her hand over her mouth, dying of laughter. "I wish I could've seen that."

"It was the best," I said. "He did it right after I lost Nashoma. To be honest, Jonah kinda pulled me out of it after he died. I don't think I'd be here if it wasn't for him."

I played with my fork. "I just... I wish I could repay him by helping him now."

"Why don't you?" Sophia asked. "Can't you stand up to his parents?"

"I can't do anything." I shook my head. "Last time I tried to defend him, his parents threw me out, and he took their side. It didn't work out too well."

"That's so horrible. I hope he wakes up soon. He needs to kick them out of his life," Sophia said.

I shrugged. "Jonah's gotta do what's best for himself, whatever that is. And he's the one that's gotta figure that out."

"I guess." Sophia put her head in her hand and sighed. "I just wish there was something we could do."

Koigni weren't the types to forget and let things go. They protected the people they cared about viciously— which meant they liked to meddle in things that weren't their business.

Sophia had to stay out of this. Messing with the Chanees would only get her hurt, as it did me.

Sophia checked her watch. "Come on. We're running late to meet Imogen." We left the dining hall and headed to the Nivita dorms. To my surprise, Jonah was there, but he still didn't look too bright.

"Liam!" We heard Imogen's voice behind us and turned. She was literally running toward us, waving a black book in her hands. Sassy and Squeaks were at her heels. "Liam, I figured something out, I—"

She stopped. Her mouth dropped open when she observed Jonah's face. He looked back at her without a smile.

"Oh, Jonah." Imogen put her arms around his neck and hugged him. Jonah stooped down and embraced Imogen, lifting her off the ground. It looked like a giant holding a doll.

"I'm okay," Jonah whispered. Imogen gave a weak whimper into his shoulder.

We might be best friends, but Jonah and Imogen shared a special bond. It was obvious he'd told Imogen more about his parents than he'd ever told me. And I felt a little awkward intruding in on their moment.

When Jonah put Imogen back down, Squeaks stepped forward. Her tail lashed and her beak clacked together in concern. She nibbled at his hair. Her big black eyes seemed so full and upset.

"I'm fine, Squeaky." Jonah rubbed her neck. He sounded like me—and it was totally unconvincing.

Squeaks nuzzled her head into Jonah. He leaned his forehead against hers, closing his eyes.

I'd noticed Jonah had been looking a lot better since he bonded with Squeaks. There was a reason he'd come in with a black eye today over any other day. If his dad tried to smack him with Squeaks around, he'd end up without an arm.

"Hey, Jonah," I said, and he looked up. "I was thinking, I kinda want to get an apartment this summer. Just for a few months before we go back into school. I'd like you to move in with me. What do you think?"

I had no intention of moving out of my parents' mansion before I graduated, but I had the money, and I couldn't handle another summer of Jonah living in that hell. I'd do anything just to get him out of that house.

"Yeah." Jonah immediately brightened. "That would be so cool!"

"We could all move together," Imogen suggested brightly. "The four of us! We could get a three bedroom."

Sophia and I glanced at each other. I knew what she was thinking. We'd only been dating for a few months. Some people would say we were moving a little fast.

It didn't seem like that to me. I wanted to live with Sophia. Waking up next to her every day in the same bed would be incredible. And it might be possible, after I cleared her name. People from different Houses living together might look weird, but since there were four of us, it wouldn't draw too much suspicion. As long as we didn't let anyone inside, it might actually be possible.

"That sounds... really amazing," I finished, and Sophia beamed. "We should look into that."

"It would be so perfect," Sophia said. "But what is it you wanted to tell us, Imogen?"

"Oh, yeah." Imogen held up the black book she'd been carrying. It was old and leather-bound. "I found something in my family's library that might help you, Liam. But I think we should show Perot, too."

"Lead the way," I offered.

We headed down to the alchemy lab. Professor Perot was brewing something in one of his vials, and he looked flustered. Baxtor was on a perch cooing to him sharply, as if calling out instructions. The peacock looked cross, too.

"Professor?" Imogen poked her head in. "Is this a good time?"

"Children!" Perot said. He wiped his forehead with a cloth and said, "Come in, come in."

We filed into the classroom, and he poured out the beaker he was working at into the sink. The noises Baxtor was making, I was sure his Familiar was swearing at him.

"Another one, ruined," he said in discouragement, before turning toward us. "What can I help you with?"

Thank the ancestors Perot didn't ask about Jonah's eye.

Imogen stepped forward. "I wanted to show you this."

She opened the book on a desk and pointed to a painting that had been copied into the book's pages. There, I saw a picture of a tall, older man with gray hair, his hand on the shoulder of a young woman, who was sitting down in a chair. The woman had her black hair in two braids, and a white wolf sat by her side. Her skin was tan, like mine, and she had dark eyes.

"I present to you Arthur and Anna Cedrick, friends to the Hawkei and builders of Orenda Academy," Imogen said proudly.

"Wait a minute..." I muttered, staring at the painting. I pointed to Anna. "That's my ancestor!"

Imogen smiled. "Precisely. She's the daughter of Arthur Cedrick, and she died young of a mysterious illness. I bet she passed away from whatever Liam has."

"That's gotta be it." Things were coming together.

"Liam, what are you talking about? How can you be sure?" Jonah asked.

"She's my spirit guide. I know her. I've met Anna several times, when I've summoned her," I said. "I just didn't know who she was."

"It seems like your illness *is* genetic, Liam. Cedrick must've married a Hawkei woman, and had Anna. Then Anna must've had a child and passed whatever ailed her down to you," Perot said. "Does the book say anything more?"

"It says that Arthur married a Toaqua after he built Orenda Academy," Imogen said proudly. "He had a daughter. And she produced a boy that became the next Toaqua chief."

"I can't believe this," I said in awe. "I'm descended from Arthur and Anna Cedrick."

"Aye." Jonah clapped me on the back. "Good to know ye've got a bit of Scottish in ye, me laddie."

Good to see he was back to normal.

"No wonder she's your spirit guide, Liam," Sophia offered. "She knew you were going to be sick, and she knew what it felt like, so she signed up to guide you."

This was incredible. "Did you find out anything else, Imogen?"

"Not much." She ruffled through the pages of the book. "It describes Anna's illness, and it sounds a lot like what you've got, Liam. But it doesn't seem like very many Hawkei had it. Only a few mixed in with the dozens of descendants Anna had. The disease is exclusively found in the Toaqua bloodline, nowhere else."

I was getting excited. Next Ancestors' Day I could try summoning Anna, maybe even talk to her! And I could get some answers on how to handle my illness. It was coming up, not even two months away.

"How long did Anna survive?" Sophia questioned.

Perot and I shared a glance. He knew what was coming. "The legends say Anna passed away before her thirtieth birthday," Perot said. "But that was in the days of Anichi, when they had people to heal her. Liam... he isn't so lucky."

I expected some sort of breakdown, but it didn't happen. Sophia just picked up Esis and cuddled him. "I understand."

She was being exceedingly calm about it. So were Imogen and Jonah. It was... weird.

"I think you should keep this book, Professor." Imogen handed it out to him. "There might be something in there that could help find a cure for Liam."

Perot took it. "Thank you, my dear. This will be crucial to my research."

When we left Perot's office, I immediately grabbed Imogen and wrapped her in a giant hug. She squeaked as I spun her around. "Imogen, thank you! I can't believe you did this for me!"

"Of course I did." Imogen gasped and coughed as I set her down. "We're friends, aren't we? I told you I would."

"I just can't believe you had the time to go through all those books at your house," Jonah said. "Babe, I've been there, and they're so... wordy."

Imogen blushed. "Well... I kind of had a lot of free time when Sophia and I were fighting."

"It's nice to see that something good came out of you two bitches going at it," Jonah said cheerfully, and he wrapped an arm around each of the girls.

Sophia giggled. "It did. But we're never going to do it again."

"Never." Imogen reached out to squeeze Sophia's hand. "I missed you too much to fight like that."

I was in a better mood than I had been in ages. I finally had some hope. This Ancestors' Day, I'd speak to Anna Cedrick. And I'd finally get some answers.

sophia

SIXTEEN

"Sophia Henley, you're up next."

My knees shook as I rose from my desk and started toward the front of the class. I'd listened to people present their Hawkei Careers projects on Monday, but it couldn't prepare me for when it finally came my turn on Wednesday. Professor Cameron thought I was about to present my topic on Fire creature care. She had no idea I'd changed my mind.

All eyes turned on me and Esis as I walked to the front of the classroom. I could connect each face with the presentation they'd given. *Doctor, lawyer, congressman, professor, dragon specialist, alchemist, Hawkei historian...*

They were all very good career choices. The only presentation anyone had laughed at was when Miranda said she wanted to be a Familiar hairdresser. And the guys who laughed were stuck-up Koigni second-years whose Familiars looked in serious need of a grooming. Miranda would hair dress the crap out of their creatures.

I reached the front of the room and placed my flash drive in the computer at Professor Cameron's desk, then pulled up my slideshow on the projector. Esis hopped down from my shoulder and sat in front of the computer to change my slides for me. Professor Cameron and her koala Familiar gave me a simultaneous nod, letting me know I could begin.

I wiped my sweaty hands on my jeans. *Just relax*, I told myself.

I glanced to my notecards, then cleared my throat and began. "Hawkei sociologist Rupert Cosper states, '*It is of our duty as Hawkei to pursue the tasks in which benefit the entirety of the tribe.*' You'll notice that Cosper used the word *tasks* rather than *careers*, and I believe he did so deliberately. In chapter six of our textbook, we read about Cosper's wife, Holly."

I shot Esis a glance, and he changed the slide to show a picture of Holly Cosper from our textbook. It was an old photo from the seventies and showed her holding a young child on her hip, surrounded by four other children. The family stood in front of their treehouse in the Nivita neighborhood. It was one of the first modern treehouses on the Hawkei reservation.

I continued. "Cosper continues, '*Many would have said that Holly did not work, but they would be grossly wrong in assuming so. My wife worked a twenty-four-hour shift seven days a week, three-hundred-and-sixty-five days per year. As a professor, I didn't even work half that.*' Cosper recognized the importance of his wife's role among the family. He did not discredit her just because she wasn't bringing an income home."

I noticed Professor Cameron's forehead crease as she wrote something down on her grading sheet. I shifted uncomfortably at the front of the room.

"Cosper's six children each went on to contribute greatly to the tribe. Their eldest son, Eli Cosper, was the head engineer who worked on the *Hozho*, ensuring that the design would be compatible with elements in flight. His daughter, Elana Cosper, pioneered various Familiar medical care tactics, particularly in dragons, which led to a ninety-eight percent survival rate from dragon flu, up from sixty-percent prior to her work. His other children took jobs in government, teaching, and medicine, all making significant contributions in their respective fields."

I glanced around the room to see most people looked bored with my presentation. One guy in the back was even sleeping.

"In his memoir, Eli Cosper says, '*If it weren't for my mother's love and constant encouragement, the* Hozho *would not exist.*'"

I took a deep breath and signaled for Esis to change the slide. It showed an old picture of me in high school that I had Amelia send me. In it, I knelt down with my friends Emily and Leah between a group of fifteen first-graders. Each of the kids held up a picture book we'd been given for Christmas as part of our Community Service Club project.

"I believe that my greatest contribution to the Hawkei will not be through any career I might undertake, but through the life lessons I can pass down to my children."

My next three slides gave an overview of what my duties as a mother would include. I didn't once mention cooking or cleaning. Instead, I focused on the emotional nurturing I would provide my children, citing various psychologists and scientific studies on the human brain. I talked about how staying home with my children would allow me the time and attention to raise them in an environment best suited to their personal growth.

"As Holly Cosper said, '*Our tribe is the present, but our children are our future,*'" I concluded. "Thank you." I had to swallow down my nerves when the presentation was finally over.

"Thank you, Sophia," Professor Cameron said. "That was a very unique, well-researched angle."

I smiled, but my smile quickly faded when a girl in the front row raised her hand. Her name was Jill, and she'd given a presentation on working as an Elementai on the *Hozho* so she could travel the world. Professor Cameron didn't even call on her before she started speaking. "Yeah, I just have a quick question. Doesn't your presentation suggest that working mothers are somehow inferior to stay-at-home moms?"

I blinked several times, taken off-guard by the question. "No. I wasn't suggesting that at all."

"Wouldn't a traveling mother have less *time and attention* to give to raise their children *in an environment best suited to their personal growth?*" Jill shot at me, crossing her arms over her chest.

"Absolutely not," I said. My palms were starting to grow clammy again. I hadn't at all anticipated that type of response. I was starting to wish I'd put some sort of disclaimer in the presentation. "Working mothers can benefit from all the psychological studies I cited."

"But if they're not home with their kids, they would like, screw them up, right?" Jill challenged. Her tone was nasty.

"No," I stated firmly. "All I'm saying is that staying home with my kids would be the right choice for *my* family."

One guy in the back leaned over to his friend and whispered rather loudly, "Lazy."

The other replied, "Trophy wife."

"How can you know what will be best for your family if you're not married yet?" Jill asked. "You're just planning on marrying the first rich guy you can find? How do you know you won't need a job to support your family?"

"I—" I gaped at her. Of course I thought working mothers were just as capable. My mom worked, and Amelia and I turned out fine. It just wasn't what I wanted for myself.

"That's enough," Professor Cameron said calmly. She stood from her desk and met me at the front of the room. "It's not your job to judge and question other students' presentations, Jill."

I breathed a sigh of relief.

"She's judging mine," Jill accused.

"I was not," I insisted.

Professor Cameron held up a hand. "That's enough, Jill. I don't think Sophia meant any offense by suggesting this was the right path for *her*. She provided a very compelling argument supported by credible sources. That's more than I can say for you."

A chorus of gasps traveled around the room. Next to Jill, a Toaqua guy froze the water in his water bottle and held it out to her. "Want some ice to cool that burn?"

"Shut up," Jill snapped at him.

Professor Cameron turned to me while the rest of the class broke out into conversation. She handed me the rubric she'd been using to mark my scores. "I would've liked to see more comparison on the role between working mothers and stay-at-home mothers, but overall, your presentation was very good. Congratulations, Sophia."

I looked down at the paper to see my grade written in big numbers across the top. Ninety-eight percent! Holy crap! Esis hopped onto my shoulder and peeked at the grade, then clapped in my ear.

"Shh..." I told him. I didn't need everyone knowing what I'd scored.

I returned to my seat, still trying to process the fact that I got an A on my presentation. Maddie had been right! It was like a huge weight had been lifted off my shoulders.

Esis grabbed my rubric from my hands and put it on his head like a veil. He paraded across the table like he was walking down the aisle.

I laughed at him and stroked his tail, thinking what it would be like to get married. In my mind, Liam stood at the end of the aisle, with Jonah and Squeaks at his side, and Imogen and Sassy on the opposite end of the altar. We were outside in warm summer air, beneath a canopy of trees that swayed softly in the wind. The sun shined down like diamonds across the aisle. Esis walked in front of me with a basket of rose petals, sprinkling them in front of me as *Canon in D* played on an unseen organ. Everyone I loved was there, including Amelia and my parents. Liam and I would be married, and soon after, we'd have kids of our own. I wondered if they'd look like me, or like him.

It seemed so perfect. Then a terrifying realization struck.

Liam was Toaqua, and I was Koigni. It was forbidden for us to be together, but we couldn't sneak around forever. Unless we could truly get the Hawkei to change their traditions— change the law— I'd have to choose between Liam and my dream of raising children.

"I'm so done with this week," I announced as I entered Imogen's room on Thursday night. I dropped my backpack on her bed and fell onto the mattress. Esis jumped off my shoulder and settled into Imogen's mushroom chair in the corner. Sassy startled on the bed and stuck her nose out to sniff my hair. I was glad the weekend was here and Imogen had invited me for a sleepover.

"What's up?" she asked as she dug through an endless pile of nail polish on her dresser.

"I presented my Hawkei Careers project. It was totally nerve-racking. Then this girl tried to chew me out about it afterward."

"Aw, man. That sucks," Imogen said. "How'd you do, though?"

"I got an A."

Imogen turned to the bed with a pile of nail polish in her hands, then sat beside me and fanned the bottles out in front of her. "What's the problem, then?"

I sat up and shrugged. "I don't know. It was just the whole topic of becoming a mom is... a little scary, to be honest."

Imogen shook a bottle of purple nail polish. "You're only eighteen, Sophia. You're too young to have kids. You don't need to be thinking about that yet."

"But... I kind of do. I mean, Liam and I are getting serious, and I need to figure out what I want with him," I said.

"I thought you wanted marriage and kids. You can't have that if you're with Liam." Imogen held out her hand to me. "Fingers, please. Besides, didn't you say his mom was calling you *shantee* when you met her?"

I stuck my bare fingers out in her direction, and she guided them onto her knee. "Yeah. What does that mean, by the way?"

"It's a Hawkei word that means *wife-in-training*, or engaged to be wed," Imogen explained. "In our tribe, the future mother-in-law of the woman to be married takes the *shantee* under her wing and puts her through wife training before she marries her son. The tradition has died out in most of the tribe, but I think Toaqua families, especially wealthy ones, still practice it."

"Oh, wow," I said, trying to take in the weight of the word's meaning. "I can't believe his mom called me that."

"*I* can," Imogen mumbled. I didn't know exactly what she meant by that.

"Anyway, I *do* want to marry Liam," I said. "I wouldn't be with him if I didn't. But the Hawkei would never let us have kids. How can I contribute to the tribe as a mother if my kids were illegal?"

Imogen bit her lower lip as she painted a streak of purple across my pinky nail, like she didn't know what to say. Finally, she said, "So... how serious are we talking with you and Liam?"

I blushed a deep shade of red. "You already know most of it."

"Most of it?" Imogen's eyebrows shot up. "Girl, you need to tell me *everything*."

My face grew even hotter. "There's something I didn't tell you about because... well, I don't know if it's weird or not."

Imogen's eyes grew to twice their size. "Oh my gosh. Did you suck the D?"

"*Suck the D?* Ancestors, Imogen. People don't talk like that, do they?"

She shrugged and returned to painting my nails.

"No, it wasn't that, but you're really close."

Imogen drew a sharp breath and made a rude gesture with her hand and tongue.

"Im!" I swatted at her. "Yes, okay."

"Sophia!" Imogen sang with a wide smile. "You're *so* bad. What was it like?"

My heart sped up as I thought back to it. Honestly, I'd never felt anything so amazing. I was nervous at first since it was out in the open, on a freaking beach, but as soon as Liam touched me *there*, that didn't seem to matter. And then his tongue was on me and just... oh, God. It was incredible.

But I didn't say any of that to Imogen. Instead, I just said. "It was good."

"Good?" Imogen repeated in disbelief. "You've gotta give me more than that, girl."

"I don't know. I was just worried about how I tasted, you know?"

Imogen started on my next nail with a light blue color. "Well, did he like it?"

"He seemed to."

"Then I'm sure it was fine," she said. "If you're ever worried about that, you've just gotta use strawberries."

My eyebrows shot up. "Strawberries? On my... Imogen, that sounds gross."

"Strawberries aren't gross!" she insisted. "I read it in a book!"

"Was this book by any chance called the *Kamasutra?*" I teased.

"Shut up." Imogen dabbed a dot of nail polish on my nose, then screwed the cap back on the blue. I gasped at her, pretending to be offended. "No, it was this fiction book I read a few years ago."

I clicked my tongue at her. "Naughty."

She rolled her eyes. "It wasn't like, erotica. It was really sweet."

"I'm sure the strawberries were, too," I joked.

"That's the point!" she cried.

"Come on, Im. I'm not putting *food* down there."

"No! You *eat* the strawberries."

"Ooh." That was a million times better. I loved fruit. "Yeah, I can do that."

Imogen took off the cap to a red color. "Okay, but if I *did* suggest you put something down there, I don't get why you're so against it."

"I could get an infection or something," I argued.

Imogen shrugged. "I think you need to get a little more adventurous."

"Adventurous?" I asked. "We're plenty adventurous. Someone almost caught us in the Commons that one night."

"Was it fun? Almost being caught?" She smirked.

"Come on, Imogen," I complained.

"Hey." She held her hands up in surrender. "Until Cade decides to ask me out, I must live vicariously through you."

"You should ask *him* out. Then you can do all sorts of crazy shit throughout the castle." I giggled.

Imogen sat up straight and breathed a sigh. "Tell you what. If you do something crazy with Liam, I'll ask Cade out myself."

"He already ate me out on the beach!" Sassy's ears perked up at the words *ate me out*. I quickly lowered my voice. "What more do you want?"

Imogen's jaw dropped. "The beach? You didn't mention it was on the beach!"

I waved my hand like it was no big deal. "It was this private little beach. No one was around."

Imogen pressed her lips together, thinking. "Then your next step is doing it where someone *is* around."

"Ew. No!" I objected. "Besides, if we're caught, we could get in a lot of trouble."

"You're not supposed to get *caught*," she emphasized. "It's just the idea of it that's fun. Look, if you suck Liam's dick in the library, I'll ask Cade out. No more excuses."

I eyed her for any signs of dishonesty. I couldn't find any. "Fine. If I suck Liam's dick in the library, you'll be the first to know. And you *have* to ask Cade to be your boyfriend."

"Deal," Imogen said happily. She didn't think I would really go through with it.

I had no intention of doing such a thing, but I really wanted to see Imogen ask Cade out. It wasn't like I wouldn't enjoy it. And I sure as hell knew Liam would.

I was going to have to seriously consider this deal...

FRIDAY WAS mine and Liam's day. I was so excited to see him that I was out of bed at the crack of dawn. Imogen winked at me on my way out of her room and said, "Don't do anything *too* crazy," before rolling back over into bed.

Liam and I met outside the dining hall for breakfast. The second I saw him standing there waiting for me, my whole world lit up. It was like I was back by our waterfall all over again, with fortune fairies lighting up the night sky with their twinkling lights. *Magical.*

Liam looked well today. His lips were full of color, he held his shoulders straight, and his eyes were brimming with life. There wasn't even a hair on his head that looked out of place. It seemed like Esis' treatments were really helping him. Maybe he really wasn't going to die. Butterflies fluttered in my stomach as Liam's eyes met mine.

"Hey, *pawee*," he greeted as we entered the room. "How were classes this week?"

I grabbed a plate. "Ugh. Don't even ask. You look bright-eyed and bushy-tailed today."

"Yeah, I'm feeling great. I was thinking that maybe we could do a bit of hiking today. You could bring your camera."

"It's already in my bag." I winked at him as I gestured to the backpack on my shoulder, which Esis sat perched on top of. Esis tugged at my hair to get my attention, then pointed to the bacon. "Yeah, yeah, buddy. I'm working on it."

Breakfast seemed to taste better this morning than most days. I didn't know if the cooks in the kitchen did something differently or if it was just because I was in an awesome mood. I mean, I was sitting across from Liam *and* my big Hawkei Careers presentation was over. How much better could the day get?

As we walked out of the dining hall, my fingers gravitated toward Liam's, but I pulled away when I saw a group of students turn down the hall toward us. We made our way down the grand staircase, then headed toward the back of the castle near one of my favorite hiking trails. My footsteps slowed as we passed the library.

Liam stopped beside me. "What's up?"

I glanced inside the double doors, thinking about what Imogen had said. The library was one of my favorite places in the castle. I'd spent a lot of time there my first semester trying to dig up what I could on the prophecy— which honestly wasn't much. But it was still a beautiful, peaceful place to hang out. It had a high ceiling covered in wooden beams, and an intricate painting of all different types of magical creatures on the entrance wall. Floor-to-ceiling bookcases lined the outer walls, while long rows of bookshelves and various study areas spanned the rest of the room. Light spilled in from a huge stained-glass window set into the far wall. The room was quiet, full of people... and pretty damn tempting.

"What do you say we take a detour?" I suggested. I wasn't sure I'd decided to actually do it until the words came out of my mouth.

Liam eyed me curiously. "What kind of detour?"

I bit my lower lip and stared up at him past my lashes. "The good kind."

Liam gaped at me, speechless.

I couldn't help but smile. I leaned into him and whispered. "That day on the beach was amazing. What do you say, Liam? Can I return the favor?"

"Uh..." Liam finally picked his jaw up from the ground. "Here? In the library?"

I shrugged. "Yeah, it'll be fun."

Liam opened his mouth, but it took a second for the words to come out. "Okay, I'm in."

Grinning from ear to ear, I led Liam inside. We passed by a librarian, who didn't even look up from her book, and by a group of Nivita students whispering softly at one of the study tables. We ducked behind one of the rows way in the back, where the books looked centuries old and were covered in a thick layer of dust.

I dropped my backpack in the corner. "Esis, go keep watch."

Esis jumped down from my shoulder and scurried around the corner, where he could see the group of students. My whole body shook in anticipation.

As soon as Esis was out of sight, Liam and I were all over each other like magnets. His lips connected with mine, and his tongue slipped inside my mouth. I clung to him like the floor had fallen out from under me and he was the only thing keeping me grounded. His hands found the bare skin just above my waistband and inched their way up my shirt. I inhaled a deep breath and bit his lower lip when they met my breasts and he squeezed. My nipples hardened beneath his touch. God, I loved the way he made me feel.

I drew away, breathing heavily, and ran my hands down his side and to his waist. My fingers paused on his zipper. "Before we do this, I have to lead with the disclaimer that Imogen basically bet me that I wouldn't."

Liam smirked down at me, looking amused. "And what happens if you do?"

"She'll ask Cade out."

"Oh," Liam said with a nod, like that made perfect sense. "Then I guess we better do this... you know, for the sake of their relationship."

"Right," I said softly. "For Imogen and Cade."

"For Imogen and Cade," Liam whispered back, but the look in his eyes said something entirely different.

The sound of his zipper dropping sounded like a stack of books falling. At least, it seemed like that to me in the silence of the library. Could the group of students in the study area hear us all the way from here? The very thought sent adrenaline coursing through my veins like a flash flood raging through a canyon. This was so forbidden. It made it even more exciting.

I pushed the fabric of Liam's jeans aside and reached for the waistband of his underwear. As my fingers grazed the top of him, heat pooled between my thighs like the warmth of a winter fire. I pulled his underwear down to expose him to the cool air of the library. Liam gasped and clutched the bookshelf behind him when I took him in my hand.

My heart pummeled against my rib cage as I lowered myself to my knees. I leaned in slowly, glancing up to Liam's face to watch his reaction. His eyes were closed, and his bottom lip quivered in anticipation. My breath brushed across his skin, and his shoulders fell to a relaxed position. He was so into it and I hadn't even started yet.

Finally, I lowered my mouth until my lips were all the way around him, my tongue rolling over his erection. Liam tangled his fingers in my hair, pulling tightly on the strands. It only made everything hotter. I took it as an invitation to go deeper. As I did, Liam's breathing grew heavier, and he pressed on my head with his hands like he wanted more. I snuck a glance back up at him to see he was biting down hard on his lower lip, like he was trying not to make a sound.

Damn, he wanted me so badly.

I released my hold on him and let my mouth do all the work. My hands roamed his hips, then reached his backside. Liam gasped as I opened the back of my throat and eased down on him as far as I could go.

And then I gagged.

I quickly drew away from him. He released me instantly and shoved his dick back inside his pants.

"Sorry," I whispered while wiping drool from my chin.

Esis poked his head around the corner, but I waved to him to let him know everything was fine.

"You okay?" Liam asked, looking concerned— and a bit embarrassed.

"Fine. Now I know better." I gave a light chuckle, then reached out for his jeans again.

He shied away, though he didn't pull up his zipper or button his jeans.

"It's fine," I whispered. "No one's coming."

Liam took my hands in his when I reached for him again. "Maybe... maybe we should stop."

I looked up into his eyes, searching them curiously. He seemed so eager for this only moments ago. What had changed?

"Okay," I said softly. "If you don't want to do this anymore, we can stop. I won't make you."

"I *do* want to do this... and I don't." He looked away from me, like he was ashamed.

"Liam." I rose to my feet beside him. "What's wrong? You can tell me anything."

He hesitated. "It's nothing, really."

"It is," I said in a low whisper only Liam could hear. "Otherwise, we wouldn't have stopped. We don't have to go any further, but if I don't know why you're uncomfortable, I can't make you more comfortable next time. Is it because I gagged? I didn't mind. In fact, I'm totally fine with it."

"No, it's not that," Liam said. His hands tensed in mine, like whatever he was about to say was difficult for him. "I... this is my first time, okay?"

"Really?" I asked in shock. I thought Mia would've done this to him a hundred times before.

"Mia always thought it was gross," he admitted, averting his gaze from mine. "She always made me feel bad for wanting one. Then here you are all eager for it, and I just can't resist you. But I... I don't want to hurt you. I don't want you to hate it."

"Liam," I said, rubbing my fingers over the backs of his hands. "You didn't hurt me. I don't think you *could* hurt me. And if you did, that's not something I would hide from you. And if I hated it, I wouldn't be doing it. In fact, I was really enjoying myself."

Liam gave me a shy smile. "Me, too."

"Do you want to leave?" I asked.

Liam didn't answer right away. It felt like he was contemplating which answer I wanted to hear, like he thought there was a right answer. Damn, Mia had seriously given him the wrong expectations about relationships.

"Liam," I stated firmly, looking him in the eyes. "I will *never* make you do anything you don't want to do. All I ask from you is honesty."

His shoulders relaxed. "Okay. Honestly, I kind of want to finish. But now it's all awkward... and it's hella hard to stay quiet."

I smirked. "That's the fun, isn't it?"

Liam nodded.

"We can start over," I suggested. "But only if you want to."

"Okay," Liam agreed. "But what about... what about when I finish? What are we going to do about...?"

I squeezed his hands in mine. "You let me worry about that. Okay?"

Liam smiled, looking more relaxed. "I'm so lucky to have you, *pawee*."

"Me, too," I whispered back. "Are you ready to try again?"

Liam dropped my hands and grabbed on to the shelves behind him. A wide smile spread across his face. "Hell yeah, I am."

I knelt in front of him again. He needed help getting hard again, but it didn't take long once I touched him. My mouth was on him again, pumping up and down as he let out soft, quiet moans above me. God, those moans were everything. To know that I was pleasuring him and not royally screwing this up gave me all the satisfaction I could hope for.

Just as I thought my heart might explode from the adrenaline, Liam's muscles contracted inside of me. A warm liquid filled my mouth. It wasn't quite like I was expecting. It was thick and tasted like... pineapple.

Awesome. I loved pineapple.

Liam pulled away from me, breathing deeply. He was so disoriented that he just let everything hang out in the open for several seconds before he opened his eyes and came back to reality. He gazed down at me with the softest look I'd ever seen him wear before. That look alone sent my stomach somersaulting in my abdomen.

Liam zipped his pants. "Fuck, *pawee*. That was amazing."

I swallowed everything in my mouth and stood beside him. "Really?"

Liam smiled at me. "Does it look like I'm disappointed?"

I beamed. "No."

"Then you have your answer."

"Hey, Liam," I said as I gathered my things and we started walking out of our hiding spot. Esis met us at the end of the aisle and jumped into my arms.

"Yeah, Soph?"

"I really enjoyed that. I think I'd like to do it again sometime."

Liam grinned. "You will, *pawee*. You will."

I really looked forward to it.

I just hoped we never had to stop.

SEVENTEEN

"Have you retrieved it yet?"

I'd tried to duck out of Advanced Toaqua Magic III as quickly as I could, but Baine grabbed my arm and stopped me before I could leave the classroom. His eyes searched me, as if he was trying to see what I would say next would be a lie or not.

"Obviously not," I said, irritated. "If I had, I would've brought it to you immediately."

"Have you gotten close?" he asked in frustration. "Or are you even trying?"

"I'm not trying to procrastinate, here," I shot back.

"I'm sorry, but I'm not convinced." Baine's tone was flat. "If Sophia does have something powerful in her possession, we're in trouble. It shouldn't be that hard to steal an item from an eighteen-year-old girl and an oversized rabbit."

"It's a kurble." I'd never used the word before, but fuck it. I wanted to piss Baine off. "You think you can do a better job, get on with it, because I'm at the end of my rope."

"You know I can't do that. If I were to be caught stealing something from a student, Koigni would know what we're up to." Baine's expression was tense. "The Toaqua Elders are done with waiting, Liam, and so is your father."

I hadn't spoke to Dad since our argument. But I honestly didn't give a shit if he was getting impatient. He knew where I stood. "This is my mission," I said. "You assigned me to get the job done, and I will."

"Liam..." Baine frowned. "You know I don't feel good about any of this. I care about Sophia as well. But I also know you won't follow through with this mission unless you're put under pressure. It's how you've been all your life."

"I get that this has to be done. But it's gotta be on my terms," I said.

"They're threatening Thalassa," Baine said, and his words were desperate. "You don't understand."

Something in me got bitter and broke. "No. *You* don't understand. You don't realize how much I fucking miss him."

I ripped my arm away from him and left. I don't think I'd ever sworn at a professor before, but dammit, Baine was really starting to get on my nerves. And it was more than usual, so that was really bad. Every time he saw me, he asked if I had gotten my hands on the totem. I had to keep telling him no, and acting like I didn't know what I was searching for. He acted more and more disappointed, and as much as I hated to admit it, it kinda hurt.

It was nearing the end of the semester, the time of my deadline. I thought in January I'd have Nashoma back by now, and he still wasn't here. I was starting to freak out that the Elders would retract their offer and refuse to bring Nashoma back at all.

It'd crossed my mind lately to try and do it myself— but how the hell did you raise someone from the dead? I wanted to ask for help— Imogen was such a killer researcher, she could probably dig something up— but that would totally blow my cover.

I'd had a lot on my mind, with Ancestors' Day coming up and figuring out what I was going to say to Anna, along with getting my hands on the totem. It didn't make it any easier that Professor Perot had told me I was going to die a few weeks ago, then I'd somehow started making a miraculous recovery. All my recent tests had come back really good, and it'd practically sent Perot into a seizure. I didn't know what the fuck my body was doing.

I wasn't hungry... too pissed off... so I went into Basket Weaving early to work on my project, but not even that helped my mood. Usually it calmed me down, but lately I kept on making mistakes. I had to tear out a lot of my work and start over several times. Professor Amber hovered over me and crooned that I needed to *let the spirit in*, whatever the fuck that meant.

After class, I had a fuck-ton of homework to do, but I didn't feel like doing it, so I headed to the Commons instead. I heard a huge roar come from one of the classrooms, and a couple of people screamed.

One of the large doors opened, and a tyrannosaurus rex, green with yellow feathers, came walking out of the classroom, carrying one of the professors. A stegosaurus and a velociraptor followed. A bunch of students came out from behind them, including Sophia and Imogen. Sophia was beaming with excitement. She saw me and left Imogen's side, hurrying over.

"Have fun in Ancient Familiars?" I asked.

"Yes! Who knew that dinosaurs weren't really extinct?" she gushed. "I got to pet a t-rex!"

Esis was in her arms. He made little movements with his arms and growled, like he was pretending to be a dinosaur.

Her enthusiasm was contagious. My eyes caught the loop around her neck that dipped into her t-shirt, hiding the totem. It was hard to concentrate on stealing the totem when all my attention went immediately to Sophia whenever she was in the room.

Also, it didn't help that she gave *amazing* blow jobs. The library had become my favorite place in the castle.

"You okay?" Sophia eyed me. "You don't talk much, but you're being... quiet. Even for you."

I shrugged. "Just Baine. He's annoying."

"Ah, okay," she said. I complained about Baine enough on a regular basis that Sophia was used to it. "So, where you headed?"

"The Commons. I was just gonna chill for a while," I told her.

"Can I come *chill* with you?" Her tone implied something more, but I wasn't in the mood. There really was something wrong with me today.

I reached out and scratched Esis' chin. His eyes rolled back happily. "Always."

When we got there, Imogen had thankfully grabbed our usual spot around the big TV and the fire. She'd started studying, Sassy bent over one of the books like she was reading, too.

I saw that Miranda was close by. She was combing the hair of a white cat that had a blue tint in its fur, which shimmered like a wave every time it moved. Her Elementai, a short, brown-haired woman with hazel eyes, watched in glee. I recognized her as Belinda. She was from my house.

"Miranda, you do such a good job with Ester's hair. I love it," Belinda said. Ester purred and leapt away from Miranda, jumping onto Belinda's lap.

"Ester's got a rather long coat," Miranda said. "She'll feel so much better if you continue to keep it groomed."

Belinda walked off, cuddling her cat and looking rather pleased. She made little raindrops form in the air and crystalize, giving Ester a diamond collar. Ester purred in happiness.

Sophia and I sat down on the couch next to Imogen. Esis hopped up on the table where Ester had been and patted his head.

Miranda laughed. "You want me to do your hair too, buddy? Okay."

Miranda picked her brush back up and started combing Esis' hair. The movement almost caused the little guy to fall over.

Sophia said, "Miranda, I wanted to tell you that your project for Hawkei Careers was really cool. I didn't even know you could be a Familiar hairdresser."

Miranda shrugged. "I don't know. I thought it was pretty good, but I only got a C, and people have been picking on me for it since."

"Really?" Sophia's eyes narrowed.

"Yeah." She sighed. "I'm Koigni. People expect me to have some fancy, important job. They think doing hair is a waste of time."

She frowned. I decided to speak up.

"They just want to show off. Power and reputation is everything in this society," I said. "I'd rather have a job where I was happy then some trumped-up position where I'm respected but miserable."

"Right?" Miranda said. She took a small can of hairspray out of her pocket. "Cover your eyes, Esis."

Esis did, and Miranda sprayed. She grabbed a mirror from the table to show him. "There. What do you think?"

Esis squealed in happiness. Miranda had given him a mohawk. He flexed his muscles and grinned, like he thought he was so tough.

"Well, you've made Esis happy." Sophia giggled.

"Yeah." Miranda sighed. She seemed a little down. "But that's not very important, is it?"

"Of course it is. We need all kinds of people in this world to make it work," I said.

"I guess so." Miranda gathered her things. "See you guys later."

Sophia and I looked at each other as she went. We were both thinking the same thing. One of the things that sucked about our world was so much of it was based off of birth, money, and status. People like Miranda, who followed their hearts and passions, were made to feel worthless because of it.

Imogen looked up from her book. She had a coy look on her face as she reached into her bag and handed something to Sophia. "I was in the store yesterday. I saw this and thought of you."

Sophia started laughing. I looked down. Imogen had given her a canned tin of pineapple.

"You like?" Imogen waggled her eyebrows.

"Oh, yes, pineapple's my *favorite*," Sophia said. Both of them burst out laughing.

I clearly didn't get the joke. I was alerted to Jonah's presence by the sound of clomping hooves, smashing objects, and drawn-out, over-exaggerated sighs.

He collapsed onto the couch, but it wasn't in his own spot. It was on top of us. Jonah literally laid on top of our laps, spread across the three of us, and threw a hand over his eyes dramatically, giving another sigh. Imogen and Sophia made groaning noises as Jonah's weight squished them.

Squeaks copied him, lying on the rug with four feet in the air. Esis jumped down and started punching her in the shoulder. She didn't notice.

"Aren't you supposed to be in class?" I asked him, irritated.

"How can I possibly go to class when Renar doesn't notice me?"

Jonah whined. "I've done *everything* over the past semester to get him to ask me out, and he just... doesn't."

"Hey, I've got an idea. How about you forget about him and find someone else?" I asked sarcastically. I pushed Jonah off, and he went rolling on top of Squeaks.

"How can I do that?" Jonah wailed from Squeaks' middle. "How can I possibly go on?"

Imogen fumbled in her bag and pulled out two mini bottles of tequila. She handed one to Jonah while unscrewing another for herself. "Here, Jonah. Have this."

"Hey, where'd the fuck you get that?" I asked, interested.

"I only brought enough for two, for an emergency," she said. "And Jonah obviously needs it."

Jonah moaned again before he downed the shot. I rolled my eyes. He was being so ridiculous.

Imogen raised the mini bottle in a toast and said, "I'm through with men. I'm dating women from now on."

"Amen to that, sister," Jonah finished. He threw the empty bottle to the other side of the room, and I heard someone shout as it hit them on the side of the head.

"Why do you need it?" I asked Imogen.

"For courage, obviously." Sophia grinned. "She's going to ask out Cade."

"I need more time!" Imogen squeaked.

"Hey, a deal's a deal," I said. I looked around to be sure we wouldn't be heard before I added in a whisper, "Sophia *did* blow me in the library, so you have to ask out Cade."

"I'm sure that was a great sacrifice on your part," Imogen snapped, and I grinned.

Problems forgotten, Jonah rolled onto his stomach to absorb the latest gossip. "What's this I hear? Sophia gave Liam a blow job in the library, of all places? How dirty."

"Yes. We made a bet that if I did it, Imogen would ask Cade out, and she hasn't done it yet." Sophia crossed her arms. "She needs to pay up."

Jonah popped up onto his feet like he'd received an electric shock.

"Well, let's get to it!" He reached for Imogen and pulled her up from the couch.

"What? No, I'm not ready!" Imogen yelled.

Jonah didn't pay attention. He carried Imogen through the Commons and out the door. Sassy gathered Imogen's things into her bag and chased after them, carrying the tote in her mouth. Squeaks hopped playfully after the group.

Sophia giggled. "Too bad Cade's in class right now."

"Like that matters to Jonah," I said. "He'll probably force Imogen to go in there and interrupt with a flash mob proposal."

"Yeah, right. She'll run away screaming." Sophia stood. "I'm kind of hungry. Let's go eat."

I shook my head. "Don't feel like it."

"Liam, you have to eat," Sophia said sternly, and she grabbed my hand to pull me off the couch. "Come on."

Sophia was on me to take care of myself better than I did. She remembered my pills and potions a lot easier, and liked nagging me about how much sleep I got and how often I actually left my dorm. It didn't bother me. I knew she did it because she cared.

She noticed as I picked at my food. I ended up feeding most of it to Esis, who was more than eager to gobble small strips of steak out of my hand. "Are you feeling okay?" she asked in concern.

I shook my head again. "I feel fine, physically. I just miss Nashoma today." *Like, ten times more than usual.*

"Oh. I'm sorry." She frowned.

"It's okay."

I checked the clock in the dining hall and stood up. I wasn't keeping track of the time. I was going to be late.

"Where are you going?" she asked.

"It's Monday. I have Hawkei Legends," I said.

"I thought that wasn't until later?" Sophia asked.

"It's an early class today, special reasons. You can come," I said. "I actually was going to ask if you wanted to. Tonight's gonna be really badass."

"Sure." Sophia got up and swung her bag around her shoulder. Esis hopped onto her other free one for a ride. "I wanted to see if it would be something I'm interested in taking next semester, anyhow."

Professor Lopez was waiting at the beginning of the path up the ancestral mountain, along with a group of other students. "Hey, Professor," I started. "Do you mind if Sophia sits in today? She's thinking about taking this class next year."

"Of course." Professor Lopez smiled at her. "I always welcome curious students, especially freshmen. This class isn't a requirement, but I think it contains very important information that every Hawkei should know."

Sophia seemed intrigued, and Esis tilted his head. Professor Lopez waved his hand and said, "Everyone follow me! Up to the top!"

We started walking up the path. Sophia kept her eye on me, but I made it up the mountain with relative ease. I didn't even have to stop to breathe or take a break. It was such a stark contrast to how I'd been at the start of the year.

When we reached the summit of the mountain where the large totem with the five House symbols was fixed, people started gathering in a circle around a fire that Lopez was building. Sophia lightly brushed her hand against mine before she drew away. This place was special to us. It's where I'd first shown Sophia the ancestors and taught her about our history. Now she was going to learn even more about it. I was so excited. I loved sharing our culture with her.

I sat next to Kira, a black-haired Nivita girl. She and I got along pretty well. Her Familiar, a barn owl named Bubo, hooted from her shoulder. Kira always had a book in her hand, which I liked. We'd exchanged recommendations often in class.

"Hey, Liam, do you have that psychic mystery book I lent you?" Kira asked.

"Yeah." I reached in my bag and handed it to her. "Thanks for that, by the way. It was really good."

Kira smiled. "I think I'm going to give it to Imogen next. We're total besties. I think she'd love it."

"Can I read it?" Sophia asked curiously.

"Sure. Just pass it along to Im once you're done." Kira beamed as she handed it to Sophia. "I'm sure I'll get it back eventually."

"I didn't know you were so into books, Liam. Imogen mentioned it once, but only in passing," Sophia said as she put the blue book into her bag.

"I read a lot, actually." I wasn't one of those people obsessed with selfies and social media (Jonah) or that could stay inside and play video games all day (Ezra). I wasn't a fan of technology. I preferred books.

Professor Lopez stood in front of the fire. By this time, the sun was starting to set and little stars were dotting the sky.

"As many of you know, Ancestors' Day is quickly approaching," Lopez began. "It is the one day of the year that we are allowed to speak with our ancestral guides, and celebrate the anniversary of when our powers were gifted to us, by them, and by the Great Spirit."

"What's the Great Spirit?" Sophia asked under her breath.

"Listen and find out," I whispered back.

Professor Lopez waved his hands. Shapes began forming from the flames, and they emerged out of the fires to become animals. A coyote stepped out of the bonfire, followed by a deer, an eagle, a bear, a bison, and a salmon. Other animals eventually joined them, wolves, raccoons, beavers. They moved around the mountainside, though when they brushed by you, they didn't burn your skin. Lopez used his Fire magic to manipulate them as he narrated.

"When the world began, all that existed was the Great Spirit, and the spirits that surrounded him," Lopez said. "But he was not satisfied. Great Spirit wanted to create life. So the Great Spirit took four parts of himself, Water, Earth, Air, and Fire, and used them to make the world. He separated into four gods and goddesses, one for each element. Fire became the Sun, Water became the Moon, Air became Space, and Earth became our planet. They all worked together to sustain life."

More figures emerged from the fire, people this time. The details that Lopez put into them almost made them look real, humans created from flames. They were dressed in traditional Hawkei clothing and twirled in circles around the animals. The animals began to dance in tune with them, and Lopez increased the speed of his hands, to continue the display in a more elaborate fashion.

"The first people, the Hawkei, rose up out of the ground fully grown. And they were protected and watched over by the four parts of the Great Spirit. But it wasn't long before things started to change." The figures picked up the dance, moving faster. "There was discord, because the Sun was in love with the Moon. They could not exist together as friends, as Earth and Space could, for they were too different. Sun kept chasing Moon through the sky, but he could never keep up with her, for she could not tolerate his heat. She was cool and calm, but he was headstrong and temperamental. They could love from a distance, but could not exist at the same time. And it was known throughout the world that Fire and Water were opposites, never to be united."

Sophia and I glanced at each other. The shadows from the fire figures reflected off our faces. Lopez's words about Fire and Water never being able to coexist, let alone be together, were heavy and ominous. Even the gods were against us. How could you fight that?

"Sun was angry that he could not love Moon," Lopez said. "Out of his anger, he created more gods and goddesses, like Coyote Spirit, to trick young people into chasing unrequited love, and to show off his power. Not to be bested, Moon, Space and Earth all created gods and goddesses of their own, such as Deer Spirit, the goddess of gentleness, and Salmon Spirit, the god of abundance, and others. These gods and goddesses, all from the same Great Spirit, continue to guide and influence the Hawkei today, as the ancestors do."

Lopez brought back the Fire figures into the blazing inferno that sat in the middle of the group, and we were all gathered around a normal fire again. A few people clapped as the story ended.

"You'll all be expected to write a paper about one of your chosen gods or goddesses for this semester's final," Lopez said. "Extra points if you choose a spirit from your House. Class dismissed."

People chatted as we rose to our feet. My mind scrambled through the different spirits I could do for my project. I thought about Whale Spirit, because I knew the most about her and it'd be the easiest to do.

Though on second thought, I might do Coyote Spirit, even though he was a Koigni god. He'd tricked me into falling for a woman I could never truly have.

Sophia stroked Esis' ears. "I know this is our culture, but is all of that really true?"

"That's something you should decide for yourself, isn't it?" I slipped my backpack on. "Though I hoped you liked the class."

"I did. It was really cool." She looked impressed. "Can an Elementai's power really be influenced by astral bodies?"

"Yes. Toaqua can gain strength from the moon, as Koigni draw power from the sun. But that's advanced magic. It's not something everyone can do," I said.

We started the walk down the mountain. "Lopez said the first Hawkei came from the ground. But didn't the first Native Americans come here by crossing over the Bering Strait?" Sophia asked.

"No, that's stupid," I said crossly. "We've always been here."

"How?"

"Great Spirit put us here, *obviously*."

Sophia still looked confused, but she wasn't going to get our history in one night, so I let it go. Hawkei religion wasn't something you could digest easily unless you'd been hearing about it for a lifetime.

When we came back to the Commons, we found Imogen slumped over a table, her head in her arms. She was making these tiny little meeping sounds. Sassy was using her paw to pat her on the back. Jonah was standing nearby, leaning on Squeaks and looking disappointed.

"What happened?" Sophia asked. "Did she ask Cade out?"

"No. She took one look at him, screamed, and ran away," Jonah said, shaking his head. "He's probably terrified of her now."

Imogen let out a loud groan. Poor Im.

"Hey, turn the TV up," someone close-by said.

The sound of a news alert ringing out caught my attention. The three of us turned toward the biggest TV in the room. Imogen lifted her head to see what was going on. The local news was playing, and people were blasting the volume. A broadcaster with a grim expression came on-screen.

Sophia's mouth fell open, and I felt like I'd been punched in the gut as we read the headline. The broadcaster spoke in a voice that was professional, but that didn't try to hide a revolted tone.

"This news may be disturbing to some of our viewers, and therefore, we ask that discretion be advised," the broadcaster began. "This morning Kelly Catori, of Nivita, and Cameron Wahkin, of Yapluma, were discovered having sexual relations in the Greenetree Apartment buildings within Nivita tribe borders. Upon interrogation by the Elementai Task Force, they confessed to being involved in an interhouse relationship."

Two people, a man and a woman, were forcibly dragged out of a Nivita apartment building by the Task Force. They were bloody, and their clothes were ripped. They'd been handcuffed, and the woman was being dragged by her hair. It looked like they were still trying to get to each other as they were shoved into metal boxes, carriages that were pulled by intimidating and mean-looking Familiars.

The announcer continued as Kelly looked desperately at the cameras, begging someone, anyone, to help. "Wahkin and Catori lived separately, and though no Hawkei marriage registration surfaced upon searching the residence, a California marriage license was found in one of the drawers at Catori's apartment, proving the couple's guilt."

The camera panned to Cameron's face. It was so swollen from the beating that his eyes were shut. Had they really been that cruel?

The announcer paused, and his voice took on a note of surprise. "We've just gotten word that Catori was raising an interbred *child*, a product of her relationship with Wahkin."

People groaned in disgust all around us. Sophia and I continued to watch as Kelly and Cameron's panicked faces were shown on screen.

"That's so fucking gross," a girl mumbled near me. "How could you give birth to an interbred kid?"

"I don't really care if you want to be in an interhouse relationship, but don't bring kids into it. You're just setting them up to be picked on and ridiculed," her friend beside her said.

"More news, just in," the broadcaster continued, and the room quieted again. "Since a child has been discovered, Catori and Wahkin have been convicted of having an interhouse relationship without a trial. Wahkin will spend life in prison. Catori, however, upon discovery that she indeed went through *willingly* with the pregnancy and birth of an interhouse child, has been sentenced to death."

Sophia's face went stark white. On the screen, an image of two Familiars fighting against a group of magical Task Force creatures came into view. One was an alicorn, the other was a white lioness. The Familiars were tackled and held down by other creatures, chained and stuffed into cages. The Elemental Task Force shot their elements through the bars at them, and both creatures screamed in pain.

"The child has been turned over to the care of the Nivita Elders," the announcer continued. "It has yet to be decided what will be done with him."

On screen, a little boy in the arms of a Task Force member stared terrified at the multiple cameras that were shoved in his face. The boy was crying and asking for his mother. The reporters kept asking him questions about his parents, questions a toddler wouldn't be able to comprehend. He didn't answer any of them, just kept screaming louder.

Sophia turned her head away. She couldn't watch. But she needed to see this, and so did I.

The announcer cleared his throat. "The Elders would like to remind everyone that interhouse relationships are strictly forbidden, and that anyone romantically involved with someone not of their own House will be prosecuted in a similar way."

There was the shuffling of papers. "We've brought in a Task Force law enforcement expert, Octavius Paddington, for his take on this highly controversial issue."

The screen stopped showing the awful images and instead showed two men dressed in suits at a desk. Paddington was fat and had a handlebar mustache, as well as an expression that told me he felt justice had been served.

"Mister Paddington, what do you have to say about the relationship between Catori and Wahkin?" the newscaster asked.

"Well, let me start by saying it's just not natural," the so-called fucking expert said. "Something like this goes against the laws of nature. These types of people are perverted. It's the result of a mental illness left untreated."

"So you're saying that this type of thing can be cured?" the newscaster asked curiously.

"Conversion therapy has worked in some cases. Though, sadly, too many of these depraved souls are too far gone to treat." Paddington shifted in his chair. At that moment, I heard someone else on camera give an outraged exclamation.

The screen panned to a young woman with blonde hair and green eyes hidden behind huge eyeglasses. She was young, but her eyes were determined as she spoke. "The law needs to be changed. Too many of our people suffer under these oppressive laws."

The broadcaster shifted uncomfortably. "Let me also introduce Jaymin Riske. She is the leader and founder of The Interhouse Alliance, a group that advocates to make interhouse relationships legal."

Riske continued before Paddington could speak. "These laws are archaic and wrong. Elementai in interhouse relationships deserve the same rights as we do, and should be allowed to marry and reproduce within our society."

"Come now, be reasonable! These types of relationships have the ability to ruin our culture and way of life!" Paddington roared. "May I suggest that *you've* participated in one of these vile unions yourself?"

Riske's eyes narrowed, as if she was insulted. "I have not. My husband is Nivita, as am I."

"Then why is it your problem? Why do you fight for people to fornicate our bloodlines and make them *weak*? Do you want to see us all die out like Anichi?" Paddington hissed.

Paddington and Riske started arguing, and I couldn't take it anymore. I walked away, and Sophia followed.

I went into an empty classroom, and Sophia came in behind me. When Esis had jumped inside, I locked the door and slid against it. I ran a hand through my hair. Shit. This was really fucked up.

I looked up at Sophia. Esis had leapt into her arms and was hugging her. She just stared at me.

"Do you believe me now?" I asked weakly.

Sophia swallowed. She seemed more scared than I'd ever seen her, even during the Elemental Cup.

She then swept a lock of hair behind her ear and said, "I don't care."

"You don't care." I made a sarcastic noise. "Well, I do."

"What, you want to break up over this?"

"No, but Sophia... fuck."

We were quiet for a moment. Sophia squeezed Esis so hard in her arms I thought his big eyes were going to pop out.

"What'll happen to that little boy?" she whispered.

I shrugged and sighed. "I don't know. He's interhouse. No one will adopt him. There's too much stigma attached to his name. Unless his grandparents take him, the Elders will probably surrender him to the U.S. foster care system. Who knows from there?"

"So he'll never know he's an Elementai, or that he needs a Familiar?"

"No. Probably not. Not unless his powers came out, and they had to bring him back in." I cleared my throat and stood up. "And that's not something I want to put on a kid."

"That's not going to happen to us," Sophia said clearly, though I detected a tone of hesitation in her voice.

"Open your eyes, Sophia! Do you want that to happen to our kids? Or do you want to have to pick someday between having an abortion or risking that no one will ever find out they're interhouse?" I snapped at her. "I know *I* don't want to make that decision."

Sophia backed away from me, shaking her head. "We're not having kids."

"I don't care how careful we are, Sophia. Accidents happen." I took a breath. "And I don't know about you, but no matter how we feel about sex, if you haven't noticed, it's getting really hard not to have it."

She gnawed on her lip. "It doesn't matter. That's years away."

"Yes it does, Sophia. We need to start thinking about this stuff *now*."

She'd asked me to proofread her project for her Hawkei Careers class before she'd turned it in. The passion in it had been obvious, and it'd made me feel guilty. Sophia really wanted kids, no matter what she'd told me about not having them in order to be with me. If we were going to be permanent, I didn't think I could resist having a baby with her, at least one, and not for very long. Sophia wanted to be a mom more than anything, and if I was honest with myself, I wanted to be a dad, too. I couldn't imagine being a parent and making a baby with anyone *but* her.

But could we put a kid through that? Being two halves of different Houses, hiding themselves forever? That wouldn't be fair.

I could tell Sophia was nervous. So was I. But it was even worse than I'd thought. They'd convicted Kelly and Cameron without a trial. Mostly because they'd had a child. That couldn't happen with us. If we got pregnant and were found out, I'd go to prison, but Sophia... she'd be killed.

I felt sick. I must've looked green, because Sophia put Esis down on a desk, then strolled up to me and took my hands. "What we're doing is worth the risk. *This* is worth it. You hear me?"

I nodded, but it felt like she was far away. It took all I had to bring myself back down to earth again and not let myself get carried away with all the terrifying possibilities of what could happen.

"We need to lie low for a while," I told her quietly. "With this on the news, everyone is going to be talking about interhouse relationships. There will be gossip. We can't risk being found out."

Her expression was disappointed, but she nodded. "Okay. I understand."

"I don't *want* to do this, but Sophia... we need to be careful."

She nodded. I hugged her close to me and kissed the top of her head. The thought of something happening to her... it was something I couldn't handle.

"You're squeezing me so tight I can't breathe," she muffled against my t-shirt. I loosened up, but only a little.

"I don't want anything to happen to you."

"I'm not going anywhere." She brushed my hair back from my face and kissed me. Then she held my head in her hands and stared me down. "Not ever."

My mouth went dry, and my throat got tight. I mentally checked off what I knew about Koigni. They were jealous types. Sophia, check. They were crazy exes— didn't want to find out. They were sex addicts and constantly horny. Sophia, *definitely* check, thank you very much.

And they were passionate, and didn't like letting go of their partners. Not for anything— not even death. Check.

Sophia would totally risk our lives so we could be together. Even still, I didn't think she comprehended what we could lose, and if she did, she didn't give a damn. That put her in terrible danger.

The biggest threat to us wasn't the Elders. It was Sophia herself.

Just thinking about it made me hold her even closer, like I could protect her if something were to happen. She flung her arms around my neck and hung on to me.

Lowly, she whispered, "We could run away."

The possibility was pretty tempting, that was for sure. But my stomach sunk at the reminder all the people we'd be leaving behind.

"We could never see our families or our friends ever again. We couldn't come back to Kinpago, or Orenda."

She buried her face in my shoulder. "I couldn't leave Imogen or Amelia. Jonah either."

"Me too." Thinking about never seeing my parents or my brothers or sisters ever again was a depressing experience. But these were our *lives* we were talking about here. Was being together worth it?

I thought it was— or at least, I wanted it to be. But it seemed the closer I got to Sophia, the more I was taking away from her. And myself, on top of it.

"We'll be okay." Sophia stepped out of my embrace and wiped a few stray tears away from her eyes. "I know we will be."

She picked up Esis and buried her face in his fur. I watched her and said lowly, "We'll be fine, *pawee*."

But I didn't know that we would be. And that scared the hell out of me.

sophia
EIGHTEEN

The following week and a half was the worst I'd ever had at Orenda Academy. After the news about Catori and Wahkin broke, Liam had been avoiding me. We hadn't hung out, or even talked, since. He wouldn't even meet my eyes in the hallway. He acted like I wasn't even alive. I understood we had to be careful. I really did. But I didn't want to be *this* careful.

I passed by Liam on Tuesday evening on my way to meet with Madame Doya. He had his hands shoved into the pockets of his jeans and his head ducked low. He didn't even look up to notice me, but I could see the color drained from his face. I didn't miss the slow, unsteady steps he took, like he was trying not to pass out.

I hurried over to him. It wasn't until I was right in front of him that he lifted his gaze. He looked surprised to see me.

"Liam, are you okay?" I asked. I already knew the answer.

"I'm fine," he lied.

"You don't look fine."

Liam glanced around the hall. "I thought we agreed to be careful."

"We are. I just wanted to check in with you. And Esis wanted to say hi." I shoved Esis into Liam's arms before he could protest. Liam took him and softly petted him behind the ears. Esis purred and placed his paw on Liam's arm.

"I appreciate the gesture, Sophia, but..." Liam glanced around again. There were a few students passing through the hall, but no one took notice to us.

"Can we hang out sometime?" I asked. "Just the two of us. It can be somewhere quiet and secluded. Please."

Liam kept his gaze on Esis. "I don't know, *pawee*. I'm really busy with finals this week. Maybe next week after the semester is over?" He sounded hesitant— like he was trying to put it off as soon as possible.

My heart broke a little at the rejection. "We could study together for Unicornology. Would tomorrow night work?"

Liam bit his lower lip, though I noticed color was returning to his cheeks now that he was holding Esis. "Sorry, but Jonah and I have plans. Rain check?"

A weight settled on my chest. Our Unicornology final was the day after tomorrow, so there wouldn't be another chance to study for it.

"Sure," I lied. "I'll see you in class on Thursday."

Liam forced a smile. "See you, Soph."

He handed Esis back and waved as he continued down the hall. Esis waved his little paw back while I watched Liam go.

"At least he'll feel better for a bit," I whispered to Esis. Not only did I never get to spend time with my boyfriend anymore, Esis couldn't heal him either if he wasn't around. It looked like Liam's health was getting worse again without Esis' magic.

Esis dropped his ears as soon as Liam was out of sight. I turned, and we started out of the castle and toward the woods. It was a long walk to the clearing, and my mind raced the whole time. Orenda Academy had started to become lonely. Not only was Liam keeping his distance, but Imogen was hard at work finalizing her project for her Hawkei Fashion Design class, and Vanessa was either studying or hanging out with Bren. Jonah was too busy chasing after Renar to be much fun. I'd spent most of my free time studying the maps Doya had given me and practicing my Lighting, but so far, I wasn't making any headway. At this point, I wasn't sure I would be able to do it.

You have to, I told myself. *For your friends and family.*

When I reached the clearing, Doya stood in the center of it with Naomi at her side. Dark clouds blocked out the stars above our heads.

She crossed her arms and tapped the toes of her shoes in the grass. "You're late, Sophia."

I ducked my head. I couldn't have been more than two minutes late. "Sorry."

Doya walked over to meet me beside the dry log near the trail entrance. "Before we get started, we have a few things to discuss." She gestured for me to take a seat.

I sat and placed Esis in my lap.

Doya smoothed out her skirt and took a seat beside me. "I'm concerned, Sophia."

My eyebrows shot up. Madame Doya? Concerned? I wasn't aware she was capable of such an emotion.

"I'm concerned you aren't taking this task seriously," she clarified.

Of course. Because no way in hell she'd ever care about me.

"Believe me," I said, "I understand exactly what's at stake."

"Do you, Sophia?" Doya cocked an eyebrow at me. "Because I've talked with your other professors. It seems you're putting quite a bit of effort into your classes, but you have yet to make any progress with your Lightning."

"I don't think any of my classes are more important than this, if that's what you're suggesting. They're easier, though."

Doya crossed her arms. "Your Hawkei Careers project didn't sound easy."

How did she even hear about that? Was she spying on me again? And why did she seem so angry about it?

"Are you suggesting I should've failed all my classes so I could do better with my Koigni magic?" I accused.

"No," Doya replied in a clipped tone. "I'm just saying that *perhaps* you should try putting as much thought and effort into this as you did researching how to be a good mother."

I gaped at her. She seriously didn't think I was trying hard enough?

I sighed and stood. "Let's just get this over with."

Doya huffed. "This is never going to work with that kind of attitude. I need you at the top of your game tonight. Focus and effort. Got it?"

I nodded. "Got it."

I took a deep breath and tried to focus on the task at hand like she said. Esis hopped down from my arms to watch, and Doya led me to the center of the clearing. Naomi watched from her side.

Doya crossed her arms and eyed me. "Let's see what you've got."

I lifted my palm to the sky and felt my heat rise within me. Each passing second seemed like minutes. Though I closed my eyes to concentrate, I could still sense Doya's scrutinizing gaze on me. And that only made my skin heat hotter. Her eyes felt like lasers. I gathered all that heat inside my chest, then sent it out through the palm of my hand. A bright orange light shot upward and a wave of heat spread across my face. My eyes shot open as Doya took a step backward. She frowned at me.

"Sorry," I mumbled.

Doya straightened and pressed her finger to her chin, like she was thinking hard.

I shifted uncomfortably in the silence.

"We need to try something else," she said, mostly to herself. "Are you sure you're focusing as hard as you can?"

"Was it easy for you to conjure lightning your first time?" I shot back.

Doya pursed her lips, but she didn't answer the question. "Ancestors' Day is less than a week away. We don't have the luxury of waiting any longer. If you cannot conjure lightning by then... well, I don't have to tell you what the Elders will do."

My shoulders fell. "I understand. Believe me, I've run the scenario through my mind countless times. And the looming threat still isn't enough to push my magic to where it needs to be."

"Forget about the threat for a moment," Doya suggested.

"Easy for you to say," I muttered. She wasn't the one who was on the verge of losing everyone she loved. I glanced to Esis on the log, who watched me with bright eyes.

Doya took a deep breath and softened her tone. "Fire is made of a whirlwind of emotions. But Lightning? It takes precision and control. For some Koigni, that control comes from honing their anger, frustrations and rage. But I don't think that's going to work for you."

It was always weird when Doya went into teacher mode instead of acting like a drill sergeant.

"Don't use your *anger* to focus your heat," she instructed.

I carefully considered her words. Was that what I'd been doing?

"Turn around and face your Familiar," Doya said.

I did as I was told. Esis fluffed his tail and waved to me. I shot him a smile.

The sound of Doya's feet retreating in the grass reached my ears. "Forget that I'm here. Right now, it's just you and your Familiar— and your Lightning. Let your senses guide you."

I nodded. I wasn't entirely sure I understood where she was going with this, but I figured I might as well give it a shot, considering nothing else had worked yet.

Inhaling a deep breath, I forced the muscles in my shoulders to relax. The sound of Doya's footsteps stopped. All I could hear was the soft breeze rustling through the trees around us and the long blades of grass brushing against one another beneath me. The air was cool but humid, and it smelled like ocean and evergreens.

Kind of like Liam.

Esis raised his nose and sniffed the air, like he too noticed the familiar scent. He stood on his hind legs and glanced around, like he thought he might find Liam standing close by. His big blue eyes searched the clearing, then lifted to meet my gaze. There was an emotion in his eyes I couldn't quite read. It held hints of sadness— like he was sad Liam wasn't around, but also of hope.

It wasn't until that moment that I realized how much Esis truly cared for Liam. It was like he knew Liam belonged in our lives, that there was no alternative for me. My heart melted thinking of the two of them.

And then it hit me. That heat that was melting my heart... *that* was what I needed to make my Lightning work. It was passion that came only from the people I loved.

I cocked a finger at Esis. He hopped off his log and bounded through the grass over to me. His ears curled back as the wind rushed across his face. He leapt, and I caught him in my arms. I hugged him tightly and buried my nose in his fur. Heat rose to my face, burning my cheeks. I held it back, waiting for the right moment.

Esis reached his paws out and wrapped them around my face in a hug. When he hugged me, it was like my mind flipped a switch. My thoughts suddenly weren't racing anymore. I was focused. I ran back through my mind every hug I could think of— when Liam and I cuddled in the cave during the tournament, when our team huddled together after we won, when Amelia came to visit, when I saw my parents in the forest and ran into their arms...

As I thought of everyone I adored and all the love they'd shown me, the heat inside my body grew fiercer than I'd ever felt it before.

Esis drew away for just a moment, then pressed his mouth to my cheek. It was the first time my Familiar had ever kissed me, and it made all the love and happiness in my chest explode.

Thrusting my palm up toward the sky, I let all the heat out of my skin.

Crack!

A blinding white light flashed across the clearing, and thunder rumbled in the sky. A wave of disbelief and amazement washed over me so fast that I stumbled backwards and fell onto my butt in the grass. As soon as the lightning came, it was gone.

I stared up at the sky, unblinking. Clouds rushed by above me, but I continued to stare, like I thought I might get another chance to witness the lightning. Esis straightened and climbed onto my shoulder. He broke the silence with a squeaky cheer.

"I did it," I said to him breathlessly. It still hardly seemed real, even after saying it out loud.

"Congratulations." Doya stepped forward. She had a look on her face that— dare I say it— actually hinted at pride. *Doya was proud of me.* She reached out her hand and helped me to my feet.

"I can't believe it," I said, still trying to process.

"You better start believing it, Sophia," Doya replied. "Because you're going to have to do it again."

"Okay," I stated confidently. Now that I'd done it once, I felt like I could do it a hundred times.

"Show me." Doya stepped back, and I raised my hand toward the sky again.

Twice more I made lightning crackle across the sky before Doya was satisfied. Now that I'd broken the code, it was easy.

Doya cracked the smallest hint of a smile. "Good job. Now that you've accomplished this, you're ready to hear more about your task."

She led me back to the log and spoke in a serious tone. "On the night of Ancestors' Day, you will enter the Anichi temple. As we've discussed in previous sessions, you must find the Summoning Room, which is where the Anichi used to summon the ancestors. You will perform an ancient ceremony that will allow you to speak with Showana Harjo."

I chewed my lower lip, unintentionally letting my uncertainty show.

"The hardest part of your training is over," Doya said. "I will now teach you the ceremony. Then you will finally be ready."

I WAS STILL RIDING the high of my training session with Doya when I returned to the castle. I felt so proud that I entered the Commons with a huge smile on my face.

I loved the Commons. It was like a picture straight out of a million-dollar home. The whole thing was bathed in wooden textures, with a high ceiling, soft lighting, and various stone fireplaces. Different colored area rugs lined the floor, separating the large room into various seating areas, and a chandelier hung low over the pool table. Between the TVs hung many paintings of magical creatures. My favorite was one of a female centaur with a unicorn horn and pegasus wings holding a sword.

The Commons were crowded at this hour, with various people crowded around the pool table and ping-pong tables, and another crowd by the TVs.

I found Imogen at one of the tables in the corner, frantically organizing piles and piles of pictures. Her project took up the whole surface. Sassy stood on a chair with her front paws on the table. Her eyes darted around the pictures, following Imogen's quick-moving hands. I sat next to her and put Esis on the chair beside me.

Imogen looked up and blew the hair out of her eyes. "Oh, good. You're here. Can you help me?"

"What are you doing?" I glanced around at the craft supplies in front of her. There were piles of magazines, endless bits of torn-up paper, scissors, glue, and glitter.

Imogen flipped through one of the magazines, then tossed it aside before picking up the next. "I'm making a collage for my Fashion Design class to go with my presentation. I have to get this done tonight."

"Im, why'd you leave it until the last minute?"

"I wasn't going to do one, but I figured it would really help spice up my presentation." She finally stopped long enough to look up. Her eyes pleaded with me.

"Yeah, absolutely," I said. "I'll help you out. What do you need?"

Imogen breathed a sigh of relief, then handed me a thick fashion magazine. "Can you cut out any pictures of scarves or boots you find?"

"Sure." I picked up a pair of scissors and flipped open to the first page. Esis stood on his tiptoes to help me look through the magazine.

"Thanks," Imogen said. "You're a lifesaver. Hey, Esis. You wanna help me out over here?"

Esis hopped onto the table and took the glue stick Imogen held out to him. She instructed him to place the glue on various pictures, which she stuck to the huge poster laid out on the other side of the table.

"You're going to ace this class," I told her.

Imogen gave a shy smile, but it quickly faded when the sound of cheers filled the air from across the room. Her eyes locked on something behind me.

I turned to see the crowd near the ping-pong tables had parted just enough that I could see Cade. He held his fists in the air like he'd just claimed a victory. Arabelle stood at his side happily. Cade was rumored to be a champion at ping-pong.

"Who's up next?" he asked, eyeing the crowd for his next challenger.

I turned back to Imogen with a raised eyebrow.

"I know," she muttered. "A deal's a deal. Just... not now." She ducked her head, turning bright pink.

"Now's a great time," I said.

"In front of all those people?" she asked in disbelief.

"Well, is he going to say no in front of everyone?" I challenged. The truth was, I wouldn't do it either, but I kind of wanted to be there to see it.

"He could," she hissed.

"You have to at least give me a time frame," I told her. "If not now, then when?"

Imogen bit the inside of her lip and pressed a picture to her poster. She stole another glance at Cade, but quickly looked away. "I don't know. Soon."

"Before the end of the semester," I insisted.

She sighed. "I know. I want to. I just... I don't know."

I set my magazine down. "Imogen, he's not going to say no."

She paused for a moment before picking up another photo for Esis to glue. She didn't say anything.

I glanced back to Cade. He was totally killing it against his new opponent, with cool moves like holding the paddle behind his back. His rival was a Nivita guy named Sam I'd seen around before. He had an alicorn Familiar named Zaria, who was black but whose fur glittered dark blue in the light. Sam missed the ball, but Zaria bounced it back to Cade with her nose. Several people laughed.

"That doesn't count," Cade said as he caught the ball. His eyes darted in our direction, like he was hoping to catch Imogen's eye. When he saw she wasn't paying attention, he turned back to his game.

Imogen kept throwing nervous glances his way while he played, but she didn't seem like she wanted to talk about him.

"I think that's enough scarves and boots," she said. "Do you think you could find me a big picture of a bow?"

"I can try," I offered, grabbing a new magazine from the pile.

Imogen looked toward Cade again, and her whole body froze up. I turned to look at what she saw, but she swatted at me and hissed, "Don't look. He's coming over here."

Imogen tried to stay calm as she placed another picture on her collage.

I ignored her instructions and glanced to Cade anyway. He had finished his game and was leading Arabelle over to us.

"Now's your chance," I whispered to her.

Imogen threw me a nervous glance, then lifted her gaze to Cade. "Hey, how's it going?"

"Great," he replied, sliding into a chair at the table. Arabelle sniffed Sassy, and their noses touched. "What are you up to?"

"Homework," Imogen said, in a voice that didn't sound like her own.

"Wow." Cade looked down at her project, which was half-finished by now. "Looks great."

She blushed. "Thanks."

"Do you need any help?" Cade offered.

"No, I—" Imogen started, but I cleared my throat and cut her off.

I raised an eyebrow and glanced between them, urging Imogen to take her shot.

"I— I guess you can help." Imogen finally caved. "But it's kind of boring."

"Pft. Don't say that," Cade replied. "Hanging out with you could never get boring."

Imogen turned a brighter shade of red than the carpet beneath us. I nudged her under the table, and she grimaced.

"Really?" she asked him shyly.

"Yeah." Cade winked at her. "You know I love spending time with you."

Imogen's mouth hung open, and her eyes darted between mine and Cade's. I kicked her again under the table, this time harder. She looked like she was too stunned to feel it.

"Maybe..." Imogen hesitated.

That a girl. Keep going.

Imogen tucked a strand of hair behind her ear. "Maybe we could hang out sometime over dinner... just the two of us."

Yes! Finally! I couldn't help but beam for her.

Cade looked like he was holding his breath. "Like... like a date?"

Imogen began rifling through her magazine pages again so she didn't have to look at him. "I mean, it doesn't have to be a *date—*"

"Why not?" Cade asked.

Imogen stopped dead in her tracks. She opened her mouth, but nothing came out.

A smile slowly crept across Cade's lips. "I think a date sounds lovely."

Imogen was practically sweating through her shirt right now. Meanwhile, my insides were all jittery and excited for her.

"Uh... okay," Imogen said, sounding relieved. "It's a date, then."

Sassy's ears perked up. She hopped on the table and nudged her nose into Imogen's hand. Imogen looked down at her. When she did, something in her eyes changed. It was like she and Sassy were having some sort of silent conversation.

"You know what, Cade?" Imogen straightened, looking more confident. "I don't want just one date. We've already gone out once before. I want to be your girlfriend. Will you go out with me?"

My jaw dropped. Esis leaned forward to wrap his arms around Imogen's wrist, like he was hugging her. She was so enamored watching Cade that she didn't even notice.

Cade looked so shocked by the offer that he could barely find his words. "You want to be my girlfriend?"

Imogen hesitated a moment, like she couldn't believe she'd just admitted it. She bit her lower lip. "You heard me."

A silent beat passed over our table before Cade finally answered. "Yeah, Imogen. I'd really like that."

Imogen beamed. This was absolutely perfect. Oh my gosh, Imogen and Cade were officially a thing! I was so happy for them!

"Hey." The sound of Jonah's voice snapped us all out of it.

I looked up to see him approaching us. Squeaks followed behind him and stepped on a canine Familiar's tail. The dog yelped, and Squeaks bowed her head to him like she was sorry. Jonah didn't look happy.

"Hey, Jonah," Imogen said, sounding like herself again. "What's up?"

"Not much." Jonah shoved his hands in his pockets and cocked his head, gesturing to the door. "Can I talk to you for a minute, Sophia?"

Panic suddenly entered my chest. What was this about? Was Liam okay?

"Yeah." I rose from my chair and scooped Esis up off the table. "Catch you guys later," I said to Imogen and Cade.

They barely heard me. The two of them were already in their own little world. Jonah led me, Squeaks, and Esis outside.

"What's wrong?" I demanded once we were in the hall.

Jonah took a deep breath and blew it out slowly. "Look, Sophia. I just talked to Liam, and he's not doing well."

I pulled Esis closer to me. "I know. We haven't had much time together lately, and—"

"This has gone on long enough," he interrupted. "Liam deserves to know what's going on."

"But Jonah, I—"

Jonah wagged a finger in my direction. "Don't *but Jonah* me. Liam has no idea what's happening to him. It's scary enough as it is being sick. Now his health is all over the place, and he has no idea why. One second he's great, and the next he's down in the dumps again. And I can sure as hell tell you those potions Perot gave him aren't doing their job. I know you've been sending Esis to heal him. He just hasn't made the connection yet."

"Jonah..." I opened my mouth to argue, but I didn't know what to say. At this point, I didn't really have an excuse anymore. "I know I'm not being fair to him."

Jonah scoffed, and Squeaks narrowed her eyes at me from beside him. Esis looked confused by their hostility. "That's an understatement. My Liam baby deserves better than this."

I hung my head and whispered, "I know."

Jonah crossed his arms. "If you don't tell him soon, I will."

That was all he said before he stomped away and entered the Commons again.

I just stood in the hall, shaking in complete shock. Jonah had never treated me like that before. Whatever he and Liam had talked about must've been serious. I suddenly felt very concerned for Liam. We'd just healed him earlier. Had it not been enough?

Just as I decided to head to his dorm room to check on him— screw the rules about a Koigni in the Toaqua dorms— I saw him coming my way. He looked better than earlier, but still worse than normal.

"Liam!" I called, rushing up to him. I put an arm out to pull him into a hug, but he pushed me away. A little piece of my heart broke in response. More than I cared to admit. I swallowed down the lump rising to my throat.

"Careful, *pawee*," Liam whispered. He glanced toward the door to the Commons, where voices were spilling out into the hall.

"I can't even touch you anymore?" I shrunk in on myself and pulled

Esis close to my chest. It felt like it'd been so long since I'd touched Liam.

"You know it's not about that. It's—" Liam cut himself off and sighed. "Have you seen Jonah around?"

"I thought you two were just hanging out."

"We were, but he forgot his homework." Liam waved a notebook in his hand.

"Uh, yeah. He's in there." I gestured to the door, but a wave of fear overcame me when Liam took a step toward it. Would Jonah tell him about Esis when he went in there? How much time did I have before Jonah broke the news to him? "Wait. Liam."

Liam turned to look at me. He had an expectant look on his face behind tired eyes.

I knew I should've told him by now. Jonah was right. I couldn't keep waiting. And the longer I waited, the worse it would be. I knew all that, but when I opened my mouth, the words just wouldn't come out.

Liam already looked so worn. This didn't feel like the right time.

"What?" he asked with a sigh.

The tired look he gave me was heartbreaking. It was a reminder of how unfair I'd been to him. And that hurt, because I wanted to be the one to heal him. I wanted to be the one to fix everything, and even though Esis and I could help, we weren't doing enough. Telling him the truth— admitting that I'd been dishonest with him all this time— that would only break him further. I didn't want to be the one who hurt him.

"I just miss you so much." My voice cracked.

All the emotions I'd been burying down this week caught up to me in one big wave. Jonah's threat piled atop my worry for Liam, and I didn't feel like I could share any of it with him. Though Liam was standing right there, I suddenly felt very alone. My eyes burned at the threat of tears.

Liam took a step back. I knew he was feeling like crap, but the distance still stung. I just wanted to snuggle up with him and make everything better. But it didn't feel like he wanted that at all.

"I want to be with you again," I whispered.

Liam's jaw tensed. "Sophia, I'm just trying to protect you."

"By avoiding me?" I hissed. "That's not doing either of us any good."

"Sophia, this is bigger than you realize! You think that I want to stay away from you?" Liam stepped so close I thought he might touch me, but he didn't. It was a perfect metaphor for our relationship as of late. So close, yet so far away.

"Yes, but we can work through it all," I said. "There are things I want to tell you, Liam. But I can't confide in you if I never see you."

Liam paused a moment. "What kind of things?"

I dropped my gaze to Esis in my arms. Now was definitely the wrong time to tell him. I needed a clear head to do it, and right now, it felt as if my whole body was being squeezed by a vice grip.

I shot a glance toward the Commons door. "Things that would be easier to talk about alone. In private."

Liam scowled. "You know what happens every time we're alone. I'm not really feeling up to that."

My mouth fell open in shock. "You think that's all I think of you?" I exploded. "I don't care about fooling around. I'd just like the chance to at least *talk* to you."

Liam hushed me.

I didn't care. "The first part of the semester, you acted like you didn't want to be together. Then you told me you wanted to make this permanent. Now you're acting like you don't want to date me at all. So what's the deal? Make up your mind!"

"You think I haven't risked enough to be in this relationship?" he said. "If I didn't want to be with you, I wouldn't have asked you out in the first place!"

"Then what are we doing, Liam?"

"We just have to give it more time," Liam insisted. "Stop being so pushy."

I blinked several times, taken off guard by his words. "I'm... I'm not—"

"You are, Sophia." Liam gritted his teeth. "Just stop pushing me."

I couldn't take it anymore. My temper erupted. "You'd never get out of bed if it wasn't for me. Someone has to pick you up every two seconds. Maybe you *need* pushing!"

Liam winced, and Esis gasped at me. I couldn't believe the words flew out of my mouth. I didn't mean that, did I?

Liam stared at me. I just couldn't handle the pain in his features. I'd hurt him. I'd hurt him *hard*, and no amount of healing magic was going to fix it. Only time.

"I..." I could barely get the words out. "I'm sorry."

I turned around and walked away from him, humiliated. I couldn't even face him right now. I was so disgusted with myself. How could I have said that to him? I didn't resent him, did I?

I didn't know what was up with my feelings right now. But even though we'd had a fight and said things we didn't mean, I wasn't losing Liam for anything. Especially not through any fault of my own. From now on, I had to let him come to me at his own pace.

No matter how much it hurt to keep my distance.

Liam

NINETEEN

"Liam! I'm not gonna let you sit in there all weekend!"

"Fuck off, Ezra."

There was hammering on the door. My brother was trying to force his way into my dorm. I stayed under my blanket and refused to move. It was quiet and dark under here, and I liked it.

"I'm coming in there!" There was the sound of the lock freezing before it burst. The doorknob fell off before Ezra pushed it open. Dyami walked in after him. The thunderbird's head was nearly up to his shoulder— he'd grown a lot in the past few weeks. He was gonna be giant when he was fully grown.

I threw my blanket off and clambered out of bed. "Dammit, Ezra, now I have to get a new lock."

"Open it next time." Ezra was clearly dealing with no shit today. "Now, are you gonna come out, or do I have to drag you?"

"I already told you. I want to be left alone." I glared at him.

"I've left you alone. For three days. It's time to come back to the land of the living," he said. "Come have a beer and chill out with the rest of us. You've barely been in the pool all semester."

"Don't feel like it."

Ezra rolled his eyes. "Come *on*, dude. Can you please make up with Sophia, for all our sakes?"

"I doubt she wants to see me," I mumbled. I'd told Ezra that Sophia and I had fought, but I didn't tell him what it was about, or what was said. He probably thought it was minor couple stuff, when really it was so much more.

"Look, I know things are kinda... tense right now," he started.

"You mean how two people from interhouse relationships pretty much got killed and imprisoned for life? Yeah, kinda," I spat back sarcastically.

"Bro, I *will* bring Jonah in here." He pointed at me. "He will carry you out with one arm."

I sighed. He totally would.

"I don't even know what to say to her," I started pathetically.

Ezra took me by the shoulders and pushed me out of the dorm. "Just say you're sorry or whatever. I fight with my girlfriends all the time, and we always make up. It's not a big deal."

Yeah, but I bet they don't basically call you weak and a burden, I thought.

I hadn't seen Sophia since our fight. I'd even asked our Unicornology professor to let me take the exam early so I wouldn't have to show up and face her. It was petty and over-the-top, I know, but I couldn't look her in the eye right now.

I thought Sophia was different from the rest of the tribe. I thought she didn't believe I was just dead weight, that I was just like everyone else. Had I been wrong?

"Whatever she said, she probably didn't mean," Ezra said, reading my face. "Just talk to her about it. You're likely blowing things out of proportion."

I had a tendency to do that, but Ezra didn't understand. I mean, I didn't tell him, but still. What Sophia had said really hurt. It was the worst thing she'd ever said to me. And the worst part about it was that I couldn't do anything to change it. I couldn't magically make myself better. It would never happen.

But Ezra was kinda right, too. We were running out of time. The semester was ending soon, and once it did we'd have to figure out how to sneak around to see each other over the summer.

Unless, of course, she no longer wanted to date me. I had no idea.

"Fine. You're right." I brushed back my hair and straightened up. "I guess it's time to put an end to this."

"There you go." Ezra slapped me on the back. Dyami cawed behind him. "I expect to see the both of you show up tonight at Ancestors' Day."

That's right. That was tonight. All of Kinpago was getting ready for the celebration. I'd almost forgotten about summoning Anna and speaking with her. Maybe she could clue me in about all the crazy stuff my health was doing lately.

I really didn't want our argument on my mind when I was supposed to be celebrating with the rest of the tribe, so I decided to seek Sophia out and talk to her. It was her first Ancestors' Day. It should be special for her, too.

I had no idea where to find her, but it was late in the afternoon, so I didn't think she'd be in the Koigni dorms. I looked in the Commons, the dining room, and the entrance hall without any luck. The longer it took to find her, the more my mind kept going. I couldn't get our argument out of my head. Hadn't for days now.

Part of the reason her words stung so much were they were kinda true. I couldn't do anything about my health, sure, but I had to agree with her when she said I had to be pushed. Baine pushed me, my dad pushed me, Ezra had even pushed me to get out of bed. I didn't do anything on my own.

It wasn't because I was lazy. I just was really scared to fail, so I never wanted to try. It was better to do nothing than to let everyone down.

But damn, I didn't want anyone feeling like they were being dragged down by me. Did Sophia feel that way? It was scary to consider.

Holy shit. Did she think I couldn't perform in bed because I was sick? I wasn't sure, but I really hoped not. I didn't feel well a lot of the time, but I still had enough endurance to last when we were fooling around. *That* I'd be able to do until I was on my deathbed, I was determined.

I didn't know. All I figured was the woman I loved felt less of me, and it was the worst feeling in the world.

I spotted Jonah and Imogen outside, playing a game. They and their Familiars tossed a ball back and forth, not allowing it to touch the ground. They were laughing. Sophia wasn't with them.

Jonah caught my eyes as I passed by, and I waved. He gave me a weak smile that looked guilty. Jonah had been acting like the argument was his fault, though I had no idea why.

I remembered how our conversation had gone the other day. I'd vented to him about how frustrated I was about my health being up and down. Normally, I'd talk to Sophia about it, but she was so on edge lately, and worried about me enough.

I didn't get why, but the conversation had turned to Sophia.

"Liam," Jonah had started. "Don't you think Sophia's been a little... forward, lately? Especially with you?"

I didn't think so... or at least, I didn't want to admit it. "She's not Mia. We don't have a bad relationship," I'd said.

"I'm not saying you do. You guys are great together. And I know she's a far cry from the wicked bitch of the east you used to date. But she walks all over you sometimes. You've got to stand up for yourself," Jonah had said. "Sophia's my good friend, and I love her, but she's not the perfect angel you want her to be."

I knew Sophia wasn't perfect. And yeah, I'd let her get away with a lot of stuff this semester and not spoken up because I didn't want to piss her off. But though she wasn't perfect, she was still perfect for me.

But Jonah's words had resonated me, and they'd come out in our argument. Sophia never pushed me when it came to sexual stuff, or much of anything else, but she did want her way, and she wanted it in ways that were dangerous. The biggest problem in our relationship was that she wanted us to go public, to fight tradition, to take a risk, and I didn't. She kept asking for more than what I could give her. It seemed like this giant hurdle we couldn't get over. It'd been an issue from the beginning.

Finally, I spotted her. She was outside near the greenhouses. Esis was sitting on one of the fountains, and Sophia was pacing back and forth, wringing her hands.

She looked nervous. And worried. I didn't understand why. Finals were pretty much over. Had I been such a shitty boyfriend that I didn't notice there was something bothering her?

I'd spied on her last session with Doya, but I'd had to leave halfway through because I got sick, and hadn't been close enough to hear what they were talking about. I watched her conjure lightning once before I had to leave. I probably missed some crucial information during the second half of that meeting, but right now, I didn't care about that. I didn't even give a shit about the totem right now.

I just wanted to fix this fight. Then, I resolved, I'd tell her everything. About the assassination contract, the sessions with Baine, what Dad had asked me to do, and how I wanted Nashoma back, but the only way to do it was to lose her. I'd come clean right now, before the Ancestors' Day ceremonies begun. Then we'd work it out together. We'd find a solution. It's what I should've done from the beginning, but I'd been too cowardly. That ended today.

I was so scared to talk to her. There was this giant pit in my stomach that was eating me alive with the thought of facing her.

But not talking to her hurt way more, and I wanted this fight to be over with. I walked over with my hands in my pockets. "Hey, Soph. Can we talk?"

She jumped as if I'd scared her. She hadn't even noticed me walk over. Her eyes scanned me quickly before she glanced at Esis. He shrugged at her.

"Um... I don't know, Liam. I'm kind of busy today." She seemed freaked out for some reason. Her eyes were huge, and they darted from side to side, like she was trying to get away. Esis looked up at her, concerned.

I practically had alarm bells when it came to Sophia being upset. Something was wrong. I was starting to wonder if she had yelled at me because she was stressed out and not because she was actually mad at me.

"What's wrong?" I asked.

"You suddenly care now?" Her eyes narrowed. Her whole body was practically shaking with nerves. Ancestors, what was wrong with her? I had a feeling this was way beyond me.

"Of course I care. I always do," I said. "You can always tell me."

"Well, I can't this time." She went to pick up her bag, but I grabbed her arm and stopped her.

"Soph, let's work this out. Please."

"You didn't want to work it out a few days ago. Why now?" She looked hurt. There was more bothering her than just our argument, but it was obvious it still weighed on her mind.

"I was being an ass then. I didn't feel well. I know it's no excuse," I told her.

Vertigo hit me, and I staggered. The world went sideways.

"Liam? You okay?" Sophia asked. She came closer and rushed forward to touch me, but hung back at the last second.

"I just need to sit down," I said. I stumbled and ended up on the fountain. Sophia sat beside me, and Esis crawled on my lap. He put his little paws on his chest and looked up at me. A soft warmth grew where his tiny paws were. I'd never felt such a sensation before. It was weird.

Sophia looked like she wanted to touch me, but she hesitated, like she was scared.

I turned away. "I hate when you see me like this."

"I don't mind."

"That's not what you said the other day."

She frowned. "I don't know why I said that. I've never thought it before. It just popped out."

"Yeah, well, it hurt a lot." I crossed my arms and tucked them tightly to my sides. The vertigo was subsiding and things were righting themselves again. I was feeling better. Esis curled up into my shirt and sighed happily.

"I'm sorry I hurt you. I know that was a horrible thing to say, and I can never take it back." She bit her lip. "But you hurt me, too. I went to hug you, and you pushed me away. It's like you didn't want me." Her eyes were watery.

"I didn't push you away because I wanted to. We were right outside the Commons. If someone had seen, that would've been it," I told her.

I looked around. "I don't think this is the best place to talk about this, out in the open. Shouldn't we go somewhere more private?"

She huffed and crossed her arms. "Worried I'll just jump you the moment we're alone?"

"I didn't mean to say that either. I was in a bad mood, sorry," I said. "I don't think all you want is sex."

"Sure seemed like it."

"Soph, come on." I got up and tugged on her arm. She followed, but only because I was yanking on her. Esis clung to my shirt and looked between us like he was tired of all the drama.

I led her through the woods. We went through plenty of open areas where it was secluded, but I didn't stop at any of them.

"Where are we going?" she asked.

"Our special place," I said. I kept walking until we reached the waterfall clearing. This time of year in May, it was already hot and the flowers in the clearing had grown even larger. Huge butterflies flew around in rainbow colors, blending into camouflage whenever we came near. The pool had risen from the melted snow up in the mountains, and the waterfall was even louder as it roared down into it.

Sophia stepped toward the tree she'd burned our initials into and ran her fingers over it. "I'll always remember that night," she said.

"I really liked you back then," I confessed.

"I didn't know," Sophia said quietly. "I thought you hated me."

I couldn't believe it. I thought it'd been obvious.

I sat by the pool underneath a shaded tree, and Sophia took a seat beside me. Esis jumped off my shoulder and ran up a nearby tree trunk, into the cover of branches.

We were silent a moment. It's like neither one of us knew what to say.

Just apologize! Ezra said in my head.

"I'm sorry," I started. "I didn't mean what I said. I was a jerk."

"I should be sorrier. What I said was completely awful," Sophia said. She stared at the waterfall and didn't look at me.

"I'm not gonna lie that it didn't hurt my feelings," I said. "But what's worse is believing you actually think that way."

"It's not about your health, Liam." She shook her head. "I didn't want to admit it, but when we talked about how we needed to be careful and stay away from each other for a while, it really hurt me. It was like you were pushing me away."

"It wasn't about that at all," I said, astounded.

"Deep down, I know that. And I knew you were just trying to protect me." Her voice wobbled. "But I can't help what I feel, and I feel like you're leaving. It's like you're avoiding me again like you did last semester. It upset me then, but it's ten times worse now. I need that time with you. I don't care what we're doing, I just need you."

That was really hard to acknowledge. I'd avoided her last semester more or less for the same reasons I was staying away from her now. I didn't think it had bothered her that much, when in reality it had bothered her a lot.

"You'll always have me," I said. I went to take her hand, but she flinched and pulled away, like she was scared to touch me.

Okay, now I knew how it felt, and it really did suck.

"You don't get it. I don't understand sometimes why you won't let me touch you, why you seem so distant."

"I just need space sometimes. It's how I am. It doesn't mean I don't want to be with you," I said.

"But you're always talking about how this is dangerous, how it can't work," she went on. "I had to fight for us to be together, and sometimes it feels like I have to fight for us to stay together. I don't know if you want to be with me as much as I want to be with you." She sniffed and wiped her nose.

"Of course I want to be with you! I'd risk anything for you." I'd reach over and brushed away a few of her tears. *Please, stop crying. I hate it when you cry.*

She shook her head. "I know you love me. But sometimes I worry that you're not ready to be in this relationship."

"Sophia, please look at me." She lifted her head, and I said, "There isn't anywhere I'd rather be right now. Promise."

I know she didn't think that I'd given up enough in this relationship. But she didn't know what I had sacrificed— my relationship with my dad, risking the Water Elders' wrath... even possibly the chance of losing Nashoma forever... to be here. I cared just as much as she did. I just didn't know how to tell her. Or how I could.

I sat back to give her some space. "What brought all this on? You were in a bad mood before we even got in a fight the other day."

She paused before she went on. "Jonah talked to me. He said something about... some stuff," she said. "He's been kinda on me all semester. He said if I hurt his Liam Baby—"

"Does he really call me that when I'm not around?" I asked scathingly.

"Yes." Sophia let out a choked giggle.

"I'm gonna kill him," I said. "Anyway, continue."

She took a deep breath. "He said that if I hurt you, I'd have to deal with him. And I know that would really suck, because then I'd lose you, and I'd lose a friend, and I know Imogen is close with Jonah too so I don't know if she'd take his side or if it would start a fight between them, and in the end I'd probably end up all alone." She looked down. "Like I was in the beginning when I got here."

"Ancestors, Jonah." I rubbed my face. "Look, don't worry about him. He's just being overprotective. And kind of a jerk. I'll talk to him."

"Please don't," she said. "He's just looking out for you."

"I know, but he needs to keep his nose out of other people's relationships. I'm doing okay," I said.

"You're not, Liam. You're barely surviving." She put her head in her hands.

"People really need to stop worrying about me," I said. "I'll get by."

"It's because they love you." Sophia wiped her face and stopped crying. "You don't know how much I love you. I love you more than anyone else in the world. Sometimes I don't know what to do about all that love."

I knew how that was, because I felt the same way about her. "Come here." I reached out my arms and wrapped her in them. I laid down in the grass, and she curled up against my chest. I ran my fingers through her hair. She closed her eyes and calmed down when she was against me.

"Nothing in this world could make me stop loving you," I said quietly. "Don't ever think that I've abandoned you, because I never will."

She made a soft sound. I didn't know what to say to make it better, so the only way to express my feelings was to show her how I felt. I put my hand on the back of her head and tilted it up so I could kiss her.

When we made out, it was usually hot and feverish, but this time I went slow. I took my time to really draw the kiss out and make it passionate. It was quiet and soft. I tried to be as gentle with her as I could and lavished desire on her lips. I attempted to make the kiss as soothing and sweet as possible.

It was like our first kiss had been. I put every bit of feeling I had for her into that kiss.

"I love you," I said quietly.

"I love you too," she said back, a little choked up.

It struck me how much she'd been dying for some attention from me, and I hadn't put in the effort to give her any... because I'd been too scared. I felt horrible. To try and make up for it, I crushed her to my body and brought her even closer so that our legs intertwined and she felt protected. I kissed her again, deeper this time, and she gave a little moan.

Despite what I'd said earlier during our argument, I was pretty turned on, and had been for days.

Sophia pulled away. "We should stop," she whispered. She went to turn the other direction and roll out of my arms, but I didn't let her.

"What if I don't want to?" I asked.

Sophia hesitated. "But you—"

"Sophia." I put a finger on her lips. "We had an argument. It's okay. We're both sorry. Let's move on."

I could feel her body relax. "Okay." She kissed me this time. She rolled on top of me as we made out in the grass, and I tried (and failed) to tell my dick to be quiet. Sophia giggled and rolled off, and I ended up swinging myself on top of her. She laughed and brushed my hair back with her hands.

I balanced myself on my forearms and said, "Now, what's been bothering you today that's got you so freaked out?"

Her carefree expression fell away. "Oh... that. It's just something I have to do tonight for Doya. But it's not until later. I have some time."

Something for Doya... that was suspicious. But I didn't ask any questions, though I was dying to.

Sophia sat up and playfully pushed me off of her. I fell to the side, and she glanced at the pool. A smile lit up her face.

"How about we go for a swim?" she asked, and she got up and walked over to the edge of the pool. She slipped off her sneakers and looked at me.

"We don't have swimsuits," I said, perplexed.

"We don't need them." Sophia grinned mischievously and pulled off her shirt. She tossed it to the side, revealing her push-up bra. "Your turn."

Ah. Skinny-dipping. An American pastime. "I gotcha." I took off my socks and shoes, then my shirt, throwing it into a pile on the ground. Her grin grew wider as she took off her bra, and I tried not to jizz in my boxers as I looked at her perfect breasts. I, in turn, slid off my jeans. When she tossed her pants to the ground, I decided to waste no time and yanked my boxers down.

Sophia was pretty impressed. She kept looking me up and down, observing.

"I've got nothing else on," I said. "Your turn."

Sophia gave a shrug and slipped out of her panties. After she tossed them to the side, we stood there for a moment, just taking each other in. We were totally naked in front of each other for the first time ever. It was kinda scary and kinda awesome at the same time.

She moved toward me first. I noticed she'd left the totem around her neck. She started kissing me. "I don't have anything on. What are you going to do about it, water boy?"

Every part of me was dying to run my hands and mouth over every inch of her. Instead, I picked her up and threw her into the pool.

She yelped as she flew through the air, and I laughed before I dived in after her. Both of us were submerged under the deep, cool water. I looked around. The pool was deeper than I thought. Though we could stand in places, some parts of it were submerged in darkness, and I couldn't see the stony bottom. It had to be at least thirty feet deep around the waterfall's end.

Sophia popped up for air and took a deep breath. "Asshole!" She splashed me in the face.

"Don't play that game with me," I warned. "You'll lose."

She gave a sneaky grin and splashed me again. A shadow fell overhead, and Sophia barely had time to look up and scream before a mini tidal wave came and crashed down on her, pushing her underwater for a second time.

When she came back up, she was completely soaked. "That's totally unfair," she said, wiping her eyes of all the excess water.

"Don't come on to my turf and talk shit," I said, grinning.

She spat excess water out of her mouth. "Guess so."

Sophia looked to the left, then said, "Race you to the waterfall."

She dived, and I went after her. I could've caught up with her easily, magic or no magic, but I stayed behind. I liked looking at certain... assets back here.

Sophia took a breath, then dived underneath the waterfall. I followed her. When she came back up on the other side, all we could hear was the roar of the waterfall in our ears, and all we could see was a small cave beneath that had been carved out to the left, a wall of crashing water behind us. It wasn't very big, just a small enclave that was forged out of rock.

"Wow," Sophia breathed, and her voice echoed in the cave. "This is beautiful."

She clung to the ledge of the cave to stay afloat. The water was deeper in here than it was in the pool. She lifted up to kiss me eagerly before she dove back down, back under the waterfall.

When we came back up, Esis was waiting by the edge of the pool. He had a piece of long bark in his paws that he pointed to eagerly.

Sophia laughed. "You want to go surfing, buddy?"

Esis nodded. He put the bark on the water and climbed on top of it. Sophia looked at me, and I manipulated the pool so that it made little waves. Esis stood up on his hind legs and rode them easily. Sophia clapped, and I grinned. He was totally hanging ten.

"Be careful, Liam. He can't swim," Sophia said anxiously.

"He'll be fine. I've got him." When Esis was safely on the other side of the pool, where the water was shallow enough for him to walk out if he fell in, I made the water collect around me so that it rocketed me upward several feet. I did a backflip in mid-air and dived down into the deepest part of the pool. I thought I saw something down there, but I didn't pay enough attention to swim down and see what it was.

"Show-off," Sophia said when I came back up. Esis gave me the hand sign to hang loose.

"I'm always swimming. There are pools in the Toaqua dorms." I shook the water out of my ears.

"The Koigni dorms have saunas. They're *amazing*," Sophia said, drawing out the word.

Esis continued to zip around on his surfboard. Impulsively, I reached out and pulled Sophia close to me.

"Hm. What's this?" she asked playfully as her fingers explored my chest and abs.

"I just can't avoid touching you for another moment longer," I said. I put my arms around her and brought my mouth to hers. She moaned and started kissing me back. This kiss was intense and sensual. I ran my hands over her breasts and ass, and she reached downward to stroke my dick. We explored each other's bodies as the waterfall thundered behind us, and I moved my mouth so that it was brushing down her neck and shoulders. She shivered, and in response ran her teeth along my skin, scratching her nails down my back.

I grabbed her by the hips and threw her upward, catching her so that her breasts were at my eye level. She laughed and wrapped her legs around my waist, tangling her fingers in my hair. I buried my face in her breasts and started kissing them, taking the chance to suck one of her nipples into my mouth.

Sophia gasped, and that just made me want her even more. I took the other one into my mouth and favored it before I kissed Sophia's mouth again. She kissed me back with a fierceness I didn't know she had, and her hips rolled on top of me.

My dick brushed against something amazing, and I realized that it'd been Sophia. And not just any part of her, either. If I thrust upward, just once, I'd be inside of her.

This was getting too close for comfort. I wanted to go all the way, but at the same time, something inside me was screaming that now wasn't the right time. But I didn't have any more self-control left in me, and she didn't, either. We were totally going to have sex, and we couldn't stop ourselves.

"Liam?" Sophia panted. I was grateful for the pause.

"Yeah?" I was astounded at how breathless my voice was.

"I don't want to go through with this until I tell you something. It's important."

"Can it wait?" I asked.

"Not really." She looked at me, and the moment was broken. "I don't feel right doing this unless I tell you."

Wow, okay. Whatever she had to say was obviously a big deal.

And I had things to confess, too. This was it. I had to tell her.

"I, um... I actually have something to tell you, too," I started. I lifted her off me so she was no longer wrapped around my hips.

We were still in each other's arms, though we were standing on the pool floor now. Sophia obviously decided to go first. "Liam—"

A deep male voice cut her off. "All right! Are we going skinny dipping?"

It was Jonah and Imogen. Both of them appeared to be smiling and in great moods. Sassy and Squeaks were behind them.

Sophia gave a shrill scream and dipped most of her body underwater so you could only see her head. I quickly used my magic to move the bubbles from the waterfall over her so she'd be covered.

I was irritated. As. Fuck. "Really, guys?" I asked. "How'd you even find us here?"

"We were looking for slappertanks and just ended up wandering in. They like water," Imogen said brightly. "We heard the sound of a waterfall and followed it."

"Cannonball!" Jonah, the ass he was, had already stripped off all of his clothes (yes, boxers too, he didn't give a fuck) and jumped in. Water went everywhere. Sophia shrieked and swam to the other side of the pool.

Squeaks did a swan dive after him— as much of a swan dive as a hippogriff can do, anyway. When she splashed down into the water, it caused a giant wave that made Esis go spiraling on his makeshift surfboard.

Sassy stood at the edge of the water and pawed at the koi fish, trying to catch them. Esis paddled his surfboard to the shore and joined her, watching the fish swim round in circles.

Jonah came up for air and swept his long hair back. "Ah. Nothing like a nice swim on a hot day, huh boys and girls?"

I rolled my eyes. Thankfully, even though Jonah was tall, the water was high enough that it at least covered his waist.

Sophia was trying to shield her gaze with her hand. "Jonah, that's more of you than I ever wanted to see."

"We're all friends here. The human body is perfectly natural," he said back.

Imogen came out of the bushes wearing a leaf bikini that she'd obviously made herself with her magic. She hopped in, then swam over to see Sophia. Imogen didn't seem bothered by Jonah's bare ass, but come to think of it, we probably all should've been used to him by now. She pointedly ignored me though, thank the ancestors. Imogen handed Sophia another leaf bikini, and she slipped it on quickly.

"So, how are we all doing?" Jonah asked innocently. Squeaks was swimming around the pool in a circle now, giving Sassy and Esis a ride. "You two looked rather cozy."

"Yeah, until you interrupted, thanks," I said bluntly.

Jonah shrugged. "Hey, I'm not getting any, so I don't feel like anyone else should, either." He glanced at Imogen. "Isn't that right, Miss, I-found-you-under-the-staircase-with-Cade?"

"Shut up, Jonah," Imogen said, and she turned red as Sassy's fur. Sophia peered closer.

"Imogen, is that a *hickey* on your neck?" Sophia asked.

"No!" Imogen squeaked. She tried to cover up a dark bruise near her shoulder with her hand.

"It is!" Sophia squealed. Imogen pushed her into the water, and the girls screamed and started splashing each other. Squeaks got excited and joined in, using her wings to create giant splashes that soaked both girls. They laughed, and Sophia had to grab her bikini top so that it didn't fall off. Sassy and Esis jumped for cover to the banks of the pool.

"Bet you're living your fantasy, huh, Liam?" Jonah asked coyly. I sent a large stream of water shooting at him, and it knocked him over.

We swam around for a while and goofed off until it started to get dark. We got dressed (and forced Jonah to close his eyes) before Sophia made a campfire in the middle of the clearing for us to dry off with. I lifted my head as I started to hear chants and the beats of drums with the sunset. The Ancestors' Day ceremonies were starting. I needed to move quickly if I wanted to speak with Anna.

I stood up. "We should get back, guys. Ancestors' Day has begun. If we want to take part in the ceremonies and get a chance to talk to our ancestors, we'd better hurry."

Sophia stood up, too. "I'll let you guys go ahead. I forgot to take care of something. I have to turn in a last-minute project."

"Now?" I frowned. She didn't want to see me talk to Anna, and possibly get some of the answers I'd been dying for these past few weeks?

"It's for Doya. I won't be long," Sophia said. "I'll meet you guys there. Be back in a bit."

Sophia jogged off into the woods, and Esis followed.

Jonah raised an eyebrow and looked at me. He was leaning against Squeaks, who squawked. "Did anyone else think that was a little sketchy?"

I thought for a moment. That *was* weird. Sophia had just taken off on us. She knew tonight was important to me. She wanted to be there. She wouldn't bow out unless...

Then I realized. She didn't have a choice. Whatever the Fire Elders had asked her to do... it was tonight. I knew it was.

This involved my mission. The night I'd been waiting for, the night I'd prayed wouldn't come, was finally here. I had to kill Sophia tonight, or I would lose the chance to get Nashoma back forever. I had to pick one of them.

No. I wouldn't make a decision. I couldn't. It was impossible. I still could have both of them. I just needed to find a way to make it happen.

I glanced toward the sounds that were coming far off from Kinpago. Some of the ceremonies were already starting. I could miss my chance to talk to Anna.

As I saw Sophia fade behind the tree line, I made a decision. Anna would have to wait.

"Where are you going?" Jonah asked as I headed off in the same direction.

"I'm following her," I said. "You coming?" It might be easier to convince Sophia to stop whatever she was trying to do if Jonah and Imogen were there to back me up.

"You're spying on her? Why?" Imogen's tone was instantly accusative. Sassy's bushy tail rose defensively.

"It's for her own good, I promise," I said. "I just want to make sure she's safe."

"Is she in danger?" Jonah asked.

I hesitated. "She could be," I said, unsure. "I think it has something to do with the prophecy."

Imogen still looked undecided, but then she glanced at Jonah and said, "All right. Let's go."

We headed off into the woods. We followed Sophia's tracks, then stood a ways back once we caught up with her so she wouldn't spot us. When she got back to the main path, she and Esis didn't head back to the school, or Kinpago.

She took another path, one that was overgrown and rarely used. The group of us struggled to get along and not be heard from behind as we trailed her through a long, overgrown path.

Eventually, the trees parted, and my breath caught as I saw where Sophia was headed.

The Anichi ruins.

TWENTY

I glanced behind myself to make sure I wasn't being followed. For a second, I thought I saw a flash of movement in the trees, but a moment later, it was gone.

You're fine, I told myself. It's not like the Koigni Elders were going to follow me, right? I mean, they said I had to do this alone.

The forest thickened the farther I walked. Soon, large mounds the size of small houses came into view. Upon closer inspection, I realized they were old huts where the Anichi tribe used to live. They were covered in vines and moss. The forest had claimed what had since been forgotten.

Almost there. My heart hammered.

Eventually, the trees thinned, and I came face-to-face with a large stone structure. I had finally arrived. My palms grew clammy as I tilted my head back to take in the temple towering above me. Esis craned his neck and whistled.

It took my breath away. Made entirely of stone, the temple was larger than any building I'd seen in all of Kinpago. It took up my entire vision. I couldn't see all the twists and turns to the building through the forest. It was shaped like a pyramid and ended in a flat, open room at the top— the Summoning Room, where I had to perform the ceremony. I could see the stone pillars outlining the room from here. The temple reminded me of the Mayan ruins I'd seen in pictures, but it had been all but eaten by the forest. It was as if one could walk straight up to the ancestors, though I knew I couldn't get to the Summoning Room from the outside.

Finally forcing air to return to my lungs, I took a shaky breath and stepped forward. Damp moss squished beneath my shoes, and broken bits of stone wobbled under me. Esis and I stopped beside a large gorge that surrounded the entire temple like a moat. It was at least fifty feet across and was dug so deep into the earth that when I peered over the side, I couldn't see the bottom through the darkness.

I took a deep breath and set Esis down at my feet. I slipped my bag off my shoulder and pulled out a flashlight, then clicked it on and shone it across the gorge. My light caught a large, open doorway set into the high stone wall.

I swept my light across the gorge. Between myself and the door stood a raised drawbridge on the other side. There was a lever beside it that would allow me safe passage back out of the temple when I finished the ceremony. Dotted all around the gorge were various small platforms not much bigger than a stovetop. They led toward the drawbridge like stepping stones, but the first two had crumbled away. The rest towered high above the bottom of the pit in uneven rows. There wasn't any way to get to them across this distance.

My knees shook. "I don't want to do this," I whispered to Esis.

He turned his big blue eyes up at me and dropped his ears. I knew exactly what he'd say to me if he could. *You don't have to.*

The Koigni Elders' threat returned to mind. *If you don't do this, your friends and your family will suffer.*

"I have to," I told him before taking another deep breath.

I glanced around, looking for possible ways across the gorge. There was a thick log nearby, but it'd be far too heavy for me to move, and it wasn't long enough to reach across anyway. Maybe there was a way down into the gorge and back up again?

I pointed my light over the edge and gazed downward. What I saw made my skin crawl. The walls of the gorge were made entirely of flat stone and plummeted straight down another fifty feet. At the bottom, a dark black sludge twisted and turned. At first, I thought that maybe the temple had been built upon a tar pit, until I realized that the large black spots were moving across the walls and the floor independently of one another. Each huge spot was attached to eight legs.

Spiders!

I shuddered. These weren't just any normal spiders, either. They were bigger than my head, just like Madame Chavis' Familiar. I'd remembered how much that thing had unsettled me when I'd met with the Koigni Elders. I wasn't about to go crawling into a pit of thousands of its cousins. Finding a way down and back up again was out of the question. Those suckers would eat me alive.

"We have to find a way across," I told Esis. "Doya said the temple would test my bravery. I guessed she wasn't kidding."

Esis looked up at me with frightened eyes. He puffed his chest out proudly and pointed to himself.

"No," I stated sternly, crouching to his level. "I'm not letting you do this for me. I'll find a way."

Esis dropped his shoulders.

"Just stay here. I'll drop the bridge so you can get across."

Esis stomped his tiny little foot, but I was already on my feet again, surveying my options. Doya had told me about the first task. She'd said it would be very physical, but what she didn't know was that the first two platforms I needed to get across no longer existed. I glanced upward and tried to think back to my senior year of high school physics to recall everything I knew about pendulums, force, gravity—all of it. Eyeing the trees and vines overtaking the landscape, I came up with a plan. It wasn't a *good* plan by any means, but it was my only option.

There was no way directly across, but I saw a way to get to the platforms, where I could hop from one to the other until I reached the other side.

Don't question it, I told myself. But I did, and I hesitated as my eyes locked on a vine twisted high above on a tall tree overhanging the gorge. My whole body came alive with nerves, and my hands shook at my sides. Esis stepped forward and placed a paw on my ankle. His ears turned down as he looked up at me, like he knew what I was about to do and didn't want me to risk it.

"If I don't get in there, the Elders will hurt my friends," I reminded him. "I have to take this risk."

Esis looked frightened, like he wasn't sure I had it in me. Heck, *I* wasn't sure I had it in me. But I had to at least try.

Go now, and don't look back.

I bent and gave Esis a kiss on the top of the head, then handed him my flashlight, and took off running. Esis' frightened cry followed behind me, but it was drowned out by the sound of my footsteps in the dirt. I jumped upward and caught a branch high above my head, then swung my leg out. My heel caught on the branch, and I used leverage to pull myself up. Esis followed me with the light, making it easier to see the branches in front of me. I climbed higher and higher until my arms began to ache.

When I glanced down below myself, Esis was just a mere dot. My head spun being up this high, and a shot of adrenaline made every muscle in my body quiver. I held on tightly to the closest branch and took several deep breaths, trying to force myself not to focus on the height. When I glanced down again, I saw that Esis was standing at the base of the tree. He'd dropped the flashlight and was starting to climb.

"Esis, don't!" I warned him. I knew he was a good climber, but I wasn't going to let him do this for me. He was safer right where he was.

Esis hesitated, then stepped away from the tree and grabbed the flashlight again. "I'm almost there," I called down to him.

Up this high, the branches were beginning to thin. I grabbed on to one above my head and began to walk toward the end of the branch I stood on, where I could see the thick vine I needed hanging off a nearby branch. I needed to unhook it so I could swing to the platforms. I was almost there.

The branch groaned under my feet, causing me to stop in my tracks. After a moment of silence, I reached out toward the vine, but my fingers couldn't grab it. I was only mere inches away. Gripping the branch above my head once more, I inched further outward. The branch beneath my feet began to bow. Then suddenly—

Crack!

The branch snapped off beneath me, and my stomach hurdled up into my throat as my feet fell. My fingers tightened around the branch

I'd been holding, clutching it for dear life. My legs flailed, trying to find a new foothold but failing. I heard Esis scream, and I squeezed my eyes shut tightly to keep the fear at bay.

It so didn't help.

"Ancestors, help me," I whispered.

I heard Esis scurry up the tree, but I couldn't peel my eyes open to look at him. The sound of his claws on the bark came near my head as he crawled onto the branch I clung to.

"Esis, I told you to stay," I snapped. "I have this handled."

His warm little paw touched my finger, and I finally opened my eyes. He stared down at me, looking worried. I didn't know how much longer I could hold on. I was in shape from all the hiking I did, but that didn't exactly help me in the upper body strength department.

I glanced around for another branch to rest my feet on, but they were all out of reach. The vine I needed to get to was close, slung across a branch only a few feet away from my head, but I feared that if I reached out for it I might fall and plummet into the gorge.

What was I thinking? I chastised myself. I didn't say it out loud, because I didn't want Esis to know how scared I was.

Esis reached down with his little paws and tried to grab my wrist, like he had the strength to save me. The truth was, I didn't think even I had the strength to do another pull-up right now, and I was losing adrenaline by the second. It was clear I only had one option, but I was still trying to work up the courage to take the leap.

"That's not helping, Esis." My voice shook.

He stood up straight on the branch and placed his hands on his hips as if to ask, *Well, what do you want me to do, then?*

"Meet me at the bottom," I said.

And then I took my chance. Taking one hand off the branch, I reached out toward the vine. My fingers just barely brushed it, and I missed. My heart leapt in my chest, and I thought this was it, that I was falling, but a second later I was still hanging on to the branch with one hand. Putting my other hand back in place, I hung there and took deep breaths, letting the last shot of adrenaline run its course. But my fingers were beginning to slip, and I was losing so much strength that if I held on much longer, I wouldn't have enough strength to hold the vine.

One shot, I told myself. *I only have one more shot.*

I couldn't waste it, or it was down into the deep, spidery gorge for me.

"Esis," I whispered. He gave a mournful sigh back to me. "If this doesn't work..."

I couldn't finish my sentence.

Esis opened his mouth to make a noise, but I was already moving, swinging my body to build up momentum. Then I launched myself forward.

My stomach bottomed out as I flew through the air. It was like speeding down the highest point of a roller coaster, only a hundred times worse because I wasn't strapped to anything and had no idea if I'd make it or not. My fingers curled around the thick vine, and I clung on as tight as I could. The vine pulled to a stop for just a second before my weight took the tree branch with us, snapping it off at the end. A high-pitched scream cut through the air, and it took me a second to realize it was my own. Wind rushed through my hair as I plummeted down and down and down... and then started to swing up again.

A sense of pride and victory swept through me as I saw a platform come closer. I pointed my toes, readying them for the impact. My feet just barely touched the top of the platform. I realized a second too late that I'd grabbed about a foot too high on the vine. My chance to jump off the vine and land safely on the platform was there and gone before I knew it. I began swinging in the opposite direction.

"No!" I cried as the platform fell away from me. High up in the tree-tops, Esis squealed loudly.

The vine slowed as it reached its peak in the other direction. I could already tell that I'd lost my momentum to make it to the platform. Without an extra boost, I'd end up hanging there over the gorge.

Luckily, the swing brought me back in the direction of the tree I'd climbed. As I swung toward a lower branch, I extended my legs and braced myself for impact. My knees bent as my feet connected with the branch at the peak of the swing. Then I kicked off with all my strength, sending me spinning back in the direction of the platforms. My pulse thundered in my ears as I lost control. I knew this was my last chance, so

I didn't give myself the opportunity to hesitate. Keeping my eye on the incoming platform, I let my instinct guide me.

"*Shiiiit!*" I cried as I let go of the vine.

My breath suspended in my lungs, and my body flew through the air. My feet slammed into the rocky surface, but my body kept moving. My legs flew out from under me, and I reached my hands out, clawing through the air for a hand-hold.

I came to a halt with my feet dangling over the gorge and my fingers curled around the rock above me. I had just enough adrenaline left that I managed to pull myself up. I sat on the towering platform, taking long, deep breaths, then looked up at Esis in the trees. He was scurrying down the trunk to get to me as fast as he could.

"I did it, Esis!" I cried.

He clapped and cheered as he bounded through the dirt toward the edge of the gorge. Finally, my heart began to slow. I couldn't believe I'd done it. For a moment there, I'd thought for sure I was a goner.

And then a creaking sound below me met my ears, and my heart went hammering against my rib cage again. I shot to my feet just in time to feel the platform teetering beneath me. Without thinking about it too hard, I set my sights on the next platform several feet away and jumped.

The sound of tumbling rock followed. I landed safely on the second platform, then glanced down into the deep gorge below. The platform I'd just been standing on had snapped from its base and landed at the bottom of the pit with an echoing *crash*.

Suddenly, the dark shadows below began to move at an alarming rate. The falling rock had seriously pissed the spiders off. As if they were one being, the dark shadows began to grow upward, covering the walls of the gorge and the tall columns the platforms were suspended on. When Esis shined the flashlight downward, I caught a glimpse of the spiders' jaws snapping in my direction. There was no time to waste.

I threw myself over the gorge again, soaring through the air until I landed on the next platform. Only a few more to go...

One... two... My feet landed on the last platform before the temple entrance, and I felt the rock move out from beneath me. Not a second too soon, I jumped forward before I could be taken down with it. The stone fell out from beneath my feet and tumbled toward the bottom of the pit.

My heart leapt up into my throat, and Esis' scream echoed across the gorge as I realized I was short of my target. I threw my hands out in front of me, and my fingers just barely caught the edge of gorge. Breathing heavily, I tried to pull myself up, but failed. Esis cried out from behind me, getting my attention. I followed the light he pointed below me to see that the giant spiders were headed straight toward me.

Panic whipped through me as the first spider reached my shoe. I felt its long, hairy leg brush up against my ankle. It snapped its large, terrifying jaws at me, like it was about to bite my foot clean off.

"Motherfu—" I grunted as I pulled back my foot and slammed my shoe into its face. The spider went spiraling downward, taking several others with it. By now, there were hundreds more only a few feet away.

Digging my toes into the side of the wall, I groaned as I pulled myself upward with every ounce of energy I had left in me. To my surprise, I pulled myself up high enough that I was able to hook my elbow on the ground and drag myself the rest of the way.

As soon as I was on solid ground again, I leapt to my feet and whirled around just in time to see dozens of spider legs poking up out of the gorge.

Then came the eyes... the endless eyes. I scurried backward, but the spiders only followed, pursuing me like I was an endless buffet table and they hadn't eaten in decades.

Thinking quickly, I pointed my palms toward the ground at them. Flames came shooting out at my command. The spiders backed away momentarily, but they snapped their jaws at me again as soon as the flames died out.

"What the hell?" I exclaimed aloud. Why weren't they hurt?

I shot flames out of my palms again, aiming at the closest group. This time, it wasn't a warning. The flames coated their hairy backs, and I thought for sure I was having fire-roasted spider for dinner, but the fire dissipated and the spiders moved forward again.

Then the closest one opened his jaws and shot a flame of his own at me. I jumped out of the way, but I wasn't fast enough. The end of a hot blue flame caught the hem of my pants, sending the bottom of my jeans up in enchanted flames. An agonizing scream erupted out of my lungs.

Fire spiders, I realized.

I quickly killed the spider's flames with my powers, but a hot, burning ache spread across my leg. Normal fire wouldn't hurt me, but this wasn't normal fire, and these weren't normal spiders. I barely had time to process the throbbing ache in my lower leg as I turned back on the creatures.

Even though my flames couldn't hurt the spiders, they still didn't seem to like them. This time, when I shot flames out of my hands, I kept them going, sustaining them like a flame torch. All around me, the spiders shied away, blinking as if I was hurting them.

It's not the heat! I realized. *It's the light.*

These were creatures of darkness. The light hurt their eyes. Finally, my breaths began to slow as I realized I'd gained the upper hand.

Keeping my flames aimed at them, I began to walk forward toward the drawbridge lever. The spiders parted, letting me pass through. A sense of victory washed through me as I tugged on the lever.

The drawbridge groaned as the centuries-old chains unwound. A puff of dirt rose into the air on the other side as it touched down.

"Come on, buddy!" I called over to Esis.

He grabbed my flashlight and dragged my bag behind him as he hurried across the bridge toward me. Esis shined the light into the eyes of approaching spiders, and they backed away to let him through. The rest of the group scurried down to the blackness of the pit. They had finally left us alone.

I bent and held my arm out to Esis. He jumped into it as soon as he was close enough, and I squeezed him in a tight embrace, burying my nose into his soft white fur. I was still trying to recover from the adrenaline rush and couldn't quite catch my breath.

"See?" I said to Esis as I set him down. "I told you I had it covered."

I swung my bag over my shoulder and turned to the temple entrance. Taking a final deep breath, I started toward it with cautious steps.

Esis shined the flashlight inside the temple doorway, illuminating the damp stone walls. All I saw ahead was a long hallway that reminded me of a cave tunnel. There were holes cut out in the ceiling to provide light, but as evening settled over the ruins, they weren't much help.

I entered the temple slowly, like I thought there might be another band of magical creatures waiting for my arrival, but I was only greeted by silence...

... Until I heard the sound of sticks breaking in the forest behind me, a few shouts, and a couple of curse words. I whirled around, thinking this was another obstacle, like some sort of giant mythical creature meant to protect the temple. Then I spotted the silhouette of a hippogriff in the trees and I knew...

My teeth gritted. I couldn't believe them!

I glanced to Esis, then back to the tree line. "Looks like we have company."

Liam

TWENTY-ONE

I was totally smushed against my teammates for what felt like the thousandth time in my life.

"Jonah, move your fat ass," I said, and I elbowed him to the side. Imogen, Jonah and I, including Squeaks and Sassy, were hiding behind a collection of ruins that we'd ducked behind just as Sophia had turned around. Problem was, the ruin was only big enough for one of us to hide behind, and space was even more hard to come by when one of the people you were trying to hide had a hippogriff for a Familiar.

"You move your fat ass! I'm suffocating," Jonah whined. We were speaking in low voices, but I was pretty sure Sophia could still hear us.

"There isn't enough room for any of us behind this pillar!" Imogen hissed. Sassy was squished against her chest, looking like roadkill.

I went to say something else, but Sophia called out from the entrance of the temple. "All right guys, come on out!"

The three of us froze and looked at each other. What did we do?

"I can see Squeaks' butt! I know you're there!" Sophia shouted.

"Uh... we're not here!" Jonah cried out in a high-pitched voice, trying to sound like a woman.

I rolled my eyes. Game over.

Squeaks stumbled. All of us went careening forward headfirst. We collapsed into a pile on the ground as Sophia stomped toward us.

"I can't believe you guys!" Sophia yelled. Esis was hot on her tail. He gave a scathing look to Squeaks and Sassy, who seemed to shrug. Esis started chittering, and the noises he made sounded a lot like swear words as he shook his fist at his friends. Sassy stuck her tongue out at him, and Squeaks ruffled her feathers, like she was offended.

I tried to give Sophia a weak smile as I untangled myself from the others and got to my feet, but she totally wasn't having it, because she was *pissed*.

"Us? What about you?" Jonah said as he brushed himself off. Squeaks worked on fixing his hair with her beak, which had fallen out of place. "You're clearly hiding something."

"Yeah, Sophia," Imogen said. She sounded hurt. "What is all of this? Why are you trying to sneak into the Anichi temple on Ancestors' Day?"

"And why didn't you tell us?" I added— though I had a pretty good idea.

"I don't have to tell you guys everything," Sophia shot back. "There's some stuff I keep to myself."

"Um, best friends here," Jonah said, and he gestured between all of us. "Whatever you're hiding is obviously a big deal."

"It's my business! Back off!" Sophia shouted.

Imogen's head went from side to side, not sure which side to take. I took the initiative. "Sophia, whatever you're doing, can't it wait?" I asked. "It's Ancestors' Day. Come back and enjoy the celebration."

"You guys don't get it. If I don't do this tonight, all of you are going to die!" she screamed.

The breath left my lungs. Jonah grabbed at his neck like someone was choking him. But Imogen didn't hesitate. "What do you mean, Sophia?"

The anger faded from Sophia's face. She dropped her head and sighed. "It's about the prophecy. The Koigni Elders contacted me at the beginning of the semester and told me on Ancestors' Day, I had to go to the Anichi temple and summon the *naderei* who made the prophecy. I have to speak to her and see what I'm supposed to do in order to fulfill it. If I don't, they're going to torture Esis— and kill everyone I care about. That includes my parents, Amelia, and you guys."

Imogen gasped. Jonah's eyes widened, and I said, "There's more at stake than just our lives. Fulfilling the prophecy... *pawee*, that's gonna start a war. It'll rip the tribe in half."

"Liam, they were going to start with you," Sophia said, and her voice broke. "Doya knows we're involved. If I fail, she'll come after you first. I couldn't live with myself if something happened to you because of me."

"My life isn't a precious thing to me," I said softly. "Sophia, please don't do this."

Sophia hesitated, and Imogen said, "Why didn't you tell us about this sooner?"

"I couldn't say anything. They swore me to secrecy. It was part of the deal," Sophia said.

She turned toward the temple. "I'm sorry, but I have to do this on my own."

I reached out and grabbed her by the shoulder, turning her around. "We're not going to let you do this alone."

"Never, Sophia," Imogen said.

"Yeah. Also, if you mess it up, that means we're dead," Jonah added. "I'd like some extra security."

"This is a bad idea in the first place," I argued. "If the prophecy comes true, thousands will die."

"We don't know if that'll happen. There's no proof. The prophecy could mean anything," Sophia said. "But if I don't do this, Liam, you *will* die. So will Imogen, so will Jonah, then they'll kill my parents and Amelia before they start with Esis. That's a fact."

I wanted to tell her the part of the prophecy that was about Toaqua facing its darkest hour. But I wasn't sure if it would even deter her.

"What are you supposed to do?" Imogen asked.

"I have to get to the Summoning Room at the top of the temple and perform a ceremony. Once I have the information from the ancestor, I'm to report back. Then they'll leave me alone," Sophia said.

They'd never leave her alone. I knew that much. I was supposed to stop this. That was the task my tribe had assigned to me.

But I was curious. If we got to the top of the temple and Sophia performed the ceremony, we could finally get some answers. Maybe the prophecy wasn't as bad as we'd thought.

At the same time, that might mean risking my chance to get

Nashoma back. If I failed and Koigni became more powerful than Toaqua... the Elders would never forgive me. I'd never see my wolf again.

Yet this wasn't about me. This was about saving my entire race.

I didn't know what to do. But I couldn't show my hand yet. I didn't have enough information. And a part of me was dying to learn exactly what the prophecy meant.

"How long will it take?" I asked. If we hurried, I would still have time to speak with Anna.

Sophia shrugged. "There are traps inside set by Koigni, but Doya told me how to avoid everything. The walk to the top and the ceremony itself shouldn't take more than a few hours."

That was plenty of time. It was a quick walk and a short ceremony. What could it hurt?

"Fine. But we're coming with you," I said.

"But—" Sophia started.

"No buts." Jonah swung his arm around her shoulder. "This is a job for the Reject Team. It's got *us* written all over it."

"I've always wanted to explore the Anichi temple," Imogen said, peering up at it. "I bet there's tons of amazing artifacts in there."

Sophia gave a pleading look at me, and I raised my eyebrow. "If you think I'm gonna walk away now, you don't know me that well."

Sophia sighed. She knew there was no convincing us. "Okay. Let's just get this over with."

She looked upward. "Maybe we don't have to go through the temple. The Summoning Room is at the top. Jonah, can you fly us up?"

"I can try." Jonah lifted his hands, and each of us rose a few inches off the ground, but we didn't get any farther.

Squeaks tried flying above the temple, and she reached the top, but once Sophia got onto her back for a ride, she couldn't get her hooves more than a couple feet off the ground.

"This isn't going to work. There's some sort of ward around it, preventing me or Squeaks from flying you there," Jonah said. "I think you're supposed to go through the temple, to prove you're worthy or whatever."

"That's it, then," I said. "Come on, guys. We gotta walk."

We headed inside the temple. The hallway in front of us was long and dark. Sophia tried to turn her flashlight on, but it didn't work.

"Dead." She threw it to the side, looking frustrated.

"Here." Jonah took down a few torches from the wall that looked ancient. He passed one out to each of us, and Sophia lit them.

Even though the torches gave light, it was still hard to see down the hallway. As we headed forward, Jonah said, "You were a total badass back there by the way, Sophia. It was like watching *Tomb Raider*."

"Hell yeah!" Imogen said. "She kicked those spiders' butts!"

"She nearly gave me a heart attack," I grumbled. We'd gotten lost in the woods, and only caught up to Sophia when she'd been right in the middle of trying to *Indiana Jones* her way to the other side. By then, we were too far away to be of much help. Watching her jump from the tree and fall toward the platform, only to grab on at the last second, had been worse than terrifying. Yeah, I suppose it would've been cool to watch, if the person being chased by giant spiders and leaping from crumbling ruins hadn't been my girlfriend.

"Nothing was going to happen to me. I had it handled," Sophia said. Esis chittered from her shoulder, and she shushed him.

We hit a door. Sophia pushed it open, and the moment we stepped inside, we were hit by musty air. I held up my torch to look around and noted that we were in a very large, very empty space, although I couldn't judge how big because it was so dark.

Sophia walked forward, toward an isolated statue directly in front of us. It was grey, nearly twelve feet tall, and took the form of a Spirit Warrior holding an ax, with various inscriptions and carvings around it. It was the same kind of unknown lettering that was on Sophia's totem.

I recognized it as a *stela*, an ancient form of Anichi art.

Sophia pushed down the ax on the warrior. As she did that, the room lit up. Torches that were all along the walls ignited on their own, illuminating the room. It was huge, three hundred feet long and just as wide, and the ceiling reaching upward to where the Summoning Room was. The walls were made of limestone and were set with carvings of Spirit Warriors and Familiars in the Anichi style. Mesoamerican architecture could be seen everywhere past the vines and ivy that overgrew the temple. Statues like the one Sophia had pressed were scattered around the room, some of which were lined with gold. The temple had been sacked by Koigni of all valuables after Anichi was overrun, but some features of the abundance and wealth Anichi had possessed still remained.

Squeaks gave a low whistle, while Esis clapped, impressed.

"This place is enchanted," Imogen said in wonder.

"Or cursed," Jonah added less-helpfully.

Sophia took out a map from her bag and scanned it. I was less patient and started heading down the nearest hallway, but Sophia called out, "Liam, we can't go down that way."

I gritted my teeth and spun around. "Why not?"

"Remember what I said about traps?" Sophia asked. "There's a fire wall down there. We head in that direction, you guys get burned to a crisp."

"Don't be in a hurry, man. This place is huge. We could get lost," Jonah said.

I was in a hurry. I wanted to get this over with so I could talk to Anna, get Nashoma back, get some answers... get back to a normal life.

"Okay." I tried to force myself to have some patience. "So, which way do we go?"

Sophia chewed on her lip. "I'm not sure. Doya marked a path, but..."

She looked flustered. I knew Sophia wasn't bad at maps, which meant that she was getting nervous.

"What would you do without us?" Imogen sighed. She took the map from Sophia and looked it over before she pointed to the left. "There. That way should be safe."

"Are you sure?" I asked.

Imogen gave me a scathing look. "I'm not sure, but this is where Doya told Sophia to go."

"Good enough for me," I said. I went through a door and led the way down to the next room. The stairs went downward, though, instead of up, which confused me.

"Why are we going down if we need to get to the top?" I asked.

"Different chambers lead to different places. There's only one right way to reach the Summoning Room," Sophia said. "You have to go a certain way, otherwise, you'll just end up wandering through the Anichi temple forever."

"This place is a maze," I muttered. Jonah had a point about not getting lost.

"Doya said nobody has been inside for years. We're the first Elementai to enter in probably decades," Sophia said.

We reached the end of the stairs, which led to— you guessed it— another heavy ass door. Jonah, Squeaks and I had to ram ourselves against it in order to get it open.

I looked. The room inside was completely empty, and about fifty feet across. Once we finally managed to get inside, the door that had been so hard to open immediately shut behind us of its own accord.

All of us jumped. Before we had time to react any further, I heard the sound of rushing water. I faced the center of the room and watched in horror as water began streaming into the room through pipes that were embedded in the ceiling. It came pouring down, and within seconds was up to our ankles.

"What the hell is going on here?" Jonah asked.

"This isn't right! Doya said there weren't any traps beside the ones Koigni set!" Sophia shouted.

"The other tribes must've put booby traps in here, too, to try and stop any Elementai from getting through the temple that wasn't of their tribe." Imogen spoke quickly, her voice panicked.

Jonah turned on the door. He started pulling on the handle, and Squeaks kicked at it quickly with her hooves, but it didn't budge.

"The door won't open," Jonah said in a high-pitched voice. He backed against it, looking scared at the rising water. We glanced frantically around the room, but there were no windows or exits— just a door twenty feet above us, with a platform that led to it.

Jonah flew himself up to the platform using his Air, but no matter how hard he and Squeaks tried, magic or brute force, that door wouldn't open, either.

"It won't budge. We're trapped in here!" Jonah screamed. He could barely be heard over the sound of the water coming in.

"Stand back, guys. I've got this," I said. I raised my hands and forced the water back to the other side of the room and froze it there into a large ice wave. But although I could push the water back, I couldn't do anything else. I tried to freeze the pipes so no more water could get through, but the force of what was coming in made that impossible. No matter how much I froze, or how much I commanded the water to stop flowing through the pipes, it wouldn't. I let cold water come splashing backwards, and it soaked our clothes.

This was freaking me out. I'd never had water disobey me before. This kind of stuff came easy for me. I didn't know what to do.

"The water's coming into the room faster than I can control it. There's nowhere for it to go," I said. An edge of alarm entered my voice.

The water was almost to our knees already. Sophia was holding up Esis, and Imogen clung to Sassy. It wouldn't take but a few minutes for the entire room to be filled with water.

Once it hit the ceiling, it'd black out all the torches and we'd all drown. And I'd go last. I'd have to watch all my friends die.

"Get me out of here!" Jonah lost all sense and started pounding on the door he was near, trying to get out. Squeaks sensed his panic and lost it, too, throwing herself against the door over and over, pounding her hooves against the stone.

Imogen was shaking and holding Sassy, who was barking over and over. There was so much going on, it was hard to handle.

"Liam! What do we do?" Sophia yelled. Esis was squeezing her for dear life, watching as the water rose higher and higher. By now, we'd all dropped our torches and they were floating in the water.

All it took was their screaming voices to put me right back in the Elemental Cup. My team was freaking out, and they needed someone to lead them. I had to take control of the situation.

"We need to figure out a way to stop the water from coming in," I said immediately. I scanned the room for clues. This was a Water task. The Toaqua Elders had to have put this here, which meant they'd put in a way of escape for someone who was a Toaqua.

"How the hell are we supposed to do that?" Jonah cried.

He wasn't helping. I ignored him and tried to block out the sounds of the water as I looked around.

The room was completely empty. There was nothing in here we could use. Except...

Up near the top, just below the torches, were four large square buttons the size of my head, decorated with artwork that didn't quite fit into the rest of the temple— a portrait of a water droplet symbol. It was Toaqua, not Anichi.

"There." I immediately focused on hitting those buttons. I shot a water ball at one of the buttons, and once it hit, the button sank in and made a low sound, like a note coming from an organ, though it rose back out almost as fast as I had hit it. I tried another button, and when my magic hit that, the button sank and made a similar sound, though the tone was different and the pitch was higher. I tried using my Water to shoot out different jets that would hit the buttons in succession, but it didn't do anything except make a lot of noise. It sounded like someone was playing a bunch of piano keys at the same time.

"I think we have to press them all at once," Imogen said quickly.

"Together. Everybody use their elements to hit the buttons," I instructed. "Sophia, you take the one on the left. I'll take the one on the right. Imogen, you've got the far-left corner; Jonah, you've got the far-right."

Jonah was shaking. I hoped he could do this, because if he couldn't, we were fucked. The girls pulled themselves together, holding on to a ray of hope.

"On the count of three!" I shouted. "One, two, three!"

We all shot at once. But although we managed to push all the buttons down at the same time, and all the tones rang out together, nothing happened. The buttons returned to their original position, and water kept coming in. It was getting close to my shoulders and had already risen to Imogen's neck.

"It didn't work!" Jonah wailed. I wasn't ready to give up yet.

"Try it in different patterns!" I suggested. I was just pulling stuff out of my ass now. The water had gotten up to six feet now, and we had to tread to stay afloat. Sassy struggled to swim, and Esis clung to the top of Sophia's head, looking nervous at the water coming in. Squeaks swooped down and grabbed both of them, bringing the Familiars back up to the platform with Jonah, but they'd only be safe for so long.

The four of us tried a bunch of different versions of hitting the buttons at the same time, but nothing worked. Although it was nothing for me to tread water, I noticed Sophia struggling to stay afloat. This had to work. We had no backup plan. Maybe there really was no way out of here.

As we were experimenting, I noticed something. The tones, playing together... it sounded like the song of the tribe.

"Stop!" I yelled, and everyone halted using their magic. We were only a few feet away from the ceiling now, almost to the platform where Jonah was. *"Earth, Water, Fire and Air, gifted to us by breath of a prayer—"*

"Singing isn't going to help us right now!" Jonah screeched.

"Shut up! If we can match the tone of the buttons to the pitches in the song—" I shouted.

"Yes! Liam, that's brilliant!" Imogen cried back.

"Imogen, you're the first tone, then me, then Sophia, then Jonah," I said quickly, trying to match up the sounds in my head. I hoped this worked. We were running out of space, and oxygen.

Sophia sputtered next to me. She was losing strength. She spat water out of her mouth and gasped before her head dipped down underwater and back up again.

I immediately swam to her side and grabbed her around the waist, lifting her upwards. I was able to keep both of us aloft in the water with my magic, but soon, there wouldn't be anywhere else for us to go. In moments, we'd be able to touch the ceiling. Those pipes filtering water were only a few feet away.

"Come on, Soph, stay with me," I muttered in her ear.

She managed to hold one arm aloft and out of the water. She struggled to conjure fire, but after a second try, a fireball blazed in her hand.

"We have one shot at this, guys!" I yelled. "Imogen, now!"

Imogen sent rocks from the temple floor hurtling at her button, and hit her target. I used the hand that wasn't holding Sophia up to blast the button on my right. Sophia hit her button with her fireball, and after a split-second of hesitation, Jonah seemed to realize this was do-or-die and pushed his button down with Air.

The sounds echoing around the room sounded exactly like the tribal song. This time, the buttons stayed down. The water stopped filtering in from the pipes and shut off. I heard a draining sound, and the water level dropped. We started drifting downward. Eventually, all the water filtered out of the room, leaving us soaking wet and shivering.

"Is everyone all right?" Jonah called from the platform. Now that the threat was gone, it looked like he'd gotten himself together.

Everyone was breathing really hard. I checked the girls over, then called out, "Yeah, Jonah. We're fine."

I dried us and the torches off, and Jonah levitated us up to the platform where he was. This time, the door opened easily. We proceeded through it, the stairs going upward this time.

Nobody said much. We were still spooked from what had happened back there.

"I told you guys this was dangerous. I didn't want anyone coming with me," Sophia said sourly. Esis sat on her shoulder, his hair standing on end.

Imogen opened her mouth to say something, but I got there first. "If we hadn't gone with you, you'd probably be dead," I snapped, before I made a sarcastic noise. "You think I *want* to be here? The last thing I wanted to do today was go through the Elemental Cup, Part Two."

"This isn't as bad as the Cup, Liam. Quit being so negative." Sophia was getting irritated with me. We'd been at each other's throats since we'd gotten in here.

"Easy, guys," Jonah said. "We still have a lot of temple to get through."

I hated that he was right. We'd just started making our way through this temple, and we had no idea what kind of traps lay ahead, or what House they'd been placed by.

The whole thing was freaking me out. What exactly was in here that the tribes didn't want anyone to discover?

I f I thought I could do this alone, I was fooling myself. There was no way Esis and I would've made it through the Toaqua's booby trap on our own. I didn't say it, but I was grateful my friends had followed me.

Even though I was dry now, I still shivered from the cold. I held Esis tightly to me and walked beside Liam, holding my torch with my other hand. I was close enough that I could feel the heat coming off him. I wanted to reach out and touch him just to show how grateful I was he saved us back there, but my hands were full.

When we reached the top of the stairs, we found ourselves in a long hallway lined with empty torch holders. I'd relit them so we could see that the hall came to an abrupt halt twenty yards ahead of us.

"Dead end," Jonah said, stating the obvious. "Maybe we missed something back in that chamber."

Jonah turned to start back the way we came, but Imogen placed a hand to his chest to stop him. "We didn't miss anything. It's another obstacle."

Imogen started forward until she stopped just a foot away from the wall at the end of the hall. It was covered in twenty-four stone tiles, each at least four inches wide and set into a square. There would've been twenty-five, but one was missing in the top right-hand corner. Each tile

379

had a different pattern cut out on it, but they didn't match up. It was as if someone had placed them into the wall at random instead of in the pattern they were intended.

Imogen reached out and touched the tiles, running her fingers over the designs. Sassy stood on her hind legs and sniffed them.

"What is it?" Liam asked. "It looks like someone glued the tiles on wrong."

Imogen shook her head without taking her eyes off the wall. The way she looked at it made me think she knew exactly what this was, like it wasn't a mistake at all but intentional. That's when it hit me.

"It's a puzzle, isn't it?" I asked.

Imogen nodded. "That's exactly what it is. This must be a Nivita obstacle."

Jonah stepped forward and studied the puzzle, but the furrow in his brow told me he didn't have a clue what he was looking at. "You think so?"

"Nivita value knowledge," Imogen said. "We read books and do riddles. It's our thing. I think we have to solve this puzzle to get through."

"But there's a tile missing," Jonah pointed out. "We'll never solve it."

"It's supposed to be missing," Imogen told him.

"Okay then. Sounds easy enough." Jonah grabbed one of the tiles and tried to pry it out of the wall. It didn't budge.

"Not like that, you dummy." Imogen swatted at him. "You have to slide the tiles to complete the picture."

Jonah frowned and stepped aside. "Well, that's dumb. We all know I won't be any help."

Imogen tapped her finger to her chin. "It just... it can't be this easy."

"What do you mean?" Liam asked. "This puzzle looks complicated."

"The last obstacle could've killed us. We could've drowned. This is just... too safe."

"Well, Nivita aren't known for being cruel," I pointed out.

"I guess you're right," Imogen agreed. "You all can just chill for a couple of minutes. This shouldn't take me long."

Imogen reached for the top tile and slid it over into the empty space.

Suddenly, grinding noises from all around us filled the air, and then came a heavy, resounding *thud.*

We all whirled around at the same time to see that a stone doorway at the top of the stairs had fallen from the ceiling, blocking our way back. Twelve compartments within the door had opened, revealing long, narrow sticks with holes straight through them like straws. My heart leapt to my throat, and I squeezed Esis closer to my chest.

Jonah jumped behind Squeaks and ducked down. "What the hell is that?"

"Uh, oh." Imogen's eyes widened.

"*Uh, oh,* what?" Liam demanded. "What are those things?"

"If I had to wager a guess, I'd say poison dart throwers." Imogen sounded pretty sure of herself. "They're very ancient Hawkei weapons, from before they settled in this area."

I finally tore my gaze off the darts and looked to Imogen. "How much time do we have?"

Just as I asked it, I noticed a small door only a few inches high had opened just above the puzzle tiles. Inside was a compartment no bigger than a safe, where an ancient-looking hourglass stood. Sand rushed through it, counting down the seconds we had left.

Imogen glanced up to the hourglass. "Ten minutes, I'd say."

Liam leapt straight back into Captain mode. "Get to work, Im. Jonah, let's see what we can do about disabling these darts."

Liam started down the hall, but Imogen stopped him. "I wouldn't do that if I were you."

"Why not?" he asked.

Imogen had already placed her torch in one of the empty holders next to her and was moving tiles around the puzzle. She didn't look back at him when she spoke. "Nivita's the smartest House. We anticipate alternatives. They probably set up second booby traps that'll go off if you try to tamper with the darts."

Liam huffed.

"Maybe we can all lie down," Jonah suggested. He made a wide, sweeping motion with his hands. "We'll all just lie flat so that when the darts come at us, they just fly over our bodies."

"Look at how spread out those things are," I said. "Esis and Sassy are the only ones small enough to avoid them. You and Squeaks will be hit no matter where you stand."

"I'll lie down just like this." Jonah shoved his torch into Liam's hands and lowered himself to the floor. He pointed his toes and fingers like he was mimicking a plank.

"And you'd be poisoned," Liam assured him.

Jonah glanced to the dart throwers. "No, they'd just whizz right over me. *Zip*." He waved his hand quickly over his nose to demonstrate.

"Dude," Liam pressed. "There's a dart thrower pointed directly at your junk."

"Huh?" Jonah took a second to process what Liam said, then quickly threw his hands protectively over his package and jumped to his feet.

"Relax," I said nervously. "Imogen will figure it out. Won't you, Im?"

Imogen bit her lower lip, concentrating hard as she slid tile after tile across the puzzle surface. "Sorry, kinda busy."

"See?" I said hesitantly. "She's got this."

I hoped.

The following eight minutes were agonizing. I sat next to Squeaks on the ground, who had curled up to wait patiently. The only sound I heard was the tiles sliding against one another and my own pulse in my ears. I'd placed my torch in the holder above me and stroked Esis while I watched the sand in the bottom half of the hourglass slowly rise. We were running out of time, and judging by the image starting to form in the puzzle, Imogen was only half-done.

Liam paced back and forth in front of me. "Come on, Imogen. We only have a minute and a half left, if that."

"Don't rush me!" she shot back.

"Okay, I give in," Jonah said with a sigh. "Squeaks and I will create a barrier. You all can hide behind us. We'll take the darts for you guys."

"Jonah, no!" Imogen turned from the puzzle for a moment to shoot him a dirty look.

"Come on, it's the only way," Jonah said. "Squeaks and I are too big for anyone to help us. The rest of you need to find a way out of here."

Imogen turned back to the puzzle. "I still have a minute left. You are *not* giving up on me just yet."

"Yeah," Jonah said. "We have a minute to prepare. Sophia, you stay right where you are. Liam, go snuggle up close—"

"No." I shot to my feet. "No one's sacrificing themselves. Imogen will figure it out." I glanced up to the hourglass. It was draining so fast that sweat began to break out across my brow. "Im, do you need help?"

"No, I've got this," she replied without looking up from the tiles. She moved three of them, only to move them back to their original position a moment later.

"Im!" Liam cried. "You have less than thirty seconds left! If you don't get this, we'll all be—"

"Stop rushing me!" Imogen shouted. Another tile slid into place, and I realized what image she was forming. It was a sapling with two leaves, a symbol of the Nivita house. But there were still four tiles in the wrong spots and only seconds left.

My heart hammered, and I leaned into Liam. He draped an arm around me and pulled me and Esis close to his chest. I buried my face between them. I couldn't watch.

"It's not your fault, Im," I told her. "You didn't know—"

"Shh," she hissed, hushing me.

I dared to steal another glance up at the hourglass. Esis looked too, and he seemed just as frightened as I was. His ears pressed back, and he clung to me tightly. Ten... nine... eight...

Liam took my shoulders and positioned me in front of him. He tried to be subtle about it, but I knew exactly what he was doing. He was acting as my shield.

I tried to step out of the way. I couldn't let him do it. But he held me in place so I couldn't budge. The sand was so close to the end now. Every muscle in my body tensed. I sucked in a deep breath and held it.

Five... four... three... two...

Imogen quickly arranged the final three tiles. "Done!"

A second later, a series of loud *clicks* sounded all over the room. The door on the hourglass compartment slammed shut, and the dart throwers retracted back into the entrance on the other end of the room. The door raised back into the ceiling, opening the hall back to the stairs. In front of us, the wall with the puzzle slid aside to reveal a dark room ahead. I let out a sigh of relief as my heart slowed.

"Im, you did it!" I rushed forward and pulled her into a hug.

"I told you I would!" She squeezed me back. Esis was squashed between us.

Jonah threw his arms around us, picked us both up in his arms, and spun us around. "Thank the ancestors!"

Imogen laughed as he set us down, then gestured to Liam to join us. Liam sighed but stepped forward and joined in on the group hug.

"Shall we?" Imogen asked once we parted.

The four of us grabbed our torches and stepped inside the next room with our Familiars at our sides. The room wasn't very big, about the size of a large bedroom, but it had three wide passageways splitting off in each direction. All around us, the room was overgrown with vines and roots growing in from little cracks all throughout the walls. Rocks of various sizes were piled neatly in the corners, like the Nivita who'd set up the last booby trap had left them behind to show they'd been here.

"Which way?" Liam asked.

I dug inside my bag and showed Imogen the map Doya had given me. She studied it for a moment, then said, "It looks like we need to take this tunnel on the right."

Before any of us could move, the sound of footsteps padding lightly across the floor met our ears. I shined my light toward the tunnel in front of us. For a second, time stood still as I held my breath, staring at the strange creature that stepped out of the shadows. It wasn't much bigger than Sassy, but it was terrifying. It had a lizard-like body with black and red stripes across its scales. Sharp, bony spikes grew several inches out of its elbows and spine, trailing all the way down its tail. A pointed barb stuck out the end of its tail, like it was some sort of giant mutated lizard-scorpion. It gazed at us with haunting midnight-black eyes.

"Shit!" Imogen screamed.

Nobody hesitated. We all took Imogen's cue and ran, sprinting down the hall she'd pointed to. My heart pounded a million beats per minute, and Liam breathed heavily beside me. I dared to steal a glance over my shoulder and saw that the lizard-scorpion was pursuing us quickly. He was only several feet behind Squeaks' hooves.

"Everybody turn your lights out!" Imogen shouted.

"But we won't be able to—" Jonah started.

"Just do it!" she cried.

Jonah sent a strong gust of wind through the tunnel, and our torches flickered out, but we didn't slow down. Pitch blackness enveloped us, and my panic went into overdrive. I wasn't afraid of the dark, per se, but I was *so* not prepared to race through unfamiliar ruins without all five of my senses. We could run into a pit or something and fall to our deaths! My arms shook, and my breaths became shallow as my legs moved quickly beneath me.

"Imogen, why are we— *ohf*!" Liam's body slammed into something hard, giving me a warning a second before I ran into the same wall. Imogen screamed from beside me as she too ran into it. All at once, Jonah grunted the same time Squeaks' feathers rustled. Imogen screamed, and Sassy let out a bark. Torches clattered to the ground.

I stumbled backward, feeling the impact across the whole front of my body. I had to rely only on sound to make sense of my surroundings. On my left, Imogen and Jonah groaned from the ground. On my right, the legs of Liam's jeans brushed against each other, and it sounded like he was getting to his feet. He grumbled and let out a few curse words under his breath.

"Get off me," Imogen said, followed by the sound of her slapping Jonah in the leg.

"I'm trying!" he shot back. "Squeaks' big butt is in the way."

Squeaks squawked, then came the sound of her heavy hooves against the stone floor. Based on the way their voices echoed off the walls, I had to guess we'd entered a room not much bigger than the last.

"Can I use my light now?" I asked Imogen urgently.

"Just a flash," she warned. "In case it's still following us."

Esis climbed onto my shoulder and settled himself on top of my backpack. I held my palm out and shot a high flame into the air for a second before it disappeared. All I saw was a wide doorway leading out into the hall and the lizard-scorpion standing in front of it with its eyes on us like it was ready to pounce. My entire body tensed.

Gathering my magic again, I shot a fireball across the space between us. Flames whizzed through the air, but the lizard was already on the move. I missed him by a long shot.

"Don't let him touch you!" Imogen cried.

I took a step back until I was pressed up against the wall. Liam did the same beside me.

"What is it?" he demanded of her.

I shot another fireball across the room, but the lizard was three feet ahead of my aim by now. I threw another three in rapid succession, trying to stay ahead of it, but it was like it could anticipate my moves and darted in the other direction.

"Stop it, Sophia," Imogen insisted.

I didn't listen and threw another fireball. The lizard was only ten feet or so from us now, and that was far too close for comfort. At least the fireballs distracted him enough to hold him off for a bit. "Imogen, it's freaking me out!"

"Jonah, try to immobilize it," Liam instructed.

Jonah took a deep breath, and a breeze passed through the room. The sound of scurrying feet zig-zagged across the floor. I couldn't tell where the thing was.

"I can't find him!" Jonah cried.

"There's not enough water in the air," Liam said. "I can't do anything. Im?"

"Shh... hold on," she said.

Everything went silent, apart from the sound of Squeaks' tail brushing against the wall behind her. The scurrying of feet had stopped. I couldn't hear the lizard at all.

"Did it work, Jonah?" I whispered.

"I didn't do anything," he replied in a low voice.

"Do you think we scared it away?" I asked.

"I hope so," Jonah said. "What *was* that thing?"

"A *hunpedzkin*," Imogen answered.

"Hump—what?" Jonah asked.

"*Hunpedzkin*," Imogen repeated. "A Mayan beaded lizard?" She was only met by silence. "Seriously, do you guys read? They're so lethal that if they touch you, you'll die within minutes."

"Then what are we doing sitting here in the dark?" Liam snapped.

"*Hunpedzkin* target your shadows," Imogen explained. "If they bite or sting your shadow, you'll get a headache so bad that you'll kill yourself just to make it stop."

"That sounds better than instant death!" Jonah bellowed.

"True," Imogen admitted.

"Let's get some light, Sophia," Liam said. "Maybe it's gone."

Holding out my palm, I used my Fire to light the room. For the first time, I had a chance to look around. The room was small, but all along the walls on either side of us were displays carved out in the stone where statues of various Familiars stood. The rest of the room was empty.

"Wow," Imogen said breathlessly, taking in all the statues. "This must've been the Familiar Healing Chambers. It's a very sacred room."

"Cool," Jonah said flatly. "Can we maybe focus less on the statues and more on keeping our eyes peeled for the humpty-thing?"

The rest of us scanned the room, and I finally relaxed when I saw no sign of the *hunpedzkin*.

"Can they really sting your shadow?" I asked skeptically. "That sounds—"

"Imogen, look out!" Liam shouted.

All eyes darted to the ceiling to follow his gaze. The hunpedzkin was hanging there like a gecko. Its eyes locked on Imogen's head, and it took aim.

Everything happened so fast that I could hardly process it. Liam jumped forward to knock Imogen out of the way, and then a stark white blur flew through the air to intercept the lizard. Sassy's bark echoed around us. My flame died out for a second before I lit my palm again.

I gasped, and Esis chirped from my shoulder like he was pleased. Sassy's bright red fur was nowhere to be seen. Instead, a pure white fox with nine tails stood in front of us, baring its teeth at the *hunpedzkin*. Golden streaks ran through her vibrant fur, and ivy vines wound around her body. Her body glowed with a strange white light that lit up the chamber. She was bigger than Sassy had been, nearly the size of a wolf instead of a fox.

Liam and Imogen laid on the floor. After a moment of disorientation, Imogen lifted her gaze and propped herself up on her elbows. She drew in a sharp breath, and her jaw dropped like she couldn't believe what she was seeing. None of us could.

"Sassy?" Imogen asked.

Sassy— or the white, nine-tailed fox that was Sassy— didn't respond.

She was too focused on the *hunpedzkin,* who cowered in fear of her. Sassy advanced forward, and the lizard creature stepped back. When Sassy barked, the sound with high-pitched and clear, echoing with magic. The *hunpedzkin* flinched, but it didn't move apart from the eyes. Its gaze darted toward Imogen, and Sassy lost it. Her nine tails stood straight up, and her fur fluffed all around her, making her look almost twice her size. The vines around her body grew, curling out toward the *hunpedzkin* until— *whip!*

Vines thrashed through the air, zipping toward the *hunpedzkin* like a collection of angry tentacles. They moved so fast that I barely saw them touch the creature. Whip marks marred his scales, and blood oozed out of the wounds. It inched away with every whip, but tried to jump back at her a second later. It didn't get far before she whipped it again and it was forced to retreat. I could barely believe what I was seeing. Sassy growled, and bricks that had fallen out of the side of the temple that were lying disregarded on the floor rolled together until they had formed one giant mass of earth, tumbling toward the *hunpedzkin* at high speed. The reptile had to jump out of the way to avoid getting hit. When the *hunpedzkin* managed to leap away from every boulder, Sassy took a deep breath and screamed at the creature. The vibrations from her loud voice were so powerful they sent the reptile flying backward.

"That's my girl, Sassy!" Imogen cheered.

At the sound of Imogen's voice, Sassy whipped harder and faster, until the *hunpedzkin* gave up and raced out of the room into the dark hall. Sassy chased after it, yipping as she whipped the creature with her ivy vines.

"Sassy, come back!" Imogen cried, scurrying to her feet and going after her.

Jonah caught Imogen by the arm before she could get out of the room. "That thing is dangerous. You said so yourself."

"Exactly," Imogen stated. "Sassy could get hurt."

Imogen tore her arm from Jonah's grip, then started for the door. But before she could disappear into the shadows, Sassy came back. She was back in her usual form, a regular red fox with only one tail, and she was dragging the *hunpedzkin* by its tail across the floor. Its rosy pink belly was on display, and its eyes stared upward lifelessly. A trail of blood followed behind it. Sassy dropped the creature at Imogen's feet and then sat, staring up at her proudly.

"Sassy, you were amazing!" Imogen praised.

"Is she okay?" I asked, concerned. If what Imogen said about the creature was true, Sassy might have been poisoned.

Imogen took a knee and ran her hand through Sassy's fur. "She looks fine. She must be immune to their poison."

"What *happened* to her?" Liam asked curiously. He still sat on the ground, with one knee up and an elbow rested on it, trying to catch his breath.

Imogen scooped Sassy up in her arms and stood. "Isn't it obvious?"

The three of us stared back at her blankly.

Imogen shot us all a broad smile. "Guys, Sassy's a kitsune!"

"A kitsune?" I repeated.

"Yes. They're clever, powerful foxes with nine tails," Imogen explained. "They were mentioned in chapter nine, page two of our Ancient Familiars textbook. Don't you remember?"

No, because we weren't assigned that chapter. I ignored the question and instead asked, "How long have you known?"

"I didn't," Imogen replied joyfully. "I had no idea until now. But this is great news!"

Jonah reached out to scratch Sassy under the chin. She relaxed under his touch. "That could've been helpful during the tournament, girl. Why didn't you tell us you had powers?"

Sassy just curled into his fingers like she was enjoying the massage. Esis jumped from my shoulder and into Imogen's arms, right on top of Sassy's belly. He threw his tiny little arms around her and gave her a hug. Squeaks came up to both of them and shoved the crown of her head into Sassy's fur to show her affection. It was sweet.

I glanced to the dead *hunpedzkin.* "Well, it looks like we're safe now, all thanks to Sassy. Should we light our torches and get moving?"

Liam took a deep breath, picked his torch up off the ground and stood. "Might as well get this over with."

I lit his torch, then mine. "Hopefully that's it for booby traps."

Jonah scoffed as he picked up his torch and held it out to me. "Sweetheart, if there's one thing I know about Yapluma, it's that we never miss a party. Hold on to your hats, boys and girls. I'll bet anything Air is up next."

Liam

TWENTY-THREE

With another look at the map, it seemed like we were three-fourths of the way through the temple. We only had one more room to get through before we reached the Summoning Room at the top.

After everything we'd been through already, I was *not* looking forward to getting through the next room.

"Guys, I think it's time we turned around," I said as we made our way down yet another hallway. "We've almost died three times now. Don't you think we've had enough?"

"You can go back if you want," Sophia said. "I'm not quitting."

Like hell. I shook my head and jogged to catch up with Sophia. "There must be another way. We can convince the Koigni Elders that you did the ceremony, make up some shit. We can buy ourselves some time."

"There is no other way." Sophia was set on it. Her eyes were fixed straight ahead, like she was on a mission. On her shoulder, Esis looked similarly serious.

"I think we should keep Sassy's real identity a secret," Imogen announced. She stooped down to pet her fox as we walked. "At least for now. Until we have to show our hand."

I nodded. "Right." Kitsunes were super rare. I'd never seen anyone have a Familiar like Sassy before. Imogen would become a target if people knew Sassy wasn't just a normal vixen.

But I didn't like the way Im was talking, either. She was making it sound like we had to be careful.

But of course, we were in deep water. We were associated with Sophia, and the Elders all knew it. There was no turning back now. We were in this together, and from this moment on, we'd have to watch our backs.

We got to another door. Everyone stopped in front of it and looked at it. It had the Yapluma House symbol on it, though you wouldn't notice if you weren't actively looking for it— which we were now. The symbol was so small you had to squint to see it in the door's design. Nobody wanted to be brave enough to push it open.

"Well?" I crossed my arms. "Who's gonna take the bait?"

"I'll do it," Jonah offered. "It's probably a Yapluma trap. I bet the task is to drink a fifth of vodka or something in five minutes. Squeakers and I got you."

Squeaks squawked in agreement and clacked her beak at the thought of chugging alcohol. Jonah pushed open the door, and we followed behind him. We entered onto a balcony with steps leading to the room below.

The room was about a hundred and twenty yards wide, and filled with a maze, with high stone walls that ended at the balcony's height. In the middle of the maze was a square, open section. You had to go through the maze to get to the other side, where stairs wound up to the second level and to the next door.

Beside the maze, the room was entirely empty. I wasn't sure what I was expecting, but this wasn't it. It seemed too simple— and too complicated to be made by a Yapluma, no offense.

"I have an idea," Jonah said. "Squeaks, try flying across."

Squeaks pumped her wings and attempted flying over the maze. She made it halfway before she collided with something invisible and went tumbling down into its walls, disappearing from view.

"Squeaks!" Jonah shouted. He took off running down the stairs, rushing into the maze.

"Jonah, stop!" I yelled. We sprinted down after him, but when we entered the maze, we found that the path split into three different directions instead of one.

"Which way did he go?" Sophia asked, frightened.

Sassy stuck her nose to the floor. She sniffed a few times before she jumped up and down and yipped, catching the scent.

"Good girl! Lead the way, Sassy," Imogen said.

Sassy darted ahead. We followed her, but the maze was confusing. It went around in circles, and the walls were covered with a reflective surface that looked like mirrors. I slammed into them a few times, thinking I was going the right way when I wasn't.

Imogen and Sophia had the same problem. Imogen slammed head-first into a wall, and I managed to grab Sophia at the last minute before she went down the wrong way and got separated from us. Esis had jumped down from her shoulder and was spinning in place, looking dizzy.

"This way, guys," Imogen said. She pointed in the direction Sassy was heading.

I caught my breath and looked at her. In the next second, Imogen had literally vanished from the spot.

Sophia screamed and jumped, clinging on to me. I was stunned. Imogen had just up and disappeared.

Then, in a different spot from where Imogen originally had been, she reappeared. She stumbled as she came into view again. Sassy gave a bark of alarm, and Sophia yelped. She was squeezing the life out of my insides.

"I didn't do that," Imogen said. Her face went white.

We didn't have any time to talk about it, because in that moment Sophia and I vanished, too. We were standing on the right side of the hallway of the maze one second, then we reappeared on the left side. Esis jumped three feet into the air in terror, and Imogen backed up against the maze wall, pressing herself into it and looking horrified.

It didn't hurt, but it had been fucking freaky. "You were just there," Imogen peeped. She pointed to the spot we'd been at. "Now you're there!" She pointed back at us.

This place was fucking with our heads. How were we going to find Jonah in here?

"Girls, hold hands," I commanded. "It's too easy to get lost in here."

I grabbed on to Sophia's hand, and she took Imogen's. Esis jumped down and hung on to Sassy's tail. We made a chain as we wound our way through the maze, looking for Jonah. At least if the three of us vanished again, we'd all end up together.

"I don't like this," Imogen commented. "If there was one *hunpedzkin*, there's another. They probably breed down here."

"Great," I said. That's all we needed.

Sassy yipped again, and she darted down a zig-zagging hallway, dragging Esis behind her. We followed her, and to my relief we found Jonah sitting in the large open area in the middle of the maze, kneeling by Squeaks. She was lying down and swinging her head around, dazed.

"Jonah!" Sophia cried, and she ran to him.

"Is Squeaks okay?" Imogen asked, immediately concerned. Sassy started licking Squeaks' feathers, and Squeaks cooed.

"She's okay," Jonah said, and he rubbed her head. "Just a little stunned."

"Jonah, you know better than to run off," I snapped at him. Now that I knew he was okay, I was pretty pissed. "You know the rules. Don't get separated from the group."

"I'm okay, *Mom*," Jonah said. "Jeez, wanna check my homework next?"

"Shut up," I barked at him. He'd called me that during the tournament, too.

Sophia snickered. "You are kind of a mom."

"I am not!" I shouted.

"Liam, you're *such* a mom," Imogen said, and she started laughing. "You worry all the time, you make sure everyone's taken care of, you're always nagging us..."

"Ancestors!" Jonah fell over against Squeaks. "It's so fucking true!"

Sophia, Imogen and Jonah lost it. They roared with laughter, and the sound echoed around the chamber. Even the Familiars joined in. Esis pointed his finger at me and laughed. I narrowed my eyes at them and thought they were being childish.

Oh, shit. Maybe I was a mom. Fuck them.

"Ha-ha," I said dryly. "Can we get going?"

The laughter died down, but they were all still wearing silly grins on their faces. Squeaks got to her feet and shook her head, looking chipper as always.

I headed toward what looked like the exit, but before I got there, a door on either side of the opening slammed shut. Behind us, similar doors appeared, preventing us from going back the way we came. We were closed off. There was no exit.

Aw, fuck. Everytime this had happened before, it was a real sign shit was about to go down.

"What's going on?" Jonah said. He stood up and turned in a circle. Squeaks copied him, her cheerful demeanor gone to be replaced by hesitation.

Before we had time to figure out what was happening, four different walls making four different rooms sprung up from out of nowhere and separated us, appearing by magic. The walls were made of glass so we could see each other, and they opened at the top so we could still hear each other, but no matter how hard we pounded against the glass, we couldn't escape.

The walls started moving inward on us. I pressed against them, trying to hold them back, but it didn't work. There wasn't enough water down here in this temple for me to use, and I couldn't climb out, as the walls were too slippery. Next to me, Sophia tried melting the glass with her fire, but it didn't work. Imogen was trying to use the stone floor to put a barricade up against the glass, but that was futile as well. Even Sassy had taken her kitsune form and was whipping out her vines to try and break the glass, but her lashes didn't make a scratch.

"Jonah, fly out!" I yelled to him.

"I can't!" he shouted. He tried pushing upward, but an invisible force, much like the one Squeaks ran into, prevented him from going any higher.

"We're going to be crushed!" Sophia screamed. She clawed at the glass. Esis dug his tiny nails into the glass, scratching at it frantically.

This was it. We were going to be pulverized. I'd pick almost any way to go but this.

Jonah looked wildly around before his eyes cleared with a moment of realization. "Guys, I think I know how to stop this!"

"We'd like to know today, thanks!" I yelled. I didn't like the panic in my own voice. I didn't sound like that often, not even during the tournament. I didn't know what to do.

Jonah closed his eyes. Then he vanished. Squeaks went with him, and there was an empty space where the two of them once were.

All of us screamed at once, thinking he must've gone to a different part of the maze. Our efforts to get out were renewed. I started punching the wall, and Imogen kicked at it, with Sassy putting her paws on it to try and hold it back. The walls grew even tighter, until I couldn't extend my arms out all the way.

Blood showed on Sophia's glass. She was damaging her hands in a desperate attempt to escape.

"Oh, fuck. We're screwed, we're so fucking screwed," I said. My organs were going to be total mush. And I thought I had at least a couple more months before I kicked the bucket. I couldn't even get Sophia or Imogen out. At least Jonah was safe somewhere.

Then I heard Jonah's voice, echoing over the maze. "Guys, I'm on the platform on the other side!" Jonah shouted. "I escaped!"

"How?" Sophia's plea was desperate. I didn't like that look in her eyes. She had given up trying to get out and was clinging to Esis for dear life. Her blood had stained his white fur. She thought she was going to die.

"You have to think positively!" Jonah shouted. "Once you do, the spell will break and you'll be transported to a safe place! If you don't, the walls will crush you!"

"What the fuck!?" I yelled. "There's no way that works!"

The walls were getting closer and closer. I felt like I was being enclosed in a small box. There wasn't even enough room for me to take a step backward now if I wanted to.

Imogen didn't question. Diagonally from me, she closed her eyes. In seconds, she and Sassy vanished, to appear ancestors knows where.

"Imogen!" Sophia screamed. Her eyes grew wide once she could no longer see her best friend. "Where are you?"

"Sophia, I'm out too!" Imogen said. Her voice bounced off the glass walls, somewhere from above. "It works! Trust Jonah! Just think happy thoughts!"

Sophia took a trembling gasp. Then she closed her eyes and buried her head into Esis' fur. She was there for a moment, then she was gone.

Once I lost sight of her, I completely. *Lost. My. Shit.*

"Aw, fuck!" I was alone. I was totally alone. I couldn't move. The walls were so close now that my arms were scrunched up against it in a poor attempt to hold them back. I was gonna die. This was it. It was the end.

"Liam, I'm okay!" Sophia shouted. I felt a bit of relief when I heard her voice, but only just a little— you know, because I was only a few seconds away from being turned into jelly. "We're right above you!"

I couldn't see any of them, but they could see me. "Where are you guys?" I shrieked. My terrified face reflected back at me in the glass, and it freaked me out a hundred times more than I already was.

"Don't worry about that! Just stop being negative!" Jonah shouted. His voice sounded calm and relaxed— how, I didn't know. "Just think you'll get out, and you will!"

"I don't believe in that positivity bullshit!" I screamed.

"It's the only way!" Imogen added.

"Aw, shit. We have to make Liam think *positively*," Jonah said. "He's surely a goner."

"Liam, please, think of something happy!" Sophia pleaded.

"Think of Sophia's boobs!" Jonah cried out.

"That's not helping!" It wasn't easy to be positive when Sophia was screaming above me and begging me to not die.

I tried. I tried to think about the first time Sophia kissed me, when I'd bonded with Nashoma, when we'd won the Elemental Cup. I tried to focus on all the good times I'd had with Sophia and my friends and tried to remember how I'd felt in those moments.

But there was a problem. Every time I recalled those memories, it just brought up more pain. Losing Nashoma. Still not being respected as a Cup champion, because I was sick and I'd fainted on-stage. Having to worry, be afraid and sneak around in order to keep my relationship with Sophia alive. I had good memories, true, but every single one of them was still tied to the bad in some way. There was always a negative consequence to my happiness. And the bad was all I could think about.

"*Liam!*" Sophia screamed. The walls were so close now I could feel them pressing me together. She really thought I was going to be crushed.

So I tried a different way. I squeezed my eyes shut and tried to imagine something better. I made up a world where Sophia and I were older, and we were married and had a bunch of kids running around. We had a house where we lived together and I felt good and people accepted us. We didn't have to hide from our tribe, because the laws had changed. People didn't think less of us or less of our children. We were normal. We were okay. And I was still sick, but it didn't matter, because I was happy.

It'd been love at first sight for me when I saw Sophia, even when I didn't want to admit it. I didn't believe in that kind of thing, either, before it had happened. But it had ended up to be true, so who was I to say that miracles didn't happen?

Okay, fine. I believed I was getting out of here, because I wanted to be with Sophia forever and no stupid wall was going to crush me before that happened.

She was my miracle. So this trap could go to hell.

Before I knew it, I stumbled out of the confining box and into Sophia's arms. I heard the walls snap together behind me just as she caught me.

I had landed on the balcony across from the one we'd entered on, on the other side of the maze— except the maze was no longer there. Now all that was in the chamber was an empty room.

Jonah was standing above me with a smug grin on his face. "Told you."

I wiped my forehead. I was sweating. "What was all that?"

"None of it was real. The vanishing, the maze, the walls. It was all in our heads," Jonah said, and he tapped the side of his temple. "The purpose of the trap is to get people so scared they die of fright and for no reason at all, or they just wander the maze forever and starve to death. Funny, isn't it?"

"Hilarious," I said as I caught my breath. Yapluma had a sick sense of humor.

"That doesn't mean we wouldn't have watched you get smushed," Jonah added. "The maze didn't vanish, and the illusion didn't break until you got out."

"But if it didn't *really* happen to him, wouldn't he still be alive?" Sophia asked. She helped me to my feet, and I swayed on the spot. Fuck this temple. I wanted to go home.

"He probably would've had a heart attack, anyway," Jonah said, and he shrugged. "The illusion would've still given the simulation of getting crushed. It would've made Liam feel like he was, even though he wasn't. The mind is a powerful thing."

"You know a lot about this stuff, Jonah," Imogen said in admiration. I tried not to throw up.

"I love psychology," Jonah said. "It's fascinating getting to know how the human brain works."

Esis clambered from Sophia's shoulder onto mine. I tried to tell him no, but in a few seconds, the pain ebbed away and I felt somewhat normal. I didn't have a lot of energy left in me to make it through this temple. I hoped it was over soon.

"What I don't understand is that it's a Yapluma trap. It didn't involve Air at all," Sophia said. She gave a wayward glance at Esis on my shoulder, and he gave her a thumbs-up back... whatever that meant.

"Most Yapluma are positive-thinkers," Jonah replied. "We're happy-go-lucky people, and we like mind games. People from the other Houses wouldn't have been able to see through the trap that it is."

"But Yapluma don't have power over illusions. How did they even manage to do such a thing?" Imogen questioned.

"The Arcanea must've set it up," Jonah said. "I bet Yapluma hired them to setup the magic, and the maze."

"Who are the Arcanea?" Sophia asked.

"They're sorceresses. Masters of illusion. They're the only magical race bound to shifters," Jonah said. "I learned about them in my Magical Races and Cultures class."

"You actually paid attention for once?" I grumbled.

"Shifters?" Sophia's face was confused.

"People who can change into animals. They're different from our magical creatures," I said quickly. "But there's no time for a lesson on world cultures. We need to keep moving."

My time was running out to see Anna. We'd already been down here for hours— more than the short walk to the top Sophia had promised. It'd taken so long because we had to stop often to figure out where we were going and outmaneuver the traps we knew of, plus walking around this big temple in the first place was taking longer than we thought. I only had a short time left before my chance to contact Anna was over.

"Whatever you say, Mom," Jonah said, cracking a grin. Sophia and Imogen died of laughter.

"I hate you all." I almost smiled, too, because a joke was a welcome thing after that horrible shit.

We went out the doors and found a staircase leading up to the Summoning Room. We stopped at the bottom so Imogen and Sophia could look at the map and I could take a breather. Jonah was petting Squeaks and still looking pretty damn proud of himself.

"Are we almost to the end? I'm tired of this crap," I said.

"It's just up there," Sophia said, and she pointed. "At the top of this staircase."

Thank the ancestors. Esis hopped off my shoulder and started scampering upward.

The Familiars went up the stairs first, sprinting toward the doors that led to our destination. Jonah and Imogen went on ahead, but I was slow going, and Sophia hung back to stay with me.

"You okay, Liam?" Sophia asked. She looked like she was hovering between indecision. Like she didn't want to go through with what she'd been asked to do, but knew she had no choice.

"I'll make it, *pawee*." Though I wasn't sure I wanted to. At the start of this, I thought that Sophia would eventually get discouraged and turn back. I never thought we'd actually make it this far.

I underestimated her. As always. Koigni didn't give up no matter what the circumstances.

We reached the top of the temple, where the Summoning Room was. We opened the door, and a blast of cool air hit my face. The Summoning Room was a large area open to the air, with stone pillars in the shape of various magical creatures that had been carved in the Anichi style. There was a large hole in the roof where magic could be channeled and where the ancestors were supposed to come down through. The area was covered with vines, and some of the pillars were crumbling.

In the middle of the room was a large, flat stone table, big enough for several people to lie on and level with my waist. I supposed the stone table was where ceremonies were performed.

Sophia started forward toward the stone table with purpose. But I wasn't going to let her get there. I walked in front of the table and planted my feet, lunging out an arm to stop Sophia from going any further. Sophia looked up at me, bewildered.

"I can't let you go through with this," I said firmly. "I have to stop you."

"What are you talking about?" Sophia asked. Esis looked at me and chittered.

"I meant what I said. This ends right now," I insisted.

"Liam, what are you doing?" Imogen asked. Both she and Jonah looked confused.

"You don't get it. I *have* to do this," Sophia said. She attempted to push me aside, but her weak effort failed. It only cemented the fact in my head she didn't want to go through with this. And I wasn't going to let her.

"No, Sophia. You don't understand." I stood in front of the summoning platform and refused to move.

"Liam, let me through," Sophia said. She tried to shove past me again, but I wouldn't budge. I grabbed her by the shoulders and held her back, looking her in the eyes.

"You can't perform the ceremony," I said. "If you do, I'll have to kill you."

sophia
TWENTY-FOUR

K ill me? Liam had to be joking.

"That's just cruel," I told him bluntly, and I ripped away from his grasp. "Now's not the time for jokes."

"*What!?*" Imogen and Jonah cried in unison over me.

Liam's jaw tensed. "I'm not kidding, Sophia. The Water Elders have plans of their own. They want me to kill you."

Ancestors! Liam was dead serious.

An agonizing pain unlike any other tore through my heart. Hot tears that felt like embers welled in my eyes. I blinked to hold them back, but I couldn't stop my voice from cracking. "Is... is that why you went out with me? To get close to me?"

Suddenly, the ceremony didn't seem so urgent— not when my boyfriend was planning to stab me in the back the second I performed it. I was so hurt by his confession that it already felt as if a knife was sticking out of my spine. My knees nearly buckled beneath me, but I held myself up by the corner of the table.

"No," Liam insisted. He stepped forward and reached out to touch my arm, but I jerked away. Esis snapped his teeth at him. Pain and regret crossed Liam's features. "It's *because* I'm with you that they asked me to do it."

"That doesn't mean you have to!" I cried.

"But..." Liam hesitated.

"Bro," Jonah said. "This is crazy."

Imogen picked her jaw up off the floor. "This is a violation of the Elder's power! What were you thinking?"

"You guys don't understand!" Liam roared at them. He quickly quieted his voice and turned back to me. "The Water Elders know how to bring Nashoma back. They agreed to do it if I killed Sophia."

"That's impossible," Imogen muttered.

A tear rolled down my cheek. I couldn't imagine losing Esis, only to be given the chance to revive him... by choosing between him and Liam.

But killing me? That was *way* too far. I couldn't believe Liam was actually considering it. My teeth clenched so hard that a headache started to form.

"You wouldn't," I whispered, unable to find the volume in my voice.

Liam raked his fingers through his hair but wouldn't meet my gaze. "I don't know, *pawee*."

The pain inside me snapped and turned to rage. "Don't call me that," I spat.

I walked straight up to him and shoved him as hard as I could in the chest. He stumbled backward a step, looking surprised. Jonah and Imogen began to protest from beside us, but I didn't hear what they said over my own voice chewing Liam out.

"How *dare* you!?" I screamed. "How dare you call me that? I thought it meant something. I thought *all* of this meant something! This whole semester, I thought..." My stomach felt as if it was trying to hold in a ton of rocks.

I shoved him again when he didn't respond. "You took advantage of me, Liam Mitoh! All this time, you were just planning to kill me. You're a coward! You should've kept your distance."

Heat waves pulsed across my skin. Liam just stared down at me, his lip quivering.

"Say something, asshole!" I snapped at him, smacking him hard in the chest again.

Liam swallowed, then whispered, "I'm sorry."

"Sorry's not good enough," I snarled. "Don't you understand that I'm doing this for *you*? I already told you what the Koigni Elders would do to you if I didn't finish this. Koigni House doesn't fuck around, Liam."

He finally burst. "Neither do the Toaqua Elders! Sophia, you can't go through with this. We can work something else out."

I crossed my arms, and Esis mirrored me from my shoulder. "What's the deal, Liam? You keep me from fulfilling the prophecy, and they find a way to bring Nashoma back from the dead?"

"Yeah, basically," he replied bluntly.

"Then let me do this," I insisted. "I'm not fulfilling the prophecy. I'm just getting answers."

"But Sophia... if you are the prophesied one—"

"*If*," I emphasized, standing on my toes to get up in his face. "We don't know anything until we talk to the ancestors."

Liam leaned down until his nose was only inches from my own. His breath was cool and uninviting across my hot cheeks. "You're being selfish."

"Selfish!?" I screamed.

"Everyone just calm down." Jonah tried to peel Liam and me apart, but I pushed him away. He jumped back from us like he'd touched a hot stove.

"I'm trying to save your life!" I cried. "Or did you not hear me the first two times I said that?"

"You're doing this because you're curious about the prophecy," Liam spat back.

"So what? Maybe I am. Aren't you?"

Liam hesitated.

"You wouldn't have waited this long to say something if you weren't," I accused.

"I..." Liam's gaze darted to Imogen and Jonah, like they might be able to help convince me.

Imogen spoke up first. "Sophia's right," Imogen said. "I think we're all curious."

Liam huffed. "We don't have to do this. We can work out a solution. We can lie to the Koigni about what happened here tonight."

I stepped away from him, feeling disgusted. "We can lie to the Toaqua, too."

Silence hung in the air a moment. I couldn't stand it.

"Fine, Liam," I snapped, opening my arms wide in a *come at me* gesture. "You want to kill me, then kill me."

"*Sophiaaa.*" Imogen dragged my out, like I was being ridiculous. I ignored her.

Liam's eyebrows knitted together tightly, and his fists shook.

"You can't, can you!?" I yelled. "The fact of the matter is, Liam, the only way to save you is by completing this ceremony. Every other alternative gets you killed!"

Imogen chewed her bottom lip and exchanged a glance with Jonah. I didn't realize the confession had come out until it happened.

Liam gaped at me. "What do you mean?"

"Sophia," Jonah said softly. "I think it's time to tell him."

"Tell me what?" Liam's fists clenched harder.

There'd never been a *worse* time to tell Liam the truth. But I was so sick of keeping secrets from him. There was never going to be a *right* time. As long as the confessions were rolling, I might as well get this one out in the open.

My skin was so hot that sweat dripped down my forehead. A lump formed in my throat, but I forced the words past it. "If you kill me, Esis dies with me. He's the only thing that's been keeping you on your feet these last few weeks."

Imogen breathed a sigh of relief, like she'd been holding her breath for that confession for months. Jonah let out a squeak, as if it was some sort of touching moment that made him tear up. Sassy yipped at Squeaks' hooves, and Squeaks danced around her. From my shoulder, Esis relaxed his hold on my ponytail and stood up straighter, like he was proud.

Liam's face went completely blank, as though he needed time to process what he was hearing. "What... what do you mean?" he asked breathlessly.

I could see the gears turning in his head as he put all the pieces together.

I dropped my gaze. "Esis has the power to heal. He's been treating you for months."

A wave of guilt tore through me. Ancestors, why was it so hard to tell him the truth?

Liam drew deep, shallow breaths, and his lips pursed tighter. The crease between his eyebrows deepened. He looked like he was trying not to explode. "How long have you known?"

"Since last semester," I confessed, unable to meet his gaze. "Esis helped you through the tournament and has been healing you ever since."

The top finally blew off his kettle. "*You just decided not to tell me!?*"

I distanced myself from him a step as his arms flailed angrily.

"Doesn't that seem like an important bit of information?" he roared. "This could change the whole course of my life!"

"I know," I admitted sheepishly. "We tried to stay away while Perot was studying you, but nothing he did seemed to help. Not like Esis could."

"That doesn't matter!" Liam growled.

He began pacing back and forth, like he was warming up for a marathon. When that didn't help, he stomped over to a statue of a bird and shoved it over. A sound like thunder filled the room, and the statue cracked into at least a dozen pieces.

Imogen gasped, then cried, "Liam, stop it!"

"Bro!" Jonah rushed forward to help calm him, but Liam just shrugged him off with his elbow. Jonah grunted and backed away, clutching his ribs.

Liam whirled back to me. "How could you keep something like that from me?"

"Because I knew you'd react like this!" I screamed back. "You think I want to stand around and watch you break things?"

Liam glanced down to the broken statue, looking guilty.

"Besides, I wasn't the only one keeping secrets! I was actually trying to *keep* you from getting killed! I wasn't the one planning your murder!" My chest hurt so bad that I thought I might go into cardiac arrest.

Liam ignored my accusation. "Why didn't you tell me when you first found out?"

I curled my arms around myself as the confession tumbled out of my mouth. "I didn't want anyone finding out what Esis was. I was scared they'd take him from me. We wanted to tell you during the tournament, but if you reacted like this then, we would've never gotten through. Then the Koigni threatened me, and Perot was treating you... it was all too risky. I tried to tell you, but it was never the right time. We always got interrupted."

"'*We wanted to tell you during the tournament,*'" Liam repeated. He turned on Imogen and Jonah, fuming. "You two knew about this?"

"Um..." Imogen looked to Sassy at her feet.

"We did," Jonah admitted. "But Sophia's right. We couldn't tell you during the tournament."

"You could've told me after!" Liam snapped. "You're supposed to be my *best friend.*"

"It wasn't my secret to tell," Jonah insisted.

"You guys totally betrayed me. All of you!" Liam started pacing again. I'd never seen him so mad before. He fisted his hands in his hair, then kicked at one of the pieces of broken statue. It went flying across the room and out through the space between the pillars. I heard it tumble several feet down the side of the pyramid.

Finally, Liam gave up. He leaned his back against a pillar and sank down to the ground with his head in his hands. The anger was gone now. It was being replaced with total devastation.

His shoulders shook in heavy sobs. I couldn't help but feel guilty for driving him to this point.

"Liam," I said softly, but he didn't look up. He sat as still as if time had frozen, like he'd given up. I knew I'd broken his heart, but I still had to move forward. "Liam, I'm doing this with or without you."

"Then do it," he snapped without lifting his head.

Fine, I thought bitterly. I turned my back to him, trying to forget he was in the room at all.

"What about you two?" I asked Imogen and Jonah. "Are you going to stop me?"

"No," Imogen answered immediately, shaking her head.

Jonah's shoulders slumped, and he glanced toward Liam. "I think you should try to get some answers."

Taking a deep breath, I turned to the summoning table. I stole one last glance back at Liam. As angry as I was with him, I couldn't let the Koigni Elders hurt him. I couldn't let them touch *any* of my friends.

Esis hopped onto the summoning table. I swung my bag off my shoulder and set it next to him, then climbed onto the table myself. I positioned myself cross-legged in the center, just below the opening in the ceiling, where the table had been stained dark. Imogen and Jonah stood beside the table with their Familiars to watch.

Taking deep breaths, I tried to cool down, but my pulse continued to race. I was so angry I could explode.

Just forget about Liam for a minute, I told myself. I didn't have the luxury of putting this ceremony off. I'd get back to Liam later.

My hands shook as I opened my backpack and pulled out a small bag of herbs Doya had given me. I tugged on the drawstring, and a strong, sweet aroma hit my nose. Doya didn't tell me exactly what was in it, just that it contained four different herbs that represented each of the four Houses. I handed Esis the open bag to save for later. Reaching into my backpack, I pulled out a washcloth and a sharp pocket knife. My heart hammered at the thought of using it.

Imogen drew a sharp breath. "What's that for?"

I glanced to her to see a worried look on her face. "The ceremony requires blood."

Jonah turned his nose up. "Just don't cut your palm. Use your arm or something, where it'll hurt less."

"I can't use either of those. The ceremony requires blood from the ears."

Imogen's eyes widened.

"It's a symbol to the ancestors," I explained, repeating what Doya had told me. "It tells them I'm opening myself to hear from them."

"Are you sure about this?" Imogen asked, looking frightened for me.

"Im, I have to."

Her expression softened slightly, so I turned back to Esis. He bit his lower lip as I lifted the point of the knife to the skin just behind my ear.

"You know what you're doing, buddy?" I asked him. Esis nodded, though his blue eyes glistened with tears. "You don't have to worry. I'll be fine."

He nodded, but it didn't look like it helped ease his worry.

"Sophia, don't." Liam's voice sounded behind me, but I ignored him.

"Here we go," I said, taking a deep breath. Then I pressed the knife into my skin.

I gasped as a sharp pain shot through my ear. Warmth trickled down my neck and across my hand. I quickly leaned over to the center of the table and watched as blood splattered across its surface. My insides twisted, and Esis squeaked nervously.

"I think that's enough," Imogen said.

But I didn't stop. Doya had warned me about using too little blood. She'd said that if I thought I was done, I still had a long ways to go. So I continued to let the blood pour out of me. The thick red liquid began to creep along the length of the table, spreading out in all directions. Esis stepped backward as it inched toward him.

"Sophia," Imogen pressed.

"Not yet," I replied.

Drip. Drip. Drip. Large droplets of blood fell into the liquid already pooled beneath me, one after the other in quick succession. I couldn't even calculate how fast the blood came. It ran down my jaw and dripped off my chin. As I leaned over further, my ponytail slid across my shoulder, and blood matted in my hair. I held my hair back and waited... my head began to spin, and a chill spread over my skin.

"Sophia!" Imogen cried again.

Finally, I pressed the washcloth to my wound and pressed hard. "Esis, the herbs."

He flipped the small bag in his hands over, dumping the herbs on top of the blood. He tossed the bag aside and scurried onto my shoulder, pressing his paws behind my ear to heal me.

Meanwhile, I lit the herbs with my Fire. Tall orange flames shot into the air, then quickly died down to a small fire. I reached for the totem around my neck, praying it would help give me the courage and the power to get through this ceremony... but it wasn't there!

I ran my fingers across my empty chest again. Panic swept through me, but I didn't have the time to worry about where I'd lost the totem—somewhere in the ruins, I was sure, but I couldn't go back to look for it now. The herbs were almost burnt out now, and I only had one chance to complete the ceremony. I was going to have to do this without the totem.

I quickly began muttering the Hawkei words Doya had taught me. *"Ei suma te ancetras por tahli ei naan ei hode. Desago ehn te solae, Showana Harjo."*

I call upon the ancestors to guide me on my path. Descend from the stars, Showana Harjo.

My words concluded as the last bit of embers died. Only one step left. I could do this.

I threw my washcloth to the ground, then turned my palm up to the sky. I channeled all of my heat down through my arm, picturing it as a rope leading up to the ancestors. It took everything I had to push Liam out of my mind and focus on the things that brought me joy. Esis gently stroked behind my ear where I'd cut myself, and his fur brushed against the back of my neck. I put all my focus on him. Liam betrayed me, but Esis never would. At that thought, heat exploded out of my palm.

Lightning flashed above my head, immediately followed by a crack of thunder. I blinked several times, blinded by the light.

When my eyes focused again, the first thing I saw was a pair of bare feet hovering just inches off the summoning table. Slowly, I lifted my gaze, unable to believe what I was seeing. A woman dressed in a long yellow skirt and an elaborately patterned top stood in front of me. She had long black hair secured in a braid down her back. Her body was slightly transparent, but she was more solid than my ancestors I'd met in the past— like she was more physically present than they ever were.

"Showana Harjo?" I asked breathlessly. My heart pounded so hard I could hear my pulse in my ears. Imogen and Jonah both gasped, but I didn't look over to them.

"Sophia Henley," Showana replied kindly, opening her arms to me. Her voice was melodic, like the sound of wind chimes in a light breeze.

I quickly got to my knees and bowed my head so low my nose nearly touched the blood at my feet. "Thank you for meeting with me."

"What can I do for you, child?" she asked.

I lifted my head. "I'm told you're the *naderei* who made the Fire prophecy."

She nodded.

"Can you tell me about it?" I asked desperately. I could still hardly believe she was standing there. A small part of me never thought it would actually work.

She smiled sweetly. "What is it that you want to know?"

Relief flooded through me, and the questions spilled out. "What does the prophecy mean? *The fated Koigni child, born on the summer solstice in the year of the dragon, shall bring glory to the greatest house.* The greatest house is Koigni, isn't it? They are the most powerful."

Showana nodded. "Yes, they are."

"And the fated Koigni child... that's me?"

She pressed her lips together. "I cannot answer that definitively. It does not have to be."

"What do you mean?"

"The answer is yes and no," she said thoughtfully. "Do you want it to be you?"

I hesitated. "I don't know. What benefit does elevating my house give if everyone else gets hurt because of it?"

She didn't answer right away. Instead, Showana knelt to my level and looked me straight in the eye. "You do not have to do this, Sophia. Other Koigni children will be born."

"I don't?" Honestly, my heart lifted in my chest a little. If there was a way out of being the chosen one, I might actually take it.

Just then, a sound like falling rock came from outside the room, as if the wind had blown the broken piece of stone further down the side of the pyramid. My eyes darted in that direction, while Jonah quickly rushed to the corner of the room and peeked over the edge. Squeaks looked over with him.

"What was that?" Imogen asked in alarm.

Jonah shrugged. "I don't see anything."

"I had hoped it would be you," Showana said, pulling my attention back to her. "You are the first child with the tools to carry the prophecy out."

"What happens if I don't want to?" I asked cautiously. "Can I prevent it?"

Showana took a deep breath. "There's a reason prophecies are given in such vague wording, Sophia. You must let your inner light guide you to its true meaning. If you are the Koigni child I spoke of, you will understand when you are ready. Once you find all the pieces to the prophecy — once you see what the future truly holds for your House— you will understand what has to be done."

I absorbed her words as she stood. "All the pieces? The pieces the other Houses are hiding, you mean?"

The Koigni Elders had been right. The other Houses had secrets, and they were each holding tight to their hand.

Showana nodded. "When I delivered the prophecy, I gave a piece to each of the Houses so that they could not use the information against each other. If you want to know what to do, you must reunite those pieces."

"That's why I'm here," I said desperately. "To get the pieces from you."

Showana shook her head slowly. "I cannot do that. There are lessons to be learned along the journey. Telling you them now would render the journey obsolete. You have much to learn before you are ready. The prophecy is only a destination. But there are many paths to the end. Your choices will affect the outcome. You, Sophia, have the power to determine the fate of the Hawkei."

I took a moment to consider what she was saying. It sounded like a huge responsibility. But it also gave me hope— hope that I could change the course of our tribe's future. "That's all I have to do? Find the pieces?"

She smiled. "Yes. You already have two."

"Two?"

"*The fated Koigni child*," she said. "That was Koigni's piece."

"Was the second piece about the magical object?" I questioned, thinking about what Doya had told me months ago. *You will have to find a powerful item that will serve to fulfill the prophecy.*

Showana crossed her hands in front of herself calmly. "That was part of the same piece. Koigni kept that half to themselves. The second piece..."

She didn't finish her sentence. Instead, she lifted her gaze to look at Liam across the room.

I followed her eyes to see that Liam was still slumped against the pillar, but he was watching us with interest.

"Liam already has the Water piece, if he is willing to share it with you," Showana said.

Liam's eyes went wide, and he stilled. My stomach sank. After everything, I couldn't believe how many secrets there were between us.

"You knew there was more to the prophecy, and you didn't tell me?" I asked him. The hurt was evident in my tone.

Liam nodded so slightly that it was barely noticeable.

Tears welled in my eyes again, but my voice was gentle. I wanted to break down and cry, but I knew I had to play nice. "Will you tell me?"

Liam chewed on the inside of his cheek, looking as if he was fighting a tough internal battle. Finally, he stood, but it looked like it caused him pain. He held on to his side and used the pillar to support himself. When he found his footing, he stepped forward with guilt and regret in his eyes. Tears began to stream silently down his face as he recited the Toaqua portion of the prophecy.

"The prophesied one will bring death beyond comprehension. It it she who shall cause Toaqua's darkest hour," Liam said.

I pressed my hand over my mouth. Beside the table, Imogen and Jonah clung to each other.

Liam gazed downward and whispered softly. "That's why the Toaqua want you dead— to save our tribe."

Tears began streaming down my face. I didn't want to be the one to hurt anyone— especially Liam. I would never destroy his House to save mine.

I turned back to Showana, my whole body quaking, but I couldn't find my voice.

"You must find the pieces each House holds," Showana said. "Then you will know. Be prepared, because if you're willing to do this, you will lose the very life you cherish."

All the air left my lungs. Beside me, Imogen began crying into Jonah's shoulder.

I didn't get a word in before Showana said, "That is all I can reveal to you now, my child. Tread carefully."

Then she was gone, like leaves being taken by the wind. It took me several moments and Esis' chirp in my ear to be brought back to reality. My mind was still racing with everything Showana had said to me.

I lifted my head and looked to my friends. "Guys... I don't think I can do this alone."

"I don't think you can do this *at all*," Jonah replied. "Didn't you hear any of that? If Koigni rules, people will die. Toaqua will face its *darkest hour*."

"How can you even be considering this?" Imogen asked, looking offended. "This prophecy sounds horrible! She said you were going to die if you fulfilled it!"

I looked to Liam, waiting for him to say something. His eyes glazed over like he wasn't really with us. He looked completely empty.

"I'm not going to fulfill the prophecy," I stated. "I would never do that. But I still think we need to do what Showana instructed. We should find all the pieces."

"So that you can go report back to the Koigni Elders?" Liam asked bitterly.

"No!" I cried. How could he think I'd do that? "So that we can use the pieces against them! You heard what Showana said. My choices will determine the fate of the Hawkei. If we have all the pieces, we'll know what we're up against. Knowledge is power, and the more we know, the more advantage we have over the Elders. We could prevent this thing from ever happening."

Imogen relaxed, and Jonah looked thoughtful, like I'd made a good point. Liam looked as if he was trying to decide if I was lying or not. But none of them spoke. It was like they were all waiting for someone else to decline the offer.

"Look, if you guys don't want to help me, then you might as well kill me now, because I can't do this by myself," I said, choked up. I was begging them now.

"Absolutely not!" Imogen cried.

"We won't do that!" Jonah said at the same time.

"I failed the ceremony," I pointed out. "I didn't get what the Elders wanted. The Koigni might still go after you. You might as well murder me to save yourselves. Liam can get Nashoma back, and the rest of you can enjoy your lives without this prophecy crap hanging over your heads."

They all exchanged a wary glance.

All I knew was that I couldn't do this without my friends. It was all together or not at all.

I picked up my knife and walked to the end of the table, then bent to shove the handle in Liam's hands. He backed away and stared down at the blade with wide eyes. I jumped down from the table and took his hands in mine, forcing the point of the blade to the sensitive skin at my navel. It dug in, but not enough to cut skin.

My heart pummeled against my chest, and I could barely breathe. Esis tugged hard on my ponytail to stop me, but I ignored him.

Tears streamed down my face as I looked into Liam's pain-filled eyes. "Do it, Liam. Save yourself."

A muscle popped in his jaw. He shook his head. "Don't make me do this, Soph."

"Sophia, stop it!" Imogen sobbed, curling into Jonah's arms. "No one's going to die!"

I didn't take my eyes off Liam's. His expression was filled with apology, and tears wet his face. He looked like he was in agony. Esis screamed in my ear, but I barely heard it. All I could focus on were Liam's soft, sad eyes.

I would miss them, but that would be all right. I'd watch him from the stars with the ancestors. With Nashoma back, he'd get better, wouldn't he? He could live a full life, one where his tribe flourished.

"Liam," I whispered. "Finish it."

"No!" Jonah shouted.

A slew of emotions flickered across Liam's features so quickly that I couldn't read them. His fingers tightened on the blade.

Ancestors, he's going to go through with it!

In the blink of an eye, Liam jerked backward, ripping his hands and the blade away from me. He tossed the knife aside, and it slid to the ground and over the side of the temple.

"No, *pawee*," he said, his chest heaving. "I won't do it. I won't kill you. I..." He looked to Jonah and Imogen momentarily before turning back to me. "I'll help you."

"You will?" I whispered breathlessly.

"Yes," he replied. "We'll find all the pieces of the prophecy together.

And we'll use them to beat Koigni. Toaqua will never see its darkest hour."

Relief washed over me like a strong ocean wave. I was so overwhelmed that my knees shook beneath me. Imogen rushed forward and pulled me into a hug, helping keep me upright. Soon, Jonah joined me at my other side, along with Liam moments later. Sassy weaved between our legs, rubbing her fur against us happily, and Squeaks spread out her wing and draped it over Jonah's shoulder. Esis threw his arms around my neck.

Tears fell from my face. Liam's offer didn't earn him immediate forgiveness, but I was grateful beyond words that he didn't do what the Elders had asked of him.

"Jonah and I are going to help you, too," Imogen said. "There's no way we're letting you search for those pieces on your own."

We all finally drew away from each other, wiping our eyes.

"We just have to be careful," Imogen said.

"Careful how?" Jonah asked.

"There's no coming back from what we've just done," Imogen said. "All the secrets, Showana's advice... not to mention the fact that Sassy's a kitsune. With a powerful Familiar like that, people would be watching me if they knew."

"People are watching us already," Liam pointed out.

"Exactly," Imogen agreed. "And if they knew we were trying to piece the prophecy together, we'd be in even more danger. We're helping Sophia, which makes us all targets. We have to be careful and watch each other's backs."

"Don't worry, guys," Jonah said. "I've got your backs. All of you."

We all looked at each other blankly, unsure of what to say next. The silence was unnerving as I waited for someone else to speak.

Finally, Jonah dropped his head.

"Come on, guys," he said lowly. "Let's go home."

KNOCK. *Knock. Knock.*

The door to Madame Doya's office swung open so fast that it blew

Doya's fiery red hair back. "Sophia! Where have you been? What took you so long?"

Doya looked— dare I say it?— concerned. She reached out into the hall and grabbed my shoulder, dragging me into the privacy of her office. It was so early that dawn hadn't yet broken. I was beyond tired and probably looked like a mess. I seriously needed a shower to wash the blood out of my hair and the dirt out of... everywhere.

But I'd been instructed to report back to Doya the second I returned to the castle. We were all so tired that we split up once we made it back. I headed straight to Doya's office instead of my dorm.

I dropped my bag on a sofa cushion, then plopped down beside it. Esis hopped off my shoulder to snuggle in my lap. Naomi hugged Doya's side closely. She limped on her front paw, which was wrapped tightly in a bandage.

"I ran into a few snags," I told Doya.

She sat in the chair across from me and raised an eyebrow. "Snags?"

"There were more obstacles than you thought," I admitted, though I didn't reveal specifics.

Doya's expression softened so that I couldn't read it. She leaned back in her chair. "Interesting. What kind of obstacles?"

I shrugged. "Things set up by the other Houses, I guess. Puzzles and stuff like that. Nothing my Fire couldn't handle."

Doya crossed her legs. Her tone was skeptical. "Really? You mean, you didn't have any help?"

What the heck? How did she know? I suddenly felt more alert and awake.

Doya's eyes momentarily darted toward the bandage on Naomi's paw, and I instantly understood. Naomi had followed me. The falling rock we heard must've been Naomi slipping as she prowled around the narrow pyramid stones. She'd hurt herself on the way down, then rushed to report back to Doya.

I pulled Esis closer to me. How much had Naomi heard? Did she hear me tell Liam about Esis' healing abilities? The Koigni Elders would be far too interested in that bit of information.

"What matters is that I got to the Summoning Room and completed the ceremony," I said.

"And?" Doya pressed.

"And... that's it." I shrugged. "Showana appeared, but she didn't tell me anything you don't already know."

"She didn't give you the other pieces to the prophecy?" Doya asked, but she didn't sound very curious. It was like she already knew.

I tried to think back to when we'd heard the falling rock. All Naomi knew was that Showana told me I didn't have to be the prophesied one if I didn't want to be.

"No, she didn't," I answered truthfully.

"Then you didn't try hard enough." Doya's accusation was like a slap in the face.

I leaned forward, my skin heating as I stared her down. "I did everything you asked of me and more. Don't you think Showana would have given me the pieces if I was the prophesied one?"

"True," she agreed. "But who knows what you might be hiding?"

Was she serious?

"*But,*" Doya emphasized. "I think you still have greatness in you Sophia. So don't think you're completely off the hook just yet."

Oh, wow. What a compliment. I guess I never expected anything less from Madame Doya.

"I have to say, I expected more from you," Doya said coldly.

I scoffed. "Like I haven't heard that one before. Why can't you just accept me as I am?"

Doya went completely still at the question, like I'd hit a nerve. Finally, she uncrossed her knees and leveled me with a heavy stare. "Just don't get too comfortable, Sophia."

I stood with Esis in my arms and walked to the door. I didn't have to take this. "Don't worry. I won't. Oh, and next time, maybe try preparing the prophesied one *a little* more than you prepared me?"

Doya smirked. "I'm sure the Koigni Elders won't make the same mistake twice."

I paused with my hand on the doorknob. "Our deal is still good, right? I did what you asked, so my friends are safe."

Doya nodded. "As long as you're telling the truth."

"Naomi heard the same thing I did. Why don't you ask her?" I asked snidely.

Doya looked at me with such disgust that it churned my stomach. "In that case, you might as well know that the Fire Council has already convened. Chieftess Westfenix and the other Elders are furious that you've failed. We should've known you weren't the chosen one when you bonded with that weak Familiar."

Bitch!

I whipped the door open and stomped out of her office. At least now I knew Naomi didn't hear about Esis' abilities.

I walked for a while, heading back to the Koigni dorms. Around the corner, I nearly rammed into Liam. He straightened from where he leaned against the wall, looking alert. Esis bared his teeth at him.

"You can relax," I told him with a sigh. I didn't know what to say to Liam— or how to feel. It was like I was looking into the eyes of two different people. The Liam I loved and the Liam who had vowed to kill me. It tore my heart in two. I could literally feel the pain clawing away at my chest. "I didn't tell Doya anything she didn't already know. The Koigni Elders don't think I'm the prophesied one anymore. They've lost interest in me. They don't know about Esis."

Liam shoved his hands into his pockets. "That's not why I'm here."

"Oh?" I asked curiously. "Then why?"

Then I knew. I already knew what he was going to say before he opened his mouth. I could see it in his eyes.

"Because this can't wait," Liam said. "We need to talk."

Liam

TWENTY-FIVE

Sophia's face hardened as she looked back at me. "Fine. Where."

"Probably somewhere private." I led her to an empty classroom, the one where we'd talked about putting some distance between each other in order to stay safe.

I'd had enough time to think about what I had to do. I'd made up my mind. This was the only way, and I was done with fooling myself... done with getting hurt.

I felt so numb. All that was inside me was emptiness. It was hard to feel anything anymore. I entered into the empty classroom, and Sophia came in behind me. She put Esis on one of the desks as I shut the door.

I didn't bother waiting around. I needed to get the words out, before I lost my nerve. "I have to end our relationship. It's over, Sophia. We're done."

Her face changed. A bunch of emotions crossed it all at once. Rage. Confusion.

And the one that hurt me the most. Absolute heartbreak.

Her mouth dropped open. "Are you serious? You just put me through a night of hell, and now you're *breaking up with me?*"

"What else are we supposed to do?" I asked her. "Do you see any way to fix this?"

"We should just take a break, not break-up." She stepped forward and put her hands on my chest. "We just need some time to think. Please, Liam."

I took her hands off of me and gently pushed her away. Her face fell again. It was practically like I could hear her heart crack.

Her expression was one of total disbelief, before it turned to anger. "I knew it," she snapped. "I *knew* you were just waiting to throw in the towel. You wanted to give up on us. I told you that by the waterfall."

"It's not like that," I mumbled. It seemed like a shitty excuse.

Esis looked between us, back and forth. He seemed so desperate, like he wanted the fight to stop, but didn't know how to make us.

"I know today was rough. I don't really want to be with you now, either, after what you did, but I still don't want to give up on us!" Sophia insisted.

"There is no us!" I shouted. "Look at what we did, Soph! We lied to each other for *months*."

"I had good reason to!"

"Did you? Did I?" I raised an eyebrow at her. "Because I realized that I didn't. And I think, deep down, you know you didn't, either."

Sophia chewed on her lip, thinking. She was trying to come up with a way to salvage what we had— trying to stop this. "I just... I can't believe you did this to me. All of it," she whispered. "I know you wanted Nashoma back, but this is just cruel."

"What if Esis died? What if someone came to you with the opportunity to get him back, you'd just have to kill me first?" I asked. "I *hope* you would take that chance, Sophia. You don't know what it's like living like this."

"I thought I meant more to you than that." The tears started coming. They were pouring from her eyes so fast they outnumbered the rain. I longed to step forward and wipe them away, but I held myself back.

"It's not like that! I didn't have a choice!" I shouted. "They would've sent another assassin after you if I hadn't agreed! I bought you *time*. Don't you understand that?"

"Are they still going to kill me?" Sophia's tears didn't stop, but she took on a fierce look that said she'd like to see them try.

"Not if I report that you aren't the prophesied one," I told her, and I stood up straight. "I'll tell them you failed the ceremony, and that the

Koigni Elders no longer think you're going to fulfill the prophecy. Then they'll leave you alone."

"Are you going to tell them about the pieces I have to find, too? After all, you're their errand boy," she shot at me.

My mouth fell open. "Who do you think I'm more loyal to?" I asked. "Everything I've done this past year has been *for you*. Yes, even the bad stuff," I said when she opened her mouth. "I lied because I was trying to protect you. My tribe abandoned me, and you didn't."

"But you're still breaking up with me. Like that makes sense." She let out a skeptical noise.

"Because there's no other option. Relationships are built on trust. We don't have that anymore. I don't think we had that from the beginning." I shook my head. "We totally betrayed each other. Both of us are to blame. It doesn't matter which betrayal is worse. What matters is that it happened, and neither of us said anything until the information came out on its own."

"You weren't trying to protect me. You were looking out for yourself," she said bitterly. "You didn't want to risk getting hurt by telling me the truth."

"You're being rather hypocritical," I said bluntly. "You had all semester to tell me about Esis, and you didn't say a damn thing."

Her face remained stony. "It was wrong to keep that from you. But I wasn't trying to *actively kill you*," she hissed.

"That was never my plan, not from the beginning," I said. "I never wanted to kill you. I didn't consider it an option."

"You did tonight," she said. "I saw the look in your eyes. You were considering it."

"And I still couldn't do it, which should tell you something," I spat back at her. "I couldn't kill you, Sophia. Not even for Nashoma's sake. You were right from the start when you said I could never hurt you. I've been trying to save your life all semester."

"What do you mean?" She sniffled, looking confused.

This was it. Time to reveal more secrets. "I've been sabotaging you, trying to make it seem like you weren't as powerful as Koigni thought, so that the Toaqua Elders would lose interest and leave you alone," I said.

"The only way to make sure that I didn't have to kill you was to convince the Elders you weren't a threat."

"Your dad put you up to this, didn't he?" Sophia asked. "I knew he hated me. When you took me to your house to meet your family, was it all an act?"

"Don't talk about my family like that," I said viciously. "All this shit is way out of our control. My dad was only doing what he thought was best for Toaqua. And my mom and siblings don't know anything about this. Not even Ezra. This was my burden to bear."

"What did you do to me?" her voice was getting high-pitched and squeaky. She started crying again. I could barely understand her.

I looked at the floor. I couldn't even look at her as I admitted it. "I poisoned the roses. The ones I gave you on Valentine's Day. I put a herb in them that weakens a Koigni's magic."

She started crying harder. "I can't *believe* you!" she yelled. "Do you realize what Doya put me through because of that? I thought there was something wrong with me. I thought it was my fault."

She put a hand over her mouth. "Did you fuck with my camera, too?"

"No," I said immediately. "That was a gift. A real one."

"You must've bought it out of guilt." Esis reached up to wipe away the tears from her eyes. She leaned down to let him.

"I didn't," I said weakly. The anger was fading from me now to be replaced with guilt. I'd done so many bad things. "I just... I wanted to make you happy."

"Well, you did." She sobbed, and forced out, "Too bad it was all a lie."

"It wasn't a lie." My voice was getting desperate. Fuck, I was seconds away from crying, too. I'd cried enough tonight. I didn't want to break down again. "I still love you."

"And I did what I did because I love you, too!" Sophia shouted. "Esis is the only one keeping you from dying. But what he can do isn't a cure. It's never going to be able to fix you. It might even stop working. I couldn't give you false hope."

"Sophia," I said gently. I moved forward and grabbed her chin gently in my hand, then lifted it so she could look at me. "I would've been okay with taking that risk."

She pulled away from me. "I wanted to tell you about the Koigni Elders. But how could I? If I had said anything, they would've hurt you. I've had to go through this the entire semester alone."

It felt like a knife was twisting into my gut as I watched her sob. I realized how lonely she had felt this entire semester, bearing this burden on her own. The signs had been staring me in the face that she needed someone to be there for her, but I ignored them.

I was the one who had made her feel alone. I'd known the Koigni Elders had put her up to something, but I'd never asked. I'd barely tried to find out. That was on me.

"We could've worked something out," I said. I tried to keep my tone as soft as possible. I couldn't bear to yell at her anymore. "Instead, you chose to keep quiet and play with fire. You trusted Doya more than your own friends."

"You spied on me and Doya?" She hardly reacted. It was like she was expecting the blows to keep coming.

"Yes. And when I reported back to Baine—"

"Baine's in on this, too?" Her eyes popped out of her head.

Shit. There were so many secrets I'd forgotten them all. I pretty much lived in a twisted web of lies. "He's on the Toaqua Council. My dad assigned him to help me with my... mission." My words faltered. "I've been misleading him all semester so he didn't force me to..." My voice dropped off.

"I can't even trust my own teachers." She started bawling harder than before. This was unbearable to watch. But I couldn't look away, because she deserved more from me.

Sophia's tears ebbed as she let out a sarcastic noise. "You know, you might've been assigned to kill me. But it sure didn't prevent you from fooling around with me on the side."

"That was special to me, too." I felt deflated. "I don't mess around with just anyone. I meant every word I ever said to you. It wasn't about getting off, or—"

"I never should've shared those moments with you. They were a mistake." Sophia cut me off. "I'm glad I didn't have sex with you. I regret letting you even *touch* me."

When she said those words... those few short sentences... the pain was worse than anything my body could put me through. I couldn't say anything in reply. The air felt so heavy. In that moment, it was difficult to even breathe. I felt a huge weight on my chest, like I was being crushed.

I'd felt it before, when Mia had broken up with me. But that pain felt like nothing when it came to losing Sophia. It was an afterthought. This was a million times worse... equal to losing Nashoma.

"This semester has been so hard." She wiped back strands of hair that had fallen in front of her eyes. "I thought the one good thing about it was you."

"You're not the only one." I forced myself to meet her eyes. "To me, you were the best part of Orenda Academy."

"Then why—?"

"Do you know how much I've suffered these last few months?" I asked. My voice was starting to break now, because I never admitted it to her, never admitted it to anyone, but I'd been in *so much pain* and she'd seen that, and said nothing. "I didn't know what was wrong with me. One week I was fine, and the next I was terrible. I thought I was dying! I spent weeks trying to figure out how to say goodbye to my family, say goodbye to you, and none of that was necessary because you were able to help me the entire time! You just didn't."

"I did help you," Sophia insisted. "Esis healed you as much as he could."

"Without my knowledge," I said. "You treated me without asking permission first, without telling me what you were doing to my body! That's fucked up. My body is the one thing I still have a say with. Doesn't matter if it works right or not."

I crossed my arms and turned away from her. "I didn't know what was going on. I didn't know what was wrong with me. I still don't really know. I had the opportunity to figure it out tonight, but I lost my chance to talk to Anna, because I was helping you." This was such a soft spot. Even talking about it was agonizing. It's why I never brought it up.

"I didn't mean to hurt you," she insisted.

"No. You had the answer to the most painful problem in my life, and you never said a word! That fucking hurts, Sophia!"

I finally broke. Tears started coming out of my eyes, and I couldn't stop them. I fucking hated this.

Her expression was shocked... like she didn't know how badly she'd hurt me. Her face was conflicted. She didn't know what to do. I kept my back turned to her, so she couldn't see. Now we were both crying. Shit, this was a mess.

Sophia's sobs lessened and became quiet. I heard her footsteps behind me. She laid a warm hand on my back. I let her touch me. "Please don't cry," she whispered.

"I'm trying not to." I wiped my face and pulled myself together. I wanted to kick something, but I was trying to show her I could remain in control of my emotions. It was barely working. I stepped away from her, so her hand was no longer on me. It was like pulling an ax out of my back.

I turned back to face her. I needed to change the subject, because if I kept talking about my health, I was going to lose it completely, and I didn't want her to see me break down. My voice steadied when I went back to business. "There's one last thing you should know. There's a weapon out there that could eliminate the entire tribe. Baine's been looking for it for years. Toaqua thinks that you're going to find it, and use it against them. It's called the *Azaimperiai*... it's a weapon that can control the ancestors."

Sophia shook her head and took a step back. "Even if I found the *Azaimperiai,* I wouldn't use it."

"I know that," I responded quietly. "But other people don't."

She looked at me. "Are the Toaqua Elders going to bring Nashoma back, now that you've proven to them I'm not the one?"

Things in my head cleared. "I... I don't know," I said breathlessly. "I hope so."

I hadn't thought about it. But I had completed my mission. I'd done what they asked. They had to fulfill their end of the bargain, didn't they? I was getting Nashoma back... today.

It made me so happy that I wanted to fall to my knees and praise the ancestors. But at the same time, it was horrible, because it had cost me

Sophia. Not her life, thank the Great Spirit. Just... us. Who we were together.

It was a horrible sacrifice. Like everything in my life that brought me joy, it came with something bad. It came with a cost.

Sophia wiped her face. "I do hope you get Nashoma back, Liam." Her voice wobbled, like she was trying not to cry again. "I hope it was worth it."

She ran off. Esis stood on the desk and watched her go before he turned to look at me. His ears were drooping, and his lip wobbled. His big blue eyes were filled with tears.

He didn't seem angry at me. Just miserable.

Esis jumped off the desk and padded after Sophia. They left the door open behind them.

The moment she was gone from my sight, I realized I'd just made a terrible mistake.

It was sunrise. I'd been up all night, but I had no intention of sleeping.

Baine was in his office, grading exam papers. I'd never seen him up so early. It was a bit weird to find him here. He must've had a lot of work to do.

I knocked before entering. He looked up, and I didn't give so much as a hello before I said, "Summon the Elders. I have information to discuss."

"It's rather early, Liam," Baine said. "Most of the Elders are still sleeping. It would be better to wait—"

"I'm the firstborn son of the chief. I have the right," I told Baine. "Call the meeting. Now."

Baine blinked at me as I left. I headed out of the classroom and started toward the beach.

When I passed the cafeteria, I saw Jonah leaning outside one of the doors, looking excited. He hadn't gone to sleep either, obviously. When he saw me, he came rushing over.

"Liam! Liam, you'll never believe what just happened!" Jonah said.

"I was just at breakfast. Guess what? Renar asked me to move in with him over the summer. Isn't that great? We don't have to live together now."

The apartment we were all supposed to get this summer— the four of us. I'd completely forgotten about it.

Jonah moving in with Renar seemed like a terrible idea. But it was his life. I didn't have any right to tell him how to live it. "That's great, man." I forced a smile, but it was so small it vanished within seconds. "Happy for you."

Jonah's grin vanished as he noticed my tone. "You look..." Jonah glanced at me, up and down. He didn't finish his sentence. "Did something happen between you and Sophia?"

"We split up." The words were out of my mouth before I knew it, and I realized they were horribly true. Sophia had been my girlfriend mere hours ago, and now she wasn't.

The fact would've destroyed my soul if I still had one.

"Oh. I'm sorry, man," Jonah said. He frowned. His tone implied he really meant it.

"That's okay. Things just don't work out sometimes, I guess," I said hollowly.

Jonah grimaced, like he didn't agree, but he said nothing. "So, where are you off to now?" Jonah asked.

"I'm reporting to the Toaqua Elders," I told him. "I'm giving them the bare minimum to get them off my back and away from Sophia. I'm not saying shit about the pieces. That's for us four to know."

"Good luck," Jonah told me. I nodded to him and walked off.

I made my way to the beach and dived in. I planned to get to Serpent Assembly before anyone else did, but I took my time. I swam as far as I could out to sea, until I didn't see the shoreline, and laid on my back as the sun came up.

One of the reasons I loved being in the water was because of how weightless you felt. You could lie on your back for hours, and it felt like your problems literally fell off of you and drifted to the ocean floor.

I thought that maybe tonight I could just swim out into the ocean as far as I could go. And just float on the water until I couldn't anymore. The bottom of the ocean couldn't be lower than I felt right now.

Just... sink.

But Nashoma was waiting for me. Possibly even this very moment. The only thing right now that could possibly make me feel any better was to have him go rushing into my arms.

I held my breath and dived downward. I rocketed myself toward the Assembly and entered through its double doors. I didn't even bother to dry myself off as I entered.

The Elders began arriving one by one, taking their place in the benches above me. They appeared disarrayed and frazzled, as if they'd just gotten out of bed. Most were confused.

Dad seemed to know what the meeting was about, though. He wouldn't meet my eyes.

Elder Malison sneered at me with his old, decrepit face and said, "You'd better have a good reason for calling us at this early hour, boy."

"I'm here for my reward," I said. "I did what I was asked to do. Now I want Nashoma back."

Dad shifted uncomfortably in his chair. Malison let out a humorless laugh and said, "You haven't yet delivered on your promise."

"I followed Sophia to the Anichi Temple last night," I began. "She performed a ceremony to talk to the *naderei* that made the prophecy, but she failed. Showana Harjo refused to tell her how to fulfill it. The Koigni Elders have lost interest in her. They no longer consider her the chosen one and are already looking for another."

"A likely story," Malison said, but Wells shushed him. Madame Wells stared at me intently, giving me the floor.

"I saw it with my own eyes. Sophia Henley told me all of this herself," I said directly. "I have no reason to lie. She's no longer a threat to you. Now give me what I came for. We had a deal."

"This is preposterous," Malison complained. "You can't believe we'll take you at your word."

"Liam is right. We've wasted our time." Baine took my side. He pounded his fist into the desk, looking frustrated. "I for one am ashamed that we focused our intentions on hurting an innocent eighteen-year-old girl."

"She is far from innocent. She is Koigni," Malison argued.

"Birth does not assign guilt! I will have no more part in it!" Baine yelled. "My duty is to protect the students of the institution where I teach. Sophia Henley is blameless, and I will not move to strike against her!"

"Treason! Treason against the tribe!" Malison bellowed.

Dad waved his hand to silence them. Everyone in the room looked to him. "My son speaks the truth," he said wearily.

"But we are no further along than we were months ago. We need security," Malison said.

"He did do as he was asked," Elder Poole said meekly, though he shrunk down in his chair as he said it.

"It doesn't matter." Malison focused his sniveling gaze on me. "The agreement was the Henley girl's life for your Familiar's. You still have to kill her. Do so, or you'll leave here empty handed. Make your decision, *boy*."

I looked desperately to the faces on the council. Dad. Wells. Poole. But no one on the Water Council moved to say anything against Malison. Not even Baine. All the Elders looked at each other with shifting eyes, as if they were hiding some sort of unspoken pact.

Everything I did over the past semester didn't matter. To the Toaqua Elders, there could only be one outcome. Sophia could have nothing to do with the prophecy, but she was Koigni, which meant, in their eyes, she deserved a death sentence. They still wanted me to execute her. They wouldn't bring Nashoma back until I did. I'd been a fool to not see it from the beginning.

I had to make a decision. Nashoma or Sophia.

But too late. My heart had already made it.

"You can take your deal and go to hell," I told them lowly. "I'm done being used by you."

Then I did it. I turned around and walked away from the last chance I'd ever have to bring Nashoma back to me. My footsteps were the only sound echoing through the shocked room.

"Treason!" Malison cried again, but no one moved to arrest me. I freely walked away and grabbed the double doors.

"Liam!" Dad cried after me. But I barely heard him. I opened the double doors and blasted through the air chamber on the other side, ricocheting into the ocean.

The water rushed around me as I forced my element to get me far, far away from here, as far as it would take me. I'd turned my back on my chief and my tribe. For what, I didn't really know. But it seemed like the right thing to do. It was a feeling in my gut, stronger than anything I'd felt in my entire life, that told me I'd done what needed to be done.

Nashoma would've wanted me to do it. He would've been proud of me.

I WENT BACK to my dorm and slept the entire day away. I didn't get up until it was dark again. I noticed a lot of things were already gone from my dorm. Ezra must've snuck in and taken some stuff back home for the summer while I was sleeping.

Jonah had probably told him about me and Sophia. I was glad, because that meant I didn't have to.

I didn't want to pack up the rest of my stuff and go home just yet, because I wanted to be alone. Also, because I didn't know how I was going to face my dad.

The school was pretty quiet. Most everyone had already gone home for the semester. I didn't know where I was going, but my feet seemed to know. I let myself wander around the halls of the school. I tried to think, but I'd been through so much in the past twenty-four hours my brain seemed to stop working.

I saw them sitting on a collection of suitcases by the door near the grand entryway— Sophia and Imogen. Sassy was curled up on Sophia's feet, and Esis was on her shoulder, stroking her hair. Imogen had her arms wrapped around Sophia and was comforting her. The entryway was empty, except for them.

I ducked behind a wall quickly so they couldn't see me. I knew I needed to walk away, but I couldn't help overhearing. And I already missed Sophia's voice, so I stuck around for a couple minutes... just to try and record the memory of the sound, so I could hold on to it a bit longer.

Sophia was crying again. "This is so awful. I feel like I'm dying. I can't believe he dumped me like that, after everything. I hate him."

I winced. Ouch. That hurt.

"You don't hate him. Sophia..." Imogen paused. "I wouldn't say this to just anyone after a breakup, because I don't want to give you false hope. But... I don't think you and Liam are going to be apart forever. You'll be together again someday. He loves you too much to stay away."

"I don't know if I want him to come back, Im." Sophia started sobbing harder. "He broke my heart. He betrayed me in the worst possible way. I don't think we could ever be together again, after all of this."

"I know. But a lot of couples go through stuff like this. They break up and get back together later, when they're ready. It'll be all right," Imogen encouraged.

"Do all couples hide that they're trying to kill each other?" Sophia wept.

"Well, no," Imogen admitted. "But... you two are different. You've got something special that only comes around once in a lifetime. You just need space right now."

"I don't know." Sophia sniffled. "I don't know how to feel."

"Just give it time," Imogen said. Sassy yipped, like she was in agreement. "Liam will come back to you, and you'll forgive him. You guys just need to find yourselves first."

I couldn't listen to more. I forced myself to get away from there. I took a back door and headed outside. For whatever reason, my body led me to the mountains.

Imogen's words repeated in my head as I walked up the path to the ancestral mountain, but it was hard to feel any emotion about them. I didn't know what the future held for me and Sophia. Right now, I couldn't imagine any possibility of us getting back together. We'd hurt each other so much.

But I still hoped. And I hated myself for that, because I was the one who had ended our relationship in the first place. I was already regretting breaking up with her. It was the worst decision I'd ever made. But it wasn't like I could reach out to her and ask her to take me back now. She'd throw me out. She didn't want me. I'd broken her too badly.

Like I'd said earlier... there was no coming back from what we'd done to each other. From what I'd done. I wanted to fix it.

I just didn't know how.

I sat on the edge of the mountain once I got to the top and looked down on Kinpago, lit up against the blackness of the night. Two dragons flew overhead, having a flaming duel, and a few perytons sparred in the skies above Orenda. The castle looked especially pretty, glowing against the outline of the mountain range, and the sea behind it.

"Liam?" A voice I didn't know said my name. I turned around, and I saw Carter standing there. Tiara was behind him, her purple scales glinting in the moonlight.

The Yapluma and the Familiar who came back from the dead. I had questions. Maybe Carter could help. Maybe he could tell me how the Toaqua Elders raised him back to life... maybe how I could do it myself.

"I've been looking for you," Carter said. "I need to tell you something."

I got up from my spot on the ledge and walked over to him. "Hey. What's up?"

He glanced down. "I overheard your meeting with the Toaqua Elders this morning," he said. "They've been keeping me and Tiara prisoner in Serpent Assembly for the past few months. I just escaped... or, rather, your dad let me out without telling the other Elders. He covered for me."

I blanked out. "I thought you were just in hiding, so your House didn't discover you were still alive."

"No." Carter shook his head. "But that's the thing, Liam. I never died."

I had to repeat his words several times over in my head, because they didn't translate right away. "Huh?"

"It was all a story. I'm really sorry for misleading you, but the Toaqua Elders said they were going to kill me if I didn't tell you what you wanted to hear." Carter's voice shook. It was like he was afraid of telling me what was really going on.

I needed to get to the bottom of this. "Explain."

Carter took a deep breath. "Well, you see, when Tiara and me crash-landed in Flight class, we were really hurt. Critically injured, you know. Tiara was taken to the hospital, but I knew if she died, I was a goner, too. I figured we were both going to die."

He gave a shaky sigh. "But then something weird happened. One moment we were in the hospital, and the next, we both blacked out. When we woke up, it was a few months later, after the tournament in December. We'd been in a coma for weeks, and had been treated by Toaqua medicine men and women. Tiara was mostly healed, and I was okay, though we still had some substantial injuries that took some time to recover from."

Carter shook his head. "I didn't realize until later that we'd woken up in Serpent Assembly, in some sort of medical prison. Toaqua had staged our deaths and made it *look* like we died, even to my parents, but we never did."

Tiara made a purring sound in agreement. I was still having trouble comprehending. "I don't understand."

"Liam, don't you get it?" Carter asked. "The Toaqua Elders never had the power to bring back people from the dead. They knew you had seen Tiara fatally injured and faked my death. They used me to get to you. You were just a pawn."

"Ancestors." My father had lied to me. Baine had lied. The Toaqua Elders never had the power to bring Nashoma back. They'd used me.

And I'd fallen for it. I'd lost Sophia because of it.

The reality was so heavy that I stumbled against the mountainside, falling against the side of a boulder. "Ancestors," I repeated.

"I'm really sorry," Carter apologized again. "But they said if I told you the truth, they'd kill my entire family."

"My dad too?" I asked.

"He was in on it. I don't know if it was his idea," Carter admitted. "I know the chief's your dad, Liam. But he did help me escape. I think he's sorry for what he did."

This was so incredibly hard to believe. Baine was supposed to be my mentor. My dad was supposed to be the one person who always protected me no matter what. And both of them had willingly gone along with a plan to deceive me in the worst possible way, to achieve a sadistic goal.

I brushed my hair back and looked at Carter.

"What are you going to do now?" I asked.

"I'm going on the run. I'll reach out to my best friend, James, and see if he and his Familiar want to come with me," Carter said. "I've already told my family I'm alive. They're leaving the city as soon as they can."

"Leaving the city?" I repeated. Fuck, I felt so dumb right now. I was being slow on the uptake, but my mind just couldn't comprehend anymore.

"Yes." Carter nodded seriously. "And if you're smart, you'll take your family and friends and get out of Kinpago, before it's too late."

"What do you mean?" I asked. My heartbeat picked up speed.

"The tribes always talked of war. But now it's getting... serious," Carter said. "My jail cell was right next to the council room. I listened in on a lot of Toaqua meetings. Liam, it's gonna get bad. People are gonna die."

"How can we stop it?" I asked.

"You can't prevent it. The tribes are just waiting for an inciting event to make the next move," Carter said. "It could happen any day now."

Carter's words were heavy. I knew there was truth to them. Things had been different in Kinpago ever since Sophia had shown up. But I didn't think I could abandon my tribe— not the Toaqua, because screw them— but the Hawkei themselves. I couldn't abandon my people. If there was a chance I could save them, I had to fight.

"There must be some way," I insisted.

"Things are getting dark around here," Carter said. "Orenda Academy is safe for now. But it won't be for much longer. Choose your side wisely."

Carter turned and headed into the night, Tiara behind him. He looked over his shoulder and moved quickly, as if he thought he was already being chased.

I slumped against the boulder and sank down to the ground with my hands cradling my head, struggling to comprehend the situation. I couldn't trust my dad, Baine, or anyone in my tribe. Carter was certain there was a war coming, and he acted like it would be the war that would end the Hawkei for good.

Like the only thing left for anyone to do was to desperately try to save themselves.

Sophia had wanted to change things. I never thought we could, but now I saw that we had to. If the tribes didn't adapt... they were going to destroy each other. We were all going to die.

I sat on something hard, and fished in my pocket. I pulled out a small totem... the totem Sophia had dropped in the temple while we were running from the *hunpedzkin*. I'd picked it up and meant to give it back to her later, but so much had happened that I'd completely forgotten about it. And now that we were broken up I didn't know if I had the courage to face her again and return it, though I knew I had to eventually.

I put my head back against the cool rock and looked up at the stars. "Nashoma, what do I do?"

I didn't receive an immediate reply back. Only silence. I closed my eyes, and I thought I heard a howl on the wind as, unexplainably, I drifted off to sleep.

I heard the sounds of drums and flutes. I was wandering through the forest, but everything was painted in sharp colors. A black wolf was ahead of me, and he ran. I darted to keep up with him, moving throughout the shapes that formed the trees around us.

Nashoma led me to a mountain. We climbed it, heading upward toward the skies. The sun and the moon chased each other up above, trying to unify in the heavens but never able to truly come together.

There was a glowing light coming from inside the mountain. It was so similar, like I'd done this all before. I'd seen that light more than once. I jumped down the rocks to get to it, scaling the mountain, and Nashoma leapt after me. Our actions caused a landslide, and the rocks came barreling toward Nashoma. I screamed his name as the landslide came down.

I immediately started awake, breathing hard. Sweat ran down my forehead, and I was gasping for breath. The totem was still clenched tightly in my hand. I put the pieces together quickly.

It was a dream. A lot of people wouldn't make anything of it, but a true Hawkei knew what it meant. Ancestors communicated in dreams. Nashoma was trying to tell me something.

The totem. That's what I'd been pulled to the day Nashoma died. It had been the mysterious light I'd followed down the mountain, the strange force I couldn't pull away from. The tunnel Sophia and I had traveled through and found the totem in during the tournament had been the same mountain Nashoma had perished on— just different entrances. I didn't recognize it as the same place because there were two separate sides. I'd been trying to get to the totem that day he sacrificed himself for me. I hadn't realized it until now.

Everything in my life had been shattered into pieces only minutes before, but now all the broken parts were falling into place. Nashoma was gone, because his purpose had been fulfilled. Mine had yet to begin.

Sophia.

This was bigger than all of us. I didn't have anything left to live for. Except her. It didn't matter that we weren't together. It'd always been her.

I was a man with nothing to lose. That made me dangerous. I wasn't going to be a puppet for anyone anymore. From now on, I made my own decisions.

Sophia was my decision. I'd promised to help her find the other pieces of the prophecy. I'd promised I'd help her fulfill her destiny, whatever that was. Nashoma had given his life to make sure that happened, and I wasn't going to let that sacrifice be in vain. When the time came, I'd return the totem to Sophia... and keep it safe for her until then.

She was my reason for existing. I was still here because the ancestors had chosen me to help her bring forth— or stop— whatever hell the future had in store for us. That's why I hadn't died when Nashoma did. It wasn't yet my time. I still had work to do. A war was coming, and Sophia was going to be right in the middle of it. Along with all of my friends.

Damn the consequences. Sophia Henley was more than just my destiny. She was my legacy, and I'd die to defend that.

So help anyone who got in my way.

END OF BOOK TWO

Turn the page to read a special excerpt from Book Three: *The Earth Legend!*

HIDDEN LEGENDS

Read more from the Hidden Legends universe! Each Hidden Legends series takes place within the same world, but in separate and unique societies. Every series stands on its own, and they can be read in any order.

SHIFTERS, FAE, & SORCERESSES

University of Sorcery by Megan Linski

WITCHES, DEMONS, & REAPERS

College of Witchcraft by Alicia Rades

SUPERNATURAL PRISON

Prison for Supernatural Offenders by Megan Linski & Alicia Rades

Never miss a new release! Join our newsletter at www.hiddenlegendsbooks.com/fanclub/

THE EARTH LEGEND
CHAPTER ONE

Liam

I could recall the day I'd bonded like it was yesterday— and I knew I'd always remember it that way.

I'd been walking in the forest on my own in late September, during the afternoon around sunset. I was in my second year at Orenda Academy, and had been feeling pretty isolated from everyone else.

I felt different and alone. I couldn't understand why. My life was pretty good. I was happy, overall. But I couldn't shake the feeling that someone... something... was missing. I couldn't figure out who. There was just this gap in me that had always been there and that I could never explain. I always felt like my purpose, my destiny, was somewhere out there... not here. I wanted to go look for it, because I was restless without it.

When I got far enough into the woods, I heard a cracking sound and looked up. My heart skipped a beat, and then froze when I saw a pair of amber eyes peering out at me from the trees.

There was a large black wolf standing there, his coat deeper than night and shadow. He held himself tall, head high, his ears perked forward as he looked at me. Some people don't believe animals can have expressions, but this one did. His look was completely serious, and though we were at least twenty feet apart, it felt like he was pulling me in, further and further to him.

The gaze we shared was unbreakable. I couldn't wrench my eyes away if I tried. Time faded away, and so did everything around me. A soft flute played a solo melody in the background that only we could hear. Nothing else mattered. The only thing that meant anything anymore was the wolf. My body felt light and airy as I began walking toward the wolf, my feet moving not of their own accord.

My ears seemed to block out all sound as I approached the wolf. He turned, glancing behind himself once before he broke into a run.

I followed. I leapt into a run, but I wasn't chasing him. I was sprinting beside him. We weaved throughout the trees together, matching stride for stride. His paws touched the ground each time my foot did, and we moved seamlessly, in unison. Everything was fast, yet it was also in slow motion. I'd never felt so connected to something in my life. What I had known before, it hadn't ever made me feel this way.

Finally, the wolf stopped running. He came to a halt beside a cascading waterfall and allowed the spray to mist his black fur.

I took a few deep breaths before I sank to my knees before him. He didn't move, but remained standing, and kept staring back. I raised a shaking hand to touch his fur. The moment I did, shock waves were sent pulsating through my body.

My entire existence was rearranged. Saying that my life was different wasn't enough. This bond went beyond the short time I would exist on this plane. Everything I thought that had mattered didn't matter at all. The only thing that mattered was the wolf in front of me. He consumed every part of me, rearranged my thoughts about myself and created a mirror that I could use to reflect who I was. Every connection in my life— my family, my tribe, who I wanted to be— came loose and tied themselves tightly on to the wolf. Whatever I cared about or loved, if it didn't relate to the wolf, it was no longer important.

We were the same. There was nothing different about us. It was like we shared the same body, the same mind. All I cared about was his beating heart, his breath. Without it, *I meant nothing*. He carried all the best parts of me within him, and I was just the body that moved throughout this earthly realm. He was me— who I really was, not who I pretended or wanted to be. I would die and be buried, but he would live on with the ancestors forever.

The connection I felt between us was like golden threads twisting and binding around each other, creating a thick rope that tangled up the two of us so I couldn't distinguish where myself ended and he began. Because that would be impossible. Cutting us apart, trying to untangle the interwoven strands that bonded me and him, would be something not even the ancestors could do. I felt warm strands wrap around me like a thick blanket, and I could no longer resist and pull away from who and what this wolf was. The missing gap in my heart filled, and for the first time in my life, I truly felt like this was where I belonged. My purpose and my meaning in life had been filled up. It was like satisfying something that could never be satisfied. Whatever I'd been looking for, I'd found it, and now I was finally at peace.

"Nashoma," I whispered, and I wrapped my arms around the wolf and held him tight. The wolf buried his snout into my shoulder and huffed. I ran my hands through his fur and over his ears. He was perfect. A scar ran over his right eye, and he had a hardened look that said he wouldn't give up, no matter what happened.

He was tough. I liked it. I stood, one hand still wrapped firmly in the fur that ran across his shoulder blades. "Come on, brother. Let's go back and tell everyone I've found my Familiar."

My whole family had celebrated with me that day. Back then, I thought Nashoma would be by my side forever.

He was, in a way. But at the same time, he wasn't. The most unbearable part of it was that I didn't just *lose him*.

I'd lost Sophia.

Continue The Earth Legend to see what happens next!

BONUS OFFERS

Find coloring pages, games, quizzes, and bonus content at www.
hiddenlegendsbooks.com

Join *Orenda Academy of Magical Creatures* on Facebook to talk to other
Elementai about upcoming books in the Hidden Legends Universe!

Never miss a new release! Join our newsletter at

www.hiddenlegendsbooks.com/fanclub

Check out the *Academy of Magical Creatures Official Playlist* on Spotify!

About the Authors

Megan Linski (left) and Alicia Rades (right) are two best friends and the authors of the *Academy of Magical Creatures* series. Both are USA TODAY Bestselling Authors and award-winning novelists for teens and young adults. Megan Linski is a disabled author who loves laughter, adventure, and fantasy worlds. She is a proud member of Koigni House. Alicia Rades is a mother who enjoys exploring paranormal realms and trying new recipes. She is a champion from Toaqua House. Both girls love nature, animals, sexy romances, and eating cheese.